THE BEST DEFENSE

DEFENSE

Kate Wilhelm

FAWCETT CREST • NEW YORK

A Fawcett Crest Book
Published by Ballantine Books
Copyright © 1994 by Kate Wilhelm

Library of Congress Catalog Card Number: 94-2039

ISBN 0-449-22314-0

This edition published by arrangement with St. Martin's Press, Inc.

Manufactured in the United States of America

First Ballantine Books Edition: September 1995

10   9   8   7   6   5

For Chris and Rosanne

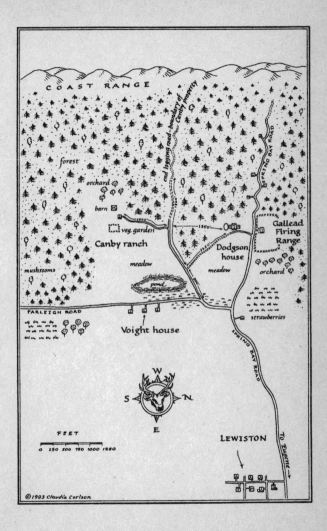

PROLOGUE

PAULA KENNERMAN IS lost, confused. Thursdays are her best days, she keeps thinking. She is off work on Thursday; there is time to play with Lori, take her to the park, or shopping, or the library. Thursdays are good days.

Packing, she was packing their things, hers and Lori's. Yes, that was Thursday. Packing. And now she is here, someplace with a curtain around her bed, needles in her arms. Thursday, she reminds herself.

"What the fuck are you doing?" Jack demands, standing in the doorway.

"Packing. Leaving. I told you."

"You're not going anywhere! Don't give me this shit."

"Leaving."

She closes her eyes and drifts away. Leaving. He took the money out of the bank. She sees herself on the floor, stunned, clutching the door frame because the floor tilts crazily. There was no pain, she realizes, puzzled, because now there is so much pain. She watches herself watching him as if from a terrible distance. He picks up Lori and throws her down on the bed. "Next time, out the window," he says.

1

Her eyes jerk open. In her head Lori screams and screams.

There was a fire, she remembers, seeing it again through a window, a kitchen blazing, flames licking against the door. Running. She took a taxi, but not to that house, another house. No suitcase. She could not lift the suitcase because something was broken, and she had to hold Lori's hand. She drifts again.

She is on the edge of a woods waiting for Lori. Another little girl comes running out. "She's sleeping," she says, and from somewhere else a second child calls, "Annie, come here. Look what I'm making." Annie darts away.

Sleeping, she thinks, standing against a tree, using it for support. She is so tired; and she hurts so much. Sleeping. What if Lori wakes up alone? What if she screams, in there alone?

"If she wakes up alone, she'll be afraid. I'd better go back." There is someone by her, she remembers, walking away from her, a woman.

"Whatever you want."

The woman is heading toward the children playing under a big bouquet. Paula moves slowly; every step brings a stabbing pain through her side, across her shoulder, down her arm. Two cracked ribs, they said. "I won't go to the hospital," she remembers crying. "I won't leave Lori. Let her come with me." The other side hurts as much as the side with the cracked ribs. From being slammed against the door frame, she recalls, thinking how crazily the floor kept tilting.

At the kitchen door. Flames. The kitchen blazing. She is running, running, like nightmare running: all that effort and so little gain. In the front door, up the stairs, screaming, "Lori! Lori!" The bed is empty. She plummets into oblivion again.

"Mrs. Kennerman, can you hear me?"

Against her will her eyes come open. Her tongue is thick and dry. "Take a sip of water," a voice says, and a straw is placed in her mouth. The water helps.

"I can hear you," she whispers hoarsely.

"Can you tell us what happened back at the Canby house? Do you remember?"

"I couldn't find Lori," she whispers. "I looked in every room, under the beds, in the closets, and I couldn't find her." She pulls against restraints on her arms. "Where is she? Where is Lori?" She is crying, her voice wild and out of control. "Where is she?"

"Mrs. Kennerman, here, a little more water." A washcloth is against her eyes, gently wiping her cheeks. It is removed and she opens her eyes.

Now she can see them, a man and a woman. She is very broad, with a broad, almost flat face; he is tall and heavy, thick through the shoulders, with thick gray hair.

"Who are you?" she whispers. "Tell me where my child is, please."

"Don't you remember the rest of it?" the man asks.

Now she does. "I kept yelling for her to come out, not to hide, because the house was on fire. I went down the stairs, and then . . . I don't know what happened. I was outside on the ground and people were all around and the house was burning, all the windows, the door, everywhere. Lori!" It was not a question this time. *Lori!*

Later the same man came back with the same woman.

"Why would she hide from you? Was she afraid of you?"

"Did you see anyone?"

"What did she say to you? Did she want to go home again? Did she want to go back to her father?"

"Why do you say you went upstairs? She fell asleep watching television, and the TV is in the living room downstairs."

"Mrs. Kennerman, you'll feel better if you just tell us exactly what happened. Believe me, you'll feel better then."

In her mind Lori is screaming, screaming. Dreamlike slow motion: Jack picks her up and throws her onto the bed. *Next time, out the window.* Lori whimpering in her sleep in a strange house, a strange bed; her every movement brings jabs of pain to Paula. Lori waking up, crying out, screaming in her sleep.

"Just tell us what happened, Mrs. Kennerman."

She told them and told them, and then she stopped telling them, and in her head Lori screamed.

ONE

FRANK HOLLOWAY FELT out of place here in the Whiteaker neighborhood; his car was too big and expensive and shiny clean, his suit, a very nice blend of silk and wool, was too well tailored. He drove slowly past the small houses, most of them well-kept and neat enough, he had to admit, past the mural wall he had read about—not exactly pretty, but impressive, he also had to admit: a jungle with unlikely creatures and more unlikely variously colored people who all seemed happy. Continuing, he passed a black beauty shop, a small appliance repair shop, a Mexican grocery store with a sale advertised in big white letters on the window: JICAMAS, TOMATILLOS, PLANTAINS, SIXTY-NINE CENTS A POUND.

He spotted *Martin's Fine Food* stenciled in white letters on a picture window out of the fifties and drove past, parked with misgivings at the curb, and sat for a moment rethinking his plan. Finally he left the car and approached the small restaurant housed in one of the old buildings. Some of the first houses built in Eugene were in this neighborhood, dating back a hundred years or more, now qualifying for historical preservation status; this probably was one of them. The structure was frame, freshly painted white, with a neat row of petunias and marigolds bordering the walkway to the entrance. Two large picture windows had been installed, and a fancy front door with a brass handle. The improvements looked hideously out of place on the building; they made him think of an aged woman wearing a Gabor wig and too much makeup. White half curtains hid the bottom of the glass panes, hid the diners from the public, but at the moment three people were standing in a tight group clearly visible, obviously yelling—a tall black man, a tall brown man, and his daughter, Barbara.

Frank drew in a breath and opened the door, entered. The trio did not glance his way, and it seemed that a squad car with siren blaring could have gone through without their noticing. Frank shook his head at another black man leaning against a door frame; he was wearing an apron and was very large and very black. There was an amused expression on his face. Frank passed him to take a seat in a booth near the rear of the dining room. There were only three tables and four booths altogether. Barbara and her two companions were by the front window, all standing up, holding down the table, as if it might float away without their intense effort.

"What's the matter, you can't walk?"

"My mother can't walk that late. I told you!"

"Don't give me that shit, man!"

"I said that's enough!" Barbara yelled, leaning closer to the tall black man.

He was yelling loudest. He was skinny, over six feet, dressed in stained chino pants and a white T-shirt. "What you mean, that's enough? He stole! He's a robber! That ain't enough!"

"You don't just want your money back, you want revenge, and I told you what the court would do. Roberto, what are you studying at LCC?"

"I'm going to be a dental technician. You know, false teeth, caps, bridges, braces, stuff like that." Roberto was also thin; he was brown, with long hair caught up in a ponytail. Barbara looked small and vulnerable between the two angry men. "I told you, I pay you back! I already paid some back!"

Abruptly the black man sat down. "You going to make false teeth? No shit?"

"Yeah. You got a problem with that?"

"Man, take it easy, okay? False teeth? Bridges?"

Barbara put her hand on Roberto's arm, and they both sat down again, and their voices faded, became too faint for Frank to catch the words. The aproned man vanished behind the swinging door to the kitchen and quickly reappeared with a tray that had two Cokes and a cup of coffee. He took it to Barbara's table, patted the other black man on the shoulder, and then approached Frank's booth.

"Just coffee," Frank said.

The waiter went to the next booth. Frank had passed it without noticing anyone sitting there. "You sure you don't want something to drink, miss? A Coke or juice or something? No charge if you're waiting for Barbara."

"No, no. I'm fine. Thank you." Her voice was very nearly inaudible.

By the time Frank's coffee came, Barbara and her clients were standing up again, but this time peaceably. She reached over the table to shake hands with the black man, and then shook hands with Roberto, and the two men walked out together. The black man was saying, "You gonna make false teeth! That's a hoot and a half!"

Frank stood up and watched Barbara without moving toward her. She looked tired, he thought with regret. It was often a shock to see her when she didn't know he was there; how like her mother she was in appearance, although not at all like her in any other way. She had fine bones, and she had let her hair grow out longer than he had seen it in years. Fine dark hair with just a touch of wave, enough to soften it. He knew there were a few gray hairs, but since he couldn't see them from this distance, he didn't have to think about them. She had lost weight in the last few months and her jeans were a touch baggy; she looked fragile, too young to be thirty-seven, thirty-eight, whatever it was. Fragile, he repeated in self-derision. She was about as fragile as a six-foot length of rebar. Actually, he didn't want to think about her age any more than he wanted to think of her hair turning gray.

She had faced the door during his swift scrutiny; now she turned toward him, her face brightening as she took a quick step in his direction. "Dad! How long have you been here?"

"Not long."

The woman in the next booth stood up and started to walk toward the door.

"Did you want to see me?" Barbara asked.

"Yes, but not if you're too busy. I mean, I'll come back some other time."

"That's just my father," Barbara said easily. "He'll wait. Won't you, Dad?"

"Yep. No problem." He sat down again and watched the woman approaching Barbara. Plump, in black stirrup pants and a red top, sandals. Not the way people dressed when they came to his office, he thought grumpily, and Barbara, in jeans and a ridiculous T-shirt, was not dressed the way anyone expected an attorney in a prestigious office to dress either, he added, and picked up his coffee. Just the father. He could wait. The coffee was very good.

Barbara had been surprised to see her father, but not terribly. She had known curiosity would bring him to her "office" sooner or later. When he sank back down into the booth, she turned her attention to the young woman, who had been crying recently. Automatically Barbara examined her arms for bruises, marks of any kind, and found only nice pink boneless limbs. She motioned to the table where Martin already had cleared away the Coke cans and glasses and her cup. Even as she was resuming her own chair, Martin came back with a tray and two cups of coffee and put them on the table wordlessly.

She mouthed her thanks to him and said to the other woman, "What can I do for you?"

"It's not me, not really. It's really for my sister, I mean." She stopped, and began adding sugar to her coffee. Her hands were trembling.

"Okay. But who are you? What do I call you?"

"Oh. Lucille. Lucille Reiner." She started to tear open a third packet of sugar and Barbara reached across the table and took it from her hands, which were icy. Lucille ducked her head and groped in her bag for a tissue.

"Just tell me about it," Barbara said after a moment.

"I was in the jail, visiting her, and it's like she's turned to stone or something. She won't talk or cry or anything, she just stares off somewhere else. They gave her a lawyer, the court did, I mean, but he thinks she did it and he says she should plead guilty. And the psychiatrist they sent her to, in the hospital, I mean, he thinks she did it, too, and he says she isn't crazy or sick or anything, she can be tried and go to prison. Or maybe even worse. But if she did it, she had to be so sick, and she's sick now, not talking, not crying, not eating, I don't think. And one of the women visitors told me to just talk to you about it. I mean, if she has a public defender, doesn't he have to work for her?"

Barbara nodded. "He does. All that means is that when a defendant can't afford to hire an attorney, under the law the court has to appoint one. And that attorney is required to treat his client exactly the way he would any other client. He'll do the best he can for her. The court will be watching to see that he does."

"But he wants her to plead guilty. I talked to him this morning, and that's what he said. And when I told her, she didn't even seem to hear me. Back in the beginning, a couple of weeks ago, when I yelled at her for not talking to him, she said what's the use, his mind's made up already, and after that she didn't talk to him or me either most of the time."

"Who is he, the attorney? Maybe I know him and can reassure you about him."

"Spassero. William, I think. He's young, real young."

Barbara shook her head. "New to me. But I can find out something about him. Do you live here in town? Can you come back in a few days, Friday? I'll find out what I can."

"We live down at Cottage Grove. I come up to see her three, four times a week, but it's hard, I've got two

kids, I mean, seven and eight, and I work four days a
week, but I'll come on Friday. I promise."

"Fine. About this same time?"

"Yeah, that's good for me, late afternoon, I mean."

Late afternoon, four forty-five. Time for a glass of
wine, time to relax, time to see what her father was after. . . . Barbara felt herself make the few internal preliminary adjustments that meant she would stand up
now and finish this last bit of business, get on with relaxing.

Lucille Reiner leaned forward and said, "If he's no
good, this other lawyer, I mean, he might be okay, but
not for her. Would you take the case for us? I have a little money, eight hundred dollars. I mean, I know you
don't charge people here, that's what the lady in jail
said, but this would be different. I mean, you'd have to
go on trial and everything."

Barbara shook her head slightly. "Mrs. Reiner, I don't
even know what case you're talking about."

"Oh, I thought I told you." She ducked her head
again. "It's my sister, Paula Kennerman."

The words *baby killer* leaped into Barbara's mind.
"Let me find out what I can about Mr. Spassero," she
said, feeling a new tightness in her throat, "and talk to
you again on Friday."

Barbara watched Lucille leave and then consciously put
a smile on her face and turned to the back of the restaurant. "You can come out now." She picked up her briefcase and laptop computer and put them on the table,
and then stretched as far as she could reach.

"Done for the day?" Frank asked as he drew near.

"Yep. One-thirty to about this time, Tuesdays and

Fridays. I want you to meet Martin Owens, the best cook in the city, and the best secretary. He keeps the coffee coming."

She introduced the two and then said, "See you on Friday, Martin. Thanks."

"Barbara, you sure you don't want to come back later on for some supper. Good red snapper, that creole recipe you like, corn fritters . . ."

"Hush. He wants to fatten me up until I'm his size," she said. "Come on, Dad. Let's blow." She picked up her briefcase and handed the satchel with the computer to her father.

"Wouldn't hurt to fatten you up a little," Frank muttered.

Martin laughed and nodded.

"Don't you guys know svelte when you see it?" Barbara said, leading the way outside. Martin's laughter followed them.

"Where are you parked?" Frank asked.

"I usually walk over," she said. "It's only three blocks."

He knew that, and he knew that two blocks beyond her house the railroad switchyards started, lined with warehouses, lumberyards, industrial buildings of various sorts. This strip north of Sixth to the river had been built early, when people still clung to the railroad and the river; those with enough money left, others moved in and stayed until they made enough money to leave, and the cycle continued. Now it had become the only real ethnically mixed neighborhood in the city, and the only reason anyone stayed on was that the cheapest housing was here. Every drug bust seemed to happen here, every knifing, street brawls—

He banished the ugly thoughts and said, "Well, let me drive you. A couple of things I want to talk about, if you're not busy."

"Free as the air," she said, getting into the car.

Frank stashed her things on the backseat, got in behind the wheel. "Mind a little detour first?"

"Nope."

He drove in silence until she asked, "You said things to talk about? Today?"

"Martin Owens. He's the football player, isn't he? Or was. He lets you use his restaurant as an office?"

"He's the one. I did him a little favor a few months ago. A legal matter. He's barely making it in the restaurant, but he seems to think he owes me. Good guy."

"Storefront lawyer," Frank muttered, and she turned to look out the window.

She did not ask again what was on his mind. She knew he would get around to it in his own way, first bring it up obliquely, then change the subject, refer to it again later with more details, talk about the weather or something, and so on until it was all out. She was content to wait. When he finally got to it in detail he would pretend to assume that she was in agreement, that since they already had discussed the matter, and he had responded in advance to every possible objection she might raise, the whole issue was already settled. She doubted very much that such would be the case, but meanwhile it was a beautiful June day and she was tired. Her two days a week as a storefront lawyer were wearing.

"God, I hate condos," he said suddenly.

She looked at him in surprise. "So do I, but what's that supposed to mean?"

"And apartments, too," he added. "I've been looking at condos and apartments."

She nodded. "An investment?"

"My accountant says I'm paying too much in taxes."

"Aren't we all?"

He was driving slowly now, watching for house numbers over the top of his half-glasses. Then he stopped. They were on Twenty-first, typical of Eugene in every respect, with tall trees, low buildings, lots of greenery, lots of flowers. "What do you think?" he asked, nodding toward the house he had located.

"I think it's green." Apple green, in fact, with rust-red trim.

"Well, it could be painted. Blue or something."

"That house will always be green no matter how hard you try to cover it up."

He sighed. "I'm afraid you're right." He began to drive again. "There's another one."

"You're going to buy a house," she said. "Is that it?"

"Might as well, seeing how much I hate condos. I've looked at a few. You buy a condo, what do you own? A piece of someone else's building. Want a place I can walk to the office from."

"You're leaving the house at Turner's Point?" Too late she realized she had played right into his hands again.

"Not exactly. See, how it's working out is that some of those old fogies get so set in their ways, they've got roots clear down to bedrock and nothing's going to change them. Old Mary Manchester, for instance, thinks I'm the only one in the office who can rewrite her will every year. I had her this morning." That explained his nice suit and tie. "It's too damn far to drive three days a week," he added glumly.

"Three days? I thought you were easing yourself out of the office, getting ready to retire."

"I am, I am. It's just more complicated than I thought it would be." He had driven through the downtown section, where traffic had thickened into what Eugeneans thought was real congestion. Five cars at a red light meant gridlock here.

At Fifth, instead of turning left toward her house, he made a right turn, and a block later he turned left on Pearl Street, where three of the four corners housed dozens of small shops selling everything from gourmet coffee and some of the best bread to be found to handmade wooden toys, books, natural-fiber clothes—Yuppie Heaven, they call it. He was heading for Skinner Butte Park, she thought then as he drove on. She had walked hours, miles along the river here, walking off trial tension, thinking, scheming. But he turned again, and she suddenly caught her breath. Once, years ago, he had driven up here with her and her mother, just looking. "This is where I want to live," Barbara had said, and Frank had laughed. "The only way you can get a house in this neighborhood is by waiting for the owner to die, and all the heirs, too. Then if the real-estate agent doesn't grab it, you might have a chance."

This was a tiny area, a few square blocks, but she thought of it as an oasis of sanity, serenity, stability. The houses were spacious, old-fashioned, with porches and gabled windows, lots of leaded glass, even stained-glass windows, detached garages. No two houses were similar, but they were all of a piece, well constructed with individual detail work, well maintained, beautifully landscaped, without a hint of pretentiousness.

He stopped before a two-story house that was dove gray, with white trim. An old hemlock tree, top bowed as if in thought, shaded the front; tall rhododendrons lined a driveway, screened the yard on one side; the other side had deep bushes, some in bloom, all mature and lovely.

"Not a bad location," Frank said. "Park and the trail two blocks away, six blocks to the courthouse, seven to the office. Not bad. Walk to the post office, the performing arts center, even the jail. Not bad." He glanced at her. "Well?"

"Not much yard," she said in a low voice.

"Big backyard, even garden space. And a rose arbor. Let's look inside."

"You just happen to have the key?"

He didn't answer, but pulled into the driveway and got out on his side. Slowly Barbara got out and they went inside the house that he obviously intended to buy. It was everything she knew it would be—white-oak floors, a modernized kitchen, bright living room, dining room ... There were stained-glass panels in the living room windows. Upstairs were three rooms, one of them small, a child's room perhaps, and a bath. Another bedroom and den were downstairs.

"It's very nice," she said after they had looked it over. "But pretty big."

"Oh, well, I get claustrophobic in those little boxes they call houses. Come on, let's go. You up for dinner?"

"You bet. But first a shower and a glass of wine or something. Take me home."

He had put down earnest money, she knew as well as

she knew what the rest of his little chat would be. And her answer? That she didn't know yet.

Over dinner he gossiped about the office, about what was going on in court, about a client or two. He did not mention Turner's Point. She asked him about William Spassero.

"Bill Spassero," he said, thinking. "Young, too young maybe. In the public defender's office, couple of years now. About thirty, if that much, but he seems more like twenty. A whiz kid at law school. Hotshot attitude. Ambitious. Why?"

"His name came up. I wondered. I feel about whiz kids the way you feel about condos."

He grinned, and she thought how well they understood each other. They both understood that it was time to get back to the subject at hand.

"Let's have some dessert," he said, "and some of that pressed coffee they make here. It's a real production number."

They watched in appreciative silence as their waiter performed; he ground the coffee at their table, brought water to a boil over a burner, measured the coffee into the glass pot, poured the not-quite-boiling water over it, and tightened the top in place carefully. Then he set a timer. Barbara laughed, and he grinned at her.

They both had cherries jubilee, and that called for a new table-side performance, but finally the productions ended and the coffee was delicious, the cherries no less so. And now Frank said, "I thought maybe it would work out for me to get a house, like I said. I really did look at condos, and apartments, and even a hotel apartment, but hated the idea of all of them. A real house,

that's what I need. I'd come in on Tuesday and go to
the office, like I've been doing, and stay over until Friday morning and head back out. Or maybe Thursday afternoon. Depends on how busy I am."

She nodded. "When do you sign the papers?"

Without hesitation he said, "Monday. But it wasn't
that cut-and-dried from the start. That other house, the
first one, that's the kind of stuff they showed me when
I finally said no to apartments, condos, and such.
Thought you should see it first, as I did." There wasn't
a trace of shame in his expression. "What I thought
might be a good idea, Bobby, is for you to move in, too.
I mean, you'd be alone most of the time, but the house
wouldn't be empty, ripe for the barbarians to sack."

"I'll have to think about it, Dad."

"Of course." He looked past her then and said in a
low voice, "Going out there was the best thing I did after your mother died. I needed the solitude, I guess. It
was good for me for a long time. Then, after you left,
it was different. I kept listening for your steps, kept listening for the car to drive in. I knew you couldn't stay,
but, Bobby, God, I've missed you."

"I'm sorry," she said.

"No, no. I didn't mean to lay it on you, honey. It's
my problem, I know that. And I think I've solved it.
You want a brandy?"

What had she said at the time, just six months ago?
A lifetime ago. What she had said was that she couldn't
stay, she had to move, and he had said simply, I know.
And he had known, had understood. No arguments, no
trying to persuade her to remain. He had understood.
What she had not said was that she couldn't look at the
river; she was afraid she would see Mike's body being

tumbled in the current; she was afraid she would see his body washed up on shore, tangled in the undergrowth.

No brandy, she said firmly, and he said none for him either, and soon they left the restaurant and he drove her home.

"Almost forgot," he said. "We had a conference down at the office today. You're still a member of the firm, you know."

"And will be as long as you're second on the list of partners," she said lightly.

"Damn right. But there's an interesting case at hand. Young playwright in town here claims one of the big studios stole his material. Maybe they did. Someone's going to be doing some fancy traveling on this one. New York, Hollywood. Meet some pretty interesting people along the way." He stopped at her house. "Should be an exciting case, probably won't go to trial, but you never know."

She laughed. "Good night, Dad. Thanks for dinner."

"They pay you anything, those folks who drop in at the restaurant?"

"Some do, some don't. I'm okay, Dad. Don't worry. You want to stay over?"

"And sleep on the floor?" He didn't hide his incredulity. "I'm at the Hilton tonight, tomorrow night." He walked to the door with her and then left.

Actually it was a futon, and she had grown rather fond of it. And yes, her clients paid her, when they could. Fifty dollars here, twenty there, free dinners, all the coffee she could drink. She stood in the doorway to her bedroom and surveyed it critically. Books on raw wood shelves supported by bricks that she had found in a heap in the backyard. More books in stacks on the floor. Several towels draped over a straight chair, overlapping too much to finish drying—she should put up a clothesline out back. Yesterday's clothes on the futon, some to be laundered, some to be folded and put away. She was a pig, she had to admit, but on the other hand this house had no room to put anything. Four rooms and a bath. One closet. Period.

She went into the small living room that held only a couch, one chair, two lamps, more shelves, more books, a tape player, and a special rack for cassettes. More than she needed, she told herself. She could sit in one chair at a time, read one book at a time, hear one cassette at a time. She sank down into the chair.

He was lonely. Of course. But he had brought it all back, and she had been so sure that her grief had passed over into acceptance finally. Wrong, Barbara, she told herself mockingly. Abruptly she jerked up out of the chair and crossed the room to check the door, knowing as she did that it was locked, that this was a meaningless motion. She made herself go to the kitchen, to get a drink of water, to turn off the lights and get ready for bed, and again it was meaningless. It would be hours before she was ready for bed; the twilight of dawn might be lightening her room before she drifted into sleep. She had refused the oblivion of sleeping pills months ago. She had been afraid to give up her grief. If she didn't feel that, what would she feel, she had wondered, and the answer had come: nothing.

At the sink, holding a glass of water she did not want, she surveyed the kitchen: ancient electric stove that had two working burners, a table that wobbled, two straight chairs, two and a half feet of counter space, a small refrigerator that dated back to the sixties. And by the back door was the ever-growing stack of newspapers destined for recycling when she remembered to take them out. The house was dingy with age and neglect and she despised it.

Spassero, she thought then, almost in desperation. Maybe he had made the news in the last month or so. She picked up a stack of newspapers and put it on the table, prepared for a long night. She had found that if she worked, the grief receded; lately she had believed it had changed to something else, but it was there, it was there. She started to go through the papers.

TWO

An hour later Barbara had the papers sorted, with sections of local news on the table. She was scanning for the name Spassero, but what she found were items concerning Paula Kennerman. At first she had read the story as it appeared, then had stopped reading about it as each day brought new facts, new revelations, new horrors. The first story, from back in April, was a paragraph or two. It said only that a child had been fatally burned the previous day and her mother injured in a fire that had burned down the house at the Canby Ranch.

The next day a more complete story had appeared. A group of women who were living at the Canby Ranch had gone out to pick chanterelles. One of the children stayed behind. When her mother, Paula Kennerman, returned to check on her, she had found the house in flames, but before she could locate her daughter, a propane tank exploded. The mother was thrown out the front door to the ground; her daughter was fatally burned in the fire. The mother was hospitalized for shock, concussion, minor burns.

The paper went on to describe the Canby Ranch and the generosity of Grace Canby, who had turned the house over to abused women who needed a safe haven temporarily. Four such women and their children had been living there when the fire occurred.

The next story was a brief report on the funeral of Lori Kennerman, aged six. And the one after that was the last story about the affair that Barbara had read. Lori Kennerman had not died of fire injuries. She had been hit on the side of the head and killed instantly. The fire had been an arson fire. The police were holding Paula Kennerman for questioning; psychiatric examination had been ordered. A public defender, William Spassero, had been assigned by the court to represent Mrs. Kennerman.

It was after two when Barbara finished reading the newspapers. The usual editorials had appeared: justice must take its course; everyone deserves a fair trial; baby-killing must stop. The usual people made the usual statements. Paula's friends and family, expressing disbelief and bewilderment; her husband, who never had touched her and was stunned by her running off, admitted that she had turned against him, had been acting funny. Concerning William Spassero she found very little; he had done the pro forma things: petitioned for a change of venue, denied; petitioned for bail, denied. And nothing else. There was a picture of him and Paula Kennerman at her arraignment. He was large, blond, baby-faced, and she looked shell-shocked. Not as plump as her sister was the only conclusion about her appearance Barbara could make—that and her lack of expression. And Spassero looked as if he should still be studying Composition 101.

Well, what did you expect? she asked herself crossly as she restacked the papers at the back door. This time she left them closer to the threshold. If she stumbled

over them a time or two, it might jar her memory
enough to get rid of them.

Even as Barbara was finally getting ready for bed, a
dozen blocks away a night guard doing a routine check
at Lane County Jail spotted a gleaming pool of blood
beneath the bed of one of the inmates. The guard summoned help, and then taped pressure bandages to both
wrists of the inmate while she waited. They took the patient to the hospital, where a doctor stitched her wrists
and debated giving her a transfusion, decided against it.
No one wanted to put blood into anyone these days unless it was absolutely necessary, and Kennerman was
holding her own for now. They would keep her overnight for observation and reconsider a transfusion if her
condition changed. At the jail, officers searched her
cell; she had been alone because of the threats against
her. They found the tool, a broken plastic comb that she
had sharpened somehow. It had not been very efficient.
She had made a number of attempts, cuts on both arms
that had not gone deep enough, but she had persevered.

The next morning Barbara glared at the coffeepot, willing it to be done, then glared even more fiercely at the
interior of her tiny refrigerator. Almost barren. A little
cheese, two eggs, juice. Some shriveled apples. She
didn't open the crisper, afraid she would find things
growing in there. She yanked out the juice. No milk,
damn it. She had meant to stop at the store on the way
home and her father had made her forget. No milk. After she showered and drank her third cup of black coffee, she went to the room she called her office; she
glared again, this time at her answering machine, which

was winking at her. The message was from her father:
"Want to see Spassero in action? He's in court today,
about eleven."

It had been a mistake to come to court, she told herself
at five after eleven. Too many people knew her, greeted
her, seemed to assume she was working again. Joe
Spender down in the jury room had yelled out as she
passed him, "It's about time you got back in harness.
We missed you." And everyone had turned to gawk,
naturally. Now she was seated in the back row of Court
Room B watching Bill Spassero do his thing. The case
seemed to be about an attempted extortion and malicious vandalism to an apartment building. She paid little attention to the details which were tedious. But
already she had learned something.

Spassero was impressive. He was larger than he had
appeared in the photo she had seen. Over six feet tall,
with more hair than seemed necessary, almost bouffant
it was so fluffy-looking, and very blond. He was not fat,
just big, as if he pumped iron an hour a day. Everything
about him looked expensive, from his clothes, which
were as spiffy as her father's, to the way he held himself, to his voice, which was so mellifluous he sounded
rehearsed, except no one would have rehearsed for a
piddling case like this one.

Ambitious, her father had said, and she understood
exactly. Spassero looked like a young man putting in
time enough to get some headlines, to get a lot of trial
experience quickly, maybe even make a name for himself in court, and then he would become the golden-
haired lad of a prestigious firm, or maybe run for office.
Senator, she thought. He wouldn't aim for less. He

would want the Paula Kennerman case over and done with as swiftly as possible, forgotten as swiftly as possible. Representing a defendant accused of murdering her child would not do him any good at all, even if his office had forced him to take the case. Defending the indefensible left a blot.

So, she told herself, she had seen him in action, and she had made a spot judgment, now what? Nothing followed, and she stood up to leave the courtroom before the lunch recess was called. Spassero glanced her way and nodded, as if to an acquaintance, or even a friend. She nodded back and left.

She had several things to look up in the records room—one of her clients was in a dispute about whose fence it was that kept falling down, and another one believed her grandfather had left a vacant lot to her and two cousins; she wasn't really certain.

It took longer than it should have, but one client had spelled every name wrong and even had the wrong street, and the other one didn't own the property in dispute. She was finishing up when she heard her name called; she turned and saw Spassero.

"I don't want to interrupt," he said, "but I did want to meet you. It is Ms. Holloway, isn't it?"

"Yes. And you're William Spassero. How do you do?" She let him shake her hand and hold it fractionally longer than called for. Close-up inspection did nothing to dispel the boyish image he projected; even his eyebrows were blond, and his cheeks were very pink.

"I've read about you," he said with a remarkably charming grin. "It's a pleasure, Ms. Holloway."

"Thanks," she murmured, and slipped her yellow pad

into her briefcase. She glanced around, checking for pens and pencils, then made a motion to leave.

"I was surprised to see you in court," he said. "You have an interest in that extortion case?"

"None whatever. Just passing by and thought I'd have a look to see if anything's changed. It hasn't."

He shrugged a little, grinned again, and then became very serious and sincere. "Lucille Reiner called me this morning, after she saw Paula. She said she talked to you. I guess she wanted you to check me out."

Barbara regarded him for a moment. He looked as open as a schoolboy denying to a big sister that he had taken her jelly beans. "I talked to her yesterday," she said. "She was confused about what a public defender is, what he does."

"You heard the news about Paula, I guess," he said. "On the radio? Television? It wasn't in the papers yet."

She shook her head.

"She tried to kill herself last night, and very nearly did it."

Barbara could think of nothing to say. She started to walk slowly, and he walked by her side.

"Her sister thinks I'm pushing her, trying to get her to plead. I suggested it as one of her options, that's all. Best thing she could do for herself, actually, but if she won't, she won't. Now this. Remorse, guilt, this isn't going to help her."

"No," Barbara agreed. "Have you seen her? Will she be all right?"

"I talked to the doctor, she'll be okay. They're keeping her sedated for now. I'll drop in tomorrow."

They walked toward the below-the-street tunnel to

the parking lot. Many other people were going that way; it was lunchtime.

"Mr. Spassero, have you considered a second evaluation of her mental condition?" she asked finally, keeping her voice neutral and low.

"What's the use? Ricky Palma is as good as they come. He says she can stand trial."

"I don't know what's the use," Barbara said. "I've read about her case. Everyone except her husband says she was a good mother to her child. If she was, she wouldn't have killed her, unless she was severely mentally disturbed. I guess that's all I mean."

"Every woman who turns up at a place like the Canby Ranch is disturbed," he said. "You know that. But they don't all kill their kids. And maybe the husband knows more about her than anyone on the outside."

She stopped walking and turned to face him, wondering why he was willing to talk about this case with her, why he seemed to be arguing about it with her. People eddied around them as if they were rocks in a river. "Will you get a second opinion?"

"No."

"And last night, was she disturbed then, Mr. Spassero?"

"She's overwhelmed by guilt," he said. The boyish look was gone, and although he looked less certain, a hard edge had come into his voice. "I don't want to stage a courtroom melodrama with two psychiatrists going at each other. Guilt and remorse drive many people to suicide, Ms. Holloway. I accept that."

"I know," Barbara said, and started to walk again. "But so do a lot of other states of mind. Despair, severe depression, fear, helplessness. Even grief."

They exited from the tunnel and climbed the stairs to the parking lot, into the sunlight.

"Good-bye, Mr. Spassero," Barbara said, and started to walk away from him. He caught up with her and she walked a little faster. He put his hand on her arm and when she stopped moving and looked at it, he hastily pulled back; she resumed threading her way among the parked cars.

"Look, you think I'm not handling this case right, take it. It's yours. You think I want this chickenshit? I won't fight a change of attorneys."

They had reached Barbara's car. She unlocked the door, glanced at him, and said again, "Good-bye, Mr Spassero."

Well, well, she thought as she left the lot, Mr. Spassero had a few things to learn, but he was on his way. He knew as well as she that he was not handling the case properly; there should be a second opinion. And he had tried one button after another to induce her to take over: remorse, guilt; the husband might be right; an uncooperative client; an interfering and distrustful sister. Why didn't he just get excused? A client who wouldn't talk to him was reason enough for the court to appoint someone else without another question asked.

All right, she told herself, and tried to put herself in his place. He knew there was no money; the state would pay thirty to forty thousand for the defense of a murder case, but who would pay expenses for a private attorney? She frowned. He knew she couldn't do it—few private attorneys could—but maybe he had goaded her in order to provoke her into advising Paula Kennerman of her right to have a different public defender, in which case the petition would come from the defendant, not him. Would that look better? She didn't see why it would, but maybe he thought so. It didn't matter much, she decided, what his motives were. She fully intended to advise Lucille Reiner to tell her sister she had the right to get rid of him and have someone else appointed. Anyone at all would be an improvement.

So he had read about her, she thought derisively. What he hadn't read was that she was out of it, out of court, out of doing battle with the giant state, money or no money. No more games, she had told her father. No more devious tricks and grandstanding, no more trying to psych out juries that more and more seemed to believe the state was the final authority, that more and more accepted as probably true enough whatever the state claimed, and that seemed more and more often to defy defense attorneys to try to rearrange their gray cells and convince them that the district attorney or his assistant might not be imbued with the wisdom of Solomon, the intelligence of Einstein, the prescience of—

"Goddamn it!" she muttered as she hit the accelerator and cleared an intersection to a blare of horns. Now she was running red lights. She took a deep breath and turned at the next corner. Something to eat first, then see if Mrs. Cleveland was ready to complete the will they had started a month ago. Mrs. Cleveland was having trouble deciding who should get her sewing machine.

After the will, laundromat, and then shopping—No, she had to clean her refrigerator first. She had made herself stop putting anything of consequence in it until she gave it a thorough scrub.

Late in the afternoon she finished the refrigerator. It

didn't look any different, she had to admit, but now she felt she could put milk and lettuce and good things like that into the box without holding her breath. She took the newspapers out to her car and then yanked the sheets off her futon and added them to the basket of laundry. And while she worked at domesticity, she mocked herself, she was avoiding the other problem that she kept pushing out of her mind. What to tell her father.

The next morning she read the news story about Paula Kennerman's attempted suicide. Lucille Reiner was quoted as saying it wasn't guilt that drove her to it. The article was fair enough, not inflammatory, and the reporter had not mentioned guilt, except to quote Lucille, but there it was. Hadn't that asshole told Lucille not to make statements, not to comment?

If this paper was doing this, she thought then, what were the other papers doing? The weeklies, the monthlies. What were the television commentators saying?

She banged her cup down so hard, coffee splashed out on the table, on her shirt. Not my business, she told herself sharply. Pulling off the shirt, she went to the bedroom for another one, then snatched up her briefcase and left the house thinking of her two appointments that morning, two more earth-shaking matters to resolve for clients. She heard the sardonic edge in her mind and shook her head. Actually, she was dealing with people for whom ten dollars was a lot to pay for advice, and for those people these *were* earth-shaking matters.

When she returned home two hours later, there was an old Datsun parked out front with Lucille Reiner behind the wheel. Barbara went to the driver's side and said hello. Lucille jumped as if she had been shocked from a trance.

"Can I ask you something? I mean, here, not at the restaurant?"

"Of course."

"I thought I shouldn't wait until tomorrow. I can wait if you're busy."

"Come on in," Barbara said with resignation. Inside the house she herded Lucille into the kitchen and sat her down in one of the chairs out of the way, then began to make coffee.

"You know she cut her wrists?"

"I know."

"It's my fault," Lucille said dully. "I was supposed to take care of her and I left instead."

Her resignation turning into fatalism, Barbara stopped fiddling with the coffeepot and went to the table. "Okay. Just tell me about it, but start farther back." But she knew, Barbara thought despairingly. She knew this story all too well.

The night her mother left home, Lucille said in a toneless voice, she had made her promise to take care of her little sister. Lucille was fourteen, Paula nine. Their father never had hit them, but that night her mother's eye was swollen shut and her jaw was swollen from a broken tooth. . . . The day Lucille graduated from high school, she had kept going and had never gone back.

"I told Paulie I'd get a job and bring her with me," she mumbled. "But I couldn't. Minimum, that's all, washing dishes, stuff like that, and then I got married. . . . She stayed until she was sixteen, and he started beating on her just like he did our mother."

Once Lucille started talking, Barbara had got up and

finished the coffee. Now she brought two cups to the table and put one before Lucille, who had lapsed into silence and was gazing into the past.

"What happened to your mother after that?" Barbara asked.

"She died. We got a letter. That's when he beat up Paula the first time."

And the district attorney would get all this into the record, Barbara thought moodily, and an expert would testify regarding the statistics that showed the frequency of battered children becoming battering parents.

"Where's your father now?"

Lucille shrugged. "Maybe still in Salem. I don't know. One time after Paula came to Eugene she was going to LCC to get her GED, I mean, she left before she finished school, and we thought she should do that, and we went to the coast and sat watching some of the boats leave. Not just fishing boats, I mean. Pretty boats, yachts. And we said when we got rich that's what we'd do, have a pretty boat and take off. Just take off."

Barbara glanced at her watch. "You said you had something to ask me, Lucille. What was it?"

"Yeah. It's just that this popped in my mind when that reporter came around asking about Craig Dodgson. I mean, did I know him? Did Paula ever talk about him? Stuff like that?"

She was losing a battle with exasperation, Barbara felt then; compassion for the two mistreated girls, sympathy for their fantasy about wealth and escape were not enough to tilt the scales. Carefully she said, "Lucille, I don't know who Craig Dodgson is. I don't know what you're talking about. What reporter? What did the reporter want?"

"He said he had a tip that Craig Dodgson was telling the police that he had joked with Paula about taking her away on his yacht. He said that Craig Dodgson told Paula that no kids were allowed on his boat."

"Oh, God," Barbara sighed. "And what did you tell the reporter?"

"Nothing. I said I didn't know anything about it."

"Did he say anything else, ask you anything else?"

"He said did I realize this gave Paula a motive for killing Lori. And I slammed the door on him. Then I got in the car and came up here to see Paula. I might lose my job. I was supposed to work today."

"And what did Paula say?"

"I told her, and she just said what difference did it make? And I got scared. It was like she was thinking about something else and just not interested. She's thinking of another way to kill herself. I know she is. She's smart. She'll find a way."

She was going to break down, Barbara realized. She said sharply, "Lucille, stop that! Wallowing in self-pity isn't going to help your sister." She took both cups to the sink and dumped out Lucille's coffee. She had not touched it. She refilled the cups and returned to the table. "Listen to me," Barbara went on then. "Have you told anyone else about this? Spassero?"

"No. I went to see Paula and came straight over here."

"What is the question you said you wanted to ask?"

"Will you see if they'll let you in? So you can talk to her, I mean? She won't talk to the lawyer, and I don't blame her, but she won't talk to me, either."

"What on earth makes you think she'd talk to me, then?"

"People do. I knew it when I first saw you, and me, the way I've been talking. She would, I know she would. Make her understand she has to tell her side."

This was a different level, Barbara understood. Explaining the system to Lucille so that she could inform her sister of her rights was Level A, but what Lucille was asking would put Barbara on Level B, and whether it was higher or lower she didn't know. Different. There was too much she didn't know, she thought then. Was Paula simply stonewalling? Was she crazy? Was she so depressed and withdrawn that she was uncomprehending? Would she grasp the fact that she didn't have to stick with Spassero? Would she understand that she had to talk to her attorney, whoever it was, if she expected any kind of fairness? In the end, would it matter who represented her? she asked herself bitterly. *Baby killer.*

"Please," Lucille whispered.

"I'll talk to her," Barbara said. "But understand this, Lucille; that's all. I'll explain her rights to her, no more than that, but don't expect any miracle. If she doesn't want to talk, that's it."

THREE

BARBARA EXPLAINED THE public defender system to Lucille then, and what Paula could do about Spassero. "All she has to do is write a letter to the judge, say she's uncomfortable with her attorney, that they are incompatible, and she will be assigned someone else. They're good people over there, for the most part. Spassero's just not for her." Then she asked, "What did you mean, if I can get in?"

"They said she's in seclusion or something. Only family and people who get cleared with her lawyer can see her." She looked eager, on the edge of her seat as if poised to take action herself, as if now she saw that there was hope. She started to say something, but Barbara waved her hand.

"Wait a minute. I want to think." She got up and paced the length of the small kitchen, not big enough by far, she thought distantly, and she hated the feel of the vinyl tiles underfoot. She stopped at the sink and stood looking out the back window at a rhododendron that had notches eaten out of every leaf, on its way to extinction. Beetles of some sort. She could call Spassero and clear it through him, but she did not want to talk to him, since she was going to advise his client to drop him like a maggoty apple. Seclusion, what did that mean? Isolation? She bit her lip and finally went back to the table.

"Where did Paula live, here in Eugene? Where are her things?"

"They had an apartment, her and Jack, I mean. He filed for divorce. I went there to get some stuff to take her, you know, pictures and shampoo, stuff like that, and he said not to come back. I guess her stuff is still there, unless he threw it out," she added, scowling. "What he can't sell, he'll toss, that's his style."

"All right. Is there anything of yours in the apartment? Anything you might have loaned her?"

Lucille started to shake her head, then she said, "Yes. My blue sweater. And a couple of books. Maybe some of the kids' stuff. Oh, and a covered casserole."

"We're in business," Barbara said with satisfaction. She went to the office for a legal pad and pen, which she placed before Lucille. "I'm going to draw up a couple of legal documents, and you make a list of everything you can think of that is or was yours that you would like to have back."

Lucille was uncomprehending but cooperative, and Barbara left her at the table and went to draw up her two documents and print them out in triplicate. When she brought them back, Lucille had finished. She signed the document without a second glance when Barbara slid it across the table and patiently told her what it meant.

"I have been retained by you to take possession of your belongings that are in the Kennerman apartment. Your sister's permission is necessary for me to gain entry, and I will try to get it from her. The other document

is for her, giving you permission to take possession of
her personal belongings and keep them safe for her until
she can claim them."

Now that Lucille was her client, she advised her very
carefully about talking to reporters, about the difference
between "No comment" and "I don't know anything
about it."

They agreed that fifty dollars was a fair charge for
the duties Barbara had agreed to do, and then Lucille
asked if she would mind holding the check a day or two
until she could take some money out of the savings account to cover it.

At the county jail an hour later Barbara argued with a
sergeant, and then with a lieutenant, and watched them
confer out of hearing, look up from her ID to her, reex-
amine the document signed by Lucille, until finally the
lieutenant shrugged, handed everything back to the sergeant, and walked away. An escort was summoned to
take her to a small conference room crowded by a table
and two chairs. She sat at the table waiting for Paula
Kennerman to be produced. "For all the good it'll do
you," the sergeant had said. "Might as well talk to a
log."

To a mobile corpse would have been more appropriate, Barbara thought, when Paula was brought in by a
lean, gray-haired matron who watched her sit down,
then went to the door. "I'll be right outside," she said.

Everything about Paula looked dead. She was as col-
orless as a body waiting for the undertaker to restore it
to a semblance of life. Her brown hair was lank and
dull. Even her dark eyes seemed dull, with purple shadows beneath them. She was terribly thin. The bandages

started around the heel of her thumb, reached nearly to her elbows.

"My name is Barbara Holloway. You don't know me, but I've talked to your sister."

There was not even a flicker of interest. Paula looked straight ahead, as if she were alone in the room.

"Lucille has retained me to go to your apartment and pick up some of her possessions. She made a list. But we need your signature."

Paula's eyes shifted to the briefcase on the table, and a new alertness enlivened her face, and vanished almost instantly.

"Unfortunately they didn't let me bring a pen in here, but I have the papers," Barbara said. What would she have attempted? she wondered. Grab the pen, stab herself in the heart with it? "I have another document giving Lucille permission to remove your personal belongings and keep them for you until you are ready to claim them. Will you agree to that?"

Paula shrugged. "What difference does it make? I don't care."

Slowly Barbara opened her briefcase and brought out the papers. Paula did not look at them. "Will you make out a list of things for Lucille to keep for you?"

"Let her take whatever she wants. Get the matron and I'll sign anything you say. And then leave me alone." The words were toneless.

"I also told Lucille that I would advise you about your public defender. You don't have to keep the one they assigned to you if you're not satisfied with his performance."

Paula did not respond.

"I won't tell you the danger you're in," Barbara said

evenly. "I believe you understand that perfectly well. The only thing the state was lacking before was motive, and now they think they have it. Do you know Craig Dodgson?"

Paula shook her head.

Fighting frustration, Barbara rose from her chair. "Well, have you thought of this? You said in your statement to the police that the house was already burning when you got there. Have you considered what that means? Someone else killed your child, Paula, that's what it means, if you told the truth."

"I can't help it," Paula said. "Call the matron."

Barbara walked to the door, but she did not knock yet. She remained motionless, facing the door for a moment, and then with her back to Paula she said in a low voice, "I keep wondering which loss is worse, the loss of someone you've had a long time, or the loss of someone you have just begun to love. I don't know. Last winter, the man I loved died. We were going to be married. I went to the coast. You know how the coast is in winter, gale winds, the surf crashing. It was raining. I stood on a cliff and looked at the water and I knew this was the way for me. I'd thought of other ways, but they didn't seem right, and this did. The water was all gray and black and foamy. I stood there a long time and then I went to a motel to think about it, to write a letter to my father, tidying up. And the next day I went back to the same place. The sea was smoother. I thought, Yes, now is the time, but I just stood there, and finally I had to leave again. I didn't want to live. He was all I had to live for, but I didn't do it. I tried once more, that same night. And I finally understood why I couldn't do it. He would have been so ashamed of me. I couldn't do anything to make him ashamed of me when he was alive, and I had to honor his memory, not do anything that would have made him ashamed, even if he was gone."

"Stop it!" Paula cried. "Why are you telling me all that? Get out of here!"

"I don't know why I told you," Barbara said quietly, not moving. "I haven't told anyone else. I tore up my letter and threw it into the ocean, and I went home."

"It's not the same," Paula whispered raggedly. "He wasn't your child."

"No. He was my life." Barbara turned to look at Paula then.

She had come to life, but the life was too painful to bear. Her face was twisted; tears ran down her cheeks. She was holding up her arms, staring at the bandages. "She was all I had to live for," she said, choking on the words. Abruptly she dropped her arms to the table and buried her face in them, sobbing.

Barbara was holding the doorknob with one hand behind her back in a position that brought sharp stabbing pains in her shoulder. She moved her hand and walked to Paula, feeling unsteady and weak, and tentatively put her hand on Paula's shoulder. She sobbed harder. Barbara leaned in close, put one hand on Paula's head, her other arm around her shoulders, and held her.

When the shudders began to lessen, Barbara went to the door and opened it to say to the matron, "Could we have some tissues, please?"

"Tissues?"

"Kleenex. I don't have any with me. And maybe a glass of water?"

The matron opened the door farther and looked past

Barbara, then at her with an incredulous expression. "I'll get some," she said and shut the door.

When Paula finally raised her head, Barbara had the box of tissues and the glass of water at hand. She eased the documents from under Paula's arm and sat down again to look them over while the young woman blew her nose and mopped her face and drank some of the water.

"I made a mess of your work," Paula said. "I'm sorry."

"Don't be. I'll just run off some more copies." Stuffing the crumpled, sodden papers into her briefcase, she asked, "Will you help yourself, Paula? Will you talk about it?"

"Yes," she whispered, and then more strongly, "but not to him. Mr. Spassero. He wants me to tell them I killed Lori, that I lost my head and hit her and set the fire." She jerked up from the chair and swayed.

Barbara grabbed her hand from across the table. "Sit down," she said sharply. "Go on, sit down." When Paula was seated again, Barbara let go of her hand. "No more for today," she said briskly. "You've had enough. I'll make new copies of everything and bring it all back tomorrow. You try to rest, and we'll talk then. Okay?"

Paula nodded. She looked ghastly; her face was blotched, her eyes red-rimmed and swollen. But she looked alive.

"What do you mean, I can't see her?" Barbara demanded of the sergeant the next morning at ten. She had been thinking there was plenty of time to wrap this up, get the signatures, help Paula draft a letter to the court requesting a different attorney, have a bit of lunch, and be at the restaurant in plenty of time for her first drop-in client. She peered closer at the sergeant's identity tag: SGT. R. T. PERRY.

"Look, Ms. Holloway, I'm just following orders. Okay? She's sleeping. Dr. Grayling said he'd talk to you if you want. You want to talk to him?"

"You bet I do."

The sergeant began to rummage through papers on his desk. "Here it is. He left a card with his number and address. He's already been here and left again, but he'll be in the office all day and he said he'd see you between patients. That's all I can do, Ms. Holloway. I'm sorry."

She believed him. He was gray-haired, florid, overweight, and, no doubt, as tough as he looked, but at the moment his expression appeared genuinely regretful. She wanted to ask him why Paula was sleeping at ten in the morning, but he wasn't the one to question, she decided, glancing at the card. Dr. Grayling was in the medical building across the street from Sacred Heart Hospital, where they had taken Paula to stitch up her arms. She nodded to the sergeant. "Thanks."

A freight train was howling its way through town behind the jail when she went out to her car. For a moment she thought of the prisoners up there behind narrow barred windows listening to the trains, wishing, wishing. . . . She shook her head and got in her car. From Fifth down to Seventh, which turned into Franklin, to Patterson, one more block to the medical office building. The hospital sprawled across two city blocks, and all around it, like the moons of Jupiter, satellites had appeared—sometimes it seemed overnight—professional buildings, pharmacies, parking structures, gift and flower shops, restaurants, wide skyways linking buildings. The complex couldn't spread out to the west, the university grounds started a block away; instead it was inexorably moving south and east, gobbling up neighborhoods. She drove into a parking structure; there was absolutely no parking on the street in the area. It took her longer to find a vacant slot for her car than the drive over had taken. Med biz was booming, she thought gloomily.

She found her way to Grayling's office, where she waited ten minutes in a large anteroom where dozens of other people were waiting to see half a dozen different doctors who shared the common reception area.

The office she was taken to was minuscule, with hardly enough room for the two chairs opposite the doctor's desk. Dr. Grayling was behind the desk; he made a half-hearted motion toward rising, then sat down again. If he moved back more than six inches, he would have been up against a window. His hair was a touch too long, dark and straight, and he wore horn-rimmed glasses that were too low on his nose although he pushed them up time and again. He was about forty, she decided; it was hard to tell because he looked tired and harried. He pushed his hair back, pushed his glasses back, shifted in his chair, and kept in motion.

He didn't register any surprise at her blue jeans and T-shirt, and she decided he hadn't noticed. She had thought briefly of going home and changing, and had decided not to. If what she had on was good enough for the county jail, it was good enough for the jail doctor.

"Ms. Holloway," he said after she took one of the chairs, "you know the system we're using over at the jail, don't you?"

She shook her head. "Tell me."

"Yes. Well, there are a couple of nurses on duty and a paramedic. In fact, one of the nurses is actually a paramedic. And I'm on call. You know, for things they can't handle, or shouldn't handle."

"You treated Paula Kennerman the other night? At the hospital?"

"Yes. They called me and I met them there and took care of her. I've seen her off and on from the start, of course. Very early on I told her that if she needed something to help her sleep, she could have it."

"Did she talk to you?"

"Not a word."

She wished he would get a haircut, and have his glasses adjusted, or simply sit on his hands, but they were in constant motion, fiddling with his glasses, his hair, a few papers, a patient's file.

"What happened last night, or this morning?" Barbara asked.

His hands came to rest on the file folder. "I don't know," he said. "This morning when I was over there they said her lawyer had brought in a private doctor for her, that she had been agitated and the doctor had given her a sedative. From now on she will be in his care." He was lining up papers, rearranging them in minute increments. "That's his right," he said hurriedly, watching the progress his hands were making. "The county encourages inmates to have their private physicians after the initial examination. That's not at all irregular."

She watched him and waited. When he remained silent, she asked, "What *is* irregular, then, Doctor?"

"I didn't say that," he said swiftly.

"I'm willing to forget this whole conversation," Barbara said. "It never happened. But I have to know why you agreed to see me, what it is you have to tell me. Not only that she has a private doctor now."

He stood up and pushed his chair back against the window; he looked with despair at the cramped office and sat down again. They hadn't even given him pacing room, Barbara thought with sympathy.

"They told me you had a breakthrough with Paula," he said then. "We all tried, but you did it. There's something we don't talk about much," he went on, sounding almost embarrassed. "The will to live. In children we say failure to thrive. Almost the same thing. She has lost the will to live. I tried to get through to her, I really tried. I don't know what's going to happen at the trial, or what will happen to her after that, but while she was my patient, I tried to help her." His hands had started their restless motions again.

"You're still trying to help her, aren't you?"

"Yes. But I'm in a funny position." He attempted a grin that failed and was only a grimace. "I can't protest what another physician does, you see. I can't override her choice of doctors. But her sister could find out if that really was her choice, or . . . But I can't really get in touch with her, either." He added almost ingenuously, "They told me you were representing the sister."

"You don't think the new doctor was her choice?"

He shrugged. "I don't think so, but I don't know for certain. Her attorney said he was her doctor."

"Who is the other doctor?"

"Peter Copley," he said in a low voice.

"And what did he prescribe?"

"Halcion."

"And the dosage?"

"The nurse showed me," he said. "Two blue ones initially, then one every four hours." He lifted the folder he had been fooling with and picked up a paper, the kind that pharmaceutical companies inserted in their medications. He held it out to her. "Just some information about Halcion," he said, not looking at her. When she took the paper covered with small print, he stood up, pushed his glasses back into place, and held out his hand. "Thanks for coming." His relief was transforming; all the indecision, the hesitation, the embarrassment had evaporated.

She rose from her chair to shake his hand. "Thank you, Doctor." She hesitated at the door. "I won't mention your name, but the sergeant knows I was coming over here."

"Sergeant Perry doesn't know anything," he said quietly.

She nodded and left.

In the parking structure, sitting in her car, she read the information sheet quickly, then read it again more slowly. "Son of a bitch," she muttered under her breath.

Home, she decided. Someplace where she could pace, curse if she wanted to. She drove home and called Lucille. Then she called her own doctor and caught him on his way out to lunch.

Without mentioning names or details, she described Paula and her condition. "A lot of stress, anxiety, fear, and grief. She lost a lot of blood and is about fifteen pounds underweight."

"Good grief."

"Tell me this. Am I right, that's double the high end of the normal dosage?"

"Probably. I don't prescribe it; I'd have to look it up."

"Exactly. I want reports about side effects, the warnings, you know the sort of thing. You guys get that stuff sent to you all the time."

"You know I can't second-guess another doctor without seeing the patient, and besides, what you want is in the library," he said.

"I need it now."

"Everybody needs whatever it is now," he said with some sharpness.

She could pick up the material at one forty-five, he agreed at last.

While talking to him she had thumbed through the phone book and found the number for the public defender's office; she punched in the numbers.

"I'm sorry," a woman said. "Mr. Spassero is out of town. He won't be back until Monday."

"He must have left a number where he can be reached."

"I'm afraid not. If you'll leave your number, Ms. Holloway, I'm sure he'll get in touch with you on Monday."

Barbara hung up. She tried his home number, got a machine, and left a message. Monday, she thought bleakly. Monday.

She walked to the kitchen and stood at the sink looking at the doomed rhododendron, but she was thinking of Paula Kennerman, who was equally doomed. Abruptly she went back to her office and again riffled through the phone book, took a deep breath, and then punched in some more numbers.

"May I speak with either Judge Paltz's secretary or his clerk?" she said to the woman who answered.

She had met Judge Paltz many different times over the years, but she never had tried a case in his court. He and her father had been close in the past, until he had become a judge and her father had moved out to the country and gradually circumstances and distance had separated them. The judge was seventy-three, she knew, one year older than her father.

He was heavily built, with thin gray hair and a deeply weathered face. A fisherman, she remembered. His chambers office looked like the ideal grandfather's study: deep comfortable chairs covered with dark mohair, fine walnut tables, an even finer walnut desk cluttered with keepsakes—a porcelain clock, pictures in silver frames, a ceramic boot that held pens and pencils. . . . A reassuring sort of a room. The only surprising thing about it now was the presence of William Spassero, who had stood up when she entered.

"Barbara," Judge Paltz said, taking her hand, enclosing it in both of his. "How have you been keeping yourself? You look wonderful."

This time she was dressed for the occasion in a navy cotton dress with a white jacket and white sandals. "I'm fine, Judge Paltz, thank you. Mr. Spassero," she said with a slight nod. His acknowledging nod was as cool as hers had been. The judge led her to a chair and saw that she was seated comfortably, as if she were his elderly aunt, brittle and frail.

He sat in a chair between her and Spassero and then, with his hands on his knees, he said, "Barbara, the mes-

sage I was given said there is an emergency situation
with Bill's client. Is there?"

"Yes, sir. I believe there is."

"All right. Naturally, I couldn't talk to you about the
defendant without her attorney being present also."

"Of course," she said. "I tried to reach Mr. Spassero,
and when I couldn't I had no recourse except to appeal
to the court. Thank you for arranging the meeting, sir."

He inclined his head fractionally. "You both understand that under no circumstance can I permit any discussion of material that has a bearing on the case of
Paula Kennerman?" It was not really a question. Barbara nodded.

"Yes, sir," Spassero said. "Your Honor, may I present
my understanding of this matter before Ms. Holloway
goes into whatever her emergency is?" When the judge
nodded, he went on, very smoothly, showing no ani-
mosity or resentment, only puzzlement. "Sir, I was in
court on Wednesday when Ms. Holloway chose to sit in
and observe me. I didn't know if I should be flattered or
intimidated," he said with his boyish grin. "But later,
when I spoke to her, it became clear that she was antag-
onistic. She questioned the way I was handling Paula
Kennerman's case, criticized me, even offered gratui-
tous advice." He spread his hands in a helpless gesture.
"I was baffled, sir. I know I don't have a lot of experience as a trial attorney, but this struck me as so unusual
that I mentioned it to one of the more experienced attorneys, and he said with some emphasis that her behavior
had been unprofessional, possibly even unethical."

Barbara watched him with great interest; his hurt-
little-boy act was very convincing.

Judge Paltz shifted his position, crossed his arms

over his chest. "I see. You wish to lodge a formal complaint?"

"No, Your Honor."

"I take it we haven't got to the emergency yet," Judge Paltz said agreeably. "Any time now. Are you through, Bill?"

"Not quite, sir. You know that Paula Kennerman has received many threats, and that the district attorney and I mutually agreed that her visitors should be screened. For her own safety. Yesterday Ms. Holloway got through the screening to see the defendant and left her in a highly agitated state. She was so excitable that I felt obligated to bring in a second doctor to evaluate her condition. It was his opinion that Mrs. Kennerman should be sedated and kept in seclusion for the next several days under his observation and care." He drew in a breath and said slowly, "Today Ms. Holloway was denied permission to see the defendant, who was sleeping. And that, I'm afraid, is the emergency."

"I see." The expression on Judge Paltz's face remained interested and neutral. "Barbara? First, are you representing a client in this matter?"

"Yes, sir. Mrs. Reiner, Paula Kennerman's sister." She withdrew the various papers she had collected, each set paper-clipped together. "This is my agreement with Mrs. Reiner," she said, handing him the documents. "I went to see Mrs. Kennerman in order to get her signature. The papers were ruined, and when I tried to get back this morning I was turned away."

"The emergency, Barbara," Judge Paltz said with a touch of irritation.

"Mrs. Reiner talked to Dr. Copley, who is now treating her sister, and she is very upset by the choice of

doctors and his treatment. Paula Kennerman is not incompetent; she can choose her own doctor and should
not be forced to submit to one who is not under contract
with the state."

"Is she being forced to submit to medical treatment?"
the judge asked Spassero.

"No, sir. As I said, she was very excitable, and it was
the doctor's decision—"

"She was restrained and forced to take a massive
dose of Halcion," Barbara said sharply. "And once a patient has been tranquilized to the extent that dosage
would induce, no further force is required."

"You questioned my competence, and now you're
questioning the competence of a distinguished doctor,"
Spassero snapped.

"Yes, I am. Your Honor, I have gathered information
from a number of sources concerning the use of
Halcion, especially the contraindications for a person in
the physical condition Paula Kennerman suffers at this
time—anemic, under great stress, anxious, depressed."
She held out the sheaf of papers she had clipped together. "These are photocopies of the original articles,
and stapled to each one is an excerpt of the pertinent
data."

With some reluctance Judge Paltz accepted the papers.

"What is it you want?" Spassero demanded harshly.
"First you tell me to get a second opinion, and then you
create an emergency because I brought in a second doctor. What game are you playing?"

"Now, Bill," Judge Paltz said.

"I asked if you intended to get a second psychiatric
evaluation, not if you intended to bring in a hack who

seems to think the only good patient is a sleeping patient."

"Now, Barbara," Judge Paltz said, only minimally sharper. "Both of you, quiet." He began to read through the excerpts, and after a moment he stood up, went to his desk, and picked up his telephone. "Doris, would you run down Dr. Grayling for me, please?"

While he waited for the call to be put through, he scanned the other excerpts and then picked up the documents Barbara had drawn up for Lucille Reiner. Spassero and Barbara waited silently.

When the phone rang, a soft melodious three notes, Barbara felt her stomach tighten.

"Dr. Grayling, good of you to let me interrupt your day. I just have a couple of questions to ask you, looking for a little information, you know." He swiveled his chair around and his voice faded so that his words no longer carried across the room. The conversation seemed to continue a long time before he swiveled back, saying, "I do appreciate all this, Dr. Grayling. Thank you so much." After he hung up, he cupped his chin in his hand in thought for what seemed a long time.

Finally he folded his hands before him on the desk and said, "A defendant who is being held in jail awaiting trial becomes of necessity a ward of the court. But a defendant who has been declared competent to stand trial is deemed competent to make independent decisions concerning certain personal affairs, such as the dispensation of belongings, a will, and non-emergency private medical treatment. Once certain treatments are initiated, however, it appears that independent decisions are not trustworthy, and for that reason I have asked Dr. Grayling to reassume his position as Mrs. Kennerman's doctor until Monday, when she will be given the opportunity to choose her own physician if she so desires. Dr. Grayling's opinion is that it will take until Monday for the medication to be out of her system enough to trust her independence in this matter."

He regarded Barbara levelly, then turned the same look of measured assessment toward Spassero. "Because her mental functions may be disturbed by the medication she has received, I order both of you not to see her until Dr. Grayling gives his permission, probably on Monday after his examination."

"Your Honor!" Spassero cried out. "I object to this entire proceeding. Ms. Holloway created a crisis in an attempt to prejudice the court for some reason which I simply can't fathom. She has done this in a way that is so prejudicial, my integrity has been impugned, Dr. Copley's reputation has been damaged, and for what purpose God alone knows."

"Well, she says she wants to get a blue sweater back for her client. Isn't that what Mrs. Reiner retained you to do?"

"Yes, sir," Barbara said meekly. She could not interpret the glint in the judge's eyes.

He stood up and gathered together the papers she had given him. "As for the rest of it, Bill, leave it alone. No one's accusing you of anything, far as I can tell. You saw your client animated, according to Dr. Grayling, and that was so unusual you made a mistake. It happens. But your doctor probably made a bigger mistake. And no one outside this room knows what went on in here." He walked around his desk. "I think we're through, aren't we?" He handed the papers to Barbara.

He ushered them to the door, and said to Barbara. "Sometime, when you have plenty of time, ask your father about that sturgeon we wrestled with over at Snake River. And, Barbara, keep in mind that the court appointed Mr. Spassero to represent Paula Kennerman. And to my knowledge neither of them has petitioned the court for a change."

The door clicked shut. Barbara and Spassero walked out silently through the offices, out to the street where the sunshine was blinding. Still not speaking, he turned one way and strode off, and she headed the other way toward her car. Only when she was inside it, holding the wheel, did she relax, and then she grinned. *Asshole.*

FOUR

SHE SHOULD PUT chairs on her porch, a few magazines, let her guests wait in comfort, she thought when she pulled up at her house. This time it was her father waiting in his car, reading a paperback book.

She tooted her horn and waved when he looked up. He met her on the sidewalk.

"I thought you were out of here," she said, planting a kiss on his cheek.

"Why do you have an answering machine if you don't intend to listen to the calls?" He looked her over. "So you really were in court?"

"Not exactly. Come on in."

"I went to the restaurant and Martin said you were tied up in court. I didn't believe him. You look pretty good."

She laughed and opened her door. "Help yourself to some wine and pour some for me, will you? I have to make one call and then I'm free as a bird."

She called Lucille Reiner and had to wait for a child to go get her, and by then Frank was standing in the doorway with a bottle of wine and a glass.

"This?"

"It's perfectly good wine, Dad, honest." Then she

56

spoke into the phone. "Oh, Lucille? She's off all medication and you can see her during regular visiting hours. I'll pay a call on Monday."

She listened to Lucille, grinning at her father, who was tentatively tasting the wine. He looked at it in wonder and, shaking his head, strolled away; by the time Barbara was finished with Lucille, he had gone out to the yard and was examining the dying rhododendron. He came in as she poured wine for herself. His glass was on the table, hardly touched.

"That rhody needs spraying."

"I know. I'll get to it. Now, why aren't you back home? What was on your message?"

"What I thought. You don't listen to the calls." He lifted his glass and sniffed, then tasted it again. "Drinkable," he said. "A beverage, not actually wine, but drinkable."

"Any time," she said, sitting at the table. There were several letters she had not got around to opening that morning; she started on them.

"And don't read your mail. Takes a personal visit to get through to you," he commented, going to the door, gazing out. "What I thought I might do is stay in town and look around for a few things, for the house. Thought I might talk you into hitting an auction or two with me, maybe do some looking around in a furniture store or two." When he glanced at her, she nodded. " 'Course, I'll just move all your stuff over. If you want me to. Even if you don't use the bed, in case I have company I'll be able to offer more than the floor."

She grinned. "Move the stuff, Dad. Let's talk about dinner. If I take you out, I can get out of these fancy duds, and we'll go to Martin's or Hilda's. Have you eaten there?" He shook his head. "Well, you should. It's awfully good, Central and South American cuisine. And very nice Chilean wines. It's on Blair, four blocks, walking distance. There are bleeding hearts and lambs' ears in the yard." She laughed at the sceptical look on his face. "On the other hand, if you take me out, I won't change."

"Flip you for it," he decided, and produced a coin. "Heads it's my treat."

She laughed harder, got up, crossed to him, and snatched the coin from his hand. "Cheat! You've been using that coin until it's worn so smooth you can't even tell it has two heads."

She took him to Hilda's, where, appropriately, they stopped to admire the flowers. The next day they drove the twelve miles to Junction City and an auction where he bought nothing, and then to an antique store in south Eugene where he considered a table for a long time and then shook his head. On Sunday, just as fruitless as Saturday had been, he said he might as well bring his own couch and other things from the Turner's Point house. He couldn't sit on foam, he explained, made his butt sore; his couch had inner springs, the way God intended. She nodded gravely. Then they went to a garden shop, where he seemed to go on a buying binge— garden implements, gloves, a straw hat, even a tiller.

"Couldn't you just have someone come in and till up garden space?" she asked.

"Could. But I want to do it."

There had always been a garden when she was growing up; her mother and father had tended it together most of the time. After her death he had sold the house, got rid of all the garden equipment, moved out to Turn-

er's Point, and he had not gardened since; Barbara
never had gardened after her one childhood attempt at
weeding, when she had hoed out every seedling carrot.
She experienced a stabbing jolt of memory: how they
had laughed, holding each other helplessly. Not right
away, but later that evening. And she, Barbara, had
marched off indignantly. No jealousy flared with the
memory, although in the not too distant past it would
have done so; now she felt only a sadness for him, pity
for his loss. She turned away before he could look up
and decipher the expression on her face. He would take
a lot from her, she knew, but not pity. Never that.

While he discussed tillers and delivery, she bought a
potted red geranium to put on her porch to keep her visitors company if they got there when she was away.

He brought up the copyright case only twice, adding
details each time, still not asking her directly to take it.
She played innocent.

He was excited about the house, she thought fondly
when he dropped her off Sunday afternoon. She was
happy for him, and still undecided about moving in. After he got settled down again with his own familiar furniture, and his garden out back, maybe then he would
realize he really didn't need her. He still was denying it,
but she bet herself that within a year he would sell his
house out on the river. And the garden would be his excuse. He would say no one can tend a garden with a
forty-mile-long hoe.

She went to bed early that night, but was still groggy
with sleep when her doorbell jolted her awake the next
morning. Eight o'clock, she groaned, and started to turn
over when the bell shrilled again.

She tied her robe belt as she made her way to the

door; when she lifted the corner of the blind she saw her father. He jabbed the bell again as she unlocked the door and pulled it open.

"What's wrong? What happened?"

He pushed his way in, slamming a rolled-up newspaper against his palm. "You tell me. Barbara, are you mixed up in that Kennerman case?"

"What's this all about?" she demanded. "What's that paper you're mutilating?"

He thrust it at her. "You were in Lewis Paltz's chambers on Friday, weren't you? That was your afternoon in court. Messing around with that baby killer's case."

"I'm not 'messing around' with anything." When she opened the paper, a tabloid she never had seen before, the banner headline leaped at her: BABY KILLER JUDGE UNFIT! The story lead-in was in bold print: *Baby Killer Kennerman, on the verge of confession, was put on hold as Judge Paltz and an old friend swapped fish stories in the judge's chambers Friday.*

"Oh no!" Barbara breathed.

"Christ on a mountain! You are involved!"

Barbara moved past him and put the paper on the kitchen table. Her hands were shaking.

"Go shower or wash your face or something," Frank snapped. "I'll put on coffee."

She stumbled from the room into the shower and let the water beat on her in full force for a long time. Why did he do it? she asked over and over. Why did Spassero do it?

Frank was at the back door facing out when she returned to the kitchen and wordlessly poured coffee before sitting down to read the newspaper. Every fact was followed by an explanation or opinion that was cruel, malicious, dangerous, and wrong. She, Barbara, had gone to see Paula Kennerman; the article added that her purpose had been to stop a confession that was in the works. She had objected to the doctor and his treatment; the paper said she was insistent on bringing in her own private psychiatrist, who would declare Baby Killer Kennermán insane. Judge Paltz had made the only reference to his friendship with her father and a fishing expedition; the paper said she had used old loyalties and affection to wheedle out of the judge (who might be senile or at the very least was said to have an eye for a pretty face) a three-day period during which Baby Killer Kennerman's court-appointed attorney could not speak with her. Time enough, it went on, for her sister, on orders from Holloway, to talk her out of confessing.

"Good God," she said when she finished the article.

"There's more," Frank said. "Back page."

She turned the paper over and saw her own face, a picture taken a year or more ago. Over it was the question: WHO IS BARBARA HOLLOWAY? She scanned the rest of the page swiftly, her stomach churning. *"A member of the law firm Bixby, Holloway . . . Dropped out of sight a number of years ago. Doing what? Organizing legal counsel for her 'sisters'? . . . Sowed so much confusion and doubt an alleged murderess had charges dismissed, but only after two innocent men died in a meaningless and avoidable accident. . . . Who is she? Single, never married, her father calls her Bobby, engaged in a man's profession, chooses to wear male clothing, no makeup. 'Nuff said? One last item: She seems to believe no woman is capable of committing any crime more horrendous than marrying a man."*

"Who is this?" Barbara cried furiously as she yanked the paper open, searching for the masthead. She stopped at a picture of William Spassero, looking like a high-school football star. His headline: RISING PUBLIC DEFENDER OUTSMARTED BY FEMALE SHARK. *"With less than two years as public defender, where he was making a name for himself, William Spassero finally met the most predatory creature God saw fit to put on earth—a female shark hungry for blood. And he lost. . . ."*

There, the masthead. Publisher, Richard Dodgson; editor, Richard Dodgson; circulation, Kay Dodgson . . . The two of them apparently did it all. She frowned at the name, but could not recall where she had heard it recently.

"Judge Paltz is senile or a womanizer, Spassero is a wimp, and I'm a shark," she said finally. The words fell flat.

"And don't forget the defendant," Frank said. "She's a baby killer." He left the door and sat down at the table opposite her. "You going to tell me anything?"

"Sure," she said. "Everything." She did so, succinctly.

"A blue sweater," he said in disbelief. "All this over a damn blue sweater? For God's sake, buy the woman a sweater and get out of it!"

"I'll see if I can get an appointment to see Judge Paltz," she said, nudging the paper away from her.

"That's the dumbest thing you could do. What would you say? You didn't talk, and Bill Spassero must be guilty? Lewis knows damn well it was one of you. Write him a letter and hand-deliver it to his secretary. No accusations, just express your dismay and include a firm statement that you talked to no one. That's all."

After a moment, she nodded. He knew Lewis Paltz, knew how he would react to all this, what he must be thinking. And Spassero would be there making his own case. Why did he do it? she asked herself again, and got no further than before with an answer.

"Thanks, Dad, that's what I'll do. I'm really sorry the firm got dragged in like this."

He made a dismissive gesture. "Look, Bobby, we want someone to handle that copyright case. It's right up your alley, you understand. It's got to be someone with stamina to make the trips to New York and Hollywood, and enough smarts to stay on top of those Hollywood shysters. In a nutshell, you."

Another time that would have brought a smile to her lips: His office consisted of upright attorneys; in Hollywood they were shysters.

"And it would keep me occupied," she murmured, and suddenly wondered, Who had told Spassero he called her Bobby?

"That, too," he admitted.

"No, thanks, Dad. Let someone else make a bundle this time. Are you going to be late for your appointment for the house closing?"

He glanced at his watch and scowled. "I'll give you a call later on. If you have those papers for Kennerman to sign, I could drop them off for her. Not out of my way."

She shook her head. "Dad, does Bessie still keep all those local newspapers on hand?" Bessie was Herman Besserman, who must be going on eighty; he had been with the firm since it started.

"Sure. Why?" He glanced at the *Valley Weekly Report* on the table and said, "Leave it alone, honey. You

can't win with a rag like that, and you've got a lot to
lose if they fix their sights on you. You know that."

"Just curious," she said with a shrug. "You know
them, the Dodgsons?" Another name swam back into
reach: Craig Dodgson, the man who claimed he had
asked Paula Kennerman out on his yacht.

"Nope. I've got to go. Bobby, will you stay out of
that mess? Please?"

"Go buy a house, Dad."

After he left, she read the paper again, more carefully
this time; there was no mention of Craig Dodgson, but
there was a bit of information tucked into the recap of
the murder: *"Baby killer Kennerman left her husband
and killed her child and thought she was rid of all ob-
stacles to a life of luxury, free to pursue a wealthy man
she believed would take her away on a yacht."*

She wrote a brief letter to the judge and then
dressed—today in a flowered skirt and blouse, panty
hose even, and sandals. Just in case she ran into the
judge, she told herself, tugging on the panty hose with
some resentment. It was going to be a hot day.

She delivered the letter without seeing the judge or
Spassero, and then returned to the jail for the third time.
Today there was no delay in taking her to the conference room, and they let her keep her pen. Paula was
brought in almost immediately. The bandages had been
changed, Barbara noted. They were no more than simple coverings to keep the wounds clean.

Paula was still pale, but her eyes were alive and there
was a light flush on her cheeks when she greeted Barbara. "I'm glad you came back," she said, taking her
seat.

"What happened Friday?" Barbara asked.

"He came to talk to me, the lawyer. He's off the case. Thank you. They'll send someone else now, I guess. Anyone would be better."

"Friday?" Barbara prompted. At least Spassero had had enough sense to bow out, she thought, before Paula asked for his dismissal.

"He came and began asking me what Craig someone was to me. Were we having an affair? Was there anyone else I was running around with? Things like that. He said this Craig would cinch it for the state, that I had to talk about him, about us. I tried to tell him Jack must have done it, and he wouldn't listen and just kept asking about affairs, and I started to yell at him to get out and stay out." She ducked her head the same way Lucille did. For just an instant she looked like her sister, then the look vanished and she leaned forward with her hands on the table.

"I kept thinking of what you said, someone else did it, and it had to be Jack. There's got to be a way to prove it!"

Barbara said quickly, "Paula, listen to me a minute before you say anything else. You know I'm not your attorney. I'm representing your sister, that's all. I have the papers for you to sign, and you can add whatever you'd like to the list of things for her to keep for you. You see, since I'm not your lawyer, there is no guarantee that anything you say to me will remain confidential. If they put me on the stand under oath, I would be required to repeat what you tell me."

"I understand," Paula said impatiently. "It's what I told the police in the very beginning; they know what I said. So does that lawyer, but he didn't believe it. I just didn't tell them all about Jack because . . . I don't know why. I didn't think of him, of someone killing Lori. I thought I was hidden from him out there at that place." She took a long breath. "He did it, he had to have been the one. We . . . he used to hit me now and then, not often, three or four times. I told him if he did it again I'd take Lori and leave, and for a long time, nearly a year, he didn't touch me. So that day I had a big tip from the night before, and I went to the bank to add it to the special account we started for Lori's school later, and all the money was gone. He took it all out. When he came home I yelled at him and he punched me." She had started calmly enough, but now she was crying and choking on the words, which came out faster and faster. "I was on the floor and he picked up Lori and threw her down on the bed and he said next time he'd throw her out the window. I was scared, more than I ever was before. He'd never touched Lori before, only me, and I knew it would be like it was with my father. I heard the hall door slam, and as soon as I could get up from the floor I grabbed Lori. She was crying, as scared as I was, and I ran out with her."

She had to stop, her sobbing was too hard for the words to be coherent. Today Barbara had stuffed a big wad of tissues in her briefcase; she put some into Paula's hand and waited, feeling sick.

When Paula was able to speak again, she said, "A long time ago, one of the girls at work told me about a Safe House, and I went there. But I was afraid to stay because he'd find us. And they took us to the ranch and gave us some clothes. But he found out anyway."

"Did you tell anyone about this?" Barbara asked.

"At the ranch? I couldn't. I just couldn't say anything

like this in front of Lori. And I couldn't leave her alone, she was so scared."

"You have to tell this to the new attorney they assign you," Barbara said. "It's very important that you tell him exactly what you told me. Will you do that?"

Paula nodded. "Can I tell you about the . . . that day? It's just what I told the police," she added in a rush, "and the psychiatrist. I haven't changed anything because there's nothing to change."

Reluctantly, Barbara nodded.

"Lori wasn't feeling good," Paula said. Her voice wavered, and she closed her eyes for a moment and drew in air. "She kept getting a stomachache, and she had to go to the bathroom, and she didn't want to go out when everyone else did, and another little girl said she would stay with her. One of the women said the best thing I could do for Lori was to act like I wasn't afraid, and that sounded right, so I went out, but I stayed at the edge of the woods waiting for her, and the other little girl came running over in a while and said Lori was sleeping. I hung around the woods for another minute or two, but finally I had to go back, to be with her if she woke up in a strange place, so she wouldn't be alone and scared again." Her voice dropped to a hoarse whisper, and she was staring at her hands on the table; they were clenched into tight fists. "I went to the back door and the whole kitchen was on fire, so I ran to the front. I ran upstairs, but she wasn't in the bed, and I looked in the bathroom and the other bedrooms and then ran down again, and then . . . I don't know what happened, they said the stove or something exploded, and someone was holding me and the house was burning up." The words were almost unrecognizable now. "I woke up in the hospital."

Barbara did not ask questions, did not try to get any more details than Paula was giving her; that was a job for her new attorney. Obviously the police had found terrible flaws in her story, and also obviously the district attorney believed he had everything he needed to convict her. She simply listened as Paula talked.

Toward the end of the hour and a half she spent with Paula, she did ask if Spassero had told her about the new attorney.

"No. I haven't seen him since Friday. Dr. Grayling told me. He said I can have my own doctor if I want, but I don't have a doctor. Dr. Grayling has been good to me. Is he all right, to just let him be my doctor now?"

"I think he's fine," Barbara said.

Paula added to the list of things for Lucille to take from her apartment, and signed the papers. Barbara was replacing them in her briefcase when a tap sounded on the door, and the matron opened it to say, "Mr. Fairchild is here to see Mrs. Kennerman. Will you be much longer, Ms. Holloway?"

"No. I'm leaving now." Theodore Fairchild, she repeated to herself: retirement age, in the public defender's office as long as she could remember, kindly, sharp in court . . .

"Will you stay, too?" Paula asked in a hushed voice.

"No," Barbara said, and stood up. "You have to have confidence in your attorney or the case is hopeless, and you have to speak to him knowing that everything you say is protected. That isn't true about what you say to me. I explained that before, remember? I can't sit in on a private, confidential talk between you and your attorney."

"What if he agrees with the other one, that the only thing I can do is confess? What will I do then?"

"Talk to him," Barbara said firmly. "Just talk to him. Okay?"

Paula nodded, and then made a visible effort to control the fear that had reappeared on her face. She closed her eyes a moment, opened them, and drew herself up straighter. Her clenched hands gave her away.

Barbara met Theodore Fairchild briefly in the corridor as he was being escorted in. They shook hands. He looked tired, she thought, older than she remembered, not quite haggard, but drawn.

"Ms. Holloway," he said. "Barbara. Always a pleasure to see you. How are you?"

"Fine, fine. And you? And Mrs. Fairchild?" A mistake, she realized too late when a shadowed look crossed his face and his shoulders sagged momentarily.

"I'm well, and my wife is getting along fine. Doing better all the time. I'll tell her you asked." He started to move away, then added, "Oh, yes. I told Bill I'd pass the word to your . . . that is, my client. He was given permission to oversee the case after all the preliminary work he put into it. Judge Paltz said that seemed fair." He was watching her closely.

She shrugged. "That's his right. Nice seeing you."

She spent the next several hours in Herman Besserman's office reading *The Valley Weekly Report*. She had come to the office when most of the people were out to lunch, but it seemed word had spread that she was here, and now and then someone opened the door to say hello, or just to check it out that she really had made an appearance. Her name was still included in the long list of attorneys that went down the length of the left margin of the official letterhead, but it was a joke, and they all knew it. She had no salary, no office, no flunky to bring her coffee. . . . The door opened a crack; she looked up to see Herman Besserman—Bessie—peering at her curiously. She had called, asking permission to use his room, read his papers, and he had given it cheerfully, although, he had added, he wouldn't be around until midafternoon. His eyes were like owl eyes, magnified by thick lenses, and he was as pink and roundly smooth as a baby. Stout, they said; never fat, just stout. But he was fat and happy with himself, with his body, with his office, and now he seemed especially happy to see Barbara at a table poring over the tabloids.

"I always say know what the devils are saying about you," he said, entering. "How are you, Barbara? Good picture of you there, I thought." Bessie would outlive them all, everyone agreed, and although he had not been in court for fifteen years, he was still respected as a smart attorney who knew a thing or two.

"Makes me think censorship might be a good idea, after all," Barbara said with disgust.

"You know what they say, homophobia, hatred of all government, misogyny, you name it, might be bad, even evil, but it's not a crime. Not yet. The Dodgsons have perfected every aspect of voicing hatred for the other."

Barbara nodded, putting the newspapers back in their bin. Reading them like this, one after another, covering a six-month period—all that Bessie kept at any one time—was like seeing particularly evil souls exposed to a harsh light that left few secrets. Evil, she repeated.

Evil people who hated women, hated gays, hated liberals, humanists, Democrats, most Republicans, feminists, agnostics, atheists . . .

"Why did they take out after Paula Kennerman like that?" she asked. "From day one, they tried her, convicted her, and now they're yowling for the death sentence for mothers who 'kill' their babies in any way—abortion, actual murder, manslaughter, neglect of the child, prenatal neglect. . . ."

"That's their style," Bessie said simply. "You mixed up in that?"

"No!" she snapped. She straightened up from restoring the newspapers to their proper place. Bessie's office was large, like her father's, with the same kind of desk, big and durable, and a round table with two straight chairs, other comfortable chairs. His office had one wall taken up with big windows, one wall with bookcases, and two walls with bins for the newspapers he collected, fifteen different papers, at least. She glanced at them. "Bessie, are others picking up that same message? Death sentence, baby killer already convicted, all that?"

"Some are." He waved at the bins. "Do you good to spend a day or two with them, see what they're really saying out there in the boonies."

She nodded slowly. "I might do that, if you don't mind. Thanks. I'll give you a call. Now, I need a shower."

He grinned amiably and waddled to his desk. His chair was custom-made, oversized, well padded. He sank into it with a little sigh that could have signified pleasure.

She had just missed her father, Pam, the receptionist,

said: he had been in and left again. Good, Barbara
thought.

But she wasn't ready to go home, she knew, as she
headed west on Sixth, toward Highway 126, the major
road to the coast in this area. It was said that from any
point in downtown Eugene a fifteen-minute drive would
take one out to the country, and for the most part that
was true. She had bypassed most of the commercial
strip, had driven past industrial strips, skirted Fern
Ridge Reservoir, dotted with bobbing small boats, and
was in open country within minutes. A few minutes
later the land became hillier at the start of the eruption
of the Coast Range of mountains that sheltered the
broad valley from the Pacific storms. Her next turn
would be onto Spring Bay Road, where the Dodgsons
lived, next door to the Canby Ranch, where someone
had killed Lori Kennerman and burned down the Canby
house.

The Dodgsons had made a statement that no one
could have passed them to get to the Canby house that
morning without being seen. They had convicted Paula
Kennerman in their newspaper. Their son had come forward to supply a motive, and altogether they just might
convict her in court.

FIVE

On her right the land was mesalike, while on her left forest-covered low hills came to the edge of the road, retreated, forming deep narrow valleys, advanced again, and beyond lay the paroxysm of the Coast Range with its rain forest. Orchards—cherries, apples, peaches—strawberry fields, pastures, fields of wheat gleaming in the sunlight, fields of grasses grown for the seed industry—all were very pretty and lush now in early summer before the usual summer drought struck. When she reached Lewiston, she slowed to the posted speed limit of twenty miles an hour. A small town, under a thousand people, it served the farming community, and it housed many people who drove the twenty-four miles back and forth every day to jobs in Eugene.

She had driven through Lewiston before without stopping, and had paid little attention to it; today she looked it over more carefully. A Dairy Queen, Texaco station, post office, grocery store . . . and the large metal building housing the Dodgson Publishing Company. It was set back several hundred feet from the street, with a manicured lawn, precisely planted red petunias bordering a white walk to the main entrance, and a wide concrete driveway that vanished under a high wooden fence which enclosed the rear of the property. No one was in sight on the grounds.

She nodded at the building, then turned onto Spring Bay Road and followed it out of town, not yet heading for the Canby Ranch, in order to look at the Dodgson house. She passed an orchard and a strawberry field on her right and a meadow on her left. The main crop of berries evidently had been picked; now the field was open to the public, and women and children were there in force.

On the other side, beyond the meadow, she caught a glimpse of the Dodgson house; it appeared to be on the edge of the forest that covered the hills and mountains all the way to the coast. She drove on until she had a clearer view of the big house, which had been featured in the newspapers when it was built, twelve years ago. It looked more like a church than a residence; a center section peaked steeply, with tall beautiful stained-glass panels. Wings extended to the north and to the south; attached to the southern wing, the dome of the swimming pool rose. The meadow continued to the landscaping of the grounds close to the house, and behind the house the forest started.

She would have turned at the driveway if she had not heard gunfire. Startled, she clicked off the radio. Gunfire. Up the road a short distance she saw a sign in the shape of a rifle fifteen feet long: Gallead Firing Range. Slowly she drove that way. A Buick with four women in it pulled onto the road from the Gallead drive in front of her. Another car stopped for her to pass. The property was completely enclosed with high wood fencing, and a heavy gate that stood open. The gunfire was coming from behind a low concrete-block building, the only thing visible beyond the open gate.

Barbara shrugged and continued driving, looking for a place where she could turn; the forest pressed in close to the roadway; the road became curvier, the grade steeper. She finally made her turn at a driveway that led to a small frame house where three VW vans were parked, two of them on blocks, one on its own wheels, all from the fifties or sixties. Apparently two of the vans were being cannibalized in order to keep the third one running.

She retraced her route and turned onto Farleigh Road, where there was marshy ground on both sides, and from here she soon turned again onto the private road that led to the Canby Ranch. The Dodgson meadow, now on her right, had been neatly cut and looked like a lawn, but the meadow on the Canby side was a real meadow with clumps of wildflowers in bloom, orange and yellow poppies, blue lupines; at the edge of the woods on the far side stately foxgloves glowed like torches. A pond at the marshy end was almost hidden by sedges and cattails. Here, too, the meadow extended to the immediate area of the buildings. She passed another entrance to the Dodgson house, a gravel drive with a closed metal gate that was posted NO TRESPASSING. A short distance farther, at the driveway to the Canby Ranch, she was stopped by a log barrier.

She parked her car as near the edge of the road as she could and then got out to walk around the log, a tree trunk twenty feet long, three feet through. Enough to stop any vehicle, she decided, thankful that the ground was dry and firm at the sides of the driveway. Her sandals were not meant for hiking through mud.

The forest came within ten or fifteen feet of the drive, which curved out of sight among the trees. From here she could see only glimpses of the Dodgson house through a scattering of firs that had been left standing when the land was cleared. She walked on to the site of the Canby house. It had been bulldozed level, and the basement filled in with dirt that already was carpeted with grasses and weeds; only the stones of the foundation testified to the recent existence of a building.

Beyond the grave of the house off to the right several hundred feet was a barn. A few fruit trees were visible; probably more were hidden by the structure. In the other direction, toward the meadow, a garden had been protected with deer fencing; weeds were luxuriant in the garden soil, some of them as high as the ten-foot-tall fence.

The house had faced the logging road, and from here she could no longer see the Dodgson house; too many trees were on this side of the road. Slowly, feeling a great sadness that she could not account for, she walked around the leveled house site to where the back door must have been.

She remembered Paula's words: They had left by the back door and headed for the woods. One of the little girls had gone to the apple tree to wait for the other two girls. Now Barbara retraced Paula's steps. At the edge of the woods she stopped again and surveyed the landscape. The entire meadow was visible, both on this side of the logging road and on the Dodgson side. The little orchard began several hundred feet away on her left against the backdrop of the deep fir forest.

She returned to the house site and then looked at the barn, which was locked. They said Paula had gone to the house, to the barn for the gas, back to the house, clearly visible each time to anyone who happened to look this way. As Barbara walked around the house site again, a tall man appeared on the driveway, striding toward her, grinning.

"Honey, what's the matter? Your old man knocking you around more than fun and games calls for? Tough shit, doll. This place is out of business."

He was lean and muscular, six feet one or two, with dark curly hair, a thick mustache, deep-set dark blue eyes. He was very tan, in his late forties or even fifties; it was hard to tell because he appeared so lean and fit—a man who valued his body and took good care of it.

"So I see," she said, walking toward the road. He was in the middle of the driveway. "You the caretaker?"

"Nope. Just a friendly neighbor. Keeping an eye out."

She continued to walk, made a slight detour to go around him; he stepped into her path.

"Honey, you don't have to be in a hurry. You got a problem, let's talk. A little cold beer would go down right, wouldn't it? A little talk."

"No," she said. "I'm leaving now." She had come to a stop, and now she took a step forward, another. He laughed and held out both hands toward her. She stopped again and opened her purse, drew out a notebook, and began to write, murmuring, "Short-sleeved blue shirt, LL Bean, three pens in pocket. Cardin jeans, faded blue, suede belt, brown. Reeboks, white. Rolex watch, ring with red stone. Six-two . . ."

He watched her, his grin deepening. "Honey, what's that for? You going to press charges or something? You don't even know my name."

"I can find out," she said, writing.

"And what's the charge? I think you're kind of cute? Is that it?"

"Harassment, intimidation, unlawful detaining, and if

you get in my way again, I'll add assault with intent to do harm, because I'm leaving now, and if you so much as touch me, I'll have you arrested."

She snapped the notebook shut, put it in her purse, and began to walk around him. He did not move. She knew he watched her all the way to her car. She had to back up and move forward in increments until she was able to head out the narrow road. As she maneuvered her car around, he came to the log barrier across the drive, where he continued to watch her, no longer smiling. Getting her license number, she thought grimly.

She did not start to tremble until she had made the turn off the logging road onto the county road to Lewiston. Not exactly fear, she told herself, and almost believed it. He had not been hyped up on anything but himself, and yet . . . It was the "and yet" that made her grit her teeth in fury. She slowed as she reached the town again, and she suddenly wondered: Where had he come from? There had been no car. She stopped at the Dairy Queen for a Coke and asked the teenage counter boy who the man was. She didn't need a full description; the boy knew. Royce Gallead, the owner of the firing range.

She had dinner with friends that night, and then went to a movie with them, and the evening was not great, but pleasantly relaxing. After the movie, turning down coffee at one of the new espresso bars, refusing a piano bar, she pleaded fatigue, and went home and to bed. She slept fitfully, and when she dressed the next morning to go to the Kennerman apartment to collect Paula's belongings, it was with a sense of relief; this was the sort of thing she should be doing, not running around the countryside daring trouble.

The apartment complex was at Eighteenth and Chambers, an area that had been developed during the last fifteen years and already was going commercial, with supermarkets and banks, a chain shoe store, other miscellaneous shops, restaurants, and apartment complexes. This one looked nice from the outside: three buildings, four floors each, in a U-shape around a parking enclosure, with thoughtful landscaping and flowers in bloom.

Jack Kennerman opened the door after her fourth ring. He glowered at her when she introduced herself.

"They told me you'd be here and my lawyer says I get a receipt for anything you cart off, and no questions. I got nothing to say to you." He pulled the door wider to admit her.

He was slightly built, with dark hair that covered his collar, dark eyes, a sparse beard several shades lighter than his hair. He was pale, thin-faced, and his eyes were dilated too much for the dim light. Shades were down in the living room; the air smelled sour, as if nothing here had been open to the outside for weeks.

"That's fine," Barbara said agreeably. "This is the list. Do you know where the things are?"

"No," he said without a glance at the list. "Never saw any of that shit." He walked stiffly to a recliner chair and sat down. She followed him.

Inside the apartment, claustrophobia set in quickly. The living room was tiny, with gray walls. The sparse furniture was rickety, made of pale wood and plastic. Newspapers and magazines and beer cans were scattered everywhere, on the furniture, on the floor. A few small rugs were crumpled up against the walls. There were several pale shadows of pictures recently removed from the dingy walls.

"Paula said there's a suitcase under the bed," Barbara said, moving toward an open door. "I'll get started." The bedroom was smaller than the living room, with hardly enough space between the bed and a chest of drawers for her to get past. A heap of clothing was near the closet door, more dirty clothes were scattered on the floor, and the sheets and a light blanket lay in a jumble on the bed. No pictures, no knickknacks.

The closet was almost empty; the few things in it were his. Barbara began to pick through the heap of Paula's things in the corner. He had savaged them, torn them, ripped them to shreds, pulled them apart: straps off bras, panties torn into halves, blouses with sleeves ripped off. . . . It looked as if he had taken a sharp knife to them, stabbing and tearing. . . . There was nothing salvageable. Slowly Barbara pulled open the third drawer of the chest of drawers: empty. No jewelry, no sequined purse, no nice leather gloves. . . . There were no books, not the big Audubon *Birds*, not the collected Andersen *Fairy Tales*, no children's books.

She went into the other bedroom. Empty. The windows were uncovered; even the shades gone. No child's furniture, no toys. Nothing to indicate a child had ever lived on the premises, except remnants of wallpaper hanging in shreds. The paper had been pink, with fuzzy colorful animals. Barbara felt goosebumps rise on her arms and rubbed them briskly.

She returned to the living room and regarded Jack Kennerman. "You're trying to erase her altogether, aren't you? All her things, her memory even. It won't work, Mr. Kennerman."

"I told you I never saw any of the shit on that list! She's a goddamned whoring liar. Let her prove she had diddly."

"She paid the rent, didn't she, Mr. Kennerman? How are you managing it alone? Three-fifty, four hundred, utilities. Crack, meth. Whatever it is. Who's footing the bills, Mr. Kennerman?"

"Get the fuck out of here or I'll stamp you down so hard you won't leave a smudge! Get out of here!" He lunged from the recliner in her direction.

"Oh, shut up," Barbara said. "I'm not some poor little scared kid you can knock around." She looked him over with contempt. "I asked some pretty good questions, Jack, and I think I'll do a little digging and see if there are answers. Be seeing you." She left without closing the door, and a moment later it slammed so hard the floor shook.

What she wanted to do, she realized as she drove home, was to pack a lunch, head out to the coast, and walk on the beach for hours. Many hours. But not today. Today she had open house at Martin's. Tomorrow, she promised herself.

In her house, an apple in one hand, a piece of cheese in the other, she roamed from living room to bedroom, to kitchen, to office, and back to living room. Now and then she took a bite of cheese, a bite of apple, cheese. She shouldn't have let her father talk her into staying here, she thought then. When she left his house for Eugene, he had asked her to stay in touch, within touching distance, not off in Arizona, or Montana, or wherever the hell she intended to go next. And because it had not mattered where she went, she had agreed. A mistake.

She had dropped out once and for five years she had

been free to roam, here, there, anywhere. Free, she mocked herself: Everything you are running away from, you find in your little suitcase wherever you open it. Suddenly a sharp picture of Mike's face, frozen in revulsion, forced itself into her awareness, and she stopped moving, stopped breathing. That day he had seen her destroy a young man on the witness stand; he had seen her as ruthless, as pitiless, as cruel and relentless as any shark in the waters. The guy lied, she had stormed at Mike later, and she had caught him at it, and that's how the game was played.

The image had immobilized her; now she moved again, this time to the kitchen, where she put the apple and cheese on the counter, and then went out back, where the rhody seemed to be accusing her. Sharks, she thought bitterly, and then, Dodgson was dead right about that if nothing else.

Her backyard was overgrown with shrubs, weeds, clumps of daylilies trying to find breathing space. A week or two ago her landlady had suggested that if she was too busy to tend it, maybe she could hire a neighborhood boy? Tomorrow, she thought, she would look into that.

She had dropped out, railing at a system that pitted the power of the state against an accused person who might luck into a decent attorney or might not. Luck of the draw. And if not, that accused person might go to prison, or be executed. Luck of the draw. Win a few, lose a few, and what's the score?

She had dropped out, but she had let herself be drawn back in; she had to admit she had allowed it to happen. Her father had not forced her, coerced her. And once back in, she had become the shark again, just like that, overnight devolution back to the briny. She realized she had become stock-still, and she took herself back into the house.

She liked being a storefront lawyer, she told herself in the kitchen. She enjoyed advising people of their rights, advising them about deeds and wills and contracts, about discrimination claims, about the pros and cons of declaring bankruptcy. The clients she advised needed and appreciated her help, and she did not have to hurt anyone, did not have to play the merciless game in court.

"So, why are you into the soul-searching routine?" she asked herself out loud.

She shied away from the question. She had fulfilled her obligation to Lucille to the best of her ability. Paula was talking and was ready to fight for her life. Two Brownie points. And she had made an effort to recover Lucille's possessions. Half a point there.

Lucille, she thought then, and without even posing the question, she knew the answer, what she had to do.

Business was slow at Martin's that afternoon. Only two people besides Lucille showed up, and they were satisfied quickly.

"I don't know how you did it," Lucille said to Barbara when she took her place at the table. "She's like a different person, fighting mad, I mean. And she says the new lawyer seems nice. At least he isn't telling her the only thing to do is confess and all that, I mean."

"Are you going back there today?"

"I don't think so. I just came by here to pick up the stuff, but I'm not surprised by Jack. Bastard. He's a real bastard."

"Could you take a little extra time and see her again?

I have something for you to ask her, if you can do it to-day."

"Sure," Lucille said. "I mean, *whatever* you want." She leaned forward with an intent expression on her pretty, plump face. She was very pink today, as if she had spent a good deal of time in the sun over the weekend.

"It's fairly simple," Barbara said. "Will you ask her if she knows Royce Gallead, or if she heard any of the women at the ranch talk about him?"

"How do you spell that? I never heard of him."

Barbara wrote the name for her. "And then I want you to remind her that I said she is to tell her new law-yer everything, about her clothes and books, every item on that list, and that I brought up the name Royce Gallead. And she should ask him if it's okay for her to answer my questions."

Lucille looked bewildered but dutiful. She repeated the instructions, using the written name as a guide. "Do you want me to come back here after? I mean, it's no bother or anything."

"No," Barbara said, smiling at her eagerness. "Just wait until after she talks to Mr. Fairchild again and then give me a call. Okay?"

After Lucille left, Barbara shut down her computer, closed her briefcase, and then said to Martin, "I'd like to bring Dad around for dinner tonight, about seven. Can you hold a table for us?"

His grin was answer enough. "Don't you want to know what's on the menu first?"

"Nope. But about wine, what do you have hidden away?" That really didn't matter much, either. What did matter was that they eat someplace close enough for her to walk home if she had to.

They discussed wines, and he asked if the old man would want any special booze. He wouldn't. Her father was off hard liquor these days, wine and beer only. She told him firmly that she had to pay for the dinner, a celebration couldn't be on the house, and he agreed with some reluctance.

"But, Barbara," he said seriously. "I would be highly offended if you added a tip."

"Fine," she said. "No problem. Oh, one more thing. We might want to sit around and talk a bit. Is that okay?" She knew he usually closed by nine-thirty or ten. His clientele was not into late dinners.

"Just until dawn," he said grandly.

She laughed. "I always suspected that what you really are is a poet. Right?"

His laughter boomed. "You, go on now, scat. I got things to do in the kitchen. See you at seven."

Frank had been very pleased with her message, he told her several times over dinner. He had been dubious at first about her choice of restaurants, but his doubts vanished with the first taste of avocado in cream with Stilton cheese melted through it. He followed that with fruit-stuffed pork loin while Barbara had a lamb dish that Martin had described with a blissful smile. "Lots of garlic," he had warned, and there was, but it was wonderful. The wine was excellent. Barbara suspected that Martin had gone on a quick wine-purchasing jaunt, but she didn't ask, merely was grateful.

Her father talked about the house with such pleasure that she had to glow along with him. "As far as suitability," he said thoughtfully, "on a scale from one to ten, it's about eleven or twelve."

The restaurant filled and Martin scurried around taking care of everyone himself. Frank studied each new group that entered with interest, but did not comment. They were a mixed bunch here, Barbara thought, surprised that she had not considered it before. Blacks, Latinos, whites, most of them in jeans, or even shorts, and most of them greeted by name by Martin. She turned her attention back to what her father was saying.

"We have a pretty interesting case on hand. It will go to the Supreme Court eventually. You never argued a case before the Supreme Court, did you?"

"Dad, come on. You know perfectly well that I haven't."

"Oh, it's an experience, I can tell you. A real thrill, especially if you win. But even if you don't win, just being there, knowing you're appealing to the highest court, knowing that every damn lawyer in the country will be following what you're doing, the possibility that you'll make history, be in the textbooks, it's a rare privilege, Bobby."

He dropped it there and began talking about redecorating the house, and how much he was relying on her for colors and such. A while later Martin came by to tell them about the desserts his wife, Binnie, had made. They both chose strawberry tart, and Martin said, "Good choice" and cleared the table.

When Martin left again, Barbara told her father about Binnie, who was as gangly as a colt and made the best desserts to be found in the city. Binnie was mute, she said, and very shy. Few people even knew Martin was married, but they adored each other.

Frank was gazing at her with an appraising look. "Honey, I wish I knew what all you know."

"Well, you don't."

"That's the truth."

He purposely had not asked her about Paula Kennerman, about Lucille and her sweater, about anything, she was thinking, when Martin brought their desserts and coffee.

"Could we just have a pot on the table?" she asked.

An almost conspiratorial look crossed his face, and he smiled and said absolutely. She hoped he wouldn't linger by the door the way he did when neither of them was certain a new client was to be trusted. It was a little after nine; the restaurant was emptying out, exactly as she had known it would do.

She waited until they had finished off the tarts. She poured more coffee for herself when Frank waved it away, looking very contented.

"Dad, you've done all the talking. My turn," she said then. Some of his contentment vanished, but she plunged in and started to tell him about her last two days, her long talk with Paula, getting the documents signed, meeting Fairchild.

"He's a good man," Frank said. "Good lawyer. His wife has cancer, you know. Makes it rough on him these days, of course, but he's hanging in there. Good man."

"I'm sorry to hear that about his wife," she said, remembering the brief conversation. Fairchild had assumed she knew. "After all that," she went on, "I drove out to the Canby Ranch."

Her father took off his glasses and began to polish them; his expression was grim. "And?" he muttered.

She described her circuitous route, and then her own movements at the ranch and her encounter with Royce Gallead.

"For God's sake, Barbara, leave all this alone. That's a dumb-shit dangerous thing to be doing, out there, no one knowing where you went, what you're up to. Leave it alone!"

"Wait," she said. "Let me finish." She told him about Jack Kennerman.

"And what's the point?" Frank demanded. "Unpleasant people, nasty people, doing rotten things? So?"

"Listen to me, Dad. You've missed the point. Someone told Dodgson you call me Bobby. Who? Spassero didn't know that. Someone told Dodgson all about our meeting in Judge Paltz's chambers. Who? And why? Someone told Jack Kennerman that I'd be coming around. Who? No one knew except Paula, her sister, her attorney, and me. Royce Gallead just appeared out of nowhere out at the ranch. I was looking around pretty thoroughly, and suddenly he was there on the driveway. If the house had been standing, if I hadn't been in front where I was, he could have walked right in, yet the papers have made a case that no one could have approached without being seen."

"You're accusing Royce Gallead of killing that child, burning down that house? Are you out of your mind?"

"I didn't say that. What I said is that *someone* could have entered that house without being seen, no matter what the papers are reporting." She added softly, "But it's an interesting point, Dad. Why is Royce Gallead looking out for that burned-down house?"

Frank took off his glasses and put them down hard on the table. He grabbed the carafe and poured coffee into his cup so fast that some splashed out. "I don't know why Gallead is doing anything," he said coldly, ignoring the pool of coffee. "And the fact is, neither do you.

And it's none of your business." He stirred his coffee furiously and in an even colder tone said, "I think you're sore because Dodgson implied that you're gay, and you're striking out blindly. Getting mad puts curtains in front of your eyes and all you can see is red."

"What you taught me, Dad, is that getting hot and fighting cool wins. I'm cool, Dad. Real cool."

"What have you done?" he demanded, suddenly stilled.

"I passed a message to Paula that no one on earth knows, except her sister and Paula and me. Let's see who finds out and how soon." She watched him for a moment and then said, "If there's a leak, there's no way she can present a decent case. Not if everyone in sight knows ahead of time what's going on. They keep stacking the cards against her. I don't know who killed that child. Paula says her husband did." Frank snorted, and she ignored him. "What I do know is that the Dodgsons seem prepared to do whatever it takes to get her convicted. Why did Craig Dodgson come forward after I got through to Paula? Why not a month ago? And who told him I got through to her?" She lifted her cup but continued to gaze at him over the top of it. "There are too many people who seem joined in one cause: to get Paula Kennerman convicted of murder and sent up. And there's something that stinks to high heavens about the whole affair."

"Stir up shit and you raise an odor," Frank said coldly. "So you're mad, and you're poking around. Why? What can you do? Go talk to Fairchild. I tell you, Barbara, he's a good man."

"Spassero got permission to supervise the case."

"Christ! So what are you thinking of?"

"I have a proposition for you, Dad. You aren't going to like it, I warn you. If my bait is taken, if it's leaked,

I'll know Paula can't trust anyone in the public defender's office, and I want her myself."

Frank was staring aghast now. He shook his head. "How? On the pennies and dimes you make in your 'office' here?" He waved at the restaurant, which was empty except for them.

"I want the firm to back me."

"You *are* out of your mind!"

"No, I'm not. I'll come back, on no salary to repay whatever the bill comes to, for as long as it takes, if I can keep on holding court here two afternoons a week."

"God in heaven," he said in soft-voiced wonder. "You're trying to bribe me."

"That's about the size of it, I'm afraid," she agreed. "But cheer up, maybe the bait will lie there and evaporate. And you'll be off the hook."

"I'm off the hook right now," he snapped. "Let's get out of here. Where's Martin? Where's the check?" He glared at the empty restaurant.

"It's already taken care of. Why don't you go on ahead. I'll walk home in a few minutes."

"You'll do no such thing! When I take a lady out to dinner, I take her home afterward."

"Okay. And, Dad, as I said, maybe nothing will come of this, but be thinking about it, will you?"

"What I'm thinking," he said, standing up, "is that you got your back up and you're making wild accusations."

"And what I'm thinking," she said in a low voice, "is that something is going on here that is beyond simple corruption. Something truly evil is going on, and Paula Kennerman has found herself in the middle of it."

SIX

WEDNESDAY. SOMETHING WAS eating her potted geranium, not the same thing that was eating the rhododendron; they left different bite patterns. Yellow, rather pretty dandelions were in riotous bloom. If she had a hoe and gloves, she would weed; if she had some spray, she would use it; if she had a hose, she would water a hydrangea that was wilting. She started a list.

She made three house calls and earned forty-five dollars. The garden center bill came to twenty-seven, a few groceries cost eight, laundry three-fifty, gas twelve. A boy offered to cut her front lawn for five dollars, and she accepted his offer. Otherwise, she had to buy a lawn mower, she had decided, or a goat. She considered a goat for a long time. The boy took fifteen minutes. On an hourly basis, he was earning more than she was, and he didn't pay taxes. She paid him and gazed at the lawn in dissatisfaction; he did not rake, did not trim. He cut. The clippings were three times as long as the grass they would surely smother. She regarded the geranium sourly; she had thought that being in a pot brought protection.

Each time the phone rang, willing it to be her father

on the line, she ran to her office to listen to her own
message, and the caller's message. Nothing.

Thursday. She considered answering a few letters,
and put them aside. She filed her fingernails; if she was
going to do weeding, it seemed best to start with them
short. The dandelions out back had turned into ephem-
eral, glistening puffs. The phone rang twice; one time
the caller hung up as soon as her machine came on, the
next time it was Sears wanting to know if she could use
a credit card. She took out the garbage, and at one-
fifteen she left for Martin's restaurant.

Again, there were only two drop-in clients, whom she
dispatched quickly. She had wondered if business would
slow down in the summer. Then Lucille came in to report. Paula never heard of that guy, Royce whatever,
and her lawyer said she could talk with anyone she
wanted to, but probably she shouldn't discuss her case
with them. Lucille seemed disappointed when Barbara
said there was nothing else for her to do.

She was chatting with Martin at three-thirty, thinking
of going on home since it appeared that no one else was
coming by. She had to transfer money from savings to
checking, she thought distantly, half-listening to Martin
talk about a new dish he was experimenting with. He
left to answer the telephone and she gathered her things
together.

"For you," he said from a little table that held a cash
register, the telephone, and a calculator. He put the receiver down, waved, and vanished into the kitchen.

She crossed the room, picked up the telephone, and
said hello.

"Gallead. Listen, bitch, and listen good because I
don't intend to repeat myself. You try to connect me

with that Kennerman case and I'll come after you." The phone clicked.

Well, she thought almost absently, that's how he pronounced it: Gul-*lee*-ed. Although her movements were slow, somewhat dreamlike, as she returned to her table and finished packing up, her heart was hammering.

She walked home slowly, deep in thought. That call was not what she had expected, she admitted. Royce Gallead had been far from her mind. What she had thought might happen was another diatribe in the Monday edition of Dodgson's paper, with enough said to let her know he had been informed of her continuing prying. But not this. And Gallead had called her at Martin's; he had known where to reach her, when. Possibly he had been the caller earlier who had hung up without speaking, taking no chances of having his call taped.

At home, she stood with her hand above the telephone. More than anything right now, she wanted to talk to her father, but he had to call her. What if he had been really wounded? Offended? What if he had his stubborn mode in full gear? He might never call. He could well have gone back out to the country house intending to stay there for a week, a month. She bit her lip and turned away from the phone. He had to call her.

Then she picked up her purse and left again, this time heading for the courthouse records room. Forty minutes later she knew a little more about Royce Gallead, knew that he had a gun shop on Coburg Road, and that he had the range out on Spring Bay Road, and that he had acquired the land nine years ago from Richard Dodgson. She looked up Richard Dodgson and found that he had bought the acreage from Grace Canby thirteen years earlier, and that the deed had a covenant attached, a

stipulation that he not develop, sell, or fence the lower
meadow.

She was forced to leave then because the courthouse
was closing shop for the day. More thoughtfully than
ever, she got in her car and sat for several minutes trying to make sense of it.

Canby, Dodgson, Gallead. An unlikely trio. A more-
than-benevolent benefactress who had turned over a
valuable piece of property for the use of women who
were hiding from a world they no longer could cope
with. Dodgson, a bigot, a zealot, a misogynist, a liar, a
man who claimed to be a born-again Christian and ex-
uded hatred with every stroke of the pen. And Gallead?
All she knew about him was that he was menacing, arrogant, and apparently fancied himself a Lothario. An
unlikely trio, she repeated as she started to drive.

That evening she made herself a sandwich for dinner,
and then, feeling guilty about the diet she was too lazy
to correct, she boiled an egg to go with it. The egg
overcooked and was leathery. She ate it anyway.

All through the scratch meal, off and on until she
went to bed, she mulled over her next move. She had
few options. She had about two hundred in her checking account and twenty-one thousand in the savings account her father claimed she was spending down to
nothing on purpose. She had not denied it, or admitted
it either, but she was going through it. And so little
came in that she figured in two years she would have
exactly zilch. "You act like it's dirty money!" Frank had
stormed at her. "It's not. You earned it, every penny.
And you saved a life."

And lost two, she had added silently.

Her father could be altogether too perceptive, she

thought as she wandered aimlessly about her small house. Dirty money. So why was she working like the devil on a case that wasn't even hers? Again, Frank had been partly right: Dodgson had got her back up, had made her as furious as she had been in years. But it wasn't only that. She thought of Paula Kennerman driven to a suicide attempt by her grief, or possibly her guilt. Whatever she had done, or had not done, she deserved a fair trial, and would not get it from any public defender as long as Bill Spassero was around.

And finally, she had been discredited in the eyes of Judge Paltz; what integrity she possessed had been destroyed as far as he was concerned. For years she had claimed, and believed, that she didn't care what people thought about her. What most people thought about her, she now amended. She cared what Judge Paltz thought because to her he represented what was decent in the system: He was a good judge; he cared about the law, about the rights of the people brought before him, about the people themselves. It mattered more than she had known, until now, that he not consider her to be dishonorable. And she couldn't go to him with the *yes he did, no I didn't* bickering of children.

To regain credibility she had to be able to demonstrate that Spassero had betrayed the trust placed in him by his appointment as Paula Kennerman's attorney. And to do that she had to find answers to the mystery of why Dodgson was involved, why his son was involved, why Gallead was involved.

She couldn't do it alone, she knew. There was too much. She needed Bailey Novell, who was the best private investigator on the coast and was not cheap. She needed a law clerk, and secretarial help, an office to op-

erate from, to have people come to. She needed the
backing of a rich law firm that could absorb the costs if
it turned out there would be no compensation.

And if he said no and couldn't be budged? She had
no answer.

Friday. By eight-thirty Barbara was showered, break-
fasted, and restless. She had not yet dressed, but was
wearing a short duster and was barefoot, trying to decide. Skirt and blouse? Jeans? Shorts? To the coast, or
the backyard and do some weeding? The courthouse?
The library? Too soon, she knew. The questions that
needed answers were not yet formed in her head. Visit
Paula? Wash windows, clean the stove, wax the kitchen
floor . . . ?

Bessie, she decided finally. He had told her he never
got to the office before one or two in the afternoon; she
could use his space, read his newspapers all she wanted
before that. She dressed and went downtown. Before,
she had concentrated on the Dodgson articles that followed the April murder of Lori Kennerman, and the destruction of the Canby Ranch dwelling. This time, when
she arrived at Bessie's office, she decided to read all the
Dodgson papers he had, six months of newspapers.

January: a long hate piece about the paganization of
Christmas, the most sacred day of the year. Paganization? Barbara mouthed the word and continued to read.
A long piece about the Brady bill and who really was
behind it—the satanic hordes who were desperate to
disarm the country and seize control. Registration of
guns was their first step, it claimed. There were letters
to the editor: "Dear Rich, Right on! Thank God we
have someone telling it like it is. Keep up the good

work, Rich!" And on the back page there was a list of the abortion clinics to be targeted in the coming month, complete with dates and addresses.

The next week had a list of the new books to be included in an ongoing campaign to clean up the school libraries. *The Lorax*, by Dr. Seuss. All fairy tales. Anything to do with Dungeons and Dragons, anything to do with magic in any form. . . . The headline of the article was in large black type: KIDS MINDS AT RISK! "Have you checked out your library? If you haven't looked over the books your children are reading, it is your duty to do so immediately. Witchcraft, satanism, homosexuality, feminism, socialism and even communism are the messages the New York elite is feeding your child! Send a stamped self-addressed envelope for the complete list of banned books."

Barbara frowned more intently at one of the articles on the hidden agenda of feminists: "How long since you heard anything about the ERA? Remember? Equal Rights Amendment. That's all they talked about a few years back. Sounds okay, doesn't it, but why have they dropped it? Recently discovered documents from the secret files of NOW lay it out there on the line. First, feminization of the male. Make him feel guilty about not doing a share of women's work—house-cleaning, baby-sitting, cooking. Then, take over his jobs. Women in the armed forces, in the police forces, doctors, lawyers, politicians, in construction. You name it, they've got quotas. And they've got the money to back up their demands, to buy a senator here, a representative there, ads, slanted news stories, television, books, magazines, they control them all, or are working at getting control. And the final goal they are pressing for? Complete

emasculation of the American male. A revolution without guns. A takeover of the entire American economy
and government. Equal rights? Forget it. Absolute
power is the ultimate goal. The American male is in a
war for his life, and the sap doesn't even know war was
declared."

Barbara left the table and walked to the window. Was
he insane? A paranoid psychotic? She shivered, more
afraid of insanity than almost anything else she could
think of. Reluctantly she returned to the same issue of
the paper, which seemed to be entirely about women.
The following article claimed that women who took the
"so-called 'morning-after pill' " were at grave risk.
Sixty percent of them required medical treatment for six
months or longer; thirty percent required hospitaliza-
tion. Fifty percent required therapy that was without
end. Fifteen percent attempted suicide. "God is speaking to those women who have murdered their babies.
He is passing judgment on them, and they refuse to hear
His words. What they are guilty of is murder. They pay
a penalty under God's judgment."

Another article was about the French abortifacient,
RU-486. Here the "statistics" bore on heart attacks, liver
problems, kidney failure, death, and madness. "Feminists
are clamoring for this deadly weapon of death. They
must be stopped. Call your representative, your senator. Call today! Call the White House. Write to the drug
manufacturers. You and only you can stop this newest
threat to the human race. Don't let them introduce yet
another way to kill our children and destroy the health of
our women!"

Barbara found herself wiping her hands on a tissue,
and realized there was a pile of such tissues at her el-

bow. Not good enough, she thought then; what she needed was a thorough scrub-down after handling these newspapers.

She continued to read, and suddenly stopped in midsentence and went back to the beginning of this diatribe. "All over the country so-called 'Safe Houses' are springing up. Women are luring women away from their husbands, away from their responsibilities, away from their children in some cases. In other cases, women are stealing the children away from their fathers. Kidnapping children." Then the tone changed, Barbara realized. The article continued: "A vast underground network has grown, maintained by 'sisters' for 'sisters,' funded by 'sisters' for 'sisters,' as secret as the vast underground railway system that operated during the Civil War, when otherwise law-abiding citizens became criminals and aided and abetted the escape of slaves from their legal owners. This is a nation of law, a nation that lives under the law of the land, and it is a criminal activity to kidnap a child, even if the perpetrator is the mother of that child. It is criminal activity to deny the visitation rights of the father. The child has no recourse under the law because that child is hidden away, is silenced, while the band of 'sisters' strives to indoctrinate a new member into their ranks."

It changed again here, back to what Barbara thought of as Rich's style: "What can you do? Be alert! Maybe there's a so-called 'Safe House' on your street. Maybe there's a little kid who wants his daddy, not a bunch of witches and pagans all around. Visit the house, demonstrate against this assault on every family value you hold dear. Write a letter to the editor, talk to your neighbors. Demonstrate. Don't let them get away with it!"

She plugged on doggedly, ignoring the spasms in her stomach and the rigidity of her muscles, ignoring the mounting anger that took her away from the table again and again. Each time she returned until she felt she had seen enough to know they were all alike. And now that she was aware of that stylistic change, she found it easy to spot over and over. Dodgson and his wife taking turns? Dodgson being fed the lines from an outside source? Dodgson on drugs? Something else?

She restored the papers to the bins and left Bessie's office before he turned up this time. In the wide corridor, heading toward the reception room, she was stopped by her father's voice. She turned to see him at his open door.

"You have a minute?" he asked.

She knew his answer was no. It was in his posture, in the somber expression on his face, the way he regarded her too politely. She headed his way, and when she reached his door, he stepped aside and let her pass, then closed the door behind them. Bailey Novell was slouched in a deep chair holding a drink.

"Hi, Barbara. How're things?" He hauled himself upright and shook her hand. "You're looking good," he said appraisingly.

"Thanks. And you?" He was a small man, hardly taller than Barbara, wiry, thin-faced, with sparse gray hair. His clothes were always baggy, as if he had bought them when he was twenty pounds heavier. Barbara had never known him to be heavier than he was, and most of the times she had seen him, he had been drinking something. It never mattered much what it was.

"Nothing changes. Same old grind." He seemed to melt back into the chair.

"Tell her," Frank said in a peremptory tone. He went to the wide window and stood with his back to them.

"Yeah, tell me, Bailey." She took a matching chair and slumped almost as much as he did. Reaction, she understood, and also understood that she had not really expected the firm to support her, but there had been that little bit of hope that now was extinguished.

"Okay. I know a few people, you know?"

She knew.

"So I asked a couple of questions and got the general picture of the case the D.A.'s making, not the details, but generally. It's really tight, Barbara. They don't need more than they already got. See, Dodgson was out on his tractor cutting that field all morning. Lots of folks will testify to that. And you couldn't get up that road without him seeing you. If that wasn't enough, his old lady was taking a walk on the private road. I mean that side's sewed up. The women were out looking for mushrooms in the woods across the field. Couldn't get in without someone in that bunch spotting you. And right up until Kennerman went back to the house, two little girls were playing around the apple trees, and they would have seen anyone coming down from the woods, and nobody did. It's good and tight. And even if it wasn't, who else would have killed that kid? The husband was out fishing with buddies. You know, start of trout season."

"The Dodgsons are unreliable witnesses," Barbara said.

Bailey spread his hands. Without turning around, Frank said in a dry voice, "You can't impeach their testimony because you don't like them."

"I can try," she snapped. "I told you Royce Gallead

got onto that property without my seeing him. Someone else could have done it, too."

"Gallead?" Bailey muttered. "He's mixed up in this?"

"No," Frank said.

"Yes, he is," Barbara said coldly. "Up to his eyeballs. Do you know him?" she asked Bailey.

"Sure. A gun nut. Said to be a mean one. You don't want to stir him up, so they say. Doubt that he's ever been charged with anything, or they'd take away his business, but there have been rumors of trouble."

She nodded and stood up. "Are you free? Have some time to do a few things?"

He glanced at Frank, who had not moved. "You or the company?"

"Me."

"I'm free, Barbara," he said earnestly. "But you know I got expenses, payroll to meet, stuff like that. Who's paying? Kennerman's got zilch, I understand."

"I'm paying. But we'll try to keep expenses down. Okay?"

"I always keep them down," he protested.

"Can you come over to my house around four? First I have to talk to Paula."

"And I'm going home," Frank said sharply. He marched from the room without a glance at her.

"Wow!" Bailey said. "The old man's really riled."

Barbara shrugged. So was she.

"Look at it from his angle," Bailey said. "This is a downer case if there ever was one. You'll be smeared by that Dodgson rag from here till Christmas. If you tangle with Gallead, that's real trouble. And for what? You know how many kids have been killed here in the county the last few years? Couple of dozen. People are pretty fed up; they'll take it out on you. There's no way you can get a jury that doesn't already know in their hearts that Kennerman killed her kid. Go after Dodgson and he starts screaming freedom of the press, First Amendment, all that."

"Am I paying for this time?" Barbara demanded.

Bailey grinned. It was a great big jack-o'-lantern grin that used every muscle in his face and made wrinkles, channels, and gullies where they had not been before. "Starting at four," he said, saluting her with his glass.

Paula looked incredulous when Barbara asked if she wanted her to take the case. "Yes! Oh, my God, yes!" Then she said, "But I don't have any money. Will the state pay you?"

"I'm afraid not," Barbara said. "So it's going to be a very tight budget, and you should know that up front."

Paula nodded. "Mr. Fairchild is a nice man, but he can't do much for me, not like you can. I'll find a way to pay you someday."

"Okay, that goes on the back burner. First, I have to instruct you about your options. I know the others did this, but I have to make certain you understand. What you have to do is listen carefully." And she began.

When she was ready to leave, Barbara warned, "Don't talk to anyone about our conferences—not Lucille, not anyone here, not anyone. Until we know where the leak is, we keep quiet. Agreed?" Paula nodded. "And I want a list of everyone you can think of who ever saw you with Lori—baby-sitters, day-care people, people in the apartment complex. Whoever you can think of. And people who knew the relationship you

and Jack had, how he was with Lori. Take your time
with it and make it as complete as possible."

"They won't let me have a pencil or pen. Nothing
sharp," Paula said. She ducked her head. The bandages
were off her wrists; red scars stood out vividly. "Dr.
Grayling said I'll be scarred. He's sorry about it," she
whispered.

"Tell Dr. Grayling that I offered to defend you," Barbara said. "Tell him I need your help. I think he'll see
to it that you get a pen and paper."

Paula nodded, rubbing her wrist lightly. She would be
scarred, Barbara thought, more than she knew at the
moment, and the worst scars would never be seen by
anyone.

SEVEN

On her way home she stopped at a bookstore and bought a county road map and a U.S. Geological Survey map of the county. She was dismayed to see that it was dated 1983. The clerk said it was the latest one available.

When Barbara admitted Bailey at four, she had the map spread out on the kitchen table. Bailey glanced at the living room with a bland, neutral expression, but she knew he had taken an inventory.

"Coffee? Coke? That's about all I have."

He said Coke and followed her into the kitchen when she went to get it; they returned to the living room to sit down. There wasn't enough room in her office for a guest and her.

"Here's a list," she said, handing it over. "You know the kind of stuff. General background and immediate details." He looked at it and whistled. "I know," she said. "I know. So don't let them know you're prying. Whatever you can find out about the Dodgsons—where they got the money for that house, a yacht, how they're doing now. That little scandal sheet can't pull in much. What does? And same for Gallead. And Jack Kennerman. About Mrs. Canby, forget the money angle. Her former husband inherited from his father, and made more. But is she involved in any way with Dodgson? Who worked at the ranch for her, when, did anyone leave mad? Who was out there the day the house burned? Who was in charge and where is she now?" This was all elementary, routine stuff, she was aware, but she didn't know enough yet to ask for anything more specific.

"Gotcha," Bailey said, and then asked, "What about Spassero? He's in the public defender's office, isn't he?"

She hesitated only a second. Her father had always confided in Bailey, she knew; he said no one could do a complete job without the necessary information, and she had always agreed. She told Bailey about Bill Spassero and concluded, "He's the source of the leaks, but why? What's he up to? Who is he working for?" She drew in a breath and went on to tell him about Royce Gallead, why he was on the list.

Bailey whistled. "Barbara, does the old man know he threatened you?"

"No. Dad's all the way out of this one. Keep it that way."

Bailey had set his Coke down to take a few notes. Now he lifted it and drank it all. "Okay," he said then. "Let's talk about money."

She handed him a check for five thousand dollars; she had called the bank to make the transfer first thing on arriving home. He stashed it away in his notebook and made out a receipt. They both knew five thousand would not last very long.

"One more thing," she said. "The map. Let me show you what I want." They went to the kitchen table, where

she pointed to a dark line she had drawn with a marker.
"This map is out of date, but it's the most recent one
there is. What I need is an aerial photograph of that por-
tion in the outline. Can do?"

"Someone can do," he said.

"See if he can do it without giving away what he's up
to, will you?"

"Barbara, how do you suggest hiding an airplane flying overhead taking pictures?"

"I bet he can, though."

"It might mean more flying time, more money," Bailey warned.

"I know," she said with a sigh. "I know."

After Bailey left, she opened the road map, which seemed
pitifully inadequate after the many details of the survey
map. She studied the route she would take the next day.

For a moment she was tempted by the idea of driving
to the coast, having a nice dinner, getting a motel
room. . . . She shook her head.

When she drove past the firing range the next morning,
there was the sound of gunfire as before, more of it this
Saturday, and although she drove quite slowly, she
could see little through the open gate: the low white
concrete building, cars parked in front of it, and what
seemed to be another fence. Customers had to go
through the building to get to the range in back.

Farther up the road, the people who collected VW
vans were in the yard today—half a dozen young people playing with a ball. Several looked up and waved.
She waved back.

Three more driveways led to small houses in small

clearings. They all had people around. She turned onto a Forest Service road and within a hundred feet, still in sight of Spring Bay Road, she stopped. The road was too steep and rocky; it would take a four-wheel-drive to navigate. She backed out and went back the way she had come.

Although she was watching closely as the meadow yielded to forest off Farleigh Road, she was unable to tell where the Canby property ended. Apparently Mrs. Canby did not like fences or KEEP OUT signs. Then she spotted the second logging road, which was the southern boundary of the property, and made the turn.

This was impossible, she knew after only two or three hundred feet. The road had not been maintained even minimally, and the winter rains had worked at undoing what the graders had done. The dirt road was deeply rutted in places, overgrown with seedling fir trees, vine maples, brambles. Now, in the middle of June, it was dry, but in April . . . She ignored the growing disquietude enveloping her and began to back out.

One more, she thought grimly as she drove again, this time to the blacktop road that led to the Canby driveway and beyond. The asphalt stopped fifteen or twenty feet past the Canby driveway, and a dirt road curved out of sight in a steep grade. Barbara stopped her car and brooded. In April the ground would have been saturated, that dirt road would have been like a sliding board. If any vehicle had driven up there, it would have been known immediately by anyone who glanced that way, and as soon as an arson fire was suspected, investigators would have been all over the scene. Maybe they did know, she thought then, and reluctantly got out of the car. She could have driven, but the thought of backing down again was more than she wanted to contemplate; she locked her car and started to walk. The curve followed a rock outcropping; immediately after the curve the road was blocked by fallen rocks. She could walk around them easily enough, but no car could have gone by. She sat on a boulder and stared into the dense woods.

He could have come up here Friday night, she thought, slept in the car, waited for a chance on Saturday to get to the house. . . . After he killed the child and started the fire, he could have gone back to the car. He had plenty of time that morning to smooth out any marks he had left on the dirt road. And he could have waited until everyone was gone, the fire equipment out, the occupants transported somewhere else. He could have waited until dark, and then backed down, turned in the Canby drive, and left. She made a note to herself to check the weather for the days following the murder. Rain could have obliterated any tracks easier than a man could have done.

Or he could have parked down on Farleigh Road and walked in through the woods, easily avoiding the women looking for mushrooms.

Or, she told herself, standing up, he could have parked down in Lewiston and walked here. It wasn't that far, a couple of miles. But how had he known about gas in the barn? Would that be a given? Farm—mowers, tillers, other equipment—equals gas in the barn?

She returned to her car and went home feeling out of sorts, as if she was wasting time that was irreplaceable and precious.

On her answering machine was a message from Grace Canby. Barbara listened to it twice. "Ms. Holloway, this is Grace Canby. It is two-thirty in the afternoon, Saturday. Will you please give me a call? I'll be in the rest of the afternoon, or tomorrow all day." She gave her number and hung up.

Barbara called the number, and Mrs. Canby answered the second ring. After Barbara introduced herself, Mrs. Canby said very coolly, "Ms. Holloway, it was brought to my attention earlier today that you are representing yourself as being in my employ. If, indeed, you are doing this, you must stop immediately, or I shall be forced to consult my attorney."

"Mrs. Canby, wait!" Barbara said. "I haven't done such a thing. Who told you that?"

There was a slight pause. "It doesn't matter who it was. I don't understand this, or why.... However, if you are not making such a claim, I apologize for disturbing you."

"No, please. Mrs. Canby, may I come talk to you? It's very important."

"I'm sorry, I'm very busy."

"Mrs. Canby, I am the defense counsel for Paula Kennerman, and there are influential people here who seem determined to interfere." She shut her eyes and gripped the receiver harder. "One of them is Richard Dodgson. May I come talk to you?" She did not open her eyes yet, and realized she was holding her breath. She let it out in the pause that followed.

"Yes. Tomorrow? Two in the afternoon? I really am very busy through the week."

"Tomorrow. Thank you, Mrs. Canby. Where?"

She would not speculate, she told herself as she speculated wildly after hanging up. It must have been Dodgson; his name had opened the door for her. He must have called Grace Canby. Maybe he thought she was footing the bill. What was the connection between them?

Mrs. Canby lived on the top floor of a condominium situated in a parklike setting a short distance west of Salem, sixty-eight miles north of Eugene. There was a security guard at the front desk, a rare sight in Oregon. When Barbara showed her ID, he checked it against a list, then escorted her to the elevator; he let her ride up alone, except for the closed-circuit television camera that moved slightly whenever she did.

The elevator opened onto a small foyer with only one door and another television camera. The door opened as Barbara approached to knock.

"Ms. Holloway, come in. I'm Grace Canby." She was in her mid-sixties, tall and thin, with ropelike muscles in her arms and a skeletal face that nevertheless was handsome. Her hair was white, drawn back in a severe bun, her eyes deep-set and pale blue. She was wearing gray sweatpants, a matching, short-sleeved sweatshirt, and running shoes.

"I put off my run until three," Mrs. Canby said as she walked ahead of Barbara into a spacious living room. The room was almost garish, with furniture covered in a material that had giant tropical flowers in brilliant colors. A heap of newspapers was on the sofa, magazines and books on several tables. Two lamps had Tiffany shades, one a bamboo shade. Scatter rugs were red, blue, yellow. "Let's sit over here by the window, shall we?"

She led the way to two facing chairs with a game table between them. Glancing out the window, Barbara saw that the park became a real woods behind the building.

"They put in a running track through the trees," Mrs.

Canby said, nodding toward the grounds. "Doesn't it look like something out of the Disney studios?"

It did. When Barbara turned once more to Mrs. Canby, she found the older woman studying her.

"What can I do for you?" Mrs. Canby asked.

"Was it Richard Dodgson who told you I was misrepresenting myself?"

"Yes." She was sitting perfectly still with an intent expression, as if she was still appraising her guest.

"And you called me right away to get to the bottom of it," Barbara said. "Will you tell me what he said?"

"In a minute," Mrs. Canby said, her expression changing subtly. She looked a little more relaxed. "After Rich called, I talked to my own attorney here in Salem. I didn't mention Rich, but I asked him about you, and his report was completely satisfying, and that's the reason I called. If Rich was telling a lie about you, I felt you should know about it. If it was the truth, I wanted you to stop."

"I'm very grateful that you did call," Barbara said.

"Yes. Well, I have tried very hard to remain neutral as far as Rich is concerned, but it is difficult at times. He demanded that I call you off, or he said he would fence in the meadow and we could slug it out in court for the next ten years." Her voice had become very dry. "If he fences that meadow, I'll hire people to tear down the fence, and *then* we'll slug it out in court."

"You've made it into a wildlife refuge," Barbara murmured, visualizing the meadow with its pond and native grasses and flowers.

"I didn't make it, it happened, and I want to keep it that way. I sold that acreage to Rich years ago, with the proviso that he never fence the lower meadow, or build on it. The deer and elk come down from the woods through the orchard and on into the meadow, the way they always have. If Rich ever fences in his piece of land, they will have to change their route, probably go out on the highway. It would be slaughter."

Her mouth was set in a firm line. She would be a formidable enemy, Barbara thought. "Did he object when you turned the ranch into a refuge for women?"

"Not really. He started to, but I told him if he printed a word about the ranch, I would start an investigation of him, his family, his publishing company, everything. I reminded him that *everyone* has something in the past better left buried. It would have been trouble for both of us, but he knew I would do what I said and he backed off. Things happened from time to time that made him angry all over again, and he has called me to protest, but he never mentioned the ranch in his paper, to my knowledge, until after that ghastly tragedy." When Barbara started to speak, Mrs. Canby tapped the table with her finger. "Wait. I have a question for you. Why does he care if you represent that wretched girl?"

"I wish I knew. I've never met him, never laid eyes on him or his family, or his paper until now. What kinds of things did he protest about?"

For a second she thought Mrs. Canby had said all she intended to say, but then she spoke again, and this time she filled in the background without any prompting.

"I thought for a time that one of my children might want to live at the ranch; they all grew up in that house, you see. But it didn't work out that way. I came here to Salem to serve on a committee and it became pointless to try to maintain the house as a residence. For several years it remained empty. Then three years ago I got the idea to use the house again, to let it be used by women who needed isolation, and safety. Refuge. Repairs had to be made, some appliances replaced, things of that sort had to be done first. Six months later we were ready to open."

"You said Rich Dodgson complained from time to time. Were they serious complaints?"

"Not at all. The first year someone used his driveway to turn around in, and he called me. I told him to stop being a fool and put up a gate, which he did. A few months later he called to inform me that the girls were skinny-dipping in the pond, a wickedness he would not tolerate or have his two grown sons witness." A rather wicked gleam sparkled in her eyes.

Barbara suppressed a grin; Mrs. Canby laughed. "I used to do that myself when we lived there. I told him the rushes made a perfect screen and anyone who saw the girls had to work at it. He hung up on me." She tilted her head, thinking. "There was one other time, last winter. This time he said they were trespassing on his side of the meadow and he would not stand for it. It seems," she said caustically, "that one of the girls got up before dawn to try to get some photographs of the elk as they moved through the orchard. She was in position at first light. The elk," she added, "relish the apples Mr. Reading leaves on the trees for them. Sometimes they even stand on their hind legs to reach them. What possible harm that girl could have done is a mystery. I asked Emma—Emma Tidball was the housekeeper/manager—to tell them to stay off his property, and that was the end of that. That's when he posted the entire acreage. Idiot. He was just looking for things to complain about, I'm afraid." She shook her head. "He's the kind of man who gives orders and expects them to be obeyed; he seems to feel the stability of the universe is at stake."

"Mrs. Canby, I'd like to talk to Emma Tidball and some of the women who stayed at the ranch. Do you know how I can get in touch with Emma?"

Mrs. Canby shook her head and pointedly looked at her watch. It was close to three. "Emma retired after the fire. I offered her a job here in Salem, but she has family down in Cottage Grove and that's where she went. As for the girls, what records we had were kept in the house and were destroyed in the fire. Tell me, Ms. Holloway, how can any of this be connected with that poor Kennerman girl?"

"I don't know," Barbara said. "The reports said another woman was there to lead the hunt for mushrooms that day. Angela Everts. Is she in your employ?"

"No. She went out to the ranch three days a week to help out with cleaning and gardening. She lives in Lewiston."

"Do you think she would talk to me?" Barbara asked, and saw the knowing look in Mrs. Canby's eyes. "I suspect that people who work for you don't talk unless you give permission," she added.

"I'll give you their numbers and give them both a call," Mrs. Canby said. "But, Ms. Holloway, I must tell you, I believe that poor girl lost her head and killed her child, just as Angela and Emma both believe. She was in great physical pain and emotionally exhausted. I know such things happen; very good, decent people can lose control. I feel dreadfully sorry for her, but I don't believe for a minute that I can be of any help in her defense."

"I think you've been a great help," Barbara said. "I'm just not sure yet what any of it means," she added honestly.

EIGHT

SUNDAY NIGHT SHE pretended she was not listening for the telephone to ring, for her father's voice. Stop worrying about him, he won't stay mad, she told herself sharply. But he might, she added. He might.

She made a list of things to do immediately. Call Fairchild first thing in the morning, ask for a copy of everything they had gathered to date: police reports, fire department reports, Paula's medical records, the psychiatrist's report, interviews with the others who had been at the ranch. . . . Call Emma Tidball and Angela Everts for appointments. No matter if they had been interviewed already, with Mrs. Canby's intercession either or both of them might be more forthcoming. Go to Bessie's office to read the latest diatribe.

She looked at her calendar with a frown. The trial date was set for the Tuesday following Labor Day, ten weeks away. And people took off in the summer, the Fourth of July holiday would interfere, as would the Labor Day holiday. It would be tight, too tight to be comfortable, but there it was. Ten weeks; countdown had started.

She turned on her computer and keyed in an account of her conversation with Grace Canby not that she was very likely to forget, but to try to clarify an elusive feeling that she had learned something important that she had not yet identified. Reading her report over, she still did not know what that elusive fragment had been. She wondered if, when Mrs. Canby called her former employees, she would refer to Barbara as a girl. She smiled to herself, and rather hoped she would.

He could be so stubborn, she thought then, and drew in an exasperated breath when she realized she was still brooding about her father. He had always been stubborn, her mother had complained. Barbara remembered how, when they fought, which was rare, neither of them had yielded until her mother had found a way to make him think he had won. She tightened her lips and shook her head. No way would she play that game with him.

Suddenly she remembered what he had told her, that after her mother's death he had not been able to sleep until he moved out to the house on the river, and there, soothed by the wind in the fir trees, and the rush of the river, he had finally been able to rest. She hoped he was sleeping now.

Her own grief had been different. She had fought sleep, not wanting oblivion, wanting to stay conscious to remember and relive everything, every moment, every word, over and over. When her body betrayed her and forced sleep upon her, she came awake again and again in tears with no memory of her dreams.

Abruptly she left her desk and went to the bathroom. No brooding, she told herself. Take a soaking bath, go to bed, be rested for the day to come. Countdown had started.

Mr. Fairchild was cooperative, as she had known he would be. He would have copies of everything made

and send it all over to the office, he said, and she told
him no, she would pick it up later.

Next on her list was Angela Everts, who agreed to
meet her at four that afternoon. As soon as she hung up,
the phone rang, and she picked it up without waiting for
her machine to answer.

"Oh, Barbara, Ted Fairchild here. Look, there's been
some kind of silly business over here. We can't find the
Kennerman file. I gave it to Bill to review on Friday,
and he's off on vacation and no one can put their finger
on it now. He could have taken it home with him, I suppose, and forgot to return it."

"Damnation," she muttered.

"I quite agree. I'm just terribly sorry, Barbara. I
wouldn't have had this happen for anything."

"I know. I know. Can Spassero be reached? Where
did he go?"

"I don't know. He has a married sister back East
somewhere, and parents in Massachusetts, and . . . I really don't know. He'll be back in two weeks," he said
in a more hopeful voice.

"Thanks," she said dryly.

She called the district attorney's office and asked for
Gerald Fierst, who would be prosecuting the case. She
had known him years ago, but had not met him again
since returning to Oregon. He was very cautious, she
remembered, and her memory was confirmed by his
reluctance to give her anything. When she hung up
she was in a black mood. He would put together something, she knew, but how much? The same stuff he had
handed over to Spassero in the beginning? Maybe,
maybe not. When, was another question; as soon as

possible, he had said, but they were pretty busy, people on vacation, you know how that goes.

Emma Tidball called her "dear" and said she could come by anytime. She had nothing if not time. They agreed on eleven that morning.

Was there time enough to go to the office and read the latest scandal sheet? She decided there was, if she hurried; she left the house and hurried. She nodded to Pam at the reception desk and went directly to Bessie's office, where on the table the newspaper was open to a big picture of Paula in manacles being led away to jail.

BABY KILLER KENNERMAN FIRES ANOTHER LAWYER

Baby killer Kennerman has fired the second lawyer provided by the court in an attempt to find one who will handle the case her way. Barbara Holloway of the firm Bixby, Holloway, and a dozen others, all high-priced and left of center, has agreed to represent Baby killer Kennerman. . . .

Barbara scanned the article quickly and lifted the paper to turn to the continuation on page four. Under it was another one with Paula's picture and the same headline. She looked at the paper she held and found that it was *The Watchman*, from Joseph County. The one under it was Dodgson's paper. The story was exactly the same.

She sat down and let her gaze roam over the many bins of small-town papers from all over the state. How many others would be offering up this same picture, this same story? Later, she told herself. Later. Now she had time only to look over Dodgson's paper. She scanned the first page, largely devoted to Paula Kennerman. Barbara was the big item on page two, and a long article about the firm, the wealthy clients it catered to, the special-interest groups it served—gays, feminists, environmentalists, foreigners. . . . She gritted her teeth, thinking of the reaction of some of the people it singled out for attention.

There were other articles that she intended to read, but not now. One about schools and the need for choice, another about a new threat to the logging of someone's private property, which was being halted by Earth First! She put the paper down and patted it. Later, she thought; later.

Cottage Grove was a pleasant little town situated in the hills twenty-five miles south of Eugene. It was an easy drive on the interstate, one that Barbara had always enjoyed because it appeared that as soon as one left the valley, the world turned into a vast forest on hills that precluded large farms with massive mechanized equipment. Here the farms were small, manageable, dimples in the forest.

In Cottage Grove she drove past the auto shop where Lucille Reiner's husband worked, past the hotel where Lucille was a desk clerk part of the time. On an unpaved street near a stream she found the address for Emma Tidball. The house was frame, as were most of them here, blue with white trim, with a neat lawn and a flower border edging a fence. The house had been built back in the twenties, apparently, with gingerbread over gables upstairs, more gingerbread on the porch railing.

Emma Tidball came to the door at the first ring. "Yes, yes," she said as soon as Barbara stated her name.

"Come in, dear, come in." She was sixty-two, Barbara learned that day, along with complete histories of her, her husband—now dead, bless his soul—the Canby family, many people Barbara never had heard of, and the town itself. Emma was twenty pounds overweight, she also confided, but she felt comfortable with it, not like some people always trying to diet and feeling bad when it didn't work out. She had curly gray hair and many wrinkles; laugh lines, she said.

They were seated on a screened back porch over-looking a small vegetable garden and more flower-beds. Emma had brought out a pitcher of iced tea and glasses, and a small plate of oatmeal cookies. "With walnuts," she said. "Always made them with walnuts. They seem naked without the nuts." They were delicious.

Barbara steered the conversation in the direction of the Canby Ranch refuge for women, and sat back with her iced tea to listen to another monologue.

Barbara learned which appliances had been replaced, how much it cost to heat in the winter, how much food those women ate, on and on. Then she listened more intently.

"Before we even opened it up, Grace brought over this psychologist, and we sat in that house and talked about it. Some of the women would be so scared, the psychologist said. Janey Lipscomb, that's her name. She said, if they don't want to talk, don't try to make them. You wouldn't believe the shape some of them were in! You just wouldn't believe it. And every last one of them scared to death the men they were running away from would come after them. . . ."

As soon as there was a break in the monologue, Barbara said, "Emma, you have such a wonderful memory, you surely remember the names of some of those women, don't you?"

Emma nodded gravely. "Some. Mostly we didn't make them say their names, you know. Some did and some didn't. But we promised not to tell anyone."

"I understand," Barbara said. "Emma, I swear to you that I will not reveal any of their names to anyone without their permission. But they've been through what Paula Kennerman went through with her husband; they understand her better than you or I can. Maybe some of them would want to help her. Maybe we should let them have the choice, let them decide."

Emma's lips tightened and she stood up. "I'll get us some fresh tea," she said.

Barbara waited, fighting her frustration and impatience. Emma was gone too long to be making tea. Calling Grace Canby for instructions? Thinking? What?

When Emma returned, she put the pitcher of tea down and said, "I had to pray over it first. A lot of those women came in in pretty bad shape, just like Paula, and some of them could have done what she did, they were that crazy. Scared to death, hurting—they can do crazy things and not even know it the next day."

Emma had written out a list of seventeen names, all she could recall, and she had snapshots of three of the women. Some of them dropped a line now and then, she said, but all the notes, cards, and letters had been in the house when it burned.

Barbara thanked her sincerely and asked, "Were any of these mixed up in any of the incidents that made Rich Dodgson call Mrs. Canby and complain?"

Emma's pleasant, crinkly face hardened. She looked

over the list and pointed to three names. "These two, Pam and Jenny, went swimming naked, and that fool had to stand on tiptoe to see them. And this one, Carol, took pictures of the elk on his property or something. At dawn. You'd think that idiot would have been in bed instead of up looking for trouble."

While Barbara made notes beside the names, Emma went on about Dodgson. "Butter wouldn't melt and all that baloney soft soap when he first started coming around wanting that property. And then he started that filthy rag of a paper. He's the kind of Christian that makes the rest of us think Buddhism might be worth looking into, except he's no Christian, not the way I understand religion. He'd see me in Lewiston shopping or something and he'd say something smirky like 'And how many wounded birds are flapping around your ankles these days? Seven?' He always knew the head count. They spied on us from the start, him and her, Kay Dodgson. One of our girls had a miscarriage last year and we had to get an ambulance and get her to the hospital, and the next day here he came, him and that son of his, worse than the father, that one, and they were yelling that we were running an abortion clinic, for heaven's sake! Well, one of the girls who'd been up all night with that sick girl screamed at them to get out of there, that the poor kid had the shit beat out of her by her husband and she might die, and if they didn't hightail it out she'd start throwing rocks at them and with any luck she'd hit one smack in the head and kill him." There was a gleam of very un-Christian satisfaction in Emma's eyes as she finished.

"What did Mrs. Canby say about that?"

"I didn't tell her. If he complained, then I'd tell her

the whole story, I decided, but until he did, well, it seemed to me that the matter had been handled just about right. I guess I didn't want to worry her any more than I had to. I mean, she left me in charge and all."

Soon after this Barbara said, "You know you'll be called by the prosecution as a witness, don't you?"

"I talked to them," Emma said. "They asked questions and I answered them as best I could. And I told them the same thing I told you about that day."

"Did they ask how Paula and her child behaved on Thursday night, all day Friday?"

"They did, and I told them Paula loved that child more than life, and Lori adored her mother. She'd go pressing against Paula's side, and you could see Paula turn ghost white, and sweat stand out on her lip, she was in such pain, but she held that little girl tight against her until she was willing to let go again. Paula was out of her mind when she did it. She was walking on the brink and she fell off, and it wasn't her fault, but his. He's the one should be locked up, not her."

When Barbara finally left, she decided to have a sandwich, then see if Paula had her list of names ready, and then make her four o'clock appointment with Angela Everts. There would be enough time if she didn't dawdle anywhere along the line. She didn't dawdle, and arrived at Angela Everts's house promptly at four.

It was a large two-story house on several acres that seemed to consist of vegetable gardens and fruit trees. The property was a mile out of Lewiston; it looked very well tended and productive.

When the door opened at Barbara's knock, a pleasing

fragrance of strawberry jam wafted out. "Mrs. Everts? I'm Barbara Holloway."

Angela nodded and moved so that Barbara could enter. "Mrs. Canby called," she said. "She said I should tell you what you want to know, but there isn't anything really. I already told it all."

"I know," Barbara said. "I'm really sorry to intrude, but I would appreciate your talking to me, too."

Angela Everts was in her forties, blond with slightly protuberant blue eyes and a little too much weight around her midsection. She was dressed in faded, soft jeans, and a tank top. Her arms were very muscular and tanned.

She led Barbara to the kitchen, a big room with a table large enough to seat a dozen people. There was a lot of counter space that appeared almost covered by jars of strawberry jam. There were kettles on the stove, another in the sink, long wooden spoons, a splotch of jam on the floor.

Barbara accepted coffee and took a place at the table. Angela looked over her kitchen with a shrug and turned her back on it to sit down with her own cup.

"Do you want to ask questions or just let me tell you what I told the others already?" Angela asked with resignation.

"Why don't you just tell me."

It was the same story Barbara had heard and read. When Angela was finished, Barbara asked, "Were you near Paula when Annie came out? Could you hear what Annie told Paula?"

"I know what she told her. Same thing she told me; Lori fell asleep watching television and Annie didn't see much point in staying in with her."

"But you couldn't hear what she said to Paula? Is that what you're saying?"

"I asked her what she told Paula and she told me." She finished her coffee and set the cup down. "Miss Holloway, I know what you're going to ask, if you can talk to Annie, and no, you can't. She's forgotten all this, the way children do. She was pretty upset at first, crying in her sleep, afraid people would blame her, and now she's put it out of mind, and I don't want to stir her up again."

They couldn't leave it at that, Barbara knew, but now she said, "Did you work for Mrs. Canby when she was living out here?"

"Yes, until she moved up to Salem. Never full-time, just two or three days a week, like I was doing when Emma was running the place."

"And you know the Dodgsons, the whole family, I understand."

"I used to work for them. After Mrs. Canby moved away, Mr. Dodgson asked me to come. I didn't stay long. They're awfully particular," she said in a flat tone.

"I hear they can be difficult," Barbara commented with as little emphasis as Angela had expressed. "You saw them both that morning, didn't you?"

"Yes. He was out on the tractor. He liked to go out there, wear a cowboy hat, smoke his cigar, and ride that tractor like it was a fancy car or something. He was out that morning. It was too wet to mow, but he was out doing it. I said to myself that he'd get stuck down in the marshy places, and he did, and revved the engine something fierce until he pulled it out again. And she was walking on the road, the way she does."

"Will you tell me about that, about meeting her, what she said? Whatever you can remember."

Angela looked away, out the screen door, and said carefully, "I don't like her, Miss Holloway, and that's the truth. And that's why I stopped. Because I don't like her, if you can understand that."

Barbara nodded. "I think I understand."

"Well, Annie saw her and scrunched down in the backseat, hiding. She doesn't like her either. Maybe it was because of the way Annie was acting, and I wanted to teach her a little lesson in being polite or something. But I couldn't pretend I didn't see her, in that pink running outfit and white sneakers. She wears pink a lot, and with her complexion she shouldn't. Anyway, I stopped and told her we were all going to gather chanterelles and I asked her if she'd like some. I knew there'd be a lot. And she asked how sick the new girl was, the one they took over to the hospital, her and her child, and I knew I'd made a mistake by stopping at all. They always seemed to know things like that, and I didn't even know a thing about it. So I said not too sick to take a little walk in the woods, and I drove on."

"When you drove to her house to use the phone, was Mr. Dodgson still out on the tractor?"

Angela nodded. "Heading toward the marshy edge again, I guess daring it to try to stop him again. Mrs. Canby asked him not to cut it so close—the ducks like to nest in the high grass and the geese eat the seeds—but he likes things neat. Real particular, both of them."

Loved by all, Barbara thought. "Was anyone else home that day when you used their phone?"

"Well, Craig was swimming and Reggie Melrose was in the kitchen. I rang the doorbell and hammered on the door, and Mrs. Dodgson opened it. She was carrying Craig's robe. I guess she was pretty surprised to see me at the front door. I thought for a minute she was going to bawl me out, but she didn't. She told me to use the phone in the family room, and she went on through it to turn off the music in the swimming pool room. Craig always blasted your ears with music in there. And she yelled at him to get out and get dressed, and Reggie came out of the kitchen to see what was happening."

"Did you see Craig?"

"Yes, I guess I did. I saw him and then turned my back. He swims naked."

"Who is Reggie? The housekeeper?"

"Was. She left. No one stays very long, I tell you. If there's a speck of dust, someone's going to lead you to it and point it out just like the world's coming to an end."

There was little more that she could add, and in a few minutes Barbara returned to the subject that couldn't be avoided any longer. "Mrs. Everts," she said slowly, "I believe you know that Annie hasn't really forgotten what happened that day. Children don't forget things like fire and death. Probably she'll never forget it. Would you consider counseling for her?"

Angela stood up. "I have to clean up all this mess and start making supper now, Miss Holloway."

Barbara rose from her chair. "I'm not a psychologist," she said, "but I have read that children who are seriously disturbed by something they witnessed sometimes revert to more infantile behavior. They might start bed-wetting again, or suck their thumbs, or forget lessons they knew previously. Mrs. Everts, would you be willing to discuss this with a trained child psychologist?"

Angela looked hard and cold and very distant. "No, I won't. There's nothing wrong with Annie! You hear me? There's nothing wrong with my little girl!"

"I think there must be something disturbing her very much if she claims to have forgotten. Please think about it, Mrs. Everts. Her entire life could be affected if she is deeply troubled and doesn't receive help now before she really does bury this incident."

"I have to be getting on with my work," Angela said, and started toward the hall that led to the front door.

Barbara followed her. At the door she tried once more. "Do you know Dr. Jane Lipscomb? Mrs. Canby hired her early on, before she opened the house."

Angela shook her head. "I never saw her. Emma talked about her a little."

"You know if Mrs. Canby hired her she must be good. If I ask her to get in touch with you, will you at least talk to her?"

Angela hesitated, then nodded. "But she can't see Annie, just me."

NINE

On her way home she bought a frozen dinner and salad makings and even a bottle of wine, which was cheap but okay. She was too tired to cope with a real meal and too hungry to care what she had.

She listened to her phone messages as she ate. Unless she heard to the contrary, Bailey would drop by tomorrow around ten. She nodded. Nothing from her father, nothing she had to do anything about. Then she called an old friend, Brian O'Connor, who had been a classmate years ago and now was a professor of law at the University of Oregon in Eugene.

She remembered Brian as a chubby, round-faced, serious boy with red hair and freckles. She had gone to his wedding seven years ago and found that he had become a chubby, round-faced, serious man with hair not quite so red. Nothing really changes, she had thought then.

Brian wanted to chat, but she was in no mood to hear about his two wonderful kids, his wonderful wife, or his wonderful tenure.

"Brian," she cut in, "I need some students to do some research."

His tone changed. "Ah, research. Students. Why students?"

"Because I can't afford professionals," she said honestly. "And it would be good experience for them. They have to be very, very discreet, and very bright."

"Students," he said again. "I suppose you mean graduate students."

"Brian, come on. You know that's what I mean. When we were in school this would have seemed heaven-sent to us. A little real work, a little money. Can you give me three?"

"Why don't we get together and talk about it? You know, I have a responsibility to my students. I wouldn't feel right unless we talk first."

She closed her eyes tightly. "Fine. Look, let me buy you—" She caught herself before she said lunch, remembering that he ate like a horse, and said instead, "A cup of coffee. Tomorrow?"

He had to explain at some length why he couldn't make it until in the afternoon, and they agreed to meet at three in an espresso bar downtown. But he would do it, she knew. He owed her; she had done enough algebra homework for him a long time ago for him to pass the course, and her little reminder of their impoverished days would jog more than one memory. He would think about whom to recommend overnight, hem and haw about it, ask too many questions, and then give her the short list.

She had to write out her activities of the day, keep her notes up-to-date, plan tomorrow, clean up her kitchen, get some sleep eventually. And this was how it would be for the long stretch ahead, she knew.

* * *

"You're not going to like this," Bailey warned her the next morning, opening his briefcase. He withdrew a file and put it on the table, pushed it across to her. She had given him a cup of coffee, which he sipped as she examined the contents of the file.

"Damn," she murmured. He had brought a collection of photocopies of articles about pro-life demonstrations. The caption of the picture she was looking at named some of the people, including Craig Dodgson, linked arm-in-arm with men on each side, blocking a women's clinic in Cincinnati. The next one was in Spokane, Dodgson in the front of the line again, his face twisted in rage. And again in Buffalo. Atlanta . . .

She studied Craig Dodgson: Lean, dark-haired, young was all she could say about him. In each photograph his face was contorted in anger.

"Well," she said when she had looked at them, nine in all. "The boy's busy, isn't he?"

"He gets around," Bailey agreed. "He's bad news, Barbara."

"I see he is. Does he organize, or just show up to help out?"

"We're working on that. There's another son, Alex, twenty-four, an intern in the office of Senator Bulmar in Seattle. Nothing more than that about him yet. And we'll get the aerial today. Our guy's made a couple of sweeps over the forest, scouting out yew trees for the drug Taxol. He'll wrap it up today."

"What else is bothering you?" Barbara asked.

He shrugged. "I just don't know where to draw the line. I sent Winnie in at the restaurant to talk to some of the women there." Winnie was Winifred Scourby, a matronly woman in her fifties who could ferret out anything she went after. "She got them talking, and they don't think Craig Dodgson's been asking anyone to take a cruise with him, not for a couple of years, and they seem to think that he did take a waitress out a few years ago, and then paid her off to go somewhere else."

Barbara looked again at the furious face in the photograph before her. "Give, Bailey. What did they say?"

"They believe he knocked her up and paid off with an abortion and cash for her to get lost."

"Find her," Barbara said in a soft voice. "Don't even think of drawing the line, Bailey, not until I tell you to. I want her."

She gave Bailey a new list, culled from the lists Paula and Emma had provided. "You might have trouble getting some of them to talk to you. Let Winnie do it, especially this one, Carol Burnside. She took some pictures last winter, near dawn, that made Dodgson Senior blow. Why? What's in those pictures?"

He looked at the list gloomily and stuffed it into his briefcase. "Okay. You're the boss. I just don't know what we're digging for."

"Worms," she said. "Slimy, loathsome worms."

She made a few phone calls, and then she went to the office to intercept Bessie before he got busy, if he ever did. Bessie quivered when she told him she would like to have three researchers go through his accumulation of newspapers.

"No, no!" he cried. "Barbara, you can't be serious. Three of them in my office? No, I can't let them do that."

"Can I have the papers boxed up, moved somewhere else?"

"All of them?" He turned anxious eyes to the many bins and quivered again. "All of them?"

"I'll bring them back, Bessie. I just want them to read, not cut them up or mark them up, just to read." She was afraid he would cry. "We could do it another way, of course, but it would be so costly, and since they're here, together . . . Bessie, we'll take good care of them."

"Oh, dear," he said in an undertone. "Oh, dear me. Not out of the offices. I haven't even finished them all yet." His face brightened and he said eagerly, "In the waiting room, that would be all right."

She knew the room he meant; it was where clients and family members and their attorneys all put in their time waiting for jury decisions, waiting to be called back to court. She nodded. That would be even better; the students wouldn't have to work in his office while he was out. They could go right through everything as fast as possible.

That afternoon she met her researchers. Although Brian had been painfully disappointed when she refused to explain what she was looking for, he had supplied two men and a woman. They looked terribly young. Sally Wesley had black hair halfway down her back, great round glasses, and a nice little snub nose. Rob Carradine, going for the poised, man-of-the-world appearance, had dressed in a shirt and tie and sports coat; the effect was somewhat spoiled by Levi's and dirty running shoes. And John Rohr, the youngest of the three, was bespectacled, tall, thin, and intense.

She had asked them to meet her at the office, and they were in the waiting room, where the bins of papers had been lined up against a wall. The coffee machine was plugged in, magazines in place on low tables, a few games on a shelf, all exactly the way it always had been as long as she could remember. She indicated the bins.

"They are far-right-wing publications; some are the religious right, others not, but they're all right of Attila the Hun. You have to read them all and make notes of the articles and editorials—you know, pro-life or anti-gay or school choice, whatever the topic is—and when you've read them all, group those under the same headings and check them out. Are they the same? Same wording, same catch phrases? Just similar? Not alike at all, except in topic? Keep good notes about dates and sources."

"You think maybe they aren't all locally written?" John Rohr asked.

She looked at him more closely. He was no more than twenty-five, she thought, and intense. He had retainers on his teeth, and wore glasses that made his gaze more like a stare. She nodded at him. "I don't know yet. That's what I want to find out. Is someone leading, others following? And if yes, who is doing which?"

It was nearly five, too late for them to start that day. "Keep your hours noted," she said. "And if you get tired, or disgusted, you know, if your eyes start to blur, take a break." She finished with a warning about not talking. "Not with anyone," she said, "except among yourselves. Okay?"

They all nodded solemnly. They looked like children, she thought with dismay, not at their youth, but at the gap that had widened insidiously and now separated her so thoroughly from students in their twenties.

As she was leaving, she saw Sam Bixby with an el-

derly couple who looked very prosperous. She smiled at
Sam and kept walking.

"Oh, Barbara, do you have a minute?" he called after
her.

She glanced at her watch and shook her head. "Tomorrow? I have an appointment in about ten minutes."

She had known Sam Bixby all her life; he and her father had become partners more than forty years ago,
and the firm they had launched had prospered. From the
start her father had done most of the trial work, and
Sam the estate planning, trust fund planning, wills, real-
estate deals. Now a dozen other lawyers did most of the
trial work, and her father and Sam coddled the rich old
folk who had come to rely on them. Sam was tall and
stooped, with scant hair that didn't cover his scalp, although he was always trying new ways to have it cut
and combed. Silly, vain old man; today his hair looked
as if he had had it styled and blow-dried. She was very
fond of him.

He took a step in her direction. "Call my secretary
for a time, will you, Barbara? Tomorrow?"

She nodded. She had thought he just wanted to pat
her on the head and voice the hope that no hard feelings
would result from the firm's decision. But this was
something else, she realized.

She walked out of the offices, out of the building, out
into the sunlight, where she debated walking the dozen
blocks to her appointment, but after a glance at her
watch, regretfully retrieved her car from the lot. No
time, no time, she muttered as she headed once more toward the Sacred Heart medical complex. Five o'clock
traffic was heavy on Pearl, but as soon as she turned off
onto Thirteenth, she was out of the worst of it. Nice

tree-lined streets with well-kept big houses framed with shrubbery and flowers gave the impression that this was a residential area, but it was commercial. Here the businesses had settled into the houses—a good women's clothing store, a hatter, one of the best restaurants in town, real-estate offices, a book store. . . . Within a block of the hospital complex it all changed; the buildings were new, concrete, ugly. Tiny circles had been left open in the concrete paving, like fishing holes in ice, for spindly trees that were doomed. Barbara didn't even look for a parking space, but drove straight to the hospital parking garage.

She had found Dr. Jane Lipscomb's number in the phone book, had called her, and the doctor had said, "Why don't we meet in the coffee shop on Thirteenth. You know it? The Roaster?" She had added almost ingenuously, "I saw your picture in the paper. I'll recognize you and wave."

As soon as she saw Janey Lipscomb waving from a table, Barbara knew she would have trouble thinking of her as "the doctor." She was dressed in wrinkled slacks with an equally wrinkled cotton shirt, sandals without hose; her permed hair was tied back with a red ribbon. She was very pretty, very dimply, with blue eyes and brilliant white teeth. Her patients must love her, Barbara thought as they shook hands.

"I'm glad you had time to see me," she said, taking a chair opposite Janey. She glanced about the coffee shop, which was crowded and noisy. "This is a good place."

"I think so. There was no way I could talk to you at the office. We're controlled by an ogre who runs appointments like Mussolini's train schedules. No appoint-

ment, you wait. The usual lag is close to three weeks."
She was grinning as she said this. "And you intrigued
me enough not to want to wait that long. You're representing Paula Kennerman, and there's an emergency
with a child who possibly will be a witness. How could
I wait?"

A waitress took their orders, two cappuccinos, one
pastry. "I have to eat something," Janey said. "No lunch
today, and dinner's a long way down the road."

"Do you do much work with children?" Barbara
asked when the waitress left.

"Mostly family practice, at least in theory, but actually it's mostly survivors." She looked at Barbara for
recognition of the term, and when Barbara nodded, she
went on. "Women and their children. Dysfunctional
families. Battered women. Children in trouble. How did
you get my name?"

Barbara caught a glimpse of shrewd intelligence that
vanished quickly from Janey's face. She told her about
Emma, and then about Angela and her daughter Annie.
"It made a difference when I said Mrs. Canby had hired
you. I think otherwise she would have turned me down
altogether."

"Ah, the magic name," Janey said with a little laugh.

The waitress came back with their order; the pastry
was as large as a dinner plate. "Ah, good," Janey murmured, and began to cut the pastry into wedges with a
knife and fork. She picked up a piece in her fingers.
"Have some."

Barbara shook her head and watched her eat. The
coffee was excellent.

Neither spoke again until Janey had eaten half the
pastry and finished her coffee. She held the cup up to

get the attention of the waitress and then leaned back. "What I would do in a situation like this," she said thoughtfully, "is go out and talk to the mother first. I don't know how deeply into denial she is, of course, but that's the first hurdle. She has to admit she has a troubled child. Step one. She might not talk, you know. She might not trust me worth a damn."

Barbara smiled. She would make a bet that suckling puppies would leave their mothers to follow this young woman. "You agree that the child must be very troubled?"

"Well, sure," Janey said. "Ah, more coffee." The empty cups were replaced with steaming cups, and Janey returned to her pastry.

"She's in Cottage Grove," Barbara said. "And she isn't to be billed. I'll pay for this."

"Well, someone better or the ogre would eat me raw." The second half of the pastry was vanishing as fast as the first half had done. Janey held a piece poised in front of her mouth. "But you have to understand that no matter who pays the piper, if that child becomes my client, I have to treat our relationship with absolute confidence. I'll make the mother understand that also."

Slowly Barbara said, "What I'm hoping for is that if she'll talk to you first, maybe then she'll talk to me."

"And if she doesn't? Talk to you, I mean."

"I don't know."

"Uh-huh. Boy, that was good!" She picked up crumbs on her fingertip and put it in her mouth. "Sorry. I was starved. I'll call Angela Everts tomorrow and see if I can go out on Thursday. My day off," she added with a rueful expression. "You know this all might take a long time?"

"How long?" Barbara asked, almost dreading an answer.

"Who knows? If the mother agrees to the whole thing, I'll have her bring the child to the office, where we are set up for children. You know—toys, dolls, dollhouses."

"You videotape the sessions?"

Janey gave her another one of her intelligent, appraising looks and shrugged. "Usually. Off-limits, though."

"Of course." Barbara thought a moment, then asked, "But would it be unethical if you let me know how you're making out with them?"

Janey laughed. "You're paying the bill. You get that much."

"Do you want a map of the area? The house and barn, all that?"

"No. If she cooperates, she'll make a map. I suspect it will be more interesting than one you could supply."

Well, Barbara thought, back in her car, not moving yet, she had set a lot of wheels aspin. She felt as if all around her things were in motion that had not been only a few days ago, and she was tired and hungry.

She drove through town without caring that traffic was heavy now, not caring how long she had to wait at the red lights. On impulse she drove toward Skinner Butte Park and the house her father had bought. She slowed down when she saw his car in the driveway. She could park, go ring the bell, and say, "Hey, I'm hungry." And he would put his arm around her shoulder and say, "Well, let's go eat." That's what her mother would have done, she thought, and they both would have pretended nothing had happened. She drove past the house and went home.

On her porch was a second potted geranium, white,

with a card that read: *One looked pretty lonesome. I watered them both.*

She returned to her car and drove back to his house. When he opened the door, she said, "Hey, I'm hungry," and he said, "Well, let's go eat." His arm felt good around her shoulder.

They walked to a neighborhood German restaurant, where they had big fat sausages, mashed potatoes, coleslaw, and dark beer. "Save room for strudel," Frank warned when they ordered. "This time of year it will be with fresh cherries." It was a hard admonition to follow, the food was so very good.

"Never told you the fish story Lewis brought up, did I?" Frank said as they ate. "Never told a soul, actually. Let's see, it was back about nineteen fifty-five, 'fifty-six, thereabouts. We were both young and full of oats. We decided to go over to Snake River and do a little salmon fishing, take a weekend off, have ourselves a boys-night-out sort of holiday. Long drive over there, of course, but that was all right. We got there before dark on Friday, and Saturday was exactly what we had planned. Good fishing, good weather, had a good supper that night of spit-roasted salmon, had some good talk. Then Sunday we decided to go back out for just a couple of hours before we headed back home. And Lewis snagged a sturgeon."

Telling his stories like this always worked magic, Barbara thought, watching him. Years vanished, leaving his face soft and vulnerable; his eyes appeared unfocused, but she suspected that his vision was extremely clear, focused sharply on the past.

"A sturgeon," he said, smiling slightly, "is really a wa-

terlogged tree trunk that breathes now and then, once
every six months or so, and moves just about with every
breath. Any fishing fool knows that all you can do if you
snag a sturgeon is to cut it loose. You try to bring it up,
it's like lifting the whole damn river bottom. Lewis knew
that as well as I did, but he decided to forget what he
knew. And another thing he forgot is that the river doesn't
like things to stay put. No way. It's forever rearranging
things to suit its own whims. And the current nudges everything downriver, toward the rapids and falls, toward
the Columbia eventually, and the ocean by and by."

His grin widened with the recollection. "And it
seemed that we interrupted this particular sturgeon during its period of activity; the damn thing decided to
move, heading out toward the middle of the river, where
the current was a mite swifter. So I'm yelling at Lewis
to cut the thing loose, and he's yelling that he's got it.
And we're drifting out and moving just a little faster
downriver, but Lewis is at the end of the boat where the
outboard motor is, and he won't listen to reason. Start
the damn engine, I yell, and he yells, I got the sucker!
And I yell, Change places with me! And we are doing
that when Lewis goes over the side. Just like that, over
the side. He said I pushed him, but I never, and he's trying to climb back in and next thing the damn boat is up-
side down and we're both in the drink. And now we can
feel the current really fine. We can't catch up to the boat,
and we head for shore. A little bit of beach, a little bit
of a cliff, some scraggly trees, and not a thing more."

He laughed. "Oh, we were a sorry couple, I tell you.
Lewis had some matches in a waterproof box, and we
pulled down some of the scrub and started a fire and
stripped to dry our clothes, and not a single word be-

tween us. Not a word. A little growling maybe, but not a civil word."

Barbara had finished her dinner while he talked; she waved the waiter away when he approached the table.

"So I was trying to calculate how long before the sun dipped behind the cliff, and trying to calculate how much firewood we'd need to last all night, and Lewis kept searching his pockets for something to eat, and we both sort of fell asleep for a little while. He woke up first and started yelling again, waving his shirt, just like a castaway. Here came one of those big rubber boats that takes thrill seekers down the rapids, with a guide and six customers, and they're heading our way and we're trying to cover ourselves. But they rescued us, all right, and took us with them down the rapids. And that's how I came to shoot the rapids in the deepest gorge in North America."

He finished the last scraps on his plate and now the waiter came to clear the table, and they waited for coffee and strudel.

"You never told Mother?" Barbara asked.

"Nope. Never told a soul, like I said. She would have worried every time I looked like fishing, and she thought Lewis was a bad influence. She said Lewis's wife, Caroline, thought the same thing about me. Bet he never told anyone either."

The strudel was too good for talk to get in the way. When Barbara finished hers, she leaned back with a contented sigh. "If I did this often I wouldn't be able to move. I was starving."

"Thought you looked a mite frazzled when you came in. I stopped by your office today and Martin says you've closed shop for a while. Busy days?" He was not quite off-hand, but neither was he probing.

She nodded.

"I've done some thinking over the weekend," he said, looking past her at a picture of hearty German women in dirndls carrying trays of beer steins. All the pictures in the restaurant were of hearty young women doing hearty tasks.

"About Judge Paltz?" she prodded when he seemed lost in contemplation of the artwork.

"About Lewis. He made a good judge, in spite of everything. He's fair and honest. He can be loose and easygoing, or he can be as tight as—" He pulled his gaze from the picture and didn't finish. All the young women wore very tight bodices over very plump bosoms. He grinned and waved a hand. "Anyway, he can be strict, allow not one inch of leeway."

"And he probably thinks I manipulated him, lied to him," she murmured.

"Hold on. Let me do this my way. See, I've known him for more than fifty years. He knows damn well that someone lied to him and threw him to the dogs. And you ended up getting what it appeared that you wanted in the beginning, and Bill Spassero ended up getting out." He held up his hand when she started to speak. "Wait. Paula Kennerman's already been convicted by public opinion, the newspapers, television, all of it. She's dead in the water as far as a defense goes, so that's not a real consideration at this moment. It seems to me that you've got yourself on two tracks at the same time, and they're going to rip you in halves. There's the Kennerman track, where all you can do is make damn certain the state proves its case, and there's the Dodgson track, where it all ends up in muck and murk and there's damn all you can do about them except make them mad. I can't see a way for you to prove anything about Spassero unless he decides to tell it himself. And with that hanging, you could be a liability, not an asset for Kennerman."

She waited this time until she was certain he was finished. "Dad, thanks," she said softly. "I really don't want you to worry about this. Maybe I've gone out on a limb, but maybe not. I don't think there are two tracks at all. Just one, and I'm following it to the end."

"Because of Lewis?"

"He's a big part of it," she admitted. "It wouldn't do for him to believe you tried to drown him and I threw him to the dogs, would it?"

He shook his head and drew in a deep breath, and returned his gaze to the buxom women. "No, it wouldn't do. What can I do to help?"

She stared at him. "What do you mean?"

"Christ on a mountain! What did it sound like? No deals. No quid pro quo. Just a doddering old fool offering a feeble, useless hand. You can't do citations worth a damn."

"Like hell! I can cite with the best of them when I want to!"

"When you want to," he muttered, "and that's rare. Real rare. Well?" He looked at her over the top of his glasses, his eyebrows drawn nearly together in his fiercest scowl.

"I probably can find something for you to do," she said, surprised at the huskiness of her voice.

"Well, let's get out of here and talk about it," he said. "Your place. I'd take you home with me, but I've only got one chair and damned if I can sit in it with a woman sitting on the floor, and I'll be double damned if I sit on the floor."

TEN

BARBARA HAD AN appointment with Sam Bixby at nine forty-five and another with her father at ten in his office. He wanted to meet "their client": She said the words in her head with satisfaction. And then he wanted to see the Canby Ranch. "I'll go with you," she had said quickly. Without hesitation he had nodded. And they had agreed that neither of them would go out there alone, not until something was done about Royce Gallead.

Now, at the office, she looked into the waiting room and said hello to her three student researchers, already at work. They had identical loose-leaf notebooks open; newspapers were spread on the table, some on the floor, another batch on an end table by an overstuffed chair. She closed the door softly and went on to Sam Bixby's office, where his secretary, Marjorie Newhouse, greeted her. Marjorie sometimes said she wished Sam would retire so she could. She was near seventy and would not even consider turning him over to someone else.

"He's waiting," she said with such a neutral look that Barbara braced herself.

Today Barbara was in jeans, a T-shirt, and walking shoes, prepared for the Canby Ranch, and comfortable enough with Sam Bixby that her clothes wouldn't matter. He had seen her in a bathing suit, in shorts, slacks, formal wear. No doubt, she had told herself that morning, in times that memory mercifully had erased, he had even seen her bare-assed. Now she wished she had chosen something else to wear, something more appropriate for a business office.

She tapped on the door and opened it. "Good morning," she said, entering, closing the door behind her.

"Ah, Barbara. Good morning, my dear. Please, take a chair. Would you like some coffee?"

She shook her head, but did take the chair opposite his desk, hating the feeling that she had been called to the principal's office.

"Barbara, you know your father brought up the matter of the Kennerman case with us, of course. And we were opposed for many different reasons, but, Barbara, it made me start to think of the somewhat irregular position you seem to be in at present."

"Barbara" three times, "my dear" once; it was worse than bad, she knew, and held herself very still.

"Barbara, my dear, this is very awkward for both of us, I'm afraid."

Her heart sank even lower. With the window behind him, the drapes open, his expression was impossible to read, even to see, but the slope of his shoulders, the way he was shuffling a few papers around, that was enough. Light reflected off his head as if it were made of porcelain. She waited, aware that her silence was making it more difficult for him. At the moment she didn't care. His conference, let him run it.

"My dear, I really think that it would be in the best interests of all of us if you simply offered to resign from the firm. Unless, of course, you choose to come back as a real member."

She let out a long breath. "Have you talked this over with Dad?"

"Of course not. I would hate to cause a rift in our partnership after so many years. I think it's best to handle this just between the two of us."

"I see. Of course, I'll resign, Mr. Bixby. You want a statement in writing, I suppose?"

"It's going to be Mr. Bixby now? Barbara, I—"

"I think I should be on my way," she said, rising. "I'll send in the letter this afternoon."

His shoulders slumped even more, but he did not get up from his chair.

They both turned to look when there was a pounding on the door and it flew open. Frank strode in and kicked it shut after him.

"Oh, Lord," Sam Bixby muttered.

"You're damn right, 'Oh, Lord!' What's this chickenshit? When's the last time one of us fired anyone without talking about it first? You yellow-bellied slinking lowlife!"

"Dad, he didn't fire me!"

"The hell he didn't!" He had come across the wide office to the desk, where he grasped the edge and leaned forward and said in a grating voice, "You got a few phone calls and turned chicken! Didn't you?"

"Calls and letters! I told you this was explosive! We don't need it!"

"Crap! Dodgson waved a stick and you ran like a yellow dog, whining, yelping, looking for cover."

"It wasn't Dodgson. Some of our clients, your clients

and mine, damn you. People are hot, Frank, and there's no moral ground to stand on."

"We faced them down during the McCarthy witch-hunts, didn't we? Both of us together. We lived through those years. Now you're like a fat cat cringing at shadows. What have you turned into, Sam?"

"I'm protecting what we built! I'm not going to let it all go down the drain for a baby killer. I'm not going to lose everything we've worked for—not for your daughter, not for your grandstanding. My God, I'm sick of the kind of people you've dragged through these offices over the years, and if you think I'll sit still and let your daughter do the same, you've lost what little sense you ever possessed. Maybe it's time for you to retire, too!"

Barbara watched them, speechless. They had argued over the years, many times, but never anything like this. Sam Bixby was on his feet yelling, her father was livid. They were saying things that wouldn't be forgotten or forgiven, she thought in despair. She reached for her father's arm; he shrugged away from her without a glance.

"Maybe it is," he said in a much lower, much more menacing voice. "And the firm goes down with me, Sam. I'll see that it does. Think about that while you're planning some goddamn tax dodge for one of your fat cats."

"You don't know a goddamn thing about corporate structure. You want a fight? You think I'm not ready for a fight? Is—"

Barbara snatched up a book and slammed it down on the desk. It sounded like an explosion. "Stop this! Stop it this minute! Both of you!" They both froze. "Look at you. Look at what's happening to you. First, Dodgson came between us, Dad. He did. On his high moral ground taking potshots here, there. Now he's between you two. Sniping away. And we're all playing right into his hands, doing exactly what he wants us to do!"

Abruptly Sam Bixby sat down again and Frank straightened, took a step backward. Sam reached for the papers on his desk; his hands were trembling. He looked at them for a moment and then folded them together. "We should discuss this at a later time," he said faintly.

"Now," Frank snapped. "How many letters, how many calls?"

"Enough," Sam said. "Four calls, one letter. All from clients who have been with us for years, all protesting the same thing, and the last caller said there would be others. I believe him."

"So do I." Frank grunted and sat down in one of the comfortable chairs facing the desk. "They've got a data bank," he said after a moment. "My God, that man's got a data bank that includes our clients!"

Sam looked stricken. "You don't know anything like that."

"He probably sent out a questionnaire," Frank went on, ignoring his partner. "Who's the family doctor, the dentist, lawyer, what's the church affiliation? And people obligingly filled in the blanks. A goddamn data bank."

"I tell you, Frank, it isn't like that. People are taking a stand. They're picking sides."

"And we can't be on both sides of the fence. Let them choose. Come on, Bobby, we've got some work to do."

"What do you mean?" Sam cried. "What do you mean 'we'?"

"Forgot to mention it, I guess," Frank said caustically, "what with all the yelling. I'm her assistant on this one. She goes, and there's no choice: I gotta go where the boss is."

"Oh, Lord," Sam moaned.

Frank took Barbara's arm in a firm grasp and propelled her from the office. He closed the door gently behind them, smiled genially at Marjorie Newhouse, who looked petrified, and walked Barbara from the offices out into the sunlight. He was humming under his breath. It sounded like a cat purring.

On the way to the jail, she said, "Dad, I'm really sorry. I wouldn't have had that happen for anything. I didn't want you to get involved."

"Don't be sorry," he said. He laughed and added, "It takes a fight with an equal to keep the blood circulating, keep the brain cells functioning. Sam liked it as much as I did. Or he will when he cools off." He laughed again.

He was cheerful when they met Paula Kennerman, who regarded him with wariness when Barbara explained that he would be working on the case, too. He might come around to ask questions, and it would be exactly as if she, Barbara, were asking them, she told Paula.

"Except I might ask harder questions," Frank added.

"Harder than hers?" Paula asked with a faint smile. "I doubt you can think of anything harder than she has."

"Well, I'm meaner than she is."

Paula's look said she doubted that, too. "I wrote out

everything I could think of," she said, and handed a sheaf of papers to Barbara.

"Good. That will be helpful," Barbara said. The handwriting was very legible; it looked like a school-girl's report. She avoided her father's glance; he knew as well as she did that she had to keep Paula thinking about the death of her child, talking about it, writing about it, or when the trial started, she might collapse when others began to talk about it.

In the car a few minutes later, Frank said, "I like her. Of course, when the moon is full she could turn into a raving homicidal maniac, but right now I like her." It was his firm belief that most killers could be very nice people as soon as the impediments to happiness were removed.

He drove past the Dodgson Publishing Company, exactly as she had done on her first trip, and then headed toward the ranch, but he continued past the turnoff, and they scanned the few houses on the left side of Farleigh Road as they drove by them. The marshy ground ended at a low ridge that followed the road for nearly a mile, and there were four houses in clear view on the ridge. Any one of them could hold a spy for Dodgson, Barbara thought. From those houses, the meadow, the pond, the Canby house and garden area would be clearly visible. Anyone up there could keep an eye on the comings and goings at the ranch. She pretended unawareness of the question *why?* in her mind. When the trees closed in, Frank turned around and drove back to the private road and the Canby property.

He walked the same path she had walked at the ranch, and then drove the same route she had taken. He had to see the layout exactly as she had needed to, she understood, and wondered how much he actually had taught her over the years, lessons so deeply assimilated that she no longer could recall when they had been delivered.

" 'Course," he said meditatively as he drove, "it could well be that Dodgson feels his reputation is on the line. He declared that girl guilty, and she must be guilty, or he wouldn't have said so. And once he's got his own tail in his mouth, no way he can back down. And he spied on the ranch because he wanted to find cause to close it down because he doesn't believe in letting women run out on their men."

"Just doing the Lord's work," Barbara murmured.

"That, too," he said cheerfully.

"And Kay Dodgson, home alone and terrified, called Royce Gallead to the rescue when a trespasser appeared—me," Barbara said.

"That makes as much sense as anything else," her father agreed. Then in the same cheerful voice he said, "Honey, you've considered, I suppose, that all the digging and prying you do may only reveal that Dodgson's part of a vast network that shares information about books to ban, when to come down hard on abortion, or homosexuals, or whatever the line of the day is. Just a foot soldier in the battle for the mind and soul of the country."

"I've considered that," she said glumly.

"Well, you've got the tiger by the tail, and there aren't a whole lot of options."

"I know. You go for the ride, or you let go and get eaten, or," she added, "you dig in your heels, tighten your grip, and you start swinging the damn beast for all you're worth."

* * *

But as the days passed, as the weeks melted into each other, she had to admit that she had not yet budged the beast. Each report Bailey brought in seemed to add to the depth and the darkness of the growing cloud that hung over her head.

She had sent her resignation letter to Sam Bixby; it was returned with a scrawled *Not accepted*. When they met in the wide corridor of the offices, he nodded curtly and did not speak. The students finished the first part of their job and were busy grouping stories, comparing language, dates. Bailey found the spy on Farleigh Road.

"You won't like it," he said gloomily in her father's office, which they were sharing for now. "Mrs. Carrie Voight. Her husband's the night watchman at Gallead's range. She's the day watchwoman over the Canby place. Three hundred plus, never leaves her upstairs rooms, which are equipped with a telescope and binoculars. Doing the work of the good Mr. Dodgson, who was sure those women were up to no good, smuggling aliens, growing dope, something like that. She saw Angela Everts drive up the road that Saturday morning, watched her stop to chat with Mrs. Dodgson, and drive on. No one else went up that road. And the day after I talked to her, one of the D.A.'s eager beavers did likewise. Their witness."

"Shit," Barbara said. "What does she do, sit and stare out the window all day waiting for the smugglers to show up?"

"Nope, they put in a sensor with a radio signal to her room, light goes on when anything breaks the beam."

She stared at him. "That's pretty heavy-duty stuff."

"Yep." He had helped himself to a drink from the little bar hidden behind a section of bookshelves. He swirled the bourbon around and watched it. "You won't like Winnie's report, either," he commented. "It's there, and a tape recording." He pointed to a manila envelope he had put down on the desk.

"Just tell me," Barbara said wearily.

"Right. Christina Lorenza, the woman Craig Dodgson took out on his boat a few years back. Winnie had a time getting her to talk, and she'll deny everything. But for what it's worth, she was pregnant, all right, and she went after him for support, and he took her out again and they talked it over. He signed a paper accepting responsibility, agreed to pay two hundred a month for support, the whole bit, and then she miscarried. So· he's off the hook, but out of the goodness of his heart, he forked over five grand so she could go to computer school down in San Francisco, which she did. She's a programmer now, good job, and she says he isn't all that bad a guy. He was young, she was young, let bygones be bygones."

"Miscarried? Five thousand dollars because he's a good guy? It stinks, Bailey."

"I thought so, but Winnie says she's leveling. For what it's worth."

He believed in Winnie the way she, Barbara, believed in him.

"Listen to the tape when you have half an hour," he suggested. "Cheer up. I got a lead to a guy who worked in the publishing plant a couple of years, up to last fall. I'll see him tomorrow. Up in Corvallis. Maybe the pendulum will start the other way."

"It had better, or I'll find me a new Sam Spade," she muttered.

Bailey grinned and finished his drink.

By late July her father had finished the move into his house. He invited her to his first dinner party. He was a superb cook and liked to show off, she thought, grateful for the invitation. First he had to show off his garden— tomatoes, beans, a hill of zucchini, green onions. . . . Then his office was open for inspection; he had arranged all the books he was using for research to write his own two books on the art of cross-examination, which he had been at for years, and she doubted would ever finish, because he kept finding new material that could not be omitted.

He had been right about the house; it was perfect for him. All through the evening she kept expecting him to bring up his invitation for her to move in, but he didn't. Instead, over iced asparagus soup he told her he had lunch with Ted Fairchild the previous day.

"You know," he said with a shrug, "we old-timers like to get together and chat."

"Gossip like magpies," she commented.

"Now, Barbara. Anyway, Ted confessed that he was not happy with the arrangement to let a youngster like Bill Spassero supervise a case Ted was handling. Not that he complained; he wouldn't. But still, pride's got to be involved in something like that. He's fretted about it. What he said was that it seemed to him the telescope was pointed in the wrong direction with the wrong eye at the working end. I thought that was pretty good."

Barbara could well imagine the luncheon, with her father being ever so sympathetic and understanding, asking about the sick wife, retirement plans, and Ted Fairchild opening like a book.

"It seems," Frank continued, "that Bill's working under a two-year contract that runs out the end of October, and he hasn't signed the renewal contract yet. But he's being close about his plans. Real close."

He cleared away the soup plates and brought a platter of beautiful vegetables—tiny carrots, snap peas, green onions, strips of red and green peppers, all brilliant, glistening from a marinade of lemon juice and olive oil. The casserole he brought out next was of small beef cubes with a lot of red onions, and marble-sized red potatoes.

"This is why I never make dinner for you," Barbara said a few minutes later. "I know when to compete and when to drop out. This is all wonderful."

"I've given you recipes for everything on the table," he said, pleased with her pleasure. "Back to Bill Spassero. Ted thinks he's got an offer from Doneally and Jensen."

"Well, that's not unusual for an up-and-coming trial lawyer," she said after a moment, trying to place the names. She did not know either of them.

"Nope. Interesting thing is that Doneally is Dodgson's lawyer. Handled a big libel case for him five or six years ago. Won it, too."

"Oh," she said softly. "What makes Ted think there's an offer?"

"Take it easy," Frank said. "Even if we know it for a fact, it doesn't prove anything. Ted saw them together a few times back before Bill went on vacation. That's not much."

She thought about it. They would know for sure

when Bill Spassero walked out of the public defender's office, crossed the street, and sat down in a different chair. November? Too long to wait.

"Eat your vegetables," Frank said, "and stop plotting. This is information-gathering time, that's all."

She resumed eating. "Ted hasn't seen them together more recently?"

"Nope. Lying low, or the affair cooled down. Who knows? The only other thing I got out of him was that Bill was due to take his vacation the last two weeks of September, and he asked to have it changed."

She considered this for a moment and then said, "I wonder when the offer was made. If it was. After he was appointed to Paula Kennerman, or before?"

"Why don't you ask him?" Frank said snappishly. "You aren't tasting a thing you're putting in your mouth."

After dinner she rinsed the dishes and stacked them in the dishwasher, and scrubbed a pot or two while they talked. Frank was following up on the students' work with the newspapers, culling out those that would be revealing, he said. He couldn't do too much at a time; the taste they left in his mouth made him go do something else pretty fast. "What I'm doing is reading for fifteen or twenty minutes every night, and then I take a bath."

"You brought them home?" she asked incredulously. "Does Bessie know?"

"Of course he knows." He laughed. "I promised I wouldn't put them in the birdcage."

When she was ready to leave, he said, "Bobby, things look pretty bad, but hell, I've had cases that looked worse than this one does, and you will too before you're done with the law."

"Did you win them when they looked this bad?"

He decided his glasses needed cleaning and got busy with that. "Sometimes. But you know as well as I do that that isn't the point. I said in the beginning you're on two tracks, one you've got to go with and the other one you want to go with. What you *have* to do is see to it that Paula Kennerman gets a fair trial, and not get so wrapped up in what you want to do that you lose sight of that."

The next day Bailey called, and sounded happy, such a rare occurrence with him that Barbara drew in her breath. "We found your missing photographer," Bailey said. "Winnie just got back from talking to her. In Sonoma, for God's sake. Sonoma! And your boy Craig is off on another jaunt; Winnie saw him in the airport and got curious. He's off to Denver this time."

Another demonstration? How many times a year did he do that? "Do you know someone in Denver?" she asked, as much out of irritation as with purpose. "Let's find out what he does on these trips. Talk about frequent flyers!"

"Denver . . . Yeah, there's a guy there. You serious?"

"Yes, Bailey. Just find out where he goes, who he sees. Is he organizing or just showing up? What about the photographer? Did she have anything to say?"

"Better than that, Barbara. We have her film. I'll drop it off to a guy I know to get it developed and printed, and then we'll see what made old man Dodgson blow his stack. Okay?"

"You bet. And call that guy you know in Denver before the plane lands and Craig gets lost in the crowd."

* * *

That night she, Frank, and Bailey examined the photographs under a strong light in Barbara's kitchen. They were arranged in sequence; the first few were dark and murky, with little detail. "My guy said she was probably doing a few random shots to get her light-meter reading right. Maybe set the stage before the animals arrived. See here, he said there's something between her and the building in this one and a couple that follow it."

There was the Gallead fence, with a faintly paler sky behind it. The elk probably came from behind that fence to get to the orchard, Barbara thought, peering at the prints. A later print showed an animal, a black silhouette against the lighter sky, emerging from the far side of the fence. Then a print with several elk bunched so that they looked like one large animal with too many heads. Then, apparently, the elk had turned and run away.

"She was pretty disgusted, never developed them, since the elk never got to the orchard where she could get a better shot," Bailey said. "But what my guy said is interesting is the thing between her and the fence. He can do things with the negatives, enhance the image, bring it out, he says, if we want him to."

Barbara nodded absently. She could almost make it out. A truck? And several figures. Not even at Dodgson's place, but in front of Gallead's fence. She looked closer. The edge of the gate was there, visible, light against dark. The gate was open. She straightened and rubbed her back. Frank was rubbing his, too.

"Let's see what he can do with them," she said. "Just these." She sorted them, choosing the ones that showed the fence, the gate, and the thing that looked like a truck.

"Is the damn fool running guns?" Frank muttered. "Illegal aliens? When can he get them done so we can see something?" he asked Bailey; he was scowling fiercely.

"I'll get back to him first thing in the morning," Bailey said as he gathered up the prints. "Take him a day or two. And, Barbara, I know where Craig Dodgson went in Denver, but what it means is about as clear as this mess. Four doctors. All obstetricians, gynecologists, you know, women's doctors. All in private practice, spread out over the city. He went in, stayed fifteen minutes, came out, and went to the next one, and then he came home. You figure it out."

"Are they pro-lifers? Do they do abortions?"

Bailey shrugged. "One pro-lifer, three do whatever comes along. Maybe he's trying to convert them."

"You put a tail on Craig Dodgson?" Frank asked. "Good God! What for? I'm going home."

"Just for today, Dad. And I don't know what for." And, she realized when they were both gone, she didn't know what for about any of this affair.

ELEVEN

DAY BY DAY the temperature edged upward; the sun shone without mercy. Nice people began to snarl and snap at other nice people. Those without enough energy to snarl bared their teeth silently. For most of July the nights were cool, alleviating the danger of mass insanity, but then the night temperatures began to climb also, and now people were saying, *If I wanted to live in a desert, I'd go down to Southern California.* Those who chose to live in the valley liked rain and mist and cool weather; they did not like snow, and they especially did not like it when the thermometer flirted with the one-hundred-degree red mark day after day.

Barbara's house was hot day and night. It did her temper no good at all to think of Frank's house with a heat pump that provided heat in winter and cool air in the summer. She read reports; she wrote out her own notes and reports; she interviewed people in the office, where the air-conditioning made her want to curl up and sleep; she raced around the countryside in her un-air-conditioned car to interview other people.

The tiger was still straining; she was still holding on, and neither of them had moved an inch.

The first week in August Janey Lipscomb called. "I

have a present for you," she said in her cheerful way. "Mrs. Everts is pretty grateful that you steered me onto Annie, and she said you could have a copy of the tape, if you think it will be useful." Her tone hinted that Barbara would find it useful.

"I'd like to see it very much," Barbara said, trying to resist the buoying effect of too much hope.

Janey said she could drop it off on her lunch hour, and Barbara arranged to meet her at the office at noon. When the young psychologist arrived, Barbara thought again how improbable it seemed for her to be a doctor of anything; she looked more like a cheerleader.

"Thanks," Barbara said, taking the tape. "Will Annie be okay?"

"She'll be fine. I told her mother not to let her testify in court," she said with charming candor. "That would be too traumatic for her right now."

"All right. Dr. Lipscomb—may I call you Janey?"

"You might as well. Everyone else does, little kids with two teeth, great-grandparents with two teeth, it's just Janey to them all. Why should you be different?"

Barbara laughed. "I wonder why that is." Then, serious again, she said, "There's one more thing I'd like to engage you to do. Go see Paula Kennerman."

Janey's dimply smile vanished as she shook her head. "I'm not a forensic psychologist, no match for the guy the state always uses—what's his name?—Ricky Palma. I don't want to butt heads with him."

"I don't want you to," Barbara said. "Just go spend an hour with Paula. Talk about the weather, knitting, whatever. I just want people to know you've been there."

Janey looked at her appraisingly. "Why?"

They were standing near the large round table in Frank's office; it was piled high with newspapers, notebooks, folders; Barbara added the tape to a heap of stuff. The accumulation of weeks of investigation appeared to be nothing more than a jumble, which was how she thought of it all. A jumble. Barbara waved at the mess.

"Out of all that stuff I'm beginning to unravel threads, one here, one there. I'm not sure yet where they lead, or if they connect. I don't know yet where that tape will fit in, or even if it will. But if it does, I may have to call you to testify. Your name will be on the list of witnesses for the defense. I'd rather have everyone think you might testify about Paula and not that child. I can't tell you more than that, because at this moment I don't know more than that."

Janey grinned again and shrugged. "Okay. I'm sort of curious about her, anyway. Thursday," she added.

"Your day off," Barbara said.

"Days off are really theoretical, aren't they? They sound good on a job description and vanish in reality. Gotta run. See you."

Barbara went back to sorting her materials. The Jack Kennerman material made up one stack. Then the Dodgsons and Royce Gallead, who obviously was smuggling something. All that space in his building, not necessary to his business, she felt certain, but for what? And the truck with the five men around it, on the way in. To do what? Dodgson probably knew about Gallead's operation, maybe had a piece of it. She could form a tenuous link between them, but she could not link that side to the murder of Lori Kennerman and the arson fire at the Canby house. It seemed that Dodgson had taken steps to make certain no one at the Canby place would ferret out his secrets, but once the steps were taken, boundaries established, he had left the Canby guests alone. And he and his wife and even their son were all accounted for the morning of the murder and fire. Gallead had been at the firing range all that morning, accounted for; his employee, Terry Bossert, had been in the gun shop all day that Saturday.

No matter how she tried to work the information she had, there remained a missing piece, and without it she had a foot on two different tracks, exactly as her father had claimed from the start.

He simply hadn't realized that one hand was clutching a third track as if life depended on not letting go. She had taken seriously his admonition that she might be a hindrance rather than a help to Paula as long as Judge Paltz believed her to be dishonorable. She could not start a trial in his court until that was settled, she understood, but every time she had tried to find a way to clear the air of that business, she hit a wall.

She frowned at the paper she was holding, undecided where to place the report on William Spassero. She sat down to consider him yet again. Everything in his life had been exemplary right up to the time he acquired Paula Kennerman as a client. Good family, money in the background, good education, good prospects. Absolutely unblemished, not a sour note anywhere. She bit her lip in exasperation. He had come to Eugene two years ago, with faultless recommendations, to take the job in the public defender's office. Not associated with right- or left-wing groups. Presbyterian. Probably would go with Doneally and Jensen in November. And Doneally, evidently, was in Dodgson's pocket.

Suddenly she stood up. "What if he didn't know?" she said softly, and after a moment she said to herself, "That's it. He didn't know."

She sat down again to think about it, but she felt certain that Bill Spassero had walked into a bear trap without awareness until it closed on him.

She examined this idea for a few more minutes, and then she called Spassero's office. She listened as someone at the other end yelled for him to pick up the phone.

"Barbara Holloway," she said when he barked hello. "I'd like to meet with you to discuss something."

There was a pause, then he said, "Ms. Holloway, what a coincidence. I was going to call you about that file. I can't tell you how sorry I am about that. We searched and searched, and just last night I found it at home, under a bunch of stuff. Why don't I drop it off?"

"Fine," she said. "I'm at my father's office. You know where it is?"

He said he did and would be by in half an hour.

She hung up thoughtfully. She had given up on obtaining the original file; the district attorney's office had sent over what they said was everything, and she believed them. It seemed complete. And now Spassero had found his file. Interesting, she thought, just interesting.

She had seen him being coolly professional in court; had seen him grinning with boyish enthusiasm and friendliness; he had been stiff and indignant and very righteous; and then furious. All the roles had been very well performed. The most important lesson he could learn at the public defender's office was self-control; he would be given A plus if that were a graded subject. Today when the receptionist, Pam, led him to the office, he was reserved and careful, open, willing to be friends but not pushing anything.

"I really do want to apologize for this," he said, handing her the bulky file.

"Things happen," she said. "Thanks. But this isn't what I called about. Please, sit down so I can."

"Of course," he said agreeably. He sat in one of the overstuffed chairs. She took one facing him. "All right," he said. "What did you call about?"

He was wearing a lightweight suit that looked to be more silk than wool; his shirt appeared to be silk, and his tie. His hair, looking more silvery than gold today, was as fluffy as a cloud, and he had a good tan. His face was set in a pleasant expression, like the going-to-Aunt-Maud's-tea-party expression he must have worn a lot as a youth.

"Let me tell you what I think happened," she said. "You found yourself saddled with Paula Kennerman's case, not a happy situation, but there it was. A day, two days, maybe a week later, you had a talk with an established attorney here in town who made what seemed like an incredible offer. No résumé required, no application, just walk out one door and in through another." His expression had changed as she spoke; it now was rigor-mortis blank. Not a muscle on his face twitched. He could have become deaf in the last minute or so for all the response he was showing. She continued, "And this prestigious attorney said it would be a good idea for him to supervise a case or two, watch you at work, give you a pointer maybe. You leaped at the chance. Who wouldn't? A heaven-sent opportunity, lightning now instead of having to wait a few years. Did you celebrate? I imagine you did. I would have." She smiled slightly, then became serious again.

"When did you suspect you were being used? When that article appeared in Dodgson's paper? I rather imagine that your new friend suggested that Paula needed a doctor, and it happened he knew the right one for her. Is that how it worked?"

"Enough," he said, an edge in his voice now. "I've heard about enough."

"No, you haven't. Not yet. I'm not finished with my summation, you see. You were taken off the case and Fairchild was put on it and you asked to supervise him, a man with more years of trial experience than you have lived. What an arrogant suggestion that was, and a suggestion that probably didn't originate with you. Did it? But then Fairchild was removed, and there were no more opportunities to spy on Paula and the development of her case. Were you scolded? Is that why you decided to leave town for a couple of weeks? Was the offer withdrawn, Mr. Spassero?"

He flushed and stood up. "Last week I signed a contract to continue at the public defender's office. So much for your fairy tale."

"I intend to take my fairy tale to Judge Paltz," she said quietly. "I don't intend to start a trial in his court with this hanging."

"Why did you tell me all this?" he asked, halfway to the door.

"To give you the opportunity to go to Judge Paltz yourself, to admit you were taken in, that you had no idea at the time that Doneally was Dodgson's attorney." He stiffened when she said the name, and she let out a breath softly and finished. "To tell him that you've had time to think about what happened, and realize now that you were too trusting."

"You're out to get me, aren't you? Why? Just a little game you play?"

She shook her head and got to her feet. "If I have to go to him, he'll question you. You will either lie or you will admit the truth; in either case you'll be ruined. If you go, you can save yourself." She regarded him levelly; his look had turned bitter. "I'll call him next Monday if I haven't heard from him by then. Good-bye, Mr. Spassero."

"Barbara," Bailey said later that day, "I can tell you a little about the truck in the pictures, but probably not enough." He looked at Frank questioningly; from his desk, Frank waved him toward the bookshelves. Bailey wandered to the section of shelves with the volumes from T through V, and opened the little bar by pushing against *Tyrants*. Frank had loved it when he had that addition made to his office. Now Bailey stood considering his options.

Bourbon, Barbara knew. It was always bourbon if he had a choice; if there was no choice, he took whatever was there. "Just tell me," she said with a touch of impatience.

"Sure, sure." He poured his drink first, closed the bar, and slouched into a chair. "Either Gallead or the guy who works for him, Terry Bossert, leaves after dark now and then in the truck, a Chevy van with no windows in the back, no markings. A couple of days later, before it gets light, the truck comes back. And then leaves again four or five days later for another two-day trip. It repeats just about every six to eight weeks. And that's it. It heads south, maybe. We know that one time, at least, it either loaded or unloaded five guys in work clothes."

"Unloaded," she snapped. The enhanced pictures showed five men heading toward the open gate, where another man was standing, evidently the one who had opened the gate. No features, no identifying marks, no way could it be told who they were, but they were five in number, and they were going in.

"You've been watching for more than three weeks now," she said, thinking. "If they're keeping to any kind of schedule, in two or three weeks the truck will take off again. Are you sure Gallead isn't on to your men out there?" Bailey shrugged. Who could be sure? She went on. "I don't want him to change his routine. We need to talk to one of the men, Bailey. Are they regulars or new people each time? Do they have papers? Are they electronics people, drug packagers, pornographers? What? I need one of them."

He shrugged again. "We'll do what we can. No guar-'antees about when it leaves again."

Frank made a growly sound. "I think it's time to call in proper help. The state special investigation team, or the D.A.'s special investigators, or even the Feds. We've got enough to interest them."

They had been through this before. Barbara hardly even glanced at him. "No, not yet." She knew a lid could be clamped down hard, that nothing to do with Dodgson or Gallead would be permitted out in the open, and her own case for Paula Kennerman might well be shot out of the water.

Bailey's source for the Dodgson Publishing Company

had said they printed everything: newspapers, magazines, posters, bumper stickers, labels, postcards, letterheads. . . . Some jobs even in other languages. The company got a lot of business by fax and modem. He didn't think Dodgson wrote much of the stuff he ran. Nothing new, Barbara had thought, listening gloomily to Bailey's report; it seemed that no matter what they found out, what theories they confirmed with a witness who would testify to the truth of the theory, all she had was a series of speculations, theories strung to theories. She was afraid that even if they got one of the men who had been delivered to Gallead, what he would tell them would be nothing more than what they already knew or suspected. Still, she told herself, she had to talk to one of them.

Bailey was being extremely cautious, they all knew. If he slipped up now, the whole operation, whatever it was, might close down overnight, everything disposed of, nothing left to point to, and there would be very hard feelings about not notifying the proper authorities, very hard feelings indeed, possibly charges. Barbara shrugged away the worry. She had to talk to one of the men.

On Friday Judge Paltz had his secretary call her. While she waited for his voice over the phone, she wiped her hands on a tissue.

"Barbara, how are you?" he began genially. "It's too damn hot, isn't it? Maybe it will break soon."

She assured him that she was fine and hoped he was, and then he got down to the business of the call. "I had a little chat with Bill Spassero yesterday, Barbara. I'm afraid he's been feeling quite perturbed over what turned out to be an innocent mistake. He confessed that he was the source for that article in the Dodgson rag. Bill believed he was confiding in a valued mentor, but it seems that his confidante was instead a snake in the grass and he only recently came to understand this. He rendered his most sincere apologies, and no doubt he will be in touch with you."

"I'm glad that's been settled," she said. "It was a worry."

"Yes, yes. I know. I think that young man will go far, Barbara. It took a certain amount of courage to face up to what he had done, and he was very forthcoming about it all. He'll go far."

Barbara grinned.

Ten days to blast-off, she thought a few nights later, staring at the aerial map of the Canby Ranch, the Dodgson property, the surrounding woods....

Time became a curious ally and enemy all at once. They had to prepare Paula for the trial; she was going to hear the most gruesome forensic details about how her child had died in a savage, inhuman attack, how severely she had been burned, the condition of her flesh, her skin, her hair.... She could not face all that without preparation; no one could. If she took the stand, another question not yet settled, she would face a grueling examination by the prosecutor; she had to be prepared for that. Few people were ever subjected to the kind of questioning that the witness chair permitted for hours at a time, days at a time.

Lucille Reiner shopped for her sister. Nothing fancy, Barbara warned her. Simple lines, no frills, washable clothes would be fine in this weather, hose, low shoes. Just keep it simple, not black, no mourning now, but not wild prints either, and long sleeves, she had added. Lucille had nodded, awed by the amount of money Barbara gave her for the purchases: three outfits, one pair of shoes, panty hose, underwear, a light-weight jacket in case the weather changed.

There was so much to do: review all the reports, listen again to all the tapes, watch one more time the video Janey had provided, reread the Dodgson papers, which had been returned temporarily to Bessie's office to his great relief. . . . It all had to be done in real time, without shortcuts. The days were too short, and, strangely, tomorrow with its new reports, new bits of information, new insights, tomorrow seemed unreachable, until all at once it had been there and was yesterday.

On Friday before Labor Day she realized how scant her own wardrobe was for this season. She hurriedly shopped for herself—two skirts, two blouses, one dress—and then she picked out a beige silk and ramie jacket that would go with everything she owned, but that wasn't why she bought it. She wanted it because the fabric was beautiful, the garment was well tailored, well designed, and most of all or maybe even the only reason was because she loved it. She grinned at herself in the mirror modeling the jacket, and knew this was not the sort of rationale that her father would understand, and it was not exactly the best way to hold down expenses, which she had agreed to do. But she loved the jacket.

Then, because time was behaving so mysteriously, she had the impression that she no sooner took off the jacket to have it wrapped, to pay for it, than she was putting it on again, on Tuesday morning. Countdown had come to an end.

TWELVE

Jury selection was completed by the lunch recess on Friday; Barbara had held out for equality, half male, half female, and that was how it ended up. She had had no illusions about finding totally neutral jurors—the public had already found Paula guilty—but she had dismissed several people whose eyes appeared too glittery, and one man for no reason that she could have stated. She had not liked him. Reason enough. This week there had been few spectators; jury selection was a boring business for voyeurs. But they would come, she knew.

Her three student researchers were there taking notes; she suspected that Brian O'Connor had assigned them this case to follow to the end. And Lucille was there, today accompanied by a thickset man who looked uncomfortable. She brought him to be introduced during the lunch recess—her husband, Dave Reiner. Would it look bad, he asked hesitantly, if he didn't come every day? It was hard to miss work. Barbara assured him that it was understandable, that no one would think anything of it.

Inwardly she was seething. He believed Paula was guilty, she realized; she would have rejected him for jury duty. And she certainly did not want her jurors to read his face, read the forced smile he directed at Paula. She hoped he stayed away altogether.

After lunch on Friday Gerald Fierst rose to address the jury. He was in his mid-fifties, gray-haired, and wore a gray suit and a bright blue tie. He was a quiet man without mannerisms, without fidgets or tics, just a cautious, methodical, almost plodding prosecutor who, if he had a sense of humor, left it at home when he went to work every day. He would have crossed all the *t*'s, dotted all the *i*'s, Barbara thought appraisingly.

The evidence would prove, he said, that Paula Kennerman struck and killed her child and then set an arson fire in an attempt to hide her crime. His remarks included only one item that Barbara had not anticipated: "Paula Kennerman spilled gasoline through the lower half of the house, lighted a fire in the kitchen, and then replaced the empty gas can in the barn in an attempt to hide her crime. When she returned to the house and tried to enter, a propane tank exploded and she was thrown to the ground outside the front door. . . ."

Barbara nodded to herself, a man who dotted the *i*'s. No gas can had been found near the house, something no report had mentioned.

When it was her turn, Barbara stood before the defense table, so that in looking at her, the jurors also saw Paula, who was deathly white. Speaking quietly, she stressed the fact that the burden of proof was on the state.

Defense would prove that Paula Kennerman had been above reproach as a parent, that her only goal in life had been to secure a decent future for her child, and that she had absolutely no motive for the murder of Lori Kennerman.

"Defense does not have to point the finger at another person. You will hear testimony that contradicts other testimony, and it is your duty to consider the motives of all those who appear on the witness stand in this procedure. Defense does not have to prove Paula Kennerman's innocence; it must only raise the specter of doubt that the state has proven its case."

When she sat down again and looked at the bench, Judge Paltz was regarding her with a remote, unreadable expression. Gone was the grandfatherly attitude, the kindly, reminiscing, old family friend; he had turned into the jurist her father had warned her about: strict, scholarly, and unflappable. He looked like a stranger.

He thanked her courteously, thanked Gerald Fierst, and instructed the jury regarding its duty in the coming days, and then called for a recess until Monday morning at nine.

Over the weekend Barbara stewed about the missing piece she knew was somewhere in the mass of information they had gathered. She reviewed reports and listened once more to the tape made by Christina Lorenza, the woman in Silicon Valley, whose education had been financed by Craig Dodgson. "So I said, hey, it's yours, too, you know. And he said, yeah, sure. I'll take care of it. Honest, I will. . . . I thought he'd want me to have an abortion, but I guess even back then he was dead set against it. Anyway, he wrote out what all he'd do and signed it. But I was too sick to care very much, you know. I guess my stomach was queasy, morning sickness that went on and on. We were going up to some islands out of Seattle, and I just kept getting sick. So he gave me some Dramamine, and that helped a little but not much. Two days later I said I had to go home, I was

too sick for anything, and he gave me some more
Dramamine, stronger this time, and we headed back. . . .
I was scared, and he was, too. Then I knew I was having a miscarriage. . . . He was really sweet to me, really
caring. Brought me tea and was anxious, you know, caring, and we made it back to Spring Bay. By then I was
feeling better, and we stood at the rail and tore up the
paper he had written and signed, and we even laughed
a little. That's when he said he'd like to do something
for me, you know, send me to school or something. And
that seemed okay to me, so we agreed that he'd pay for
two years of computer school, and he did." There was
a silence; Winnie asking a question? Then Christina's
voice was back: "Look, I was twenty-one and he was
twenty-four, but we were like two scared little kids. . . ."

Winnie had believed her, and Barbara had to admit
that she did, too. Dead end. A sweet Craig Dodgson
was the last thing she intended to introduce at this trial.

The weather continued hot and dry; grass was dying,
leaves turning brittle on the trees; a forest fire started in
the Willamette National Forest and smoke from it
drifted across the valley, making the light a peculiar
dirty yellow. Bailey had nothing to report about a truck
leaving Royce Gallead's firing range.

Sunday afternoon she had a conference with Paula
and warned her again about the bad days to come. "Are
you sure you don't want to use a mild tranquilizer? It
would help."

"Dr. Grayling said he'd give me something if I
needed it. I don't want anything. You know, I feel sort
of like I have to be there, really be there, for everything.
I told Janey that and she understood."

Barbara nodded; she understood too, all too well.

* * *

Every morning Barbara had driven to Frank's house and
they had walked the half mile to the courthouse. On
Monday morning when Frank came out to meet her, she
said, "I have stuff to carry." He looked with interest at
the Kmart plastic bag she held, along with her bulging
briefcase and purse. He took the bag, hefted it, then
shrugged, and they began.

Even his shady neighborhood was muggy that morning; it would be a hot walk home. They passed Yuppie
Heaven, deserted at this hour, passed the first two-tiered
parking structure where automobiles were lined up to
enter, stopping traffic. Ahead, across Seventh, a fire
truck was diverting traffic as it backed into the munic-
ipal building fire department. That building and the
courthouse across the street from it were like a matched
pair, four stories high, stable looking with old well-
weathered concrete and many windows. But the fire department really shouldn't hold maneuvers at this hour,
Barbara was thinking, when Frank caught her arm in a
hard grip, drawing her to a stop. They were even with
the middle of the county parking lot where another line
of cars had come to a halt awaiting entrance.

Framed between two cars, visible through an opening
in the stopped traffic, was the courthouse entrance
where twenty-five or thirty people were milling about,
shouting, some with signs: DEATH SENTENCE FOR BABY
KILLERS! LET BABY KILLER KENNERMAN HANG! One man
had a heavy rope tied into a noose that he carried sus-
pended from a pole. Television crews were there in
force; police had put up a barricade and were trying to
keep the demonstrations behind it. The traffic light

changed, the cars began to move again, and the scene was obliterated.

"My God," Barbara whispered.

"Hold it," Frank snapped, still clutching her arm in a hard grasp. "They've got garbage to throw. Come on." He pulled her behind a car waiting to enter the parking lot. They stayed behind cars to the entrance of the tunnel under Seventh that led to the courthouse. The tunnel was crowded as usual at this hour.

As soon as they emerged within the building, a bailiff met them. "Judge Paltz wants you," he said to Barbara.

And she wanted him.

Gerald Fierst was already there when she was admitted to Judge Paltz's chambers. Both men were grim-faced. Judge Paltz looked her over quickly and motioned to a chair, and then seated himself behind his desk.

"This won't do," he said.

"I request that the jurors be sequestered," Barbara said. "Those people have tomatoes, who knows what all."

"I know that," the judge said. He turned to Gerald Fierst. "How long is this trial going to take?"

"I'll wrap up my end in three days," Fierst said. "If there's no hindrance from the defense."

"I don't know how long it will take," Barbara said. "But if it takes a month, the jury has to be protected from a mob like that. There can't be a fair trial with that kind of demonstration outside the door. It's a vigilante mob out there. And we all know some of them will be inside the court today. Ask them if they intend to delay anything." She drew in a deep breath. "If the jury is prejudiced or frightened by a mob like that, it's an automatic mistrial."

"Don't tell me my business," Judge Paltz said softly. "We have a situation on our hands, and we have to deal with it. Once the jury is inside and accounted for, they will be protected. And there will not be any demonstrations in my court. The principals in this case will all be escorted to the courthouse door for the duration of this trial. You will be picked up by an unmarked police car and brought here, and taken back at the close of the day. No attorney in my court is going to appear with tomato or eggs on their clothing. A room will be set aside for lunches to be brought in, or you may choose to bring your own food, or eat in the cafeteria. There will be no disruption of these proceedings. I advise both of you to expedite this trial. Before today's opening I shall speak to the jury and explain the situation to them. Is that satisfactory?"

After he dismissed them both, Barbara found Frank waiting outside the door. She told him what arrangements Judge Paltz was making.

"How did he sound?" Frank asked.

"He never raised his voice."

"Yep. Mad as hell. Don't blame him, either. Well, that's life."

The courtroom was packed to capacity that day. The three students were there, but for the most part the audience was middle-aged or older, and they were for the most part well dressed and silent. To Barbara's eye they looked like vultures waiting for the first blood.

"Did you see all those people?" Paula whispered when she was led in to take her place by Barbara.

"Don't worry about them. The judge is handling things."

Paula nodded, but she looked very frightened.

If the panel of jurors had been upset by the demonstration, whatever the judge told them seemed to have had a calming effect; they were impassive and attentive when Gerald Fierst called his first witness.

Willis Jacobson testified that he was with the volunteer fire team that got to the fire six or seven minutes after the call came in. "It had been burning maybe ten minutes by then; the whole building was burning, up and down. The defendant was crying that her baby was upstairs somewhere, and I was suited up, so I went in with a hose to look for her. But it was too smoky by then to see anything and I had to back out again. We had the pumper on the house, and had the fire out within ten minutes, and we looked again for the child, and found her body on the first floor, in the living room."

"Exactly what did Mrs. Kennerman say when you got there?"

"Well, she was sort of out of her head, crying and screaming, and fighting to get back in. Two women were holding her back. She was bloody and burned some herself. She said, 'My baby's upstairs somewhere. For God's sake, she might be under a bed or in a closet hiding.'"

Barbara had no questions.

The next witness was the state fire marshal. Gerald Fierst had him describe his background, his position, his years of experience, and then asked, "Mr. Conkling, what time did you arrive at the Canby house?"

"Twelve-thirty."

"I see. And who called you?"

"The chief of the volunteer fire department, Walter Dixon."

"And why did he call you?"

"When there's a suspicious fire, it's routine to bring in an investigator. Chief Dixon suspected arson fire and called me."

"All right. Tell us, please, exactly what you did at the scene."

"Yes, sir." He was a solid man, forty-three years old, six feet tall, and very broad, slow speaking, deliberative. He took his time describing his investigation. Gasoline had been present in the kitchen, in the hallway, and in the living room. The kitchen door had been closed, and when the tank of propane exploded, it blew the door open and blew out the front screen door, and the fire spread to the living room and on up the stairs."

"How do you know it was gasoline and not kerosene, or even motor oil?"

Conkling went into a very technical explanation of the different ways combustibles burned, the different ash left, the different smoke. He explained the flash effect of the blast against the door; the same effect had been through the hall and on the frame of the screen door, and to a lesser extent on the front wall of the living room.

"So you can tell exactly what burned, and where it started, even after the firemen have soaked the house?"

"Yes, sir. We can tell."

"What did you determine about the living room where the child's body was found?"

"Someone had thrown gasoline on some of the furniture, but mostly on the floor and on the rugs. And the girl's body had been covered with gasoline. There was gas under her and over her."

Paula made a low sound, but did not move, and Barbara did not turn to look at her. She listened intently to the marshal as he continued to describe what he had found.

"It was as if the person had stood in the room and splashed out gas in several directions, making a ray pattern."

"How do you know the child's body was soaked in gasoline?" Gerald Fierst asked in a low voice. He sounded as if he hated this as much as anyone in the room.

"I examined her body and her clothing."

"Can you just tell us the conclusions you drew from your examination?"

"Yes, sir. The fire flashed over her, consuming all the gasoline, and it ignited her clothes and her hair. . . ." He kept his gaze fixed on Gerald Fierst. His voice was without expression.

Someone in the seats behind Barbara began to sob in a loud voice, and there were mutters, and one voice calling out in a harsh whisper, "Oh, God! Oh, God!" Barbara did not turn to look. She did, however, glance at Paula, who was like a carving, except that her eyes were closed and tears were coursing down her face. Barbara stood up. "Your Honor, may we have a recess?"

He already had his gavel raised, and brought it down hard as she spoke. "Ten minute recess," he said. "The bailiff will clear the courtroom." He stalked out.

When they resumed, Judge Paltz said icily in a very soft voice, "If there is any further demonstration of any kind in this courtroom, the persons responsible will be charged with contempt of court and will be denied reentry. Mr. Fierst, please."

Gerald Fierst surprised Barbara then by changing the direction of his questions. "Mr. Conkling, as part of your investigation did you try to find the source of the gasoline?"

"Yes, sir. We found three gas cans in the barn. One five-gallon can and two one-gallon cans. The five-gallon can was half filled, the others were empty."

"No further questions," Fierst said. "Thank you, Mr. Conkling."

Barbara rose and walked to the front of her table. "Mr. Conkling, can you estimate how much gas was spilled in the house that day?"

"At least a gallon," he said without hesitation.

"Could it have been more?"

"It might have been more, but no less than a gallon."

"Mr. Conkling, I have here a floor plan for the Canby house." The drawing was admitted. She handed it to Conkling. "Is this correct as far as you can tell?"

"Yes, ma'am. That's the house plan."

"What I'd like you to do, Mr. Conkling, is try to show us where the gas actually was, starting with the kitchen. Can you do that?"

"Yes, ma'am."

She handed him a red felt-tip pen. "If you would just indicate where the gas was spilled, please. And describe to the jury where you are marking the floor plan."

He began to draw jagged red marks in the kitchen, explaining as he went. He looked up at her. "There wasn't any gas on the kitchen door. Out in the hall, it was sort of splashed back and forth, not quite to the walls. Then in the living room."

When he finished, she took the house plan and studied it a moment. "There wasn't any gas on the stairs?"

"No, ma'am."

"You show that it stopped several feet away from the living room door, and there isn't any shown for several feet into the room. Is that correct?"

"Yes, ma'am."

"These other two doors in the hallway, one to a bedroom, and the other to an office, were they splattered at all?"

"No, they weren't."

"Mr. Conkling, as part of your investigations into arson fires, do you sometimes reconstruct the actions of the arsonist?"

"Frequently we do that."

"And could you do it for us with this fire?" She walked to the jury and held the house plan drawing up so they could see it and follow what he was saying.

"Yes, pretty much. Someone went to the kitchen and splashed the gas around and tossed a match in, and then closed the door and went through the hall splashing it around for about fifteen feet. Then the arsonist went into the living room and stood about where I put a circle, and threw the gas around the room and on the child's body, and then went out."

"You're assuming the child's body was on the floor already?"

"Well, the gas was all over her."

"But you said earlier that it was under her as well. Didn't you?"

"Yes. It was."

"So it had to be on the floor already when she was struck and then covered with gas. Is that right?"

"Objection," Fierst called out. "This is getting out of the range of expert opinion into pure speculation."

"The witness has been testifying as an expert from the start; this is what he does for a living, reconstruct what happened," Barbara said quickly.

"Overruled," Judge Paltz said. "You may answer."

"This is a difficult question," Conkling said. "Some gas could have flowed under the body, or she might have fallen where gas already was in place, or she might have rolled into it, or been placed on it. Without observing her body in place, I couldn't say which one is correct."

Barbara nodded. "All right. Would you expect anyone throwing around that much gas to get some on his or her clothing?"

"Very likely."

Barbara nodded and went to the defense table, where she had placed the large plastic bag. She took out a gas can. "Mr. Conkling, is this like the cans you found in the barn?"

She handed it to him, but he was already nodding. "Yes, it is," he said.

She took the can back and walked with it to the jury box to show them. The can was red, with a short spout and cap and a top handle. She returned to the witness stand with it. "Mr. Conkling, would you mind demonstrating how you believe the arsonist threw the gas around?"

"Objection," Fierst said. "This witness can't know the movements of the arsonist. This is pure speculation."

Judge Paltz was eyeing the gas can with a slight frown. He waved toward Fierst and said, "I think I would like to see such a demonstration. If you will, Mr. Conkling?"

Conkling stood up, went to the front of the bench, and took the can from Barbara. He regarded it for a moment.

"We'll pretend the kitchen door is here," Barbara said, drawing an imaginary line. "The door is closed now."

"Well," Conkling said, grasping the can in both hands, "I think you'd want to walk backwards, so you wouldn't walk through the gas." He walked backward a few steps, tilting the can with one hand, guiding it with the other in a sweeping motion.

"And now the living room," Barbara said. "Let's pretend this is where you drew your circle, where you think the arsonist stood."

He paused in thought again and then looked at her. "I think you'd want the cap off," he said. "You couldn't throw it out very well through the spout." She nodded, and he removed the cap and, using both hands, pantomimed throwing gasoline. When he was done, he replaced the cap.

"Thank you, Mr. Conkling. When you examined the gas cans in the barn, were the caps on them all?"

"Yes they were." He looked hesitantly at the witness chair and she nodded. He reseated himself.

"Did you examine the clothing worn by Paula Kennerman that day?"

"Yes, ma'am, I did."

"Did you find any traces of gas?"

"No."

"Did you also examine Paula Kennerman?"

"Yes."

"Please tell us what you found."

"She had flash burns down one side of her face and

her body, a first-degree burn where her skin was exposed."

"One side of her face and body? Which side?"

"Down the left side. Her hair was slightly charred on the left side, also."

"Thank you, Mr. Conkling. No further questions."

Fierst asked from his table. "Mr. Conkling, when you said that likely the person would get gas on her clothing—"

"Objection," Barbara snapped. "Pronouns, Mr. Fierst."

"Let me rephrase the question," Fierst said with a glance at Judge Paltz. "If a person were being very careful, then would it be likely that he or she could avoid splashing gas on himself or herself?" From someone else the question would have hung heavy with irony, but from Fierst it simply showed caution.

"It probably could be avoided."

The prosecution's next witness was the medical examiner who had performed the autopsy on the body of Lori Kennerman. Dr. Voorhees was sixty-four, thin-faced, with a raspy, high-pitched voice. He started by describing the condition of the body. When he went into detail about the extent of the burns, Barbara gripped Paula's arm. It felt like steel. In his irritating voice Voorhees continued to give a detailed report on what he had done, what his conclusions were.

"What exactly was the cause of death?" Fierst asked.

"A blow to the neck, just below the anterior region of the right ear, with an instrument sharp enough to puncture the skin and sever the carotid, and to cause a break between the third and fourth vertebrae."

"A broken neck, is that the common term?"

"Well, I suppose it is."

"Was the wound caused by a knife?"

"No, nothing that sharp. It broke through the skin, but didn't cut it as a knife would do."

"Something like the edge of a square-cut fireplace poker?"

"That could have done it, or anything with a straight edge wielded hard enough."

Barbara glanced again at Paula, who had her eyes closed and her fists clenched tight enough that blood was showing on her hands. Fierst finished his questions, and Barbara stood up.

She picked up the gas can once more and approached the witness chair. "Dr. Voorhees, could something like this have caused such a wound?" She indicated the bottom of the can. He peered at it.

"Yes, that straight edge might have done it, too."

"Dr. Voorhees, would such a wound as you describe cause copious bleeding?"

"Oh my, yes. She was very nearly exsanguinated."

"And would there have been a spurt of blood from such a throat wound?"

"I should think so."

"Would you expect a person standing close enough to cause such a wound to have that blood on his or her clothing?"

"It's difficult to say for certain, but I think so."

"Would death have been very fast from such injuries?"

"Instantaneous unconsciousness and death immediately following would result from such injuries," he said.

"As part of your examination, did you look for indications of previous accidents or injuries, signs of abuse in the past?"

"Yes. There were none."

Barbara thanked him and turned back to the defense table. Paula had her head buried in her arms.

Fierst stood up for his redirect. "Dr. Voorhees, would a long weapon afford enough distance to avoid being splashed with blood?"

"If it's long enough, or if the killer was in motion, I guess he could avoid it. But blood would have spurted."

Fierst had no further questions and the doctor was excused.

"In view of the hour, we will be in recess until two," Judge Paltz said then.

Everyone except Paula rose as he left the bench. She tried, but sank back down into her chair. As soon as the judge was gone, a murmurous group voice rippled over the courtroom. Paula looked up at Barbara; her face was ashen.

"How could you do that?" she whispered. "How could you talk about her as if she weren't even real?"

"I'm sorry," Barbara said. "Paula, you've come through this much. Don't break now. It won't get any worse than today."

THIRTEEN

TODAY EMMA TIDBALL was dressed in a dark blue polyester suit with a white blouse and a strand of large pearls. Her face was as wrinkled as Barbara remembered.

Gerald Fierst asked her to describe the Canby Ranch, what it was used for, and her position there, and she did so in a rambling way that took a long time.

Fierst finally stopped the flow and asked, "Will you just tell us what you remember about the morning of Saturday, April nineteenth?"

"Angela—that's Angela Everts—she called at about nine-thirty and said the mushrooms were up thick and did we all want to go get some, and I said sure, it would be good for everyone to get out in the woods for a time. You know, we had all that rain, and finally the sun was out and it was nice and warm. But Paula didn't want to go out, and Lori wasn't feeling good. Poor little thing, she said her stomach hurt, but I told Paula it would be good for them to go out for some air, and that Lori wouldn't be so afraid as soon as she saw that her mother wasn't so afraid, so Paula said they'd go. At the last minute Lori said she had to go to the bathroom, and Angela said why didn't I go on ahead with everyone else since I knew as well as her where the mushrooms were, and she'd wait, her and Annie, that's Angela's girl. And Fern, one of the other little girls, said she wanted to wait for Annie, and that seemed all right, so that's what we did."

"Where were you when the fire started?"

"Off nearly to the other logging road, half a mile maybe."

"Did you hear the explosion?"

"We heard something, but we didn't know what it was. And then Angela was screaming, closer by, that it was a fire, and we all hurried back."

"Then what happened?"

"Well, Angela got there first, and when I came up she was holding Paula back from going in the house. And she yelled for me to hold her and she would call the fire department, and she got in her car and raced off, and me and one of the others held Paula."

"It took two of you to hold her?"

"Yes, it did. She was fighting to go back in, screaming, crying, pulling. Out of her head."

"Mrs. Tidball, you said there were four women and their children at the ranch, and then Angela Everts and her child came. Did you see anyone else at the ranch that morning?"

"No, I didn't."

"You said that Mrs. Kennerman was irrational when you arrived at the scene of the fire. Was she irrational before that? In the morning before you left the house?"

"I said she was out of her mind. Which she was. Screaming and yelling."

"Earlier that morning how did she appear?"

"Like before, scared out of her wits, and hurting."

"But not out of her mind?" He didn't smile, but Emma Tidball stiffened as if she heard a smile behind the words.

"She was quiet, but as sane as you or me."

"Thank you," Fierst said.

Barbara stood up and approached the witness stand. "Had you been working at the ranch from the time it opened for women?"

"Yes, from the very first day."

"And was there any resistance from neighbors about opening the ranch for troubled women?"

"Objection," Fierst said. "Irrelevant."

"No, it isn't," Barbara said. "There could be a number of people who might have wanted the ranch put out of business one way or another."

Judge Paltz nodded. "Overruled."

Emma described the times that Dodgson had objected, and how Mrs. Canby had handled them all. "Except I never told her that him and Craig came over that time yelling about abortions."

"So he seemed to know who was there and what was going on much of the time?"

"He knew everything going on there, and he didn't like any of it," Emma said, her wrinkles deepening in a scowl.

"Did anyone else cause you any trouble?"

"No. Only them, the Dodgsons."

"Mrs. Tidball, did you give Paula Kennerman a tour of the property on Friday?"

"No. I offered to, but she didn't want to go outside. They stayed in their room most of the day."

"You observed Paula and Lori together Thursday

night, on Friday, and Saturday morning. Could you describe how they acted with each other?"

Mrs. Tidball did at length; a frightened child clinging to her mother, and a mother who never took her eyes off the child, who paled at a touch, but held her. One of the women in the jury was wiping her eyes when Mrs. Tidball finished and sat back in her chair.

"When she was fighting so hard when you held her, Mrs. Tidball, what was she screaming?"

"Let me go. She's in there. Let me go. I have to find her. Things like that. Like she thought if she could get back in the house, she could save her baby."

"That Saturday morning, were you inside all the time until you left to gather mushrooms?"

"Yes, every minute."

"And when you left the house, did you go straight across the property to the woods?"

"Well, yes. We wanted to get at the mushrooms."

"Did you happen to glance back at the house at all?"

"No. We went straight to the woods and the trail."

"Thank you, Mrs. Tidball," Barbara said.

"This is hellish," Barbara grumbled at lunch with Frank. They were in a small room that held a desk and two straight chairs, and now had a table set up with a tablecloth. Someone from the office had brought in sandwiches, a thermos of coffee, and a basket of fruit. Barbara regarded the food with distaste and crossed the room to pull open a blind. The room overlooked the skyway across Pearl Street and the state and federal buildings on the other side. The sun was shining. People were in summery clothes. She saw two people coming toward the courthouse and she let the blind close. *Them.* She felt as if she were in jail.

"What's happening out on the street?" she asked.

"They're picketing," Frank said amiably. He unwrapped a sandwich. "Ah, good. Liverwurst and onions. Too bad you can't eat onions."

"That's disgusting."

She sat opposite him, glowering. What she needed to do was walk, not eat. She always walked during the lunch recess. She picked up the other sandwich—roast beef—and took a bite.

"It's going about like I expected," Frank said after a moment. "Not bad so far."

She put down the sandwich and went back to the window. *They* were walking away from her. She hoped their legs fell off at the hips. "At least no one's fighting," she said, returning to the table, where she poured coffee.

"Not yet. Wait until you go haring off after the Dodgson crew."

She put down her cup and went to the door. "I'll be back in a few minutes."

It did not surprise her that Frank did not object. He knew she needed to walk as well as she did. He always had walked during the lunch recess. He nodded and rewrapped her sandwich, and recapped the thermos.

Compared to Emma Tidball, Angela Everts was taciturn. She identified herself, described her employment at the Canby house, and added not a word beyond what was required. Gerald Fierst had her tell about the morning she had gone there to pick mushrooms, and the following events, and was finished with her very quickly.

When Barbara stood up for her turn, she produced her aerial map and had it introduced as an exhibit. It was very clear, two feet by three, and showed the Canby property, the Dodgson acres, and across the road from them the orchard and Gallead's firing range. Enough of the forest behind the properties was on the map to make that part complete. Farleigh Road made a definitive boundary, with Carrie Voight's house across the road at the bottom of the map. She stood an easel where the jury and Judge Paltz could see it and placed the map on it.

Pointing with a pen, she asked, "Is this the private road to the Canby house?" Angela said it was. "And where did you meet Mrs. Dodgson on the road?" She traced the road until Angela said that was it, right about there. Barbara drew a red circle midway between the Dodgson gate and the road entrance.

"You were previously acquainted with Mrs. Dodgson?"

"I used to work for her."

"Was she facing you when you saw her?"

"She was walking in my direction."

"You told us earlier that you offered to bring her some chanterelles. What else did you talk about?"

"She asked me if the new girl, the sick girl, was well enough to go out in the woods."

"She knew there was a new woman at the ranch already?"

"She knew, and she knew there was another child there, too."

"Was she pleasant to you and Annie that morning?"

Angela's lips tightened a fraction. "She didn't see

Annie. Annie was looking for something on the floor in the backseat. She was pleasant enough to me."

"Did you happen to notice what time it was when you stopped to talk to Mrs. Dodgson?"

"Ten-thirty. I told Emma I'd be there at ten-thirty and I would have been if I didn't stop first."

"All right. They were waiting for you at the Canby house. Did you leave right away?"

"No. It was about ten minutes after I got there that I told Emma to go ahead and we'd catch up. We waited a few minutes and then Paula and me started. She stopped at the woods and leaned against a tree. I went on ahead of her. But I got uneasy about leaving her and the three little girls, and I went back just about when Annie came running out and said something to Paula and Fern called her, and she went tearing off to see what Fern was up to."

"Mrs. Everts, could you point to where Paula Kennerman stopped? Where you were when Annie came out again?"

She looked hesitant and moistened her lips. "I just don't know for sure."

"Try. For instance, this is the house. You have reached the woods with Paula Kennerman. Where?"

With great reluctance Angela left the witness stand to approach the map on the easel. "We come out this way," she mumbled after studying the map for a second or two. "Fern, she went off up this way, to the apple tree. And I went this way, along the edge of the woods, sort of waiting for the girls to come along."

"Then you saw Annie running toward Paula Kennerman. Where were you when you saw her?"

"I don't know."

"How far away do you suppose you were? As far as from here to the back of the courtroom?"

"More. Oh, I know. Just about even with the end of the garden. That's right." She put her finger on the map.

Barbara drew a small red circle.

"From that spot you couldn't see the house or the driveway, could you? Wasn't there too much shrubbery?"

"Yes, there was. I saw Annie after she got past the bushes."

"And looking that way, you would have seen the barn but not the woods beyond it. Is that right?"

"Yes."

"Thank you, Mrs. Everts. You may sit down again." She waited until Angela was back on the witness stand. "So you were here, and Annie ran out. Did you go to her right away?"

"I waited a little, not much. Then I started to walk to them."

"Where were you when Annie reached Paula?"

"I don't know," she said, almost in anguish. "Annie was running. She runs like a deer. And Fern yelled at her, and she ran off that way by the time I got to Paula."

"Did you hear what Annie told Paula?"

"I thought I did," she mumbled, "but I just don't know."

"Were you as far from them as from here to the back of the courtroom?"

"No. Maybe almost that far. I don't know."

"Was Annie facing you?"

"No. She was looking at Paula and then at the apple tree. Fern was yelling to her."

"I see. So she came out and said something, and at the same time the other little girl was calling her. Was Annie yelling?"

"No. Fern was yelling. And Mr. Dodgson was revving up his mowing machine something awful. He was stuck in the marsh."

"So it would have been very difficult for you to hear what Annie told Paula?"

"It would have been hard."

"When you reached Paula Kennerman, where was Annie?"

"At the apple tree with Fern."

Barbara put her finger there on the map. "And what did Paula say?"

"She said Lori was sleeping, but she didn't want her to wake up alone in a strange house and maybe she should go back, and after a minute she started to go back."

"And where did you go?"

"Over to the girls at the tree. And Annie said Lori fell asleep watching television and she didn't want to stay in the house with her. I told them since Lori's mother would be with her they could come with me if they wanted to, but they didn't, and I started through the woods."

"Did you look back at Paula or the house after that?"

"No, I just went into the woods and headed down toward Emma and the others." She paused, then added without prompting, "And in just a second Annie yelled that they were coming, too, so I slowed down and waited for them, and we all went on together."

Barbara nodded at her reassuringly. "When you

reached the house after the explosion, what exactly was Paula doing?"

"Well, she was on the ground, sort of on her hands and knees, dragging herself, sort of. I helped her get up and she tried to pull away and go to the house, but it was blazing everywhere and I held her."

"Was she fighting you?"

"No. She was sort of dazed and real wobbly. She couldn't hardly stand up alone, but she kept pulling."

"Now, when you drove to the Dodgson house to call the fire department, who let you in?"

"Mrs. Dodgson."

"You went to the front door?"

"Oh, yes. It was closer, going in the front, so I never gave it a thought, but she looked real surprised and not very happy about it."

"Did you see anyone else?"

"Reggie Melrose came out to see what was happening."

"She's the housekeeper?"

"She used to be."

"Anyone else?"

"Craig Dodgson was in the swimming pool."

Angela described going into the family room to use the phone. "Mrs. Dodgson went to the pool and yelled at Craig to get out and tossed his robe down and turned off the music. Then she came back and closed the door while I was talking to the fire department. She went to the door with me, and I left and went back to the house."

"You say she threw down his robe. Where did she get it?"

"She was carrying it when I got there, I guess. She had it when she opened the door."

"You can see into the pool room from the family room?"

"Yes. There's a door, and a hall, and the door to the pool room right opposite. Both doors were open. That's why the music was so blaring."

"So she went into the pool room and then what? Did you watch her?"

"Not really. It's just that the telephone's on a table so that you look at a wall or that way. I saw her."

"She threw down his robe and yelled at him to come out?"

"No. She went to one of the tables and chairs and turned off the music and put his robe on a chair and then yelled at him."

"Did you see Craig Dodgson?"

"Yes. When she turned off the music, his head popped up out of the water. That's when I turned my back."

Barbara thanked her and sat down.

When Fierst approached her for his redirect examination, he carried a sheaf of papers. "Mrs. Everts," he said in a quiet, almost sad voice, "when you made your preliminary statement you said that Annie ran out to Paula Kennerman and said that Lori fell asleep watching television. Was that correct?"

"That's what she told me happened."

"Let me read from the statement you made, Mrs. Everts. The question was: 'What happened then?' You answered, 'Annie come running out and said that Lori fell asleep watching television, so she didn't want to stay in with her. Then her and Fern decided not to look for mushrooms but to keep on making garlands with the apple blossoms, and I went on to catch up with Emma and the others. Paula Kennerman went back to the house.' " He looked at her for a moment and then asked, "Do you remember making that statement?"

"Yes, I remember that day."

"And you read it and signed it because you thought it was correct?"

"I signed it. I don't remember now just when Annie said that."

"Mrs. Everts, wouldn't you say your memory of what happened was clearer that soon after the events than it is now, nearly six months later?"

"Objection," Barbara snapped.

She was overruled, as she had known she would be.

"Mrs. Everts, do you remember the question?" Fierst asked.

"I remember it. I just don't know." Her voice had become fainter again, more muffled, and she had paled.

He read another bit of her statement and asked her if she remembered that part; she said yes. He read another question and answer and asked her again, and again she said yes. Patiently, he kept at it until he had covered most of what she had said in her preliminary statement.

"Mrs. Everts, why is it that you recall so well everything in your statement except this one incident? Can you explain that?"

"Your Honor, I object. Mr. Fierst knows very well that no one can explain the capriciousness of memory."

"Sustained," Judge Paltz said quietly. "Mr. Fierst, perhaps you can get on to something else?"

Fierst bowed slightly. And suddenly Barbara wondered if he saw himself as Job, much put-upon, forced to endure the obstinacy of defense counsel and his own witness.

"No further questions," he said. The look he gave Angela was long and very sad. He shook his head slightly and sat down.

After Angela left the stand, Fierst asked permission to enter a statement made by Annie Everts in the presence of her mother; Sergeant Gary Durham; Ms. Rogene Lancaster, an assistant to the district attorney; and Mr. William Spassero, who at that time was the defense counsel for Paula Kennerman. He read the statement in his dry, almost inflectionless voice, sounding ludicrous as he repeated the child's words.

Sgt. Durham: "And when you reached Mrs. Kennerman, then what did you do?"

Annie: "I don't know."

Sgt. Durham: "You told her something, didn't you?"

Annie: "Yeah, I guess so. Mom was coming."

Sgt. Durham: "Did you tell them where Lori was?"

Annie: "Yeah. Sleeping. We watched television and she went to sleep. She sucked her thumb."

Sgt. Durham: "And you told them that?"

Annie: "Yeah, I guess so."

Ms. Lancaster: "Did you tell Mrs. Kennerman that?"

Annie: "Yeah. I told everybody. And me and Fern made some more crowns."

Spassero was not quoted as asking anything.

Judge Paltz called for a ten-minute recess, and when he was gone, Paula whispered, "She didn't tell me that. She didn't."

"Shh," Barbara murmured. "We'll get our turn. Go take a break for a minute. Remember, we'll get our turn."

That their turn was coming was all Paula could cling to now, Barbara thought, watching her being escorted from the courtroom by a police matron. Paula knew how damning that one little point could be: Had she known Lori was downstairs sleeping in front of the television instead of upstairs in bed? Paula was so pale—jailhouse pallor—but she walked out with her back straight and her head up. Good girl, Barbara thought at her. She was seething at Spassero, who had stood mute while that inane questioning had been taking place.

"Let's get some coffee," Frank said close to her ear. "The Dodgsons have arrived in force, all three of them."

FOURTEEN

BAD TIMING, BARBARA thought, at ten minutes before four when Kay Dodgson was called by the prosecution. She walked briskly to the front of the courtroom and swore to tell the truth, and seated herself. She was dressed in a dusty-rose, raw silk suit with perfectly dyed shoes and hose to match. Her blouse was creamy white. She had a lapel pin with rubies, and earrings with rubies, and rings on several fingers. She was trim, moved like a dancer or an athlete, very attractive, with dark hair skillfully coiffed, skin a touch too swarthy for the delicate colors she wore, but beautifully made up. The jewelry was overkill, the makeup perfect. A very rich-looking lady, Barbara thought.

But it was bad timing. Whatever Kay Dodgson said would go undisputed overnight, leaving a long time for the jurors' minds to assimilate it, to embed it in concrete.

Gerald Fierst was not exactly deferential to her, but his tone was not what it had been with Emma and Angela, either. He treated this witness with a respect they had not received.

He led her through the background of purchasing the land, building a house, how long they had been there, what she and her husband did, the fact that their son, Craig, lived at home with them.

He led her to the day of the fire and asked her to tell, in her own words, what she had done that morning.

"Like most Saturday mornings," she said, "Craig was swimming laps, and that morning Rich was mowing the grass when I went out to take my walk." She filled in the rest briefly.

"Thank you," he said. "Now, for the record, did you notice what time you left the house, when you met Angela Everts?"

She shook her head. "I'm sorry," she said. "I just didn't notice. It was just so routine." She looked regretful. Then she brightened and said, "Oh, yes, it had to be after eleven when I got back to the house. Mrs. Melrose had arrived; her car was parked in the driveway."

Barbara jotted a note and handed it over her shoulder to Frank. *What did she do before Dodgson?* Actress? Model? Something that gave her a public poise that few people had, something that made her aware of timing, of gestures, that let her control her expression too artfully.

"Mrs. Melrose is your housekeeper?"

"She was. She always arrived punctually at eleven."

"Very well," Fierst said. "When you were walking, in which direction were you going when you met Angela Everts?" He finally left the table and crossed to stand in front of the jury box, so that, in facing him, she was also facing them. It was a way of saying, Now we come to the important part.

"Toward the end of the road at the pond. I was almost there."

"And you went to the end of the road?"

"Oh, yes."

"What did you do then?"

"As I said, I turned around and went the other way, to the other end where the pavement stops. And then I went back home."

"So you were facing in the direction of the Canby house and the length of the road?" He crossed to the map. "Ms. Holloway has kindly furnished us with a map of the area." There was not a trace of irony in his voice. "If you were walking this way, the entire area of the Canby property was visible to you, was it not?"

"Yes. Up to where the woods start."

"Did you see anyone other than Angela Everts that morning?"

She shook her head. "No, I did not." She smiled and added, "Except Rich, out on his mowing machine."

"It has been suggested, Mrs. Dodgson, that you and your husband objected to the use of the Canby Ranch as a refuge for women. Is that correct?"

"No," she said indignantly. "May I explain our position?"

"By all means, please explain."

"Well, when Mrs. Canby told us what she planned, we discussed it among ourselves at home and decided there was no harm in it as long as the women were quiet and well behaved. They might not have been the neighbors we would have chosen, but we made no objections then, and later when there were minor incidents, Rich went directly to Mrs. Canby to talk them over. We never printed a word against using the ranch like that. We never talked about it with anyone. We accepted the situation. We believe very strongly that one should have the right to use personal property in any way he chooses, without interference, unless he creates a public nuisance or a danger to others."

She said this in a rush that left her almost breathless, as if her indignation had overwhelmed her.

"I see," Fierst said. "Did you spy on the Canby property?"

"Of course not! We believe in the sanctity of marriage, as very few people seem to these days, and we feared that the domestic squabbles that made women run away from home might follow them to the ranch and cause trouble that could possibly spread. As it turned out, we were right."

"Objection," Barbara said. "I ask that the editorial be stricken from the record, and that the witness simply answer the questions put to her."

"Sustained," Judge Paltz said before Fierst could speak. "Everything following 'Of course not' will be stricken. Mrs. Dodgson, please, just answer the questions."

"Exception, Your Honor," Fierst said with his first show of anger.

"Noted," Judge Paltz said. "Now, let us move on."

"Mrs. Dodgson, did you hire someone to look out for your property?"

"Not hire, not in the usual sense in that she was a paid employee on a regular basis. We asked a neighbor to keep an eye out for trouble and let us know if there was any when we weren't there ourselves to protect our property. That certainly is not spying."

"Did you pay her?"

"We gave her a little something now and then. Certainly. She is practically bedrid—"

"Objection!" Barbara snapped.

"Sustained. Mrs. Dodgson, just answer the questions," Judge Paltz said in a voice so soft and low it sounded ominous.

"Mrs. Dodgson, are you acquainted with Paula Kennerman?" Fierst asked, as courteous as before, but without the note of deference.

"No. I never laid eyes—" She glanced at the judge, clamped her lips, and shook her head.

"Did you know Lori Kennerman?"

"No."

"No more questions," Fierst said and nodded to Barbara. His face was expressionless.

So he disliked his witness, Barbara thought as she rose. Too bad. But stitch by stitch he was sewing up the Canby property nice and tight.

Before she could speak, Judge Paltz said, "In light of the hour we will adjourn until nine tomorrow morning." It was four-forty.

"Be careful with him," Frank murmured after the judge left, and the others in the courtroom rose and started the usual buzz. "Lewis doesn't like her and her crew, and that will make him be fairer than fair."

She nodded. Like Angela, she remembered, stopping just because she disliked Mrs. Dodgson so much. She turned to give Paula a few words of encouragement. "Still their inning, but hang in there. I intend to fry that . . . woman."

"Bitch," Paula muttered.

"You got it. See you in the morning."

Outside, the police were keeping the demonstrators back with ropes. There seemed to be a lot of uniforms, and a lot more yelling people, still with signs that waved back and forth dangerously. They could brain each other, Barbara thought with disgust. She ignored the TV cameras, the news reporters shouting questions. The bailiff went with them to introduce their driver, Heath Byerson, a cheerful lanky police sergeant, out of uniform for this mission. "You tell me where to, and that's it," he said when they entered his car.

"Home," Frank said, and gave the address.

"Okay. We'll just drive around a few minutes first." He whistled softly between his teeth as he drove in the wrong direction.

"I need to get out of these clothes and take a long brisk walk, maybe even a run, and I have to look up something at the office," Barbara said.

"You will need dinner eventually. Pick you up at the office later? Seven-thirty?"

She nodded. She could almost see the citation she wanted.

"What I need is a glass of very good wine," Frank said as they drew near his house.

Heath Byerson slowed down and surveyed the street carefully before he stopped. "See you in the morning. Quarter to nine okay?"

They said it was and got out; he left.

"Honey, if you tell me what it is you want to look up, maybe it will come to mind," Frank suggested when they walked to her car in his driveway.

"Back East somewhere, a witness lied so often that finally all his testimony was thrown out. State appellate upheld the decision. That's all I can think of right now."

"You mean Stanley," Frank said with a grin. "Good old Stanley. *State of Rhode Island* versus *Stanley*, back around 'forty-eight or so. Everyone knows good old Stanley."

She laughed and kissed his cheek.

As she got into her car, he said, "Bobby, the catch to Stanley is that first you have to prove the lies. Remember that."

"How many does it take?"

"More than one or two. Pick you up around seven?"

She nodded and drove home.

Bill Spassero was waiting for her at her house. She recognized him instantly; at least, she corrected herself, she recognized his hair, which looked like a dandelion gone to seed. He was on the porch, stiffly upright, watching a neighborhood happening: a dozen or more people had gathered to paint the Delgados' house. There was loud music from a boom box, a keg of beer on a table, and a lot of children running around. She waved to her neighbors, and Spassero came down to meet her at the car door.

"Can we talk?" he asked.

"Why?"

"I'm not sure. I just feel we should talk, if you're not too beat."

"I'm going to change clothes and take a long walk," she said, heading for the house with him at her side. "That's about all I'm in the mood for. Sorry." Now she saw his car, a low, sleek Nissan-something that cried money.

"Let me walk with you, then."

She eyed his expensive suit and shoes. "You're not really dressed for a walk on the bike path, are you?"

He nodded. "I'll wait here and let you decide. Okay?"

She shrugged and entered her house and locked the door behind her. Now what? she thought irritably.

She took off her silky jacket and hung it up, eyeing it with dismay. Of course, it would wrinkle like that, she told herself, and took it to the bathroom to steam later. She would have to press it, she knew, and pretended not to know. She hung up her skirt and tossed the blouse and panty hose into her laundry basket and dressed again, this time in jeans and a T-shirt. When she went back out, ready for a brisk walk, he was waiting.

She led the way, set the pace, and he stayed at her side without speaking. She didn't look to see if he was taking in his surroundings. The hell with it, she thought, but if she had spoken, she would have said, *This is where most of your clients come from, bozo. Look!* In silence they crossed the train tracks; a short distance away a freight train was being tortured with great crashes and screams of metal on metal. She had not heard the switching yards for a long time; today it was eerie, like being in a futuristic world where the metal beasts were dominant and coupled with shrieks of anguish. At last they reached the bicycle path, which led off in both directions. She turned left. The path paralleled the river, and they had to keep to the edge because of the cyclists, the people running dogs on leashes, and hordes of teenagers who appeared in a dead heat and passed them the same way. It was relatively cool here, and the river sparkled and was beautiful, giving no hint of the continuing drought that was plaguing the county. A pall of smoke discolored the sky.

At last he said, "I keep thinking that any day now you'll tell me what you want."

She didn't respond. She was walking faster than she would have done if she were alone; a film of sweat covered her arms; she could feel it on her face, down her back. It felt good.

"I keep trying to figure it out," he said. "I looked you up. I know everything there is to know that's public knowledge, and it's no help."

"Look, Mr. Spassero, I don't want anything. So you can go now."

"Why did you do it, then?"

She nodded to a man and woman approaching. The man had a small boy on his shoulders; the child had both hands full of the man's hair. They were all grinning.

"I tossed a coin," she said. "Heads you were in collusion, which I probably never could prove; tails you were bone ignorant. Tails won. I'd have done the same thing for a kid brother. Now go home."

"I'm thirty-two," he said.

"You've been sheltered."

"That's true. Do you want me to tell you about it?"

"No."

"But I want to. The day after I got the Kennerman case Doneally showed up. You called it: They had been watching me; they were interested; they wanted a new man in the office, the whole works. I was flattered. And, yes, bone ignorant. It simply never occurred to me to question why this had come up now."

Barbara maintained her steady, too-fast pace and didn't even glance at him. Now and then she nodded at others on the path, and now and then moved aside to let others pass her, and now and then noted the ripeness of the blackberries that still clung to the brambles that were thick along the side of the path.

"Okay," he said, "I should have suspected something; I can see that now, but there wasn't any reason to at the time. I thought Kennerman was guilty. I still think she's guilty. I believed Doneally was giving me guidance; no one had ever done that before. Doneally told me Copley was his own doctor; I never even questioned what he was prescribing."

He lapsed into silence, and she began to get a sense of how difficult this was for him.

"Then, after you got the case, I took the file and went away to think. I read everything again and again, and it still didn't make sense, not until I got back and did a little research on Dodgson and found out that Doneally was his attorney."

She looked at him now. He was walking steadily, his gaze on the ground before him, frowning.

"I still don't understand it," he admitted. He caught her arm. "Could we take it a little slower? This isn't the easiest thing I've ever done, and I need all my breath."

She slowed down thankfully.

"So I called Doneally and told him I'd reconsidered and decided to stay on at the public defender's office. He said that was just as well, because they had decided not to expand after all, not just now."

She remained silent. He had not told her a thing she had not already known or guessed. She waited for the hook.

"Then you did what you did. Judge Paltz was really very generous, you know? I didn't expect that. I met him in the hall a couple of days ago and he asked me if I'd spoken to you."

Now we have it, she thought, regret tinged with bitterness. If the judge asked again, he could answer yes and look schoolboy innocent.

When he spoke the next time, his words were slower, more hesitant. "I realized that you hadn't said a word to him when he called you. I didn't expect that, either."

He touched her arm again and stopped walking; she stopped also. "Look," he said, "I know I'm bugging you. You need time alone, to think, to relax. I'm sorry. I just want to tell you that I'm extremely grateful. Not that I won't still be waiting to see what you want, but there it is. I'm grateful. Thank you." He looked as if those words cost him more than he could pay. Abruptly, he turned and almost ran in the opposite direction.

She watched him for a second or two, and then continued on her walk. *What was he after?*

Later, when she told her father about the meeting, he said, "Maybe he said what's on his mind—he's sorry, he was wrong."

"Right," she said. "Why didn't he come forward when he knew what was up?"

"Scared, probably. A decade of life gone down the tube. When you're his age, a decade is one third of your life. That's hard."

She made a snorting sound that even to her ears sounded exactly like the kind of noise he made when disgusted.

"You know," he went on, "most of the time it's easy enough to spot when you've made an enemy, but it takes a lot of experience to recognize when you've made a friend."

The next morning she drove to Frank's house; Heath Byerson arrived promptly at eight forty-five and drove them to the courthouse, where *they* were present in force. She ignored *them*.

Today Kay Dodgson wore a soft pink dress with a matching jacket, and pearls, and looked even more expensively turned out than she had previously.

Judge Paltz reminded her that she was still under oath, but before Barbara could start, Gerald Fierst said, "Your Honor, the witness spoke to me before court this morning and said she would like to make a statement. She misspoke yesterday and wants to correct the record."

Judge Paltz eyed Kay Dodgson with a distant look. "Is that so, Mrs. Dodgson?"

"Yes, sir," she said. "I made a mistake. I realized last night that it might look bad, and I thought I should fix it as soon as I could."

So, Barbara thought, Doneally, Dodgson's attorney, knew about *Rhode Island* v. *Stanley* along with everyone else.

"Proceed, Mrs. Dodgson," Judge Paltz said.

"Thank you, Your Honor. You see, when he asked if we paid Carrie Voight, I was thinking of paying, like you do people who clean the house, and the people who work at the press, you know, on a weekly basis, or hourly, or whatever. Then I realized that since Rich is helping support Carrie, that might look like we're paying her. But it's not the same thing." She hesitated, and cast a swift glance at the jury, then plunged on. "We give—donate, that is, two hundred fifty dollars a month to help support her."

Judge Paltz nodded. "Thank you, Mrs. Dodgson. Ms. Holloway, if you will."

"That's a very generous gift, Mrs. Dodgson," Barbara said, rising, moving toward the witness stand. "Is Carrie Voight related to you or your husband?"

"Of course not."

"So you can't even claim her as a dependent on your income tax, which makes it even more generous. How long have you lived in your present house, Mrs. Dodgson?"

"Twelve years."

"And when did you start this act of generosity with Carrie Voight?"

"I really don't know for sure." Kay Dodgson glanced again at the jury box and raised her eyebrows. "I mean, we just like to help people. We don't make notes about it."

"You said earlier that you're the general manager of the Dodgson Publishing Company, didn't you?"

"Yes."

"So you keep the books? Do the accounts? Make out the payroll? Are those your functions?"

"Yes," she said sharply. "I said that."

"I know you did, Mrs. Dodgson. I know you did," Barbara said easily. "Yet you don't know how long you have been paying, excuse me, *giving*—Carrie Voight two hundred fifty dollars a month?"

"No, I don't." She turned her gaze to Gerald Fierst, as if to seek his intervention. He made no response.

"Mrs. Dodgson, what kind of arrangement did you

have with Carrie Voight? Did she report personally when something was out of line?"

"No. I never met her."

"How did she communicate when she suspected a problem?"

"She called us sometimes to say what was going on."

"I see. Did you take those calls?"

"No. She talked to Rich. I never had anything to do with her."

"Did you share your husband's feelings about the seriousness of the incident when two women from the ranch went swimming nude in the pond?"

"Yes! Absolutely. I have to protect my own children from that sort of thing." Her mouth had become very tight, her lips almost invisible, and two spots of red appeared on her cheeks as she answered.

"How old are your children, Mrs. Dodgson?"

"Craig is twenty-seven and Alex is twenty-three."

"And this happened two years ago when they were twenty-five and twenty-one. Do they ever swim nude, Mrs. Dodgson?"

"No! Of course—" She stopped herself and said, even more tightly, "In the privacy of our home, not in public, they might."

Barbara went to her table and opened a file, extracted several glossy prints. "Your Honor, I would like to introduce into evidence photographs of the pond we are talking about."

"Objection," Fierst said, and already he sounded tired. "This is irrelevant to the case we're hearing."

"Your Honor," Barbara said, approaching the bench, "this witness is prejudicial to the use that was made of the Canby property, and that prejudice may have extended to my client. In cases of extreme prejudice witnesses sometimes misspeak, misinterpret what they see, or fail to see what is clearly before them. It is my intention—"

Judge Paltz held up his hand and overruled the objection, and Barbara continued.

"This is a photograph of the pond taken from the private road leading to the Canby property. Do you recognize the pond?"

"Of course not! I can't even see the pond!"

"This one was taken from Farleigh Road. Do you recognize the pond from this one?"

"No!" Kay Dodgson snapped.

"And finally, another one taken from your driveway off the private road. Can you recognize the pond here?"

"You know I can't see the pond in those pictures."

"Yes, I know that. And yet the swimming incident was one of the problems your husband raised with Mrs. Canby, wasn't it?"

"Yes. That pond is in public view, even if those pictures don't show it."

Barbara went to the aerial map and traced the outline of the pond. "Three-fourths of the ground around the pond is overgrown with rushes that grow six to eight feet high by midsummer." She pointed to a narrow strip without vegetation. "This one area is open, and it faces the woods that are on the Canby property. Would you call that public, Mrs. Dodgson?"

"Yes. Swimming naked in public is indecent, and they were there to be seen by anyone who looked."

"When your two sons swim nude, what is to prevent your housekeeper from glancing in and seeing them?"

"She knows better. If they have the music on, she doesn't go near the pool room."

"So, if those two women had played music, that would have been enough to warn off possible voyeurs?"

"They had no business swimming naked out in the open like that! Not around impressionable young boys."

"Mrs. Dodgson, did your sons make it a habit to trespass on the Canby property—here in the woods, for example?"

"Never! They knew better than to go over there."

"Could they have seen anyone in that pond from your property?"

Kay Dodgson hesitated and Fierst objected.

"The witness can't testify about what someone else might have seen."

"I withdraw the question," Barbara said. Then she asked, "Did you see the women swimming that day?"

"No."

"When did you hear about it?"

"I don't remember. After dinner, after Rich got home. I'm not sure."

"Your sons didn't report it to you?"

"No. Rich told us."

"Was he at work that day?"

"Yes."

Barbara led her through the incident with the gate. Did she see anyone actually turning around on their property? Was Rich home when it happened? Was Craig?

"If no one saw it, why were you so upset? Was any harm done to your landscaping?"

"No. We were afraid one of those women would decide to take a shortcut through our driveway out to

Spring Bay Road. You just don't know what irresponsible women like that will do. We wanted them to stay off our property, and we put up a gate to see that they did stay off."

"How can you be certain it was one of those women who turned in your driveway that day since no one in your household saw her?"

"We knew. We just knew."

"Did Carrie Voight tell you?"

"Not me. She might have told Rich. Not me. I told you, she didn't call me."

During the first recess Frank handed Barbara a report from Bailey. She read it and grinned. Kay Dodgson had been a dancer in a casino in Las Vegas when she married Rich Dodgson. Frank winked at her. "You're wearing her down just fine," he commented.

She nodded. "Not enough, not yet. But I'm working on it."

When they all filed back into the courtroom, she heard Frank's voice in her ear. "Someone opened up her spine and filled it with starch." Kay Dodgson was almost rigidly straight, with high color, as if she had been given a swift kick. Barbara hoped that had happened.

"Mrs. Dodgson," she asked, "have you ever met any of the guests at the Canby Ranch?"

"No, of course not!"

"Yet earlier you labeled them irresponsible. Why?"

"They left their husbands, didn't they? That's irresponsible."

"Do you think there is ever a legitimate cause for a woman to leave her husband?"

"Rarely."

"Do you accept that some men beat their wives?"

"If they fight, it takes two."

Fierst objected on the grounds that a criminal trial was no place to conduct a philosophical discussion. Barbara agreed, thinking, testing, just testing.

She led Kay Dodgson through the incident with the woman photographer and concluded by asking, "So no one could have seen her, since you say your family rises at about eight or eight-thirty. Is that right?"

"Yes."

"And she didn't make any noise that you heard? Is that right?"

"Yes."

"She didn't leave any trash behind, did she?"

"I don't know."

"If she had, wouldn't that have been part of the complaint?"

"Maybe. I don't know."

"So no one saw her, or heard her, and probably no one found anything she left behind. How did you know she had been on your property?"

"Rich told me."

"And did Carrie Voight tell him?"

"Yes."

Later: "Mrs. Dodgson, how did your husband and son learn that a woman had miscarried?"

"I don't know."

"Did you know they were going to the Canby house to confront Mrs. Tidball, to accuse her of running an abortion clinic?"

"I knew. We all talked about it first."

"Do you and your husband support someone in the emergency room of Sacred Heart Hospital?"

"What do you mean?"

"Do you have a spy in the hospital who calls you when there's a suspicious emergency?"

"We don't have spies!"

"You say you help out Carrie Voight. Do you 'help out' someone in the emergency room of the hospital?"

"No," she said harshly. "We were suspicious from the start, that's all."

"Yet you didn't go to Mrs. Canby this time. Why not?"

"It was just a miscarriage, that's all."

"How did you know that?"

"Emma Tidball told Rich." She drew in a quick breath. "And they threatened him and Craig, just like we always knew they would."

"You knew that Paula Kennerman and her daughter had arrived at the ranch. How did you know she was injured?"

"I didn't know that."

"What did you say to Angela Everts that Saturday morning?"

"I said I'd like some mushrooms. That's about all."

"Did you mention the new woman and her child?"

"I don't know. I might have. We wanted them to know we were keeping an eye on them, that's all."

"Did you ask if the new woman was well enough to go into the woods?"

"No! I didn't. I didn't know she was hurt." The red spots on her cheeks had spread down her face. Angela Everts had been right; pink was not a good color for her. And the stage training that had given her poise yesterday had deserted her today.

Barbara walked to her table and leaned against it with her arms crossed. "You said as long as they were quiet and behaved themselves, you had no objection to women using the Canby Ranch as a refuge. Is that right?"

"Yes, that's what I said. That's what we agreed from the start."

"Were they quiet?"

"I don't know. I guess so."

"Your house is about how far from the site of the Canby house?"

"I don't know, not very far."

Barbara went to the pile of stuff on her table and pulled out an acetate sheet. "This is an overlay with distances marked to scale with the aerial map." It was accepted as an exhibit and she carefully positioned it over the other map. "Let's see the distances we're talking about," she said. "Your house here is two thousand fifty feet from the site of the Canby house. About half a mile. Wouldn't you say there was little chance of hearing anything from such a distance?"

"I guess so."

"Mrs. Dodgson, when did you and your husband sell the other parcel of land? Over here, across Spring Bay Road?"

"Objection," Fierst cried. "Your Honor, that is irrelevant. What difference does it make to this trial?"

"It isn't irrelevant," Barbara said swiftly. "If they objected to noise, it is highly relevant to ascertain to whom they sold that property, and for what purpose. I maintain that noise had nothing to do with their objections."

She was allowed to continue. Kay Dodgson moistened her lips. "When did you sell that piece of property?" Barbara snapped at her.

"About nine years ago."

"And to whom?"

"Royce Gallead."

"What is Mr. Gallead's occupation?"

"He owns a gun shop and a firing range, I think."

"Don't you know he owns a firing range, Mrs. Dodgson?"

"Yes. He does."

"Have you ever objected to the noise from the firing range?"

"No, I haven't. We don't hear it much."

Barbara returned to the map and overlay and put her finger on the Dodgson property, and then on the range. "This shows four hundred fifty-five feet from your front door to his back door. That's less than half a city block. But it doesn't bother you to hear gunfire. Is that what you're saying?"

"I never paid much attention to it."

"Is Mr. Gallead a friend of yours?"

"No! He's a neighbor, that's all." She shot a swift glance at the courtroom and then looked down at her hands clenched before her.

Good heavens, Barbara thought. She's terrified of him. To give herself time to consider this new datum, she walked back to the table and took a sip of water. Later, she thought. Later. She returned to the map. "Mrs. Dodgson, the Canby house was screened by evergreens and rhododendrons, wasn't it?"

"Yes." She looked up from her hands and then put them in her lap.

"So your spy—that is, your helpful neighbor— couldn't really see what was going on once a car got near the house. Is that right?"

"Objection," Fierst said. "She can't testify as to what someone else could see."

Barbara nodded and didn't demur when the objection was sustained. She was playing for time now; she didn't want to get into that Saturday and then break for lunch. She said, "If you were on the private road, you couldn't see the house, could you?"

"No."

"Your vision was obscured by the shrubbery around the house and then by the trees on the side of the driveway. Is that right?"

"Well, when I got near enough I could see more."

"Even if you were up here, near the end of the road, you still couldn't see through the dense forest, could you?"

The map showed the forest to be almost solid. Kay Dodgson looked at it for a second or two, and then said, "I could see someone if someone was there."

"But I didn't ask you that, now did I?" Barbara said in a kindly voice. "Do you have exceptional vision, Mrs. Dodgson? X-ray vision, perhaps? The ability to see through a tree?"

"Objection!" Fierst yelled. "Counsel knows she can't harangue the witness in such a manner."

"Ms. Holloway, that is quite enough of that," Judge Paltz said. "Sustained. Since it is almost noon, we will recess until two."

When she turned to look out over the courtroom, *they*

were there staring at her with hatred. Standing against the back wall was Bill Spassero. He nodded, and left.

"Well, sometimes you have to put your paw in the door before someone will close it," Frank said with a grin as he examined his sandwich in the little room that made Barbara feel like a caged animal.

She looked out the window. *They* were patrolling the crosswalk. *They* were in the cafeteria, she knew. She had the second floor of the building to pace in; at least *they* were not allowed here.

"I've been thinking about disguises," Frank said thoughtfully. "A beard for me, maybe a red wig for you, funny clothes . . ."

She snarled at him and went out to pace the second floor.

FIFTEEN

"MRS. DODGSON," BARBARA started that afternoon, "as bookkeeper and general manager of Dodgson Publishing, do you handle the employee records? Deductions for taxes, health insurance, that sort of thing?"

"Yes, of course," Kay Dodgson said. The break had been good for her; she was in her very cool mode, gazing past Barbara as if bored.

"How many employees do you have?"

"Seven at the company, four full-time, three part-time."

"And you keep all their records?"

"Yes."

"Do you have a grounds maintenance person?"

"Of course. He's part-time."

"Does he also work at your residence?"

"Yes."

"So you work with numbers a great deal. Do you keep separate accounts for what he does at the company and what he does at your home?"

"No. Yes, I mean."

"Is your son Craig a paid employee?"

"Yes. He's learning the business."

"And your other son, Alex? Is he a paid employee?"

Kay Dodgson stiffened, then shrugged. "He's an intern in the office of Senator Bulmar in Seattle. He doesn't work for us."

"Is he a paid intern?"

"I don't know."

"Well, do you give him an allowance?"

"Yes."

"So you're tracking seven employees, three family members here, and the allowance of another son. Does your husband handle any of the financial affairs of the company?"

"No. I told you, he does the editorial end; I do the business."

"Yes, so you did. But he handles the donations, is that right?"

"Yes."

"Does he draw from company funds to do that?"

"No. That's his personal account." She had become more and more wary as this line of questioning continued. Now her gaze flicked from Barbara to the jury, back to Barbara.

"Does Mr. Dodgson draw a monthly salary?"

"No, not really. He just has some personal money that he can use any way he wants."

"Is that in a separate checking account?"

"No. It's just his money. I don't question what he does with it."

"But you balance the account monthly? You process the checks?"

"Yes," she almost cried. "I keep the books. I told you that."

"Do you write the checks for the taxes on your property?"

"Yes."

"And for insurance, on the company property and your personal property?"

"Yes. That's all part of doing business," she said with a more pronounced edge in her voice.

"Do you publish material other than the newspaper?"

"Yes."

"What kind of material do you print?"

"Objection," Fierst said. "This line of questioning is leading into matters that are entirely irrelevant to the case at hand."

"I agree," Judge Paltz said. "Sustained." The gaze he turned on Barbara was not angry, or even cold, simply formal and distant.

Barbara nodded, and said to Kay Dodgson, "The kind of work you do takes a concentrated focus, doesn't it?"

"Yes, very much so."

"And are you accustomed to estimating the cost of a job? So many work hours, plus material, plus overhead, and so on? Is that part of what you do?"

"Yes, I make the estimates."

"So you are used to dealing with numbers. You notice details. Would you say that's correct?"

"Absolutely."

"According to the overlay on the aerial map, the total distance from your house to the private road, up to the woods, down to the juncture with Farleigh Road, and back to your house is a mile and a half." Barbara traced the route with her finger as she described it. "Would you say that's about right?"

"I don't know. I never tried to measure it."

"How often do you take that walk?"

"Several times a week usually, unless it's raining."

"That's your exercise program, to walk a mile and a half?"

"I like to take a walk and that seems a good distance."

"Do you wear your regular clothes, the clothes you wear to the office, for instance?"

"No. The driveway is gravel. It would ruin my shoes. I dress for the walk."

"In what, Mrs. Dodgson? Running shoes, sweatpants?"

She hesitated briefly. "I wear walking shoes, Nikes, and an appropriate outfit."

"Blue jeans?"

"Of course not. Walking outfits, I suppose you could call them sweatpants."

"Do you always walk in the morning?"

"Yes. Right after breakfast."

"All right. Do you make it a real workout? Walk briskly?"

"Not always," she said cautiously. "Sometimes."

"How long does it usually take you to walk a mile and a half?"

"I don't know," Kay Dodgson said almost triumphantly.

Barbara permitted herself a small smile and shook her head. "You mean, you never noticed what time you left and what time you returned? Never?"

"No, I didn't." She raised her chin slightly and glared at Barbara. "I don't have to be bound by the clock, and I'm not."

"That's very fortunate," Barbara murmured. "What time do you usually arrive at the office?"

"At ten o'clock. Weekdays, that is. Saturday we go in

at one or two to get the paper out for Monday morning."

"So, ten o'clock. And you said earlier that you get up at eight or eight-thirty. Is that correct?"

Barbara could almost see her doing the numbers in her head.

"Closer to eight," Kay Dodgson said.

"You misspoke when you said eight or eight-thirty?"

"It's closer to eight, that's what I meant before."

"All right. Do you make breakfast?"

"No. Just coffee."

"Do you read the paper, chat with your family?"

"No. I just make coffee and get dressed and go for a walk."

"So if you were out of the house by eight-thirty at the latest, you would allow yourself an hour and a half for the walk, for a shower, and then to get dressed in time to get to the office by ten. Is that about what your schedule would be?"

"I don't know. Something like that. It only takes five minutes to get to the office." She appeared to have forgotten there was a jury and a courtroom full of spectators. She kept a narrow-eyed gaze on Barbara, as if waiting for the trap she suspected was there and had not yet identified.

"Do you go to the office approximately dressed and made up the way you are now, Mrs. Dodgson?" Barbara looked her over appraisingly.

Kay Dodgson flushed slightly. "Yes, I do."

"So it must take you at least half an hour to shower and dress and put on makeup, make yourself presentable?"

"I don't know."

Barbara nodded and glanced at the jury. One of the women was nodding slightly also. She knew, Barbara thought. She went to the defense table and picked up a slim volume, which she introduced. "This is a standard exercise manual published by the United States Department of Health for adult fitness," she said after it was labeled. "According to the manual, a city block is approximately one-fifth of a mile. The mile and a half we are talking about here would be like starting outside at the corner of Seventh Street and walking south to the middle of the block between Twelfth and Thirteenth Streets. Mrs. Dodgson, I ask you, would it take you an hour to walk from here to Thirteenth Street?"

Kay Dodgson's mouth tightened and her eyes narrowed even more. "It might. I don't know."

"Again, according to the manual, the average person simply walking—not running, not hurrying—walks a city block in five minutes or less. That means the average walker covers a mile and a half in about thirty-five minutes. Mrs. Dodgson, does it really take you twice as long as the average person to walk that distance? Is that your exercise program?" She made no attempt to disguise her disbelief.

"I don't know how long it takes! I told you I don't go by the clock."

"Your Honor," Fierst said, "I really have to object to this long and drawn-out go-nowhere line of questioning. Mrs. Dodgson has said repeatedly that she doesn't know how long her walks take. And the whole matter is irrelevant."

"It is highly relevant," Barbara said. "It is vital to my client to know how long Mrs. Dodgson was on that private road the morning her child was killed."

Judge Paltz allowed her to continue.

"Mrs. Dodgson," she said, "you stated earlier that you left your house that morning no later than ten, and possibly earlier than that. Is that correct?"

"I keep telling you—"

"Mrs. Dodgson, just yes or no. Is that what you said?"

"I don't know. I suppose—"

"Is that what you testified earlier, Mrs. Dodgson? We can have the court recorder find the question and answer if you are not certain."

"Yes. I said that. It's the truth. I don't know—"

"The answer is yes," Barbara said. "You stated that your son Craig went in for a swim before you left the house. Is that correct?"

"Yes. He did!"

"Did you see him enter the pool?"

"Yes. No. I heard him splash when he dived in, and the music was on."

"Was the door open?"

"Yes."

"You didn't close the door to the pool room?"

"No. I was on my way out."

"You stated that you left by the back door at ten, with the view of the private road before you, and you turned toward Farleigh Road, where you met Angela Everts. Is that correct?"

"Yes, I did. I don't know what time—"

"Mrs. Dodgson, will you please just answer yes or no," Barbara snapped. "I'm not asking for explanations or excuses."

"Objection."

"Sustained. But, Mrs. Dodgson, you must simply answer the questions put to you. Do you understand?"

She moistened her lips and nodded. "Yes, sir."

"Mrs. Dodgson," Barbara asked, "didn't you, in fact, head in the opposite direction on the private road, and weren't you, in fact, nearing the end of the walk when you met Angela Everts?"

"No! No! I wasn't!"

"You claim that you took half an hour to walk from your door to this point?" She pointed at the circle. "A distance of slightly over a quarter of a mile? A seven- or eight-minute walk for an average walker?"

"Yes!"

"What were you doing all that time?"

"Just walking. Taking my time."

"Or is it possible that you left your house at twenty-two minutes past ten, that you walked at a normal pace to the point where you met Angela Everts at ten-thirty?"

"No. It was ten. Or before, even."

Barbara went to the map once more. "From your door to the private road is thirteen hundred fifty feet. In this direction, facing the Canby property and westward," she said, pointing, "it is heavily forested, isn't it?"

"Not that thick," Kay Dodgson said through tight lips.

"The map shows that it is heavily forested," Barbara said scathingly. "Didn't you leave those trees standing in order to insure privacy?"

"We left a few."

"You have to get nearly to the end of your driveway before you can see the entrance to the Canby property," Barbara continued, moving her finger along the driveway. "For two-thirds of that time you could see only the lower end of the private road, is that not true?"

"No. I could see more than that."

"The map indicates otherwise," Barbara snapped. "Then, when you reached the private road, you had your back turned on the upper section. Didn't you?"

"Yes, but you can sense if someone—"

"Your Honor, I ask that everything after 'yes' be stricken from the record."

Judge Paltz ordered it done.

"Then, after ten-thirty until you returned to your house at eleven-ten or thereabouts, you were facing the upper road no more than half the time. Is that right?"

"I was looking more than that!"

"How?" Barbara demanded. "You stated that when you reached Farleigh Road, you turned and walked back to the end of the private road; then you turned and went the other way, with your back to the woods, and then you turned again into your own driveway, which put your back to the Canby property, and you went home. Did you walk backward part of the time?" She traced the route as she spoke, and was not at all surprised when Fierst objected to her sarcasm. "Withdraw the question," she said, satisfied.

She crossed to stand by the jury box, facing Kay Dodgson, who had made a mess of her lipstick. "You stated that you had the private road in view for an hour, Mrs. Dodgson, but the fact is that even if you were walking for an hour, you couldn't have seen the upper section for more than twenty-five minutes. Ten minutes from your own driveway—and then only by turning your head to look that way deliberately—and another fifteen minutes during which you walked toward the woods. Isn't that true?"

"No! That's a lie! I would have seen anyone on that road! I was looking around all the time."

Barbara ignored her and went to the table. Recess time, she thought. Paltz took care of his court; he knew as well as she did that Kay Dodgson was losing it. He called for a ten-minute recess, and she smiled to herself. When she looked up, beyond her father, beyond Paula, the little bit of pleasure vanished as she registered a sea of faces, some of them twisted in hatred. *They* were keeping the faith.

As soon as they were in the little room she was beginning to think of as hers, Frank hugged her. "Doing good," he murmured. Then he drew back with a troubled expression. "We might have a problem," he said, and pulled a paper from his pocket, handed it to her.

She read: *Dodgson won't be called. As soon as they're through with C. all three will take off on a long trip.* She read it again, and turned it over, looking for a clue. There wasn't any.

"Where did it come from?"

"Messenger left it at the office, addressed to both of us. I think it's some kind of a trap. Something to rattle you."

She shook her head. It didn't make any sense, she thought, and absently accepted the cup of coffee he had poured for her. She read the message once more. "We can't risk it," she said finally. "I can't let them go. Subpoena Dodgson as a hostile witness for the defense, and I'll have her put on hold for recall."

Frank shook his head. "I think that's what they think you'll do. You simply don't have cause to haul in

Dodgson, and if you try a fishing expedition, Lewis
Paltz will shoot you out of the water. I think they don't
want you to cut Dodgson in little pieces the way you're
doing her, and they're baiting you."

"What can Judge Paltz do?" she demanded.

"Contempt of court, reprimand. But worse, if Fierst
makes a case that you're on a private vendetta, Kay
Dodgson's testimony might begin to look pretty good
again. You've cut her to ribbons; this might be a way to
piece her back together again."

"Damn Doneally," she muttered.

"That, too," he agreed. "He's a smart lawyer."

Her thoughts tumbled. Under cross-examination she
could have nailed Dodgson a dozen ways to Friday, but
under direct, even as a hostile witness, she would have
to link him to the murder and fire. Rousing the rabble
after the fact wasn't enough, she knew. She could keep
Kay Dodgson on ice, but would he leave then without
her? She suspected that he might.

Finally she said, "If they get away, they'll wait until
it's all over, months maybe, and come back and pick up
where they left off. Gallead might decide to take a vacation now. If they leave, it's over. You know that."

"I know that," he agreed soberly. "But, Bobby, you
can't connect Dodgson, and you know *that*."

"I can't let him get away," she said. "Dad, I can't just
let it go on, whatever it is. Subpoena him."

"Mrs. Dodgson," Barbara began, "you stated in your direct testimony that you had been in your house only a
minute or two before Angela Everts arrived. Is that correct?"

"I . . . I think it was longer than that."

"You misspoke? Is that what you are saying?"

"I think so. It was longer than a minute or two."

"How long was it, Mrs. Dodgson?"

"I don't know. I didn't look at the clock."

"Did you hear the explosion?"

"No."

"Yet others who were far more distant, with many trees between them and the house, heard it. Do you believe you were already inside your house by then?"

"I must have been." She had repaired her makeup, but already she was moistening her lips; the lipstick wouldn't last long.

"According to the fire marshal, the explosion occurred at about five minutes after eleven. And you were already inside your house. What did you do when you returned from your stroll, Mrs. Dodgson?"

"I was in my room, laying out clothes to put on."

"Did you enter by the back door?"

"No. No. I went in through the front and straight to my room."

"Did you see Mrs. Melrose?"

"No."

"Where were you when Angela Everts arrived to use the telephone?"

"In my room."

"It took you ten or eleven minutes to pick out clothes?"

"Yes, if it was that long!"

"Were you surprised to see her at the front door?"

"No! I mean, yes. She never came to the front door."

"How did you know your son was still swimming?"

"When I came out, I saw the door open and heard the music, and when I called him, he was in the pool."

"When did you pick up his robe, Mrs. Dodgson?"

"I didn't."

"Mrs. Everts testified that you were carrying his robe when you answered the door. Were you?"

"No! Why would I? I was in my room."

Barbara went to the map again and pointed. "This is where Angela Everts met you. About five hundred feet in from the juncture with Farleigh Road. Is that correct?"

"Yes, I guess so. About there."

"And in your testimony you have stated several times that you continued to the end of the private road. Is that correct?"

Kay Dodgson moistened her lips again before answering. "Yes, I did."

"Did you pass the 'No Trespassing' sign?"

"I don't remember."

"You know there is a sign here, don't you?" Barbara held her finger on the map and regarded Kay Dodgson evenly.

"I know we posted the property some years ago, to keep out trespassers, yes."

"Did you know about this particular sign?"

"I guess so."

"Yes or no, Mrs. Dodgson. Did you know about this particular sign?"

"Yes, then! I did."

"And were you aware that this particular sign housed a motion sensor directed across the private road?"

Kay Dodgson cast swift glances about the courtroom, toward the jury, the prosecutor's table; then she raised her chin and said almost defiantly, "I knew all about it. I told you, we were determined to keep an eye on those women and what they were up to, and since we were gone so much, we needed a surveillance system. I knew all about it!"

"On your morning strolls, did you stop short of the system, Mrs. Dodgson?"

"Yes, of course."

"I see. So you didn't really walk to the end of the road, did you? The sign is in three hundred feet from the end of the road."

"I walked to the sign."

"So we have to reduce the distance you strolled by six hundred feet, don't we?"

"It isn't that far!"

"Of course not," Barbara agreed. "But three hundred feet from the sign to the end of the road and three hundred back—that does add up to six hundred feet, I'm afraid." She walked to the end of the jury box, very near Paula. "Mrs. Dodgson, is it possible that you have misspoken about when you finished your morning walk? Is it possible that you turned and went back to your home after speaking with Mrs. Everts?"

"No! I told you. I went to the other end of the road first!"

Barbara nodded. "Your Honor," she said, "I have no further questions for this witness at this time. I request the court to advise Mrs. Dodgson that she is to hold herself in readiness to be recalled as a hostile witness for the defense after we have had the opportunity to hear testimony from other witnesses."

"Objection!" Fierst cried. "Defense counsel can ask any questions she chooses to at this time. This is a delaying tactic, meant only to harass this witness."

"Your Honor, there will be other testimony in direct

conflict with the statements Mrs. Dodgson has made repeatedly."

Judge Paltz held up his hand for silence, and Barbara stopped. "You wish to call this witness as a hostile witness for the defense?"

"Yes, sir. I will call her as a hostile witness."

He regarded her thoughtfully for a second, then said, "It is the opinion of the court that defense counsel has the right to do this. It is so ordered. Mrs. Dodgson, you will be recalled to the stand when the defense presents its case. Now, Mr. Fierst, do you wish to—"

"I can't stay," Kay Dodgson said in a furious voice. "We have plans. We are taking a trip. I can't stay."

Judge Paltz looked at her levelly. "Mrs. Dodgson, you must change your plans and hold yourself in readiness to be recalled to the stand. Do you understand what I am telling you?"

"But we can't just cancel everything!" She looked about wildly. "When will I have to come back?"

"Ms. Holloway will determine that when she presents her case," Judge Paltz said. "You will be notified in advance."

"Why are you letting her do this to me? This is persecution!"

Judge Paltz rapped his gavel. "Mrs. Dodgson, you must remain silent. Mr. Fierst, do you wish to redirect at this time?"

"No, sir. I'll hold my redirect for her recall."

"Very well. Court is adjourned until nine tomorrow morning."

The courtroom buzz sounded like a wasp nest, with her on the inside, Barbara thought, after the judge left and the jury was escorted out. She did not turn to look behind her. The noise rose and rose, with whispers, and hisses, and indignant shrill cries.

"I'll come around to see you later," Barbara told Paula as the matron approached. "You okay?"

Paula didn't look okay; she was far too pale and had become thinner. "I'm okay," she said in a low voice. "As long as *they* can't get to me."

"No one's going to get near you," the matron said firmly. "Don't you worry about them. Riffraff, that's all they are."

Barbara still didn't make a motion to rise. Behind her, Frank was gathering his things, making rustling sounds. She felt his hand on her shoulder and shook herself and shuffled her own things together, back into the briefcase. Paula had walked out ramrod stiff, and she would do no less.

"Home?" Heath Byerson asked when they were escorted to his car. Before he could engage the clutch, a tomato splattered against the windshield. Wordlessly he turned on his windshield wipers; the blades made streaks as they moved back and forth. He started to drive.

"Home," Frank said heavily.

"Then I have to come back to see Paula," Barbara said, watching the blades move back and forth.

"I don't think that's a good idea, if you don't mind me saying so," Heath Byerson said. "They'll grab that bozo who tossed the tomato, but there are others. Yesterday they hung out around the jail, too."

"Jesus," she muttered. "It's a state of siege. I have to talk to my client, no matter what *they* are doing."

In the end he drove them to the jail, around to the

back entrance, and Frank stayed out to keep him company when she went in to talk with Paula.

"The state will wrap it up tomorrow," she said. "But it's going to be bad again. I doubt they'll call Carrie Voight, and we'll call her later if they don't. I don't think they want to hear any more about spies and motion sensors. But your ex will tell lies about you, and Craig Dodgson will, and then they'll have the psychiatrist on hand to explain your mental state. It will be tough going."

"All those people out there," Paula whispered. "They hate me so much! They all think I did it, and they want me to die."

"They think whatever Rich Dodgson tells them to think," Barbara said. "Pull yourself together, Paula. Think of them as puppets, with him pulling their strings. That's all they are."

"Are you going to make me testify?" Paula asked then. "I'll have to see them, face them. . . ."

"Undecided. It depends on what the shrink says. I don't want you on the stand, you know. That's an ordeal I'll spare you if I possibly can. What I'll want you to do tomorrow is make notes when your ex is talking. Every time he lies, I want you to make a note of it. Will you do that?"

Paula nodded, and some of the despair faded from her face. The first day, during jury selection, Paula had said wonderingly that she was the least important person in the courtroom; in a sense she had been right. Everything was out of her hands at this point, but she needed to do something, anything, not just sit there day after day and listen to people who wanted her convicted. After Dodgson's puppets had appeared, Barbara had asked Lucille not to attend the trial until she had to testify. No incidents, she thought. Someone was certain to know that Lucille was Paula's sister, and she might be targeted. Instead, she had suggested, Paula could tell her everything that happened, everything that was said; and that had given Paula a little bit of responsibility, something to do. But most of all, Barbara wanted her occupied tomorrow when her ex-husband began to lie about her, about their relationship, about their dead child.

She stayed for half an hour, and then went out to find her father and Heath Byerson in a conversation about roof shingles.

"What we thought would be a good idea," Frank said, too casually, "would be to go to your place, let you pack up your things, and move you into my house for the rest of the trial. Just a precaution."

"Dad," she started, but Heath Byerson turned in the front seat and gave her a long serious look, and she didn't finish her protest.

"They know your place," he said. "You're too easy to find. Not many know the house your father has now." He had cleaned the windshield; no trace of tomato remained.

They were right, she admitted to herself. Gallead had known where to find her. Spassero knew where she lived. It seemed that everyone knew where she lived. With reluctance, hating the feeling of defeat she had to acknowledge, she nodded and then said to her father, "So you win."

He shook his head. "Just until this thing is over. I don't want you because you have to move in. I want you to want to move in. There's a difference."

SIXTEEN

SHE HAD NOT slept well; all night dreams had brought her near the wakeful state, and then let her slip back into sleep, but when she came wide awake, it was the dreams that bothered her even if she couldn't remember the context. She blamed the bed: the same bed she had slept in as a child, then as a teenager, when she was home from school, and, finally, in the river house. The same bed she had slept in with Mike.

"Right back," she said at the breakfast table after toying with her eggs and toast, and drinking coffee. She ran upstairs to finish her makeup, gather her purse and briefcase, give a final scowling glance at her image in the mirror, and then went down again to find her father and Heath Byerson in a solemn conversation. Roof tiles? Floor tiles? Sump pumps? They broke it off when she entered.

"Ready?" Heath asked, his cheerful countenance in place again.

"As ready as I get," she muttered. "Let's do it."

When they stopped at the courthouse her father said he would go on to the office, see if Bailey needed a nudge, see what was up. "Won't be long," he said as she got out of the car.

She nodded to her police escort, ignored the shouted questions of reporters, the eye of the television camera, the hisses and hoots, the names being yelled by the many people with their evil signs, and entered the courthouse.

Almost instantly she was plunged back into the melodrama being enacted in the courtroom. It was as if this was the only reality; all else outside this room was simple busywork, no more than a distraction.

Fierst called Craig Dodgson, and this was the reality, seamlessly attached to yesterday's reality.

Craig Dodgson appeared younger than he did in the photographs she had seen; he was tanned to a dark handsome shade, sunlamp tan, not the uneven, leathery tan of an outdoors man. He had dark, wavy hair neatly cut and natural-looking, not coiffed to any noticeable extent. He was dressed in a sports coat, nice slacks, loafers, well dressed without the show of ostentatious wealth his mother had exhibited. He looked handsome and healthy, the ideal son that a mother could be very proud of.

Today Fierst acted like a man in a hurry. He did not linger over Craig's background, but led him quickly to the case. "You stated that you were kidding around with the defendant, Paula Kennerman, and you asked her to go out on your boat. Is that correct?"

"Something like that," Craig said. "It wasn't a real invitation. But she seemed to think it was."

"Tell us in your own words about this incident, Mr. Dodgson," Fierst said.

"Well, I liked to go to the Olympus and listen to the jazz. And I kidded around with the waitresses, most of them, not just her. You know, they wear those cute little

skirts and heels and they're fun to kid with. A little
flirting, that's all." He shrugged and looked almost bewildered as he continued. "So I said something to her
about going out on the boat; but no kids, I said, and no
husband. That's what I always said. She laughed, and I
thought that was that. I never gave it a second thought
until a couple of weeks later, near the end of March, I
think, the next time I was in there, and she came to my
table and said, 'When?' Just like that, when. And I
didn't know what she was talking about. I said something like, 'Any time,' but I was uneasy because she
wasn't laughing. She looked serious and came back a
few minutes later even more serious, and she said if she
got rid of the old man and the kid, she'd hold me to my
word. She put her hand on my arm and said, sort of in
a whisper, it would be great, just the two of us. Then
she got busy and I left. I didn't go back."

"I see," Fierst said with a sober expression. "Mr.
Dodgson, did you offer to take other waitresses out on
your boat?"

"Yes I did. Just kidding. You know, it was a little flir-
tation, that's all. They knew it wasn't serious."

"You had a picture of the boat with you?"

"Sure," he said with a grin. "I'd bring it out and say,
'Hey, honey, want a little ocean cruise? Isn't she a
beaut!' And I'd show them the boat, and they'd laugh
or pretend to be interested, and we just had fun." He
spread his hands in a way that seemed to imply helplessness.

"And you said Paula Kennerman didn't take it as fun
and games? She was serious?"

"Yes, sir. When she put her hand on my arm, she really dug in. I mean, she gripped hard. She was serious,

all right." All traces of boyishness, of helplessness, of bewilderment vanished, and he was more like the grim-faced man in the photographs.

Fierst had a few more questions and then nodded to Barbara and sat down.

"Mr. Dodgson," she said, "how old are you?"

"Twenty-seven."

"And you own the boat we're talking about?"

"No. My dad owns it; he lets me use it."

"Something like the family car?" Barbara suggested with a slight smile.

"Yeah, about like that."

"How many people will the boat sleep, Mr. Dodgson?"

"Eight."

"Is it an oceangoing ship?"

"It could be," he said more cautiously.

"Well, have you taken it to Hawaii, for example?"

"Yes."

"Can one person run the yacht?"

"Yes."

"How often do you take the ship out, Mr. Dodgson?"

"I don't know. Two, three weekends a month in the summer."

"Do you take groups of people with you?"

"Sometimes."

"Do you ever take a single woman companion out with you?"

"No! Dad wouldn't let me even if I wanted to."

"I see. The family car again. Do you always inform him when you are going out and tell him who is going with you?"

"Yes, every time. It's his boat."

"And you have his approval for your various cruises?"

"Yes."

"Do you ever go out alone, Mr. Dodgson?"

"Yes. I like to go out alone."

"Where do you go alone, Mr. Dodgson?"

"No place in particular. Sometimes up to Seattle and pick up my brother and we cruise the inland waterway up there."

"Where else?"

"Just up and down the coast, not too far out."

"All the way down to Mexico, for example?"

"Yeah, or up to Alaska, if I feel like it."

"What do you do for a living, Mr. Dodgson?"

"I work for the Dodgson Publishing Company."

"That's who pays your salary, I believe," Barbara said. "But what do you actually do?"

"Objection," Fierst said with annoyance. He had started so briskly, and now she was delaying everything again, he seemed to be complaining. "Irrelevant."

"I am simply exploring areas already touched upon by Mr. Fierst," Barbara said, "in order to test whether this witness, at his age, has had enough experience to evaluate the reactions of waitresses to his advances."

When Judge Paltz allowed her to continue, his face revealed nothing. She never had worked before a judge who could hide himself so thoroughly, she thought, and turned again to Craig Dodgson, and proceeded to take him step-by-step through his duties at the press.

"You don't do any of the writing or editing," she said, "but do you agree with the paper's editorial content?"

"Absolutely. One hundred percent."

"Do you draw a salary from anyone else? Any other group?"

"No."

"Do you volunteer your efforts for the national pro-life groups?"

He hesitated and Fierst objected again, this time jumping to his feet and even raising his voice.

"Your Honor, counsel for the defense knows this is irrelevant. What Mr. Dodgson does outside the confines of this case is entirely irrelevant."

"Ms. Holloway, do you have a point to make?" Judge Paltz asked courteously.

"Yes, sir, I do. I intend to demonstrate that Mr. Dodgson is highly biased, that his testimony here is so prejudicial that it may be without value."

"For heaven's sake!" Fierst burst out. "Is everyone who might testify against the defendant to be labeled prejudiced?"

"Mr. Fierst, please," Judge Paltz said, just a touch more sharply than he had done up to this moment. "Ms. Holloway, you may proceed. Overruled."

"Exception," Fierst snapped.

Judge Paltz nodded. "It will be noted."

"Mr. Dodgson, do you volunteer your services for pro-life organizations?"

"Sometimes. It's something I am very concerned about."

"Is this your picture, taken in October of last year?" She had nine newspaper photographs from a year ago to April of this year. One by one she produced them and he admitted that it was his picture.

"That's nine," Barbara said. "Were there other demonstrations in which you participated?"

"There might have been," he said, and added, "It's a deep moral issue with me. I care enough to try to do something."

She asked that everything following "there might have been" be stricken. Craig Dodgson moistened his lips, and she thought, *At last.*

"How many others, Mr. Dodgson?" she asked.

"Several. Three or four."

"Making it twelve or thirteen demonstrations in the six months from October through April. Is that all?"

"Yes. I think so."

"Do you fly first class, Mr. Dodgson?"

"Objection!"

"Sustained."

"Do you organize the demonstrations?"

"No. I just go to them."

"And how do you know about them in advance?"

"People tell us things. We know a lot of people. We keep in touch."

"Mr. Dodgson, isn't there a national network that issues such information?"

"There might be."

"Do you know if there is?"

"Yes. I think there is."

"Do you know there is?"

"Yes. I said yes."

"Do you subscribe to such a service?"

"Me? No."

"Does your company, the Dodgson Publishing Company?"

"Yes. I think so."

"Does your company, the Dodgson Publishing Company, subscribe to such a service?" she asked.

"I said yes." His answer was even sharper than her question.

"How long are you gone from home when you attend the various demonstrations?"

"A few days, maybe a week."

"So in a six-month period you devoted up to twelve or thirteen weeks of your time to this cause. Is that right?"

"Maybe. I wasn't keeping track."

"Did you accompany your father to the Canby Ranch and accuse Emma Tidball of running an abortion clinic?"

He moistened his lips again and nodded, then said, "Yes. We thought it was true."

"Had you thought they were running an abortion clinic for a long time?"

"We suspected it from the beginning," he said, his voice harsh and even menacing.

"Did you think you had confirmation finally?"

"Yes we did."

"How did you know a woman had been taken to the hospital with a miscarriage, Mr. Dodgson?"

"I don't know. Mrs. Voight said something about it."

"But all she knew was that an ambulance had taken someone away. Did you leap to the conclusion that it was for an abortion mishap?"

"I don't remember why we thought that," he said. "It just seemed the likeliest thing."

"In those newspaper articles," Barbara said, "it states again and again that many of the clinics you were picketing did not perform abortions. Yet you demonstrated against them. Why?"

He was starting to look about the courtroom, as if

seeking help or relief from some quarter. Mercifully, Fierst was staying quiet. Barbara was grateful that he was a methodical plodder who would not force a confrontation with the judge who had agreed to this line of questioning. In his place, she would have been raising holy hell.

"Why, Mr. Dodgson?" she prodded.

"Because they were advising women to have abortions, to commit murder of innocent unborn children," he said in a rush, as if to get it in before she could object.

"Did you believe anyone at the Canby house was advising women about abortions?"

"Yes. We know they were."

She was walking slowly back and forth from the witness stand to the defense table, back to the stand, forcing him to move his head to keep his gaze on her. She stopped midway, at the center of the jury box.

"How do you know that, Mr. Dodgson?"

"We just did, from the start." Now he looked like the hate-distorted man captured in the newspaper photographs.

"That's a serious accusation, Mr. Dodgson," she said. "Did you have some evidence, some proof? Or did you just make an assumption?"

"We know the kind of women who went there. Women who swim naked out in the open are the kind of women who'd have abortions. We knew that."

"Did you see any women swimming naked, Mr. Dodgson?"

"No. But they did."

"So you assumed that the Canby Ranch was provided

for the kind of women who would have abortions. Is that correct?"

"Yes, that's right."

"And you assumed that a woman who had been severely beaten and suffered a miscarriage was in fact having an abortion. Is that right?"

"I said we were wrong about that. I admit we were wrong that time."

"But that was your original assumption, wasn't it?"

"Yes." He ran his hand through his hair and fidgeted and now he was wetting his lips frequently.

"Did you agree to back down that time and wait for a more telling incident to occur, something you could take to Mrs. Canby and demand that the house be closed?"

"Yes. I mean no. We didn't want to close them down. We just wanted them to behave."

"But you didn't go to Mrs. Canby that time, did you?"

"No. I said we were wrong that time."

"Did you come to believe you had been wrong from the start, that the house possibly had nothing to do with abortion counseling?"

"No! When women like that get together, they talk about abortions. We knew that. We just waited for something we could prove."

"In order to close down the house?"

"No. We never said that."

"What did you want proof for?"

"Just to make her keep a close eye on what was going on. For discipline, to screen who came and went."

"I see. Mr. Dodgson, is abortion ever justified in your opinion?"

"Never! It's murder!"

"Do you agree with the philosophy that maintains that women who have abortions are criminals?"

"Yes, absolutely."

"And should be punished under the law?"

"Yes!"

"And the doctors who perform abortions are criminals?"

"Yes, they are accessories."

"And those who counsel women concerning abortion, are they accessories also?"

"Yes."

"And those who stand by and do nothing to put a stop to this activity, are they accessories?"

Too late he realized where she was heading. He cleared his throat and licked his lips. "If they really know. Not just suspect, but actually know, then yes."

"You said you *knew* what was happening at the Canby Ranch, that you *knew* abortions were being discussed, that women were being counseled. You have flown all over this country to demonstrate—why didn't you demonstrate at home, Mr. Dodgson?"

"We were waiting to get some real proof," he mumbled.

"And then what would you have done?"

Fierst finally objected.

"I withdraw the question," Barbara said. She raked Craig Dodgson with a look of scorn and turned her back on him, walked to her table. Her father was in his seat; she had not noticed his arrival. She faced the witness stand again. "Mr. Dodgson, you testified that you kidded around with Paula Kennerman back in March. You came forward with your statement months later. Why did you wait so long?"

"I just didn't want to get involved," he said. The line was so fluent it sounded rehearsed.

"You have had your picture in papers all over the country, in magazines, and here you didn't want to get involved," she said. "Why did you come forward at all?"

"I had to. My conscience made me. I realized it was my duty."

"Have you been back to the restaurant since the time you say you talked with Paula Kennerman?"

"No, not once."

"How often did you used to go there?"

"Not often, once or twice a month."

"For dinner."

"No, to hear the music. Sometimes for dinner, maybe."

"Don't you know?"

"I had dinner there once in a while."

"Alone?"

"Usually alone. Not always."

"When you said you kidded around with Paula Kennerman, were you alone?"

"Yes."

"And when you returned, the last time you were there, were you alone?"

"Yes."

"Did you have dinner those nights?"

"I don't remember," he said after a hesitation.

"Come now, Mr. Dodgson, you said you recall how she put her hand on your arm, the exact words she uttered. Surely you know where that happened. Was it next to your salad or by your drink?"

"It was in the dining room," he said. A mean new edge had appeared in his voice.

"I see. If you called and made a reservation for dinner for one, we can check the records at the restaurant and find out exactly when that was, can't we?"

"No. I didn't have a reservation."

Barbara shook her head. "They don't seat anyone in the dining room without a reservation, Mr. Dodgson. Perhaps you misspoke?"

"It must have been in the lounge," he said, sounding so furious now that he had difficulty in controlling his rising voice. "I don't remember where I was, only what she said and how she gripped my arm."

"Mr. Dodgson, earlier you said the waitresses wear those cute little skirts and heels and they are fun to kid with. Do you remember saying that?"

"Yes," he all but snarled at her.

"You kidded them; they kidded back. Is that what you meant?"

"Sure. They know they get bigger tips that way."

"Do you think they dress provocatively?"

"Sure they do, flouncing around, sassy-like. Teasing."

"Did you know them by name?"

"No. You don't ask girls like that their names."

"Girls like that? What do you mean, Mr. Dodgson?"

"I mean they're ... flirts, out for the tips. Names don't matter because once you're out of there, they're out of mind. It's a game men and women play." He added almost savagely, "Most men and women. Maybe you never played games like that."

Barbara turned to Judge Paltz, but he had anticipated

her. "The personal remarks will be stricken from the record. We will have a ten-minute recess at this time."

"Get hot, fight cool," Frank murmured as he poured coffee for her in their little room. "You're a good learner, honey."

"Oh, I'm hot enough," she said, looking out the window at *them*. "What a creep!" She let the blind drop into place. "Where have you been all morning?"

"Things are happening," he said. "I had a talk with Bailey. He wanted to know how much he could spend, and I gave him the green light." Frank sighed theatrically. "He's been tracking down migrants who picked berries at the orchard earlier in the summer, and one of them came through. Seems he worked with a guy who said he'd been there before, back in the winter sometime. Gallead's place."

"No!" she breathed. "He's a marvel, that Bailey. Where is this guy now?"

"Up north, picking apples, maybe Hood River, maybe already in Washington. Bailey needed to know it was okay to go find him. I said go."

"They aren't going to move now," she said, thinking of Gallead and his secret missions. "They'll play it cool and wait us out, won't they?"

"Wouldn't you?"

"This might be our only chance."

"There's a hell of a lot of apples up north," Frank reminded her. "And a hell of a lot of migrants to sort through. It's not done yet."

"He'll do it," she said. "What else is going on?"

"Oh, not much. Doneally dropped by for a little chat."

She eyed him narrowly. "And?"

"We have twenty-four hours to pull that subpoena. He's terribly sorry, he said."

"Or else?"

"Dodgson will slap us with a suit, harassment or some damn nonsense. But it won't matter what it is. And another one after that, and then another one. I sure didn't think I'd spend my few remaining years fighting off lawsuits."

"He's acting stupid," she said, nodding. "He's scared."

"I don't know about that. Mad, that I give you. But scared? I know I'm scared. He's mean enough to do it. And apparently rich enough to keep at it."

When they resumed, Barbara went directly to the Saturday Lori Kennerman had been murdered.

"Mr. Dodgson, you stated that your mother made a breakfast of waffles and sausage and that the three of you ate in the dining room. Is that correct?"

"Yes." He had recovered his boyish good looks during the short recess.

"And you just happened to notice that it was ten minutes before ten when your father went out to mow the grass. Were you wearing your watch?"

"Yes."

"Were you dressed?"

"Yes."

"Then you and your mother cleared the table and carried things into the kitchen. It took a minute or two at the most, you said. What did you do next, Mr. Dodgson?"

"I said I went to the dressing room and got undressed to swim."

"No, you didn't say that. What you said was you went swimming. Now you say you went to the dressing room first. Is it off the swimming pool?"

"Yes."

"And how long do you estimate it took you there?"

"A minute maybe."

"All right. Then you dived into the water? Is that right?"

He hesitated. "I looked out in the hall and saw that Mother was at the back door, ready to go out, and then I dived in," he said triumphantly.

"How is the pool situated, Mr. Dodgson? Where is the deep end?"

He hesitated again, a bit longer this time.

"Mr. Dodgson, it's a simple question. Is the shallow end near the hall or at the far end of the room?"

"It's near the hall."

"I see. Why did you look out into the hall before you entered the water?"

"I don't know. I thought I heard her call me or something."

"When did you turn on the music, Mr. Dodgson?"

"I don't remember. Probably when I went into the pool room."

"And you play it loud to warn people that you're in there? Is that right?"

"No. I like music when I swim."

"Did you swim naked that morning, Mr. Dodgson?"

"Yes," he snapped. "I usually do at home when I'm alone in the water."

"So you opened the door and looked out into the hall toward the back door. Is that right?"

"Yes. I said that."

"Yes you did," she said. "Mr. Dodgson, where is the dressing room situated? At the far end of the pool room or near the hall door?"

"At the far end." He looked mean again.

"And how long is the pool?"

"I don't know."

"Let me refresh your memory," Barbara said and went to the table to rummage through papers. "When your house was built it was featured in the local newspapers, with photographs, the layout. . . . Ah, here it is." She picked up the printed floor plan and took it back to him. "Is this your house?"

She had the photographs and the house plan admitted, and then she said, consulting the plan, "The pool is forty feet long, with a twelve-foot apron on three sides and fifteen feet on the side that has doors to the dressing rooms. So, you went into the pool room, turned on the music, walked back to the dressing room and got ready to swim, and then, naked, you walked back fifty-two feet to the door to look out. Is that what you did?"

"If you say so," he said sullenly.

"No, Mr. Dodgson, not what I say. Is that what you did?"

"Yes. So what of it?"

"Why didn't you dive into the deep end of the pool when you came out of the dressing room?"

"I told you already. I thought I heard my mother call me."

"Over the music? At the far end of the room?"

"Yes! So I was wrong."

She nodded. "Then you say you went to the hall door and opened it to look out and saw her at the end of the hall at the back door. Is that right?"

"Yes. How many times—"

"Mr. Dodgson, please, just answer the questions. Was her hand on the doorknob? Was she opening it already when you saw her?"

"Yes. She had started to open it."

"And you left the hall door open to the pool room, raced across the twelve feet to dive into the shallow end. Is that right?"

"I didn't race," he muttered.

"I know your mother says she is a slow walker," Barbara said scathingly, "but how long could it take her to open a door and step out? She says she heard you splash."

"Objection!" Fierst yelled.

"Sustained. The jury will disregard counsel's remarks. Ms. Holloway, confine yourself to proper questions."

And that, she knew, was a rebuke. There was no mistaking it. She said, "Yes, Your Honor. Mr. Dodgson, was your mother always very particular about keeping the door to the pool room closed?"

He shrugged. "Not really."

"Did she complain about the smell of chlorine penetrating the rest of the house?"

"Not seriously. Sometimes we forgot to close it, that's all."

"You estimated that you were in the water no later than five minutes before ten and she was outside by then. Is that right?"

"Yes. I looked at my watch, and nothing took even five minutes after that."

"And you were still in the pool at eleven-fifteen when Angela Everts arrived. Were you swimming laps all that time, Mr. Dodgson?"

"Yes," he said. Then quickly he said, "No, I mean. Not that long. I was practicing some strokes part of the time."

"An hour and twenty minutes is a long time for laps and practice, isn't it? Do you work out that hard often?"

"Yes," he snapped. "I try to keep fit."

"Where did you leave your robe that morning?" She asked it almost casually, and was startled to see him stiffen even more.

"I don't know."

"Did your mother bring it to you in the pool room?"

He hesitated and moistened his lips. "I don't remember."

"When you got out of the pool, did you shower and get dressed?"

"Not right away."

"Did you get out of the pool and put on a white terry-cloth robe?"

He shrugged. "Yes. I remember. I had it in the pool room, on a chair."

"When did you put it there?"

"Before I got in the water."

"You mean after breakfast you went back to your room and collected your robe?"

"Yes!"

"Mr. Dodgson, did your parents ever tell you not to swim for an hour after a heavy meal?"

His look was murderous now. "I didn't eat that much," he said.

"Waffles and sausage, juice, coffee. That's a heavy meal just before you swim laps. Isn't it more likely that you sat at the table reading the paper for nearly an hour after breakfast, and then you took your swim?"

"No! It wasn't like that."

"Did you actually see your mother leave the house?"

"She was opening the door to go out."

"Ah, yes. She heard you splash and you saw her at the door. But, Mr. Dodgson, my question is: Did you see her leave the house?"

"No. She was opening the door to leave."

"Mr. Dodgson, just a simple yes or no! Did you see her go out?"

"No!"

"Thank you. No more questions."

While Fierst took him back over the few points he wanted the jury to hear again, she wrote *robe* and circled it. She had hit a sore spot and had not even a clue about why it was there or what it meant.

SEVENTEEN

JACK KENNERMAN WAS a frightened man that afternoon; he was thinner-faced than Barbara remembered, neatly dressed in a suit and tie, polished shoes, but he acted as if the clothes were not his, did not quite fit. He stretched his neck repeatedly to ease the constraint of his shirt; he worried a hangnail; his gaze flicked here, there, everywhere except at Paula. He had had his hair cut, but now it was too short, where it had been down over his collar before.

In a brisk, businesslike manner Fierst had Kennerman give some background, details about his marriage, where he was employed now—as a pizza delivery man—and then describe the last evening he had seen his wife and daughter at home.

Paula was screaming at Lori, Jack Kennerman said, throwing things around, tossing stuff into a suitcase, and when he tried to get her to tell him what was wrong, she pushed him and started screaming harder at Lori, who was crying and scared. He tried to pull her away from the baby and she hit him and he pushed her away harder than he meant to and she fell over a chair. He left, hoping she'd cool down and talk to him later. When he got home again about eleven, she was gone.

"You had a scene like that with your former wife and you just left her alone? Is that right?"

He ran his finger under his collar, his gaze shifting rapidly from Fierst out over the courtroom and back. "Yeah, it wasn't the first time. Usually she just cooled off and that was the end of it."

"Did you fight with her often?"

"Yeah, I guess so. She had a temper, and she'd start in on me, and we'd yell, and sometimes she pushed me and I pushed back."

"You said she was yelling at your child, Lori. Did she do that often?"

"Yeah. She'd yell at her." Now he was picking at the hangnail.

"Did she hit the child?"

"Not much. She'd say things like she was going to leave her in the woods and let the bears eat her, scare her like that. She'd make her sit on a spot on the floor and if she moved, sometimes she slapped her pretty hard."

"Mr. Kennerman, did she ever threaten to leave you?"

"Yeah, in the last year she did. She met this other guy, she said, and he was rich, and he liked her a lot, and as soon as she had some money saved up, she was taking off." He seemed absorbed now in the wood grain of the witness stand.

"Did you believe her?"

"Not at first. But I got to thinking about it and then I did. And when I seen how much money she was stashing away, I knew it."

"What do you mean?"

"See, I was out of work and we were doing without

stuff," he said in a rush. "Lori was doing without stuff that she needed, and Paula had all this money in the bank. She was saving up to take off."

Paula was scribbling furiously. Barbara didn't interfere with the examination; now and then she glanced at the scrawling words Paula was writing so hastily. Finally Fierst got to his last questions.

"Where were you all day Saturday, April nineteenth, Mr. Kennerman?"

"Fishing. I went up early on Saturday morning, and me and three other guys were up the North Fork of the Willamette for the opening of trout season. We came back Sunday night."

"And you were with three other men all weekend? Who were they, Mr. Kennerman?"

He named them, and Fierst said he was finished.

"Mr. Kennerman," Barbara began, "isn't it true that your former wife supported you and your child for the last five years?"

"No! That's a lie. I worked, too."

"You were unemployed in April. Were you collecting unemployment insurance?"

"No. They wouldn't give it to me."

"Why not, Mr. Kennerman?"

"That's how the system works," he said. "They make you quit and then you can't collect. It happens all the time."

"So you quit your last job. How long were you out of work?"

"I don't know," he mumbled, looking everywhere but at her.

"Well, make a stab at it," she suggested. "A month, three months?"

"Maybe four or five months. I couldn't find anything."

Fierst objected often, but she was allowed to take Kennerman back over his work experience.

"So you quit every job you had over the past five years," she said. "And out of that period you worked a total of sixteen months. Doesn't that mean that your former wife supported you?"

"I worked when I could," he said, almost whining.

"Five years ago when you quit your job delivering flowers, did you try to start your own business? A salvage business?"

"Yes," he said too eagerly. "That's right. It was a chance I couldn't pass up."

"And did you buy twenty-five hundred dollars' worth of scuba equipment and take scuba lessons to further that business?"

"Yeah, something like that."

"Did you start the business?"

He looked past her, at Fierst, at the ceiling. "It didn't work out. The other two guys chickened out on it."

"Did you charge the equipment on a credit card?"

"I don't remember."

"Who paid for the equipment, Mr. Kennerman?"

"We paid it off. Me and Paula."

"But you were out of work. How did you pay anything?"

"When I got another job, I helped pay," he said, clearly whining now. "I sold the stuff to a guy and used that."

"Three years ago did you try to start another business of your own? A photography business?"

Fierst objected, and Barbara said, "One side of their

domestic problems has been shown by the prosecution; the defense is entitled to show the other side."

"Overruled," Judge Paltz said.

Painstakingly she forced Jack Kennerman to admit to the four times he had gone deeply in debt with one venture after another that never came off. When a recess was called, she felt as weary and haggard as Jack Kennerman looked.

Today her father did not comment, but produced a small box that he handed to her. It was filled with expensive chocolates. She wanted to cry. They shared the candy and coffee in silence.

"How long have you had your present job, Mr. Kennerman?"

He hesitated, then said, "About three weeks."

"Are you still living in the same apartment you shared with your former wife and child?"

"Yeah."

"Paula Kennerman wrote a check to pay for the rent in April, but who paid the rent from May until September?"

"I did," he said, working with the hangnail again.

"How did you manage that after being unemployed for so long?"

"Some guys helped me out. I borrowed a little. I got by."

"How much is your rent every month?"

"Three eighty-five."

"You mean three hundred eighty-five dollars a month?"

"Yeah."

"So for four months that comes to over fifteen hundred dollars. What about your utility bills, your food?"

"I said some guys helped me out, and I worked a little. Odd jobs here and there. I sold some stuff."

"What guys, Mr. Kennerman?"

"I don't know," he said. "I never seen them."

"Then how did you receive donations from them?"

"A guy came over and said these guys wanted him to take the collection for them, and he brought it to me."

"Who paid for your divorce, Mr. Kennerman?"

"Nobody. He said he'd do it as a favor, that he had to do something now and then for free."

"An attorney did you the favor. Was he the same one who collected from your benefactors?"

"What do you mean?"

"Did he collect the donations and give you the money?"

"Yeah. They got in touch with him and he came around."

"Who was that man, Mr. Kennerman? What was his name?"

He looked around desperately. "I don't know. Don something. He said it too fast."

Barbara walked to the defense table and then back to the stand, thinking hard. "So a strange man came to you with money from other strange men and you simply accepted it. Did this ever happen before, Mr. Kennerman?"

"No. Nobody ever gave me nothing before. He said they did this, a bunch of guys who thought a guy was getting the shaft. They helped him."

"Getting the shaft? What does that mean, Mr. Kennerman?"

"A guy whose wife was giving him a hard time, running around, playing him for a dope, stuff like that."

"How much money did they give you?"

"I don't know," he mumbled. "Thousand, a little more."

"Did they give you enough to pay your rent for several months?"

"Yeah."

"Was it enough to pay your utility bills? Electricity, water, things like that?"

"Yeah. I couldn't find a job right off."

"Was it over two thousand dollars?"

"Maybe. I don't remember."

"Did you ask what they wanted in return?"

"Nothing. He said they didn't want nothing."

"But he was friendly, talked to you?"

"Yeah, some. Not much."

"Mr. Kennerman, do you remember what he talked about with you?"

"No! Nothing much, like I said."

She walked away, and only glanced at the jury. Some of the jurors were regarding Kennerman as if he were an alien insect found in the garden.

"Did he talk about Paula?"

"No! Just about women, how they treat their men, stuff like that. And these guys were fed up with it."

Enough, she decided, and changed the subject. "Mr. Kennerman, are you an avid fisherman?"

"I guess so. I like to fish."

"Do you tie your own flies?"

"Yeah."

"And on Wednesday, April sixteenth, did you go to a

sports shop and pick out waders, a tackle box, a fly rod, several flies?"

He was darting glances around again, or stretching his neck, running his finger under his collar, scratching, every time he spoke. His twitchiness was getting on her nerves.

"Yeah, I needed some stuff," he mumbled after a long pause.

"What kind of flies did you buy?"

He shrugged. "I don't remember. Just some flies."

"Did you have any equipment for a fishing trip when you agreed to go?"

"Yeah, sure, just not enough. I just needed a few things."

"Mr. Kennerman, didn't you try to charge three hundred forty dollars' worth of fishing equipment on a credit card Wednesday?"

"I don't know. Not that much."

"Weren't you turned down when the credit card charge was rejected?"

"Yeah. They wouldn't let me use it."

"And on the next day, Thursday, did you go to the bank and withdraw four hundred eighty dollars from your joint savings account?"

"No!" he cried. "It was four seventy-five."

Barbara nodded. "And did you use that money to pay for the equipment you had selected on Wednesday?"

"Yeah, some of it. I had to go fishing with the guys. One of them was going to give me a job."

"Were those three other men friends of yours?"

"Yeah, sure."

"How long had you known Gus Hormeier?"

"A couple of years. We used to work together."

"And Michael Selby?"

"A few months, maybe."

"I believe you said the third man was named Mr. Wentworth; how long had you known Mr. Wentworth?"

He looked around the courtroom again, as if searching for an escape route. "I just met him."

"So they weren't really your friends, were they?"

"Gus is my pal."

"The four of you rented a cabin, didn't you? Planning to stay up there Friday night and Saturday night. Was that the plan?"

"Yeah."

"But you didn't go until Saturday. Why was that, Mr. Kennerman?"

"I was looking for Paula on Friday. I got worried when she didn't come home Thursday night."

"Did you go to her sister's house in Cottage Grove?"

"Yeah. She wasn't there."

"And did you go to the Olympus restaurant and try to collect her paycheck?"

"No! I just was looking for her."

"Did you ask Cindy Truman for Paula's paycheck?"

"No! I might have said I'd put it in the bank for her or something like that. I didn't want it. I was trying to find out if she'd been there."

"Did you go to a house on South Polk Street looking for her?"

He hesitated a long time, studying his fingers intently. "Yeah. I went there."

"Who lives there, Mr. Kennerman?"

"I don't know, just a bunch of women."

"Isn't that what they call a safe house for women?"

"I don't know what they call it," he mumbled.

"How did you know about that house, Mr. Kennerman?"

"Guys talk, you know. I heard about it."

"What time did you drive up to the North Fork on Saturday morning, Mr. Kennerman?"

"I don't know, nine or a little later."

"Did you find your three friends?"

"Yeah, sure."

"Mr. Kennerman, did you see Gus Hormeier that morning?"

"Yeah. He didn't see me. He was busy, fishing."

"Did Michael Selby see you?"

"No, not right away. He was with Gus, down the river, with a lot of other guys all around them. It was crowded there."

"Who did see you?"

"Mr. Wentworth. I went by him and stayed awhile."

"What time was that?"

"I told you, nine-thirty or ten by then."

"How long did you stay by Mr. Wentworth?"

"Hour, hour and a half. I don't know."

"Was it cold and overcast?"

"Yeah."

"Where is Mr. Wentworth now?"

"I don't know. Back in California, I guess. He just come up for the opening of trout season."

"So the only person who saw you was Mr. Wentworth, who is out of state."

"We were all together later on," he said quickly.

"At what time were you all together?"

"I don't know. In the afternoon sometime."

"Mr. Kennerman, did Mr. Wentworth tell you to go away and not bother him?"

"How'd you— No! We just fished."

"Didn't Mr. Wentworth say something like you were an amateur and had no business out there?"

"No! No, he didn't say that."

"What did he say?"

"Nothing like that. He said he didn't want to talk business. He came to fish."

"Mr. Kennerman, didn't you buy a lot of new gear and go out there in order to impress Mr. Wentworth? And didn't he treat you with contempt?"

"No! He was a little uppity, that's all."

"And was it still overcast and cold when you left him?"

"Yeah. He didn't want to talk and I was cold."

"Mr. Kennerman, I have here the newspaper report of the opening day of trout season this year." She went to her table and produced the paper. "It says the weather was clear and warm all day; there wasn't a cloud in the sky. Yet you say it was cold and overcast. What time are you talking about, Mr. Kennerman? Before the sun rose?"

Fierst objected on the grounds that the question had been asked and answered several times. He was overruled.

"I don't know what time it was," Kennerman said. "I was cold."

"Didn't you get in your car and drive back to town then?"

"No! I didn't! I stayed out there and fished."

"Didn't you drive out to the Canby Ranch and have a look around?"

"No! I didn't know nothing about the place!"

"But you knew about the Polk Street Safe House, didn't you?"

"Yeah. I knew that one, but not the other one."

"When did you first start noticing that Paula was abusing your child?"

"She wasn't, not that way. She'd yell at her and punish her, that's what I mean." He was gripping the stand with both hands; beads of sweat lined his upper lip, sweat shone on his forehead.

"When Lori was an infant? In diapers?"

"Yeah, it started back then."

"Did you try to stop her?"

"Yeah, sure I did."

"How?"

"Like I said, I'd pull her away, keep her away from Lori."

"Did you hit her?"

"No! I'd just try to pull her away."

"Mr. Kennerman, did your former wife have to have a root canal in July of a year ago?"

"I don't know."

"Didn't you slap her hard enough to loosen a tooth, which then abscessed?"

"No!"

"Did you and Paula talk to a marriage counselor a year ago in August?"

"Maybe. I don't know when it was."

"And didn't Paula tell you then that if you hit her again, if you didn't straighten yourself up, she'd leave you? Do you remember that?"

"No!"

"Did you ever hit Lori?"

"No!" he cried in anguish. "I never."

"Did you tell the counselor that you and your former wife would open a savings account for Lori's education?"

"We talked about it, yeah. We never had a chance, Paula and me. We wanted things better for Lori."

"Why did Paula punish Lori? How did she misbehave?"

"She didn't. She was a good kid."

"Did she yell, race around the place, make a lot of noise?"

"Yeah, sometimes. And Paula made her sit still on the floor." He was very pale; his hands were trembling, and he was staring in a fixed gaze beyond her.

"What else did Lori do?"

"Sometimes she wet herself."

"And she was punished for that?"

"Yeah, she said she'd take her to the woods and let the bears eat her."

"And did she threaten her in any other way?"

"Yeah, with a curling iron. She said she'd burn her." He began rubbing his chest, still staring, blindly, it appeared.

"Do you have a scar on your chest, Mr. Kennerman?"

"No! She never burned me."

"Who are you talking about, Mr. Kennerman?" Barbara asked in a low voice, moving in close to the witness stand.

He broke then. Both hands flew to his face and his body shook out of control. Barbara walked back to the defense table, turned, and regarded him with pity. The silence in the courtroom was complete.

"You're not talking about Paula, are you, Mr. Kennerman?" she asked after a moment.

"No," he said, choking, his hands concealing his face.

"Did your mother burn you with a curling iron, Mr. Kennerman?"

"No! She didn't do that. She wouldn't do that!"

"Your former wife never threatened your child, did she?"

"I don't know. No. No, she didn't."

"Mr. Kennerman, the night you had your last fight with Paula, did you pick up Lori and throw her on the bed?"

"Yeah, I guess so," he said from behind his hands.

"Did you threaten to throw her out the window?"

"No! I didn't mean it. She knew I didn't mean that. I wouldn't hurt Lori. I loved her. Oh, God, I loved her!" He stopped, and this time he buried his face in his arms on the stand.

Judge Paltz rapped his gavel. "The court will recess for fifteen minutes," he said quietly.

"He was crying," Barbara said softly to her father in the little room. "Paula was crying. Half the jury was crying. I might cry."

"You might *want* to cry," Frank said, putting his arm around her, "but you won't. Not here, not now. Maybe later." He gripped her shoulder. "You know you had to do it, Bobby. You know that."

She nodded. She knew that. What she wanted to do, she thought then, was go to the coast, stand on the cliff over Little Whale Cove, and explain to Mike that she had to do it. She patted Frank's hand and went to the window to watch *them* on the crosswalk.

* * *

"Mr. Kennerman," she said when they resumed, "when Paula was in the hospital after the tragedy, you went to visit her several times. Then you stopped. Why was that?"

He had washed his face and looked as if he had taken something that had a remarkable calming effect. He was pale but composed now. "I knew she must have done it," he said dully.

"What made you think that?"

"The paper said she killed Lori and set the fire, nobody else could have done it; and I got a letter."

"What newspaper are you referring to, Mr. Kennerman? The daily paper here in town?"

He shook his head. "Some paper I never seen before."

She went to the table and picked up a copy of the *Valley Weekly Report.* "Was it this paper?"

"I don't know. Maybe. Like that one."

"Tell us about the letter, Mr. Kennerman."

"It just came. It said she was seeing this rich guy and making a fool out of me. That's all." Whatever he had taken had numbed him so much that now his voice was a monotone and all his restlessness was stilled. He looked almost asleep.

"Do you have the letter or the paper?"

"No. I tossed them."

"Mr. Kennerman, a year ago didn't you and your former wife see a counselor who advised you to continue with counseling?"

He shrugged. "I don't know. I didn't pay any attention. It was for her."

"You mean you went because Paula insisted?"

"Yeah."

"And did Paula say she would give you one more chance? Only one more chance?"

"I don't know. I don't remember."

"When you arrived home that Thursday evening and found her packing, was she angry because you took the money out of the savings account? Is that what you fought over?"

"Yeah. She was sore."

"And did she say you had had your last chance, that you had blown it?"

"I don't know. Maybe."

"When you went to the Polk Street house, did you threaten to break down the door if they didn't send her out?"

"No. I didn't mean anything like that."

"Did you say it?"

"I don't know," he said.

"Did you threaten to burn down the house?"

"No! I didn't say that!" Sudden animation made him look at her; he was wild-eyed.

"Did you yell that you would burn down the house and make all those bitches go back home where they belonged? Did you say that?"

"I could of!" he cried. "I might of. I didn't mean it! And I didn't burn down no house!"

"No more questions," Barbara said.

"Dad," she said, in the car with Heath Byerson behind the wheel, driving what seemed to be a random route, "remember that wildlife refuge up past Junction City? Off Ninety-nine? I think I'll change my clothes and go up there and do some hiking." No people, she thought, not on a weekday at this hour, this time of year.

"Fine," he said. "I'll go with you. But there's something we have to see to first."

Heath Byerson had made many turns, and she realized that they had entered the Whiteaker neighborhood, her neighborhood. They passed Martin's restaurant, and she had a surge of nostalgia for it, for holding court in the dining room, advising people about wills and fences and property lines. . . .

Heath Byerson turned down her street and stopped at her house; she gasped. The windows were boarded up, and the front of the house was covered with red paint.

"Those sons of bitches," she cried. "Those goddamned sons of bitches!"

EIGHTEEN

FRANK PRODUCED A key for the padlock, and they entered the house. Every window had been broken; it looked as if a high-pressure paint sprayer loaded with red paint had been used inside and out. Silently she looked at her futon, covered with red paint that looked like blood. In her office her file cabinet was streaked red, the desk was covered. Nothing in the living room was salvageable.

"Let's go," she said tightly.

"We think it happened about three or four in the morning," Heath Byerson said back in the car. "Probably when a train was going by, since no one heard anything. Some of the paint was still wet when the investigating officers arrived a little after eight. A lot of people saw the windows and junk this morning, and called us."

She kept her face averted, her gaze out the window although she was seeing nothing.

"Insurance people will be out tomorrow," Frank said, "and a patrol car will roam up and down until this whole thing is over."

She said nothing, not then, not when they reached Frank's house, and the two men exchanged glances.

"See you in the morning," Heath Byerson said, and left them.

Inside the house, she started up the stairs.

"Bobby, wait a damn minute. Loosen up. It's a mess, but you've seen messes before."

She stopped nearly halfway up. "I don't want to fight with you," she said, not looking back at him. "Just don't protect me anymore. Okay? You've known about this since morning, haven't you?"

"What the hell good would it have done if I'd told you? You had a tough day to get through. You didn't need this on top of it."

"Just don't make my decisions for me. Don't shoulder my load. Stop trying to protect me! Do you understand what I'm telling you?"

"No," he said. "You're dealing with maniacs, people who've let the alligator brains take over. Someone's using them, trying to rattle you. What if you'd been in that bed? Sure, we could have gone over there first thing, you could have seen it before court, and then what? You did a brilliant job today. Would you have been able to do that with fire in your eyes, murder on your mind?"

"Don't decide what I can or can't do," she snapped. "Let me mess up by myself!" She ran up the rest of the stairs.

She drove alone to the wildlife refuge with little memory of getting there, and then she started up the three-mile trail. No one else was in the area, which had been designated a wilderness, untouched except for the several trails. It was very still in the early evening; the trail was dusty.

Noble firs, Douglas firs, an occasional yew made up the forest here. Sunlight found an opening rarely, slanted in on columns of dancing dust motes, and touched with gold what it could reach, but most of the trail was in deep shadow. Fir forests were dark, forbidding to many people who dreaded the menace of the shadows, the stillness. The bears, she thought with a shudder. Jack Kennerman's mother had threatened him with bears in the woods.

She should whistle, make a noise, warn the bears that she was coming. The only sound she made was the fall of her rubber soles in the dust of the trail. She climbed for half an hour, and was drenched with sweat when she stopped to rest and look out over the valley she could now see. Below, the refuge was dotted with many ponds. Geese came here, and ducks, herons, gulls, even a pelican now and then. Refuge.

She should be thinking about what had happened in court, who had said what, the nuances, the changing expressions, the meanings behind the evasions, the destruction of her house and the implications—Gallead? Dodgson?—just another warning or had they thought she was there? Instead, the words she had used, the words her father had used played the loop. *Alligator brains, rattle you, don't protect me, murder on your mind, let me mess up myself. . . .*

She started to walk again, this time following the trail at the crest of a hill that afforded a glimpse of the valley, twisted back into the forest, returned to give another view. . . .

The next time she stopped, she sat on a fallen tree trunk that was being absorbed back into the ground but now afforded a mossy resting place. She said out loud,

"Put it behind you, kiddo. He's wrong, and so are you. Leave it for now." She nodded at the wisdom of the words and then brooded some more. He did want to help, that was part of the problem. But she had asked him to help, she reminded herself. Not this way, she retorted in the silent dialogue.

It occurred to her abruptly that the shadows now were not from the forest, but were shadows of dusk; no more sunlight slanted through the trees, and the sky had taken on a pale violet color, streaked with the muddy gray smoke from forest fires. She stood up and made her way on the remaining trail, which was all downhill now. It was nearly too dark to see the pond when she was on level ground again; where the water began, the grasses and rushes ended was impossible to tell. She skirted it with caution, and was vastly relieved when she reached her car and got inside.

No bears, no dunking in the water, no mishaps. Her legs were throbbing, and she could feel the clammy touch of her shirt on her back where sweat had soaked it through. She began to shiver, and turned on the engine, waited for the heater, and tried to imagine the state of mind Jack Kennerman would experience alone in the woods. Did he still have that fear?

All the way home she thought of Jack Kennerman and his brutalizing mother, of Craig Dodgson and his mother, of Paula and her child, her hopes. And she realized she was thinking of her father and herself. Doing the best we can, she thought then. Most of us, some of us, somehow or other, trying to do right by their children; children trying to do right by their parents.

When she got back to the house and entered, the

study door was open; her father was in his old brown chair, which was a bit disreputable.

"Dad, I'm sorry," she said from the doorway.

He looked up at her over the top of his glasses. "All right. Let's bring all this up again at a later time."

She nodded.

"Hungry?"

"Starved. I'll make something."

"I had Mexican pork stew. A little spicy, but not bad."

His pork stew was heavenly, and he knew it. "I'll heat it up if there's any left."

"Plenty left." He turned to his book again. "Won a bet with Heath Byerson," he said. "Five bucks. Not bad. He thought you'd cry over that mess. I said you'd get madder than hell."

She felt her cheeks burn. "I'll go shower first," she muttered. Shower, eat, and then work for several hours, she thought as she went up; a grin began to twitch at the corners of her mouth. Damn him.

Good, she thought the next morning when Fierst was well into his plodding examination of Enrico Palma. Fierst was going to cross every *t*, dot every *i*. She sat back to listen.

"Exactly what is a forensic psychiatrist?" he asked after Palma's credentials had been explained in infinite detail. Palma had a gray beard that was closely trimmed and neat. His hair was gray, and his eyes were a piercing black. He was fifty-one, and had been doing forensic psychiatry for sixteen years.

"We often work in cases such as this one, in order to determine the state of mind of the accused at the time of the crime, and to evaluate whether the accused is fit to stand trial."

He had examined Paula Kennerman, he said, in Salem, at the state mental hospital. Paula Kennerman had been taken to the hospital because she had withdrawn into silence and was uncooperative, and it was feared she was suicidal.

He had got her to talk to him, he said; one almost always could with the right approach. She had cooperated up to a point. He went into a very lengthy report of her childhood, adolescence, her adult life, her marriage. A recess was called, and after it, he picked up exactly where he had left off and brought his testimony up to the date he had concluded his examination.

"Exactly what do you look for when you examine persons accused of committing a crime? Criminal insanity?"

His smile appeared and vanished almost too fast to be identified. "No. I'm afraid that term has little meaning in the medical world. We look for a dissociative personality, for diminished capacity to resist a compulsive urge, for a delusional personality, or even schizophrenia, for a sociopathic personality, for an inability to distinguish right from wrong. There are other signs we seek, but those will do, I think. Of course, we have to eliminate brain dysfunction due to substance abuse, and we give a battery of tests to determine if the person is intelligent enough to comprehend the proceedings."

Fierst was about to speak when Barbara said, "Objection. The witness has used terms that are quite unfamiliar to most people. I suggest he explain them."

"I was going to ask him to," Fierst said with a touch of irritation.

And that would take them right up to lunch, Barbara estimated, when the doctor went into a long, detailed explanation. What a pompous little man, she thought; he was not quite preening, but was clearly happy with his performance.

At lunchtime, before Paula was led out, Barbara held her hand for a moment. "Relax," she murmured. "I don't think I'll need to call you. I'll explain later."

"Where is that Bailey?" she demanded when she and her father entered their room. She stopped just inside the doorway. A vase with many red roses was on the table. She looked at Frank, who went to it and extracted a card, handed it to her.

I'm sorry about your house. Bill. Wordlessly she picked up the vase and went back out with it and handed it to a woman emerging from a nearby office. "I'm allergic to roses," Barbara said. The woman looked at her blankly, turned, and reentered her office carrying the flowers.

"That asshole," Barbara muttered, inside their room again. "I'm getting fed up with their head games."

"Bobby, I wish you wouldn't call him that," Frank said, lifting the cover of a large bowl.

"I bet he's used to it. What do you suppose kids called him all through school? With his name, it's a sure bet. What's that?"

It was a beautiful seafood salad with tiny pink Pacific shrimp, chunks of salmon, bits of crab. . . . Today she sat down and ate with her father before she prowled the second floor of the courthouse.

Fierst picked up where he had left off. "Dr. Palma, you've explained the psychiatric terms, and we know

now what you were looking for. What were your conclusions after you examined the defendant?"

"She was suffering from situational depression."

Before he could continue, Fierst looked at Barbara with some bitterness and said, "Will you explain that term, please?"

And he was off with an explanation of the differences between manic-depression, clinical depression, and situational depression. "It's quite temporary," he finished. "Time and rest are the only treatment needed."

"Did you determine her state of mind before the death of her child and the fire?"

"Yes. I determined that she was absolutely normal."

Fierst had a few more questions and then Barbara stood up.

"Sir," she asked. "What is your name?"

"Enrico Palma," he said promptly.

"Thank you. You said Paula Kennerman was ordered to undergo psychiatric examination because she had become silent and uncooperative. Is that correct?"

"Yes. She had refused to answer questions, refused to speak at all."

"Did you have access to her medical records and the police investigators' records?"

"Yes, I did."

"And you read them all before you spoke with Paula Kennerman?"

"Yes, I did."

"You're familiar with Sergeant Sanderson's interrogations of the defendant?"

"Yes, I am."

"Do you recall how many times the sergeant questioned the defendant?"

He frowned slightly, then shook his head. "I'm sorry, I can't tell you. I don't recall now."

"Oh. What did you say your name is, sir?"

"Enrico Palma," he said, clearly and slowly.

She nodded absently. "We have here Sergeant Sanderson's final report in which he states that he interviewed the defendant seven different times. This was his seventh time. Of course," she added, "we have the notes from the first six interviews also. Did you have access to all seven interviews?"

"Yes, I did. I read them all."

"In each one he asked the defendant to tell exactly what she did that morning, and six times she told him that. On the seventh time, she became silent after saying, 'What's the use.' " She looked at Palma. "Did you read that report, the notes and everything?"

"Yes, I did."

"I'm sorry, sir. Will you please tell us your name again?"

He glared at her and turned to look at Fierst, who was already on his feet to object.

"Your Honor, counsel is trying to provoke the witness."

"Sustained. Ms. Holloway, please get on with it."

"Yes, Your Honor. Dr. Palma, did it render you speechless to be asked the same question only three times? Did you begin to feel it was hopeless?"

"Objection!" Fierst yelled.

"Sustained," Judge Paltz said. "The jury will disregard all the questions involving the witness's name. Ms. Holloway, you will cease this form of questioning."

Barbara did not look at him for fear he would see the gleam in her eye. *Tell them not to think of elephants.*

"Did you talk to the defendant's sister, Dr. Palma?"

"No, I did not."

"Or her ex-husband, Jack Kennerman?"

"No, I did not."

He wasn't being paid by the hour, she thought distantly, but by the word. "You have told us in great detail about her childhood, her marriage, her entire past history; you have even quoted her, and you got your information from the defendant. Is that correct?"

"Yes, it is."

"Did she tell you about the day her child was killed, about the fire?"

"Yes, she did, up to a point."

"Did she describe her actions of that day, Dr. Palma? Please, *sir*, just yes or no."

"Yes, she did," he said.

"Did you ask her to repeat the various incidents with her ex-husband?"

"No," he said.

He knew exactly where she was going, she thought as she pressed on. "Did you ask her to repeat the various incidents with her father?"

"No."

"But you asked her to repeat the most tragic story of her life, didn't you? How many times? Was it more than three, *sir*?"

"Objection! Counsel must ask one question at a time."

"Sustained."

"Did you have her repeat an account of her actions of that day, Doctor?"

"Yes, of course. Sometimes—"

"Dr. Palma, please just answer the questions," Barbara snapped. "How many times did you ask her to tell you about that day?"

"I don't know," he said. "I didn't—"

"Your answer is that you don't know," Barbara said. "Is that correct?"

"Yes, it is."

"Did she tell you about it more than once?"

"Yes."

"More than twice?"

"Yes."

"Dr. Palma, did you explain to Paula Kennerman that it was not your duty to treat her in any way, but that you had been hired by the district attorney's office to evaluate her mental condition?"

"Of course! Yes, I did."

"And she talked about her past, whatever you asked her?"

"Yes. Up to a point," he said with determination.

"What did she tell you about that day?" she asked almost casually.

Fierst objected.

"On what grounds?" Judge Paltz asked.

"Privileged information between a doctor and patient. He can't be forced to reveal what the defendant may have told him. She is trying to turn this witness into a witness for the defense."

Barbara shook her head and approached the bench. "Your Honor, Dr. Palma is not and has never been my client's physician or psychiatrist. He was acting as an agent of the district attorney's office. He has repeated verbatim what she told him in many instances. The prosecution cannot make an arbitrary decision now that he cannot continue to reveal what he learned."

Judge Paltz nodded and overruled.

Dr. Palma told what Paula had said to him, that she had gone to the back door and had seen flames, had run around the front and upstairs, searching for her child. The jury appeared to be frozen with concentration.

"Is that what she said to the investigating officers?"

"Objection!"

"The witness has testified that he read all the reports. He based his interrogation on them. The reports are stipulated as exhibits. He knows what he read or didn't read in them."

Dr. Palma was instructed to answer the question.

"Substantially," he said.

"What do you mean, 'substantially'? Was it the same story?"

"I mean there might have been some variation," he said.

"Dr. Palma, we have the police officers' reports. Shall we read them and compare them to your account? Or can you recall in what respects they vary?"

"A matter of wording," he said. "It was basically the same."

"Thank you," Barbara said. "Dr. Palma, what do the letters BWS mean on your report?"

"It was a technical note to myself," he said, "to remind me to examine for battered-wife syndrome."

"And what does that mean?"

"It's a complex system of behavior that includes violent interactions when a woman is emotionally dependent on the man she is living with."

"What do you mean by 'violent interactions'?"

"Most often the couple quarrels and that leads to

physical violence during which the man beats the woman. Sometimes severely."

"When you use the letters BWS as a memo to yourself, does that imply you are searching for a pattern of behavior, predictable behavior, that is?"

"Generally that would be true."

"Does seeking help from a marriage counselor fall into that predicted pattern?"

"No, it does not."

Barbara started back to the table, then paused to ask, "Dr. Palma, is there a term comparable to *BWS* used for men?"

He hesitated, then said, "No, there is not."

"No more questions," Barbara said.

Fierst was already on his feet to repair some of the damage. "Dr. Palma, was the defendant dissociative?"

"No, she was not."

"Delusional?"

"No, she was not."

"How would you describe her mental condition?"

"Absolutely normal, completely rational."

"Your report described her as uncooperative. Is that correct?"

"She became highly uncooperative."

"Doctor, is it standard procedure to ask a patient, or an accused person, to repeat a statement several times?" Fierst asked.

"Yes, it is. Absolutely."

"Why is that, Doctor?"

"Sometimes people simply forget part of the significant series of acts. Talking about the events might free something that has been deeply repressed. Sometimes they omit something because they think it has no significance. Sometimes, of course, they have lied, and there is a very high probability that they will contradict what they said earlier."

When Fierst finished with Dr. Palma, he said the state rested its case. Barbara, as a matter of form, requested that the case be dismissed, and was denied.

"Is the defense ready to proceed?" Judge Paltz then asked.

"Yes, Your Honor."

"Very well. Court will recess for twenty minutes, at which time the defense will present its case."

Barbara remained at the table to speak with Paula after the courtroom had been cleared. "Did he leave out anything important?"

Paula shook her head. "I don't think so, but he made it all sound so textbookish, like a statistic."

"That's his job, and he's a pro. But he presented your side thoroughly and that means you don't have to."

"You made him do that somehow, didn't you?" Paula said wonderingly, and then she said, "Oh. That's why Janey came to visit me, isn't it? They thought— Oh."

"Exactly. Go on now and get some coffee, do some breathing exercises or something. See you in a few minutes." She nodded to the matron who had started to shift from foot to foot, just out of hearing distance.

"Everyone in the business knows that character witnesses don't mean a damn thing," Frank had said many times over the years, but he always had called them. The jury didn't know what a meaningless ritual it was. He also said that cross-examination of character witnesses was no more than a test of the intelligence of the prosecutor; he'd be a damn fool if he went after them with spurs and whips.

Barbara had character witnesses lined up for the rest of the afternoon, for most of the next day, and she planned to wind up on Friday with Carrie Voight, to let the jurors mull over the Dodgsons and their spy all weekend.

And give Bailey time to find and bring home the migrant worker.

And to reveal as little as possible about her defense before a long weekend set in.

And give her time to consider Rich Dodgson; consider the direction this case would take next week, time to discover what the best defense would be.

NINETEEN

On Friday the parade of character witnesses continued
with few interruptions from Gerald Fierst, who knew as
well as Barbara that his best policy was silence now.
When one of the waitresses from the Olympus restaurant was on the stand, he asked her if Fridays and Saturdays were very busy, and she admitted they were. So
the fact that she had not seen Craig Dodgson for several
years did not mean he hadn't been there, only that she
hadn't seen him. She admitted that was correct. She had
come to court dressed in the uniform the lounge waitresses wore—a knee-length black skirt, long-sleeved
white blouse.

Cindy Truman, the manager of the restaurant, followed her. She was a statuesque woman, broad in the
shoulders, beautifully proportioned, with satiny skin and
dark hair streaked with gray.

After establishing that Paula had worked there for
four years and had an excellent work record, Barbara
asked where she had worked in the restaurant.

"In the dining room."

"Will you describe the layout of the restaurant,
please?"

She did so succinctly, and when she was finished,

Barbara asked, "So the dining area is completely separate from the lounge?"

"Yes."

"Did Paula Kennerman ever work in the lounge?"

"No. She was an excellent food server; she would have been wasted in the lounge."

She said she knew who Craig Dodgson was and that he had not been in for several years.

"How can you be certain?" Barbara asked.

"About four years ago he came to the lounge with his younger brother, who was a minor at the time. I had to ask him to leave, and Craig Dodgson made a scene. In our business you remember those who make trouble."

Barbara asked her what the food servers wore, and she stood up to show her uniform—a black skirt that came to mid-calf, and a white blouse. She tied on a white apron to complete the outfit.

"Do you know Jack Kennerman?"

"Yes. He used to come in sometimes and wait in the lounge for Paula to finish work."

"When was the last time you saw him?"

"On Friday, April eighteenth."

"Will you tell us about that, please?"

"At first he said Paula had sent him," she said, "and I told him I couldn't release her check without written authorization from her. He said he wanted to put it in the bank to cover checks they had written. Then he demanded to know where she was, if she was hiding somewhere. I told him to get out."

"What was his attitude, his manner?"

"He was loud and almost incoherent at times, contradicting himself again and again. He looked and behaved like a madman," she said flatly.

"When was the last time you saw Paula Kennerman?" Barbara asked, standing by the jury box.

"On Wednesday night of that same week," Cindy Truman said. "She came looking for me because a gentleman at her table wanted to see the manager. When I went to the table, a party of eight, the gentleman said that they had paid the tab with a credit card and added a generous tip, but that they wanted to give Paula a special tip, just for her. He gave her twenty-five dollars in addition to the tip on the credit card."

"Was he flirting with her? Was that his reason?"

Cindy Truman smiled slightly. "I hardly think so. He and his wife were there with their three sons and their wives to celebrate their fiftieth anniversary. He was simply happy with the service."

"Did Paula keep the twenty-five dollars?"

"Yes indeed. She offered to put it in the pool to share the way all tips are shared, but I told her she had to honor his wishes and keep it for herself. She said she would put it in the special savings account for Lori's education. She was very happy because that would take it to five hundred dollars."

When Barbara was finished, Fierst hacked away at Cindy Truman. She couldn't be in the lounge, in both dining rooms, in her office, and the kitchen simultaneously, he pointed out, and she couldn't know what was happening in any of the rooms where she was not present. Could she?

She said quietly that she knew what was happening in her restaurant.

"Mrs. Truman," he said, "on a Friday night you get an influx of customers when the performing arts center closes, don't you?"

"Yes, quite often."

"What does the lounge look like then?"

"People are standing at the bar, others clustered around the piano, or the trio, whoever is performing jazz, and every table is filled, every chair, with other people standing around, moving around. It settles down again after a bit."

"Yet you claim that you know who is in a crowded room like that. Do you have X-ray vision, Mrs. Truman, that lets you see through people, or magical vision that permits you to see around people?"

Barbara objected vehemently and was upheld, and she thought, Touché, Mr. Fierst.

"No more questions," Fierst said with overly theatrical disgust.

Day-care people, kindergarten teacher, baby-sitter, people from the apartment complex, even a librarian who had known Lori and Paula, a woman who worked at the Polk Street safe house, all drew hardly a comment from Fierst. Then, at three-thirty, Barbara called Carrie Voight. It was earlier than she had wanted, but Fierst was acting as if it were his mission today to demonstrate how a trial could be expedited.

Carrie Voight weighed more than three hundred pounds. It was painful to watch her slow progress down the aisle of the courtroom, and it was evident that she could not possibly be seated at the witness stand. Instead a bench was provided, and she sat down at eye level with the jurors.

Her face seemed to have been mashed in, with a protruding forehead and chin, receding nose and mouth. Her hair was cut short and hung straight on both sides of her face, with bangs that covered her eyebrows. She was dressed in a green tent—Barbara could think of nothing else to call her garment.

She was a querulous witness, and Barbara gave her the freedom to talk about herself for a good while. She and Hermie, her husband, had lived in the Farleigh Road house twenty-four years, and today was the first time in six years that she had been outside.

When she had gone on long enough, Barbara interrupted her to ask, "But in spite of your infirmities, you managed to hold a job, too, didn't you? Will you tell us about it?"

She was happy to. "It was like this, see. Mr. Dodgson came by one day and said he heard about me and my troubles, and he wanted to give me something to do, let me feel useful again. He said him and his wife came out to the country for the peace and quiet after living most their lives in big cities, and he didn't want to see that go, the peace and quiet. And he said Mrs. Canby was going to let a lot of women start living in her house and he hated the idea of a lot of loose women making trouble in the neighborhood. And I said Mrs. Canby wouldn't let nothing like that go on. She used to bring me fruit from the trees over there. I said she was a nice lady and he said maybe she was, but she wouldn't be there and who knew about the women who would be there, and I said I was sure I didn't. He was afraid they'd be doing bad things, like abortions maybe, or fighting with men, or screaming and carrying on, or noisy parties, or something. He said alls he wanted me to do was let him know who went in and out, that's all. And I said that I could look over there now and then, but I didn't see what good that would do, and he said, no, they'd rig up something so I could really tell. And they brought this little light that sat on top of my dresser, and when anyone went in the road over there, the light come on. And they brought me this telescope that was on a stand at the window and I could see license plates and everything. I liked that telescope. You know, it kind of opens the world wide open. And he paid me two hundred fifty dollars a month just to tell him who went in there. Just that."

"What did you do when the light came on?"

"I'd write down the license number, if it was a car or truck, something like that, or write down what it had on it, like the telephone company truck. And if it was a person, I'd just write down something like a girl with long hair, or two women, or whatever came to mind, and say if they was just taking a walk and going back, or going out to the orchard, or on his place. You know, sort of what they were doing."

"And then what did you do?"

"Well, if it was daytime, I'd call him on the telephone and tell him what I seen. If it was late, I'd wait until the next day and call him up and tell him."

"Just him? Did you ever call Mrs. Dodgson?"

"He said not to call her, just him, and that's what I did."

"Do you know what turned on the light in your room?"

"I figured it out," she said with a nod that sent her flesh quivering. "I seen that Mrs. Dodgson never went past that sign they put up; No Trespassing sign it is, first one ever on any of that property. And one day I watched one of the girls go past it and sure enough the light come on, so I knew."

"So you could see the cars that entered. Could you see inside the cars, see the people?"

"Oh, sure. After I got the hang of the telescope, I could see right in. And the same car usually brought in the new girls, so I knew to watch those times. I could see them, all right."

"What did you do about nighttime, when it was dark?"

"They bought me some special binoculars, heavy thing it was, and I could see at night with it. Sometimes deer or elk or even a coyote made the light go on, but he didn't want to hear about them. But I looked, just the same."

"Mrs. Voight, just how much could you see from your room?" Barbara went to the stand with the aerial map and moved it closer. "Here's your house," she began, but Carrie Voight was shaking her head.

"That's not right," she said. Her jowls were in motion, and her mouth was pursed so tightly her lips had vanished.

"This map was made from a photograph taken by an airplane," Barbara said. "This is how it all looks from above."

Carrie Voight looked at it with suspicion and shook her head again.

"All right," Barbara said in resignation. "You just tell me what you could see and I'll try to locate it on the map."

It was laborious because Carrie kept backing and filling. She had not been able to see much of anything on the private road past the Canby driveway—too many trees. Neither the Canby house nor the Dodgson house had been visible—too many shrubs and trees. Some of the Dodgson driveway had been visible, not much—too many trees. None of the Gallead property; the fence was too high and he left too many trees out front.

"Are you still employed by Mr. Dodgson?"

"No, ma'am. Couple days after the fire he sent someone to take away all the stuff—the telescope, the light, everything."

"While you were employed by him, did you tell anyone what you were doing?"

"Hermie knew, that's all. Mr. Dodgson said I shouldn't talk about it, people wouldn't understand, and I didn't."

"Did he ask you not to talk about it after you stopped working for him?"

"Well, he said he'd appreciate it if I didn't, but he's not paying me nothing now and I don't have to do what he says no more. Anyways, when people come around asking about it, I figured he must have told—I mean who else would have?—and so I did, too." She lifted one hand in a gesture that seemed meaningless; her hand was tiny, as were her feet, as if inside her hulking monstrous body was a doll-like creature.

"You were in your room on the morning of the fire at the Canby house?" Barbara asked finally. "Will you tell us about that, please?"

"Well, sure," Carrie Voight said. "The light came on and I was already by the window in my chair, the kind that has a motor to help you get out of, and so I just looked out and seen it was Angela and didn't pay much attention. I mean, she worked there, and she stopped to talk to Mrs. Dodgson. And I started to get up, but the chair takes a while, and when I looked out again, Angela was already on the Canby driveway and Mrs. Dodgson was fooling around with the gate to her driveway. I thought she was going in, but maybe not, because next time I looked she was near the No Trespassing sign again. And I didn't look out again until the fire engines come."

Wrong! Barbara wanted to say, but she walked to her table in thought instead. This wasn't what Carrie had said earlier to Bailey. She said, "Let's take it a little slower, Mrs. Voight. The light came on and you looked and saw Angela's car. Did you see her?"

"No. But I knew the car just fine."

"Did you see her daughter Annie?"

"I didn't see nobody in the car."

"And then you started to get out of your chair and didn't look out again for a few minutes. Is that right?"

Carrie Voight sighed and made the small gesture with her small hand. "That's right."

"When you did look out again, you saw the car in the Canby driveway and Mrs. Dodgson by her own gate, doing something to it? Could you see what she was doing?"

"Like I said, I thought she was opening it, going in, done with her walk."

"Did you see her open the gate?"

"No. I said she was fooling with it, like she was going to open it, that's all."

"Is that gate usually locked?"

"I guess so. I seen her unlock it and go out and lock it again after she took her walk. Plenty of times."

"All right, then what did you do?"

Carrie's mouth pursed tight again. "Nothing. Just wanted to get up."

"How long do you think you were out of the chair?"

"Long enough ... I don't know."

Oh, Barbara thought suddenly. "Where is your bathroom, Mrs. Voight?"

Her lips had vanished again. "Down the hall a ways. Not far."

"Did you go to the bathroom when you got out of your chair?"

"I might have."

Ten minutes? Fifteen minutes? "Mrs. Voight," she said kindly, "did you go out of your room, go down the hall to the bathroom and stay there a few minutes, and then return to your chair?"

"Yes." She raised both hands and let them drop gently. She had no lap for them to rest on; they stopped moving where they landed.

"When did you look out the window again, Mrs. Voight?"

"Right when I got back. She was right near the No Trespassing sign. Couldn't miss her in that pink outfit. Then I got myself in place for the chair to take me down and lean me back and I turned on the television, and I didn't look out again. I watched 'I Love Lucy'; it's just a rerun, but I like it. It come on at eleven, so it must have been eleven," she finished in triumph.

"What was Mrs. Dodgson doing when you saw her that last time?"

"Nothing, just standing there. I seen her back, that's all. Oh, then she was tying her shoe, I guess. You know, she bent down like she was tying her shoe. And I didn't look again."

It was twenty-five minutes before five when Barbara finished with Carrie Voight.

Fierst implied that Carrie Voight was a spy, and everyone knew spies were not trustworthy; he implied that everything she had said was a fabrication, an attempt to get even with the Dodgsons because an easy income had been stopped. Barbara objected and he retracted a bit, and then came back meaner, right up to five minutes before five, when he asked. "Did you see anyone else on that private road that morning?"

"No," she said in a near whisper. Everything about her was quivering, her jowls, her hands, the tentlike garment, even her feet.

"Did anyone except Angela Everts set off your light that morning?"

"No," she said, shaking her head.

"No more questions," he said brusquely.

Barbara returned to the only three things of interest to her now: Was Kay Dodgson near the pond when Angela Everts stopped? Was she at her gate, fooling with it, about five minutes later? Was she again near the pond at about eleven?

"They knew," she fumed, back in Frank's house. "That's why they didn't call her. She should have been their witness."

"Well, they found out," Frank agreed. "And by then they were pretty much committed. Way it goes. What I'm going to do is get on my shorts and weed the garden, and later on broil a couple of steaks, and cook plenty of veggies."

She went up to change her clothes, and when she returned, Frank was out in the garden, a ridiculous figure in shorts that were baggy and came down to his knees, sneakers without socks, and a wide-brimmed straw hat. He had put the telephone on the back porch. She went outside and walked the length of the brick path that led from the house to a storage shed at the end of the property, fifty feet away. It was a pretty backyard, with the vegetable garden on one side, backed by a fence covered with vines in bloom. On the other side was a rose arbor, a flower border, shrubbery. Pretty, but too short. She walked back and forth for several minutes and finally stopped near where her father was weeding a row of lettuce.

"What's wrong with it?" she demanded.

He looked up and said, "It's flabby, that's all."

She nodded. Flabby.

"Honey, you made a very good opening statement; pity you didn't listen to what you said. Got it on tape if you want to play it."

"You're taping," she said, and shook her head. "For heaven's sake, they're going to catch you at it. You know that."

He shrugged. "Maybe. Anyway, what you said was you don't have to point a finger at anyone else; all you have to do is raise enough doubts about the case the state's making. You're doing a good bit of that."

"But not enough," she muttered. "Not enough yet."

"Try me," he suggested, and started to wield a strangely shaped hoe, like an elongated diamond.

"Okay. Access. They said the place was sewed up; I showed that it wasn't. Kay Dodgson's story is blown out of the water, and Carrie Voight couldn't see enough."

"Coming down the back woods means a lot of trouble," Frank said, not looking up from his task. "Means someone already knew about the gas, or happened on it. Always risky, counting on happenstance. Why would a

stranger come out of the woods to kill a child and burn
down a house? And vanish without leaving a trace?"

"You're getting into motive," she complained, walking slowly again. "Not a stranger, Jack Kennerman. He
had motive, as much as Paula. She was a perfect
mother."

"Yep, proven by every word in court most of the day.
But she was a battered wife. She was pushed too far
and snapped. The child said something like, 'I want to
go home, where's Daddy,' and she broke."

Barbara scowled at him. "Jack."

"He might have wanted to burn it down," Frank said,
"force her back home, but he's afraid of the woods.
Can't prove he knew the place existed. Not reasonable
to think he'd go fishing, drive back directly to the
house, and conveniently find it empty, or wait for it to
get emptied, and do the deed. Why not do it first and
then set up the fishing alibi?"

"He wouldn't have known it was empty," she said,
coming to a stop. "He wouldn't have known how many
people were supposed to be there. Even if he saw Paula
leave, he didn't see Lori."

Frank stopped hoeing and regarded her thoughtfully.

"Oh," she whispered. "Right back." She ran to the
house and her briefcase with the names, addresses, and
phone numbers of all the witnesses, and she called
Angela Everts.

When Frank shouldered his hoe a few minutes later
and joined her on the porch, she had the phone to her
ear. She held it out so he could hear the ringing.
"Honey," he said, "even if you can't prove Jack did it,
and I sincerely doubt he did, you are still raising all

kinds of questions about the state's case. That's all you have to do. Paula deserves a fair—"

She was looking at him absently, then said into the phone, "Mrs. Melrose?" She paused, then said, "This is Barbara Holloway. I have to see you. There are a few questions I really have to ask. When would be a good time? An hour, this evening some time?" She listened, and nodded. "Fine. At ten in the morning. Thanks."

To Frank she said, "The gate wasn't locked when Angela went up to the Dodgson house to call the fire department."

He waited.

"Why didn't Kay lock the gate that morning? As careful as they were, it should have been automatic with her. We've been asking the wrong question." She stood up and stretched. "For heaven's sake, it's so obvious."

"You planning on letting me in on what you're thinking?" he asked aggrievedly, hefting the hoe as if ready to go back to the garden.

"You going to stop messing around in the dirt and sit down so I can tell you?"

He leaned the hoe against the porch rail and sat down.

"We've been asking why she would lie for a stranger. That's the point Fierst will hammer home when he sums up. What difference did it make to the Dodgsons who did it as long as the Canby place was put out of business? But what if she saw someone and recognized him? What if she is terrified of that person? That would be reason enough for her lies."

In her mind's eye she saw again the look of terror flash across Kay Dodgson's face when she said that Royce Gallead was not a friend, merely a neighbor.

TWENTY

"No DETAILS," SHE said. "Let's try a broad outline and see what's missing. Kay is afraid of Royce Gallead. Maybe he's been threatening, demanding they get rid of the women at the Canby Ranch. After all, his truck and his workers, legal or otherwise, were in sight the morning a photographer was out there. Next time, who knew what might happen? So, Kay learns the house will be empty and she runs home and calls him and tells him to take care of it himself. Then she has to go back out and see if he actually does anything. She must have seen him, or why lie?"

Frank made a grunting sound that she ignored. "She thought there were two little girls," she said. "She never saw Annie. He must have waited until two girls were out. That's why the long delay, why she couldn't just go back in as soon as she saw him. Or maybe she didn't see him until he finished and left."

For a while neither spoke as they considered the problems her scenario solved, and the holes it opened. Finally Frank rose and picked up his hoe again, regarded it as if it were an alien object, and leaned it against the rail once more.

"Gallead was in sight at the range all morning," he

said heavily. "Dozens of people in and out of there on Saturdays. They'll alibi him just fine."

"The more the better," she said. "It wouldn't have taken longer than ten minutes. No one person saw him every second. They were there to learn how to shoot guns, and he doesn't give personal instructions. Ten minutes out of sight, who would have noticed that? Remember when he appeared on the driveway the day I first snooped around the Canby place? He can cover ground, all right."

"You can make up stories all you want," Frank said with a new sharpness in his voice. "Suppose this, imagine that, and it doesn't matter. You can suppose an army moving in. So what? You can't prove a thing playing mind games this way."

"That's what weekends are for," she said. "Damn that Bailey! Where is he? I guess Winnie will do. I have a few notes to make." She got up to reenter the house.

"I'm going to finish weeding," Frank said. "God almighty, God almighty!"

She heard Frank come into the house later and went down to talk to him. He passed her carrying a small basket filled with vegetables—tomatoes, string beans, lettuce, a cucumber.

"No doubt half that jury believes Rich Dodgson is doing God's work against mighty odds; you *might* convince half of them that Dodgsons collectively are scum and lowlife," he growled on his way to the sink. "But you won't convince even that many that not liking your neighbors is reason enough to conspire to burn down a house and kill a little girl. And you can't connect them to whatever scam Gallead's got going. You can't bring in a new suspect at your summation, and you know it.

And there's no cause on earth to call him as a witness. You can't subpoena him and just ask outright, By the way, sir, did you commit murder and arson." He began to wash his vegetables with scrupulous care.

"Dad, relax," she said. "I know all that. I can't prove anything, and I don't have to. But I do have to present an alternative scenario that will make the jury take notice. Not just Jack Kennerman. We both know Fierst will make hash out of that." At least, she thought, if there were two alternatives, she could convince the jury that the state's case was incomplete and even sloppy. Enough doubt? Reasonable doubt? She hoped so.

"What are you planning?" he asked gruffly.

She was surprised at the surge of relief that washed over her, and she thought, Good old Dad, he knew exactly how this could work. "I have a list of things I need to find out. Who was actually at the range that morning? And what is the usual procedure? And to make sure Gallead isn't a total stranger, I have to find a way to connect him to the Dodgsons. And talk with Reggie Melrose. It's possible she saw something or heard something and isn't even aware of it. Maybe she'll connect the Dodgsons and Gallead. And I have to go out there tomorrow and see just how good the line of sight is from the end of the road to the woods. Why did Kay dally there, why not up farther?"

"Not alone," he said. He turned to face her; he looked harder than she had seen him in years, tougher. "Listen a minute," he said. "You have to write out everything you guess, everything you surmise, everything you know already. Two copies, two envelopes. One addressed to Lewis Paltz, one to Sam Bixby. And a big envelope they'll both fit in. After dinner we'll go to the office and put them in the safe."

"You've done this before?"

"I've been here before," he snapped. "And you don't go anywhere alone until this is well behind us. Not to the post office, not shopping, nowhere. Especially not out to the Canby place. You've been warned off; your house was trashed; pay attention. That man threatened you directly; if he thinks you're stepping on his toes now . . ."

She nodded. "That goes for you, too, Dad. We stay together until it's over."

"Agreed. Go on and write your letter and I'll make us some dinner."

"Thanks. And, Dad, I think we're actually homing in on something. My toes are tingling."

"Christ on a mountain," he muttered, and attacked his vegetables again.

Barbara called Winnie Scourby, who arrived at nine, raised her eyebrows at the list of things Barbara needed to know right now, and left again with a noncommittal "I'll try."

They talked until nearly midnight, when Frank went to bed, and she paced and thought for another hour or so, too tense and wound up to even think about sleeping yet. Finally, a soaking bath, a cup of cocoa, and exhaustion unkinked her enough to let her drop into bed and instant deep sleep.

Mrs. Melrose lived with her married daughter and her family in the southwest hills. The house was two-story, with a small apartment that had been converted from a garage, her apartment.

She was a plump, birdlike woman, with a comfortable bosom rounding out her front, and a comfortable bottom balancing her nicely. Her daughter didn't want her to keep working, she said, but she couldn't just sit around, could she? She had a pair of professors now, she said, pointing to chairs for Barbara and Frank, settling herself on a small sofa covered with a handmade quilt. "Four days a week, not hard work, but they're messy—papers and books everywhere, and none of it can be touched. Not easy to clean around papers and books," she said with a nod. Then she asked, "Why did you want to see me? I already told everything I know about the fire and that poor little girl, and what I know is as near nothing as you can get."

She needed little prompting when Barbara said vaguely, "Just background information. What was it like working for the Dodgsons?"

"Oh, them," Mrs. Melrose said with a sniff. "They weren't easy, believe me. Once when I was about five minutes late, not my fault, but a wreck on the road in front of me—why, I thought they'd fire me on the spot. Eleven to eight, my hours, and they wanted me there at eleven sharp."

It was a repeat of what Angela Everts had said: they were fastidious and made a fuss out of every little detail they thought wasn't exactly right.

"But I'm a good housekeeper," she said complacently. "They never found much to fuss about."

The name Royce Gallead meant nothing to her, except that she had seen his sign every day on her way to work. She never set eyes on the man, she declared positively.

Gradually Barbara steered the conversation to the Saturday she wanted to hear about. Mrs. Melrose told them she always drove around to the side of the house and went in the back door. She didn't see anyone that day. "It was like most Saturdays, except she left me a note to clean the refrigerator. She left me notes the days she wasn't going to be there, but not usually on Saturday. Lot of nonsense that was. I always cleaned the fridge on Tuesday and it didn't need a thing. But I got right at it. I knew they'd come in sniffing around to make sure I did."

"Was the door open to the pool room when you got there? Could you see it?"

"No, you can't see it down that hall, but it was open. Chlorine smell all through the hall, and the music was just blasting out."

"And then what? You were cleaning the refrigerator, but you went out to see what was happening? What made you suspect anything was happening?"

"The music stopped, and I heard Angela on the phone yelling at the fire department man. That was a surprise, I tell you, her going in the front door, tracking in dirt and all. I guess she never gave it a thought." She didn't wait for a question this time. "Well, she finished on the telephone and told me, and then she ran out. And Mrs. Dodgson told Craig to go get some clothes on, and she said she would get dressed, and she said as soon as I got done in the kitchen I might as well go on home. She was too upset for anyone to be messing around all day, she said."

"Was Craig in the white robe then?"

"Yes, he was. A hundred dollars that robe cost them. Can you believe it? He came out of the pool and put it on, I guess, and he was standing in the hall in front of the door to the pool. Closed it first, but too late; the smell was already out. And he was dripping water down his hair. He went across the rug to his room in his wet bare feet and I thought she'd tell me to vacuum out his footprints, but she didn't, and it wouldn't have done no good anyway, what with all the other footprints already there."

"Then what?" Barbara prompted.

"Nothing. I went back to the kitchen and finished up, and I checked the dressing room to pick up towels and stuff, but there weren't any, and I went home."

"Nothing was disturbed in the dressing room? Were Craig's clothes in there?"

"Not a thing."

"How long after that did you quit?"

"I didn't quit. Oh, I threatened to many a time, but they were gone most days, and I liked the hours, being away when the kids are here at supper. They're good kids, but they can get loud, you understand? Anyway, on Tuesday—I never worked on Sundays or Mondays there—so when I got there Tuesday, he, Mr. Dodgson, met me in the kitchen and grabbed my arm and steered me right to the pool, yelling like a maniac. Look what you did! he was screeching. One of those gallon plastic jugs that floor stripper comes in was floating in the water. He said the water was ruined, they'd have to have the pool pumped out and cleaned, and it was my fault. He said I didn't go on home like Mrs. Dodgson told me to, that I was in there messing around and knocked over that jug. But I didn't."

"You left right away? You didn't stay at all?"

"Oh, I left, all right. I told him what he could do with his temper fits and his pickiness, and, I guess, a few other things that don't come to mind right now." She looked quite self-satisfied.

Barbara asked a few more questions about what she

had seen or heard that day, and listened to her for another hour.

In the car again, driving to the Canby Ranch, she said grumpily, "So, if the Dodgsons and Gallead didn't want to broadcast that they were associates, they wouldn't be seen together. All right?"

Frank did not say a word.

At the Canby private road she got out near the pond and watched her father's car as it continued up the road. From here, at this time of year, she could not see past the rushes and cattails, which were high, far over her head. She walked up the road until she could see the barn, and stopped almost even with the NO TRESPASSING sign. Frank had stopped at the Canby driveway, and he walked up the road and vanished almost instantly, hidden by the trees. She did not see him again until he appeared at the car once more, stepped over the log barrier, and started toward the house site. There, too, as soon as he got past the car, he vanished. Slowly she walked up the private road, pausing only long enough to look at the padlock on the gate to the Dodgson driveway. A shallow ditch was on each side of the driveway, bone-dry now, but no doubt little rivulets in the spring. She met Frank at the site of the burned house.

Silently she walked to the edge of the woods and kept going until she was near the end of the barn, not far from the orchard. Nowhere along the walk would she have been able to see anyone leaving the house by the back door, she realized. Shrubbery, the house itself, the barn, all would have been in the way.

"What's wrong?" Frank asked when she returned and opened the car door to get in.

"Nothing," she muttered. "Nothing." But she knew she would have to tell him that she had just blown her own scenario. Gallead wouldn't have been able to see when the coast was clear.

It was nearly three when they got back home. They had stopped for lunch, and now Frank said he was going to take a nap. She turned on the answering machine, and they both froze when Bailey's voice drawled, "Reeling him in. We'll be there about ten. You'll need an interpreter. See you." Barbara let out a long breath.

"What kind of interpreter?" she muttered. "Where are they? Why ten?"

"Good God, Bobby, relax! If you can't relax, run up and down the stairs a few times—with your shoes off." He went down the hall to his room and closed the door.

Interpreter, interpreter, she repeated to herself, walking through the first-floor rooms as she thought of who it would be. Roberto, she decided, the young man who was learning how to make false teeth. She phoned him, then went upstairs to the room her father had designated her office by putting a desk, a chair, and a file cabinet in it. It was a fine office, she had to admit, and then forgot about it as she began a methodical review of her case.

She was jolted when her father said from her open door, "You didn't hear a thing, did you? For God's sake, Bobby, leave it be for a while. It's nearly six. Let's talk about dinner over a glass of wine. Downstairs." He turned and walked away.

After restacking some papers, she went down. "Dad, you really don't have to baby-sit me," she said, accepting a glass of wine. "I mean, I've lived all these years without starving myself."

"Someone has to watch over you," he said in a growly voice. "When I was in your state, your mother watched over me like a hen with one chick to guard. She saw to it that I ate, slept, washed. She reminded me to shave. I know where you're at because I've been there."

Barbara had a flash of memory of how her mother had looked after him, shielding him at times from his only child. How jealous that child, Barbara, had been.

"Every man needs a good wife," she murmured.

"Don't be ridiculous," he snapped. "It's got nothing to do with male/female roles. When one sees the need, he or she tends to it, and the other one accepts. With a pretense of graciousness, if that's possible."

"What would it be like to be married to another attorney, with two cases going at the same time?"

"One of them better be making enough money to hire a nanny who'd see to both of them. Scrub them, feed them, remind them to brush their teeth, and then get out of the way."

She laughed. "So let's go out somewhere. And you'll tell me the story about when you were threatened by someone in a case you were handling."

"I will not. My stories are too good to waste on someone who's only half-listening."

He took her to an Italian restaurant, and when they returned home at eight forty-five, he said, "Well, at least you've been well fed with decent food even if you don't know what it was, and didn't taste a bite."

Roberto arrived at nine-thirty. He was lankier than she remembered, and he looked embarrassed and shy when she greeted him at the door and introduced him to her father. In the study, Roberto said, "Barbara, we all miss you. A bunch of us were in Martin's place, and we made a committee so when they clean up your house and get it fixed again, we'll patrol, not the cops, not anyone else. We'll do it, our committee. You're coming back, aren't you?"

She nodded. "Yes. As soon as I can. You didn't tell anyone this address, or that you were seeing me, did you?"

"No! Not even my mother. You say tell no one, I tell no one. Like that."

"Thanks. Now, how about something to drink? A Coke, wine, coffee, beer . . ." He said coffee would be nice, and she left to make a pot. When she returned, he was talking earnestly to Frank about the need to have a trade, a life-long profession.

At five after ten Bailey arrived with Miguel Torres, who was carrying a canvas duffel bag. Bailey looked exhausted. He introduced his companion, who smiled and said not a word. "Drove down from an orchard out of Hood River," Bailey said. "We stopped to eat. He's okay; he slept most of the way, but I need some shut-eye. He'll want a place to sleep."

"We'll take care of that," Frank said. "Does he speak any English?"

"Not that you'd notice. He's a good guy, take care of him. I'm off. I'll call tomorrow." Frank went to the door with him.

"Señor Torres," Barbara said, *"por favor . . ."* She pointed to a chair.

He smiled and sat down. *"Gracias*, señorita." He was muscular, in his thirties, and very dark.

"Roberto, ask him if he'd like something to drink, or wants to use the bathroom. You know."

There was a swift exchange of musical language and Roberto said no, Miguel was comfortable. "He says you're very beautiful," he added. Roberto could hardly contain his excitement at his role in this adventure; his cheeks blazed and his eyes flashed.

Barbara felt her cheeks go hot, and Miguel's smile broadened. Roberto spoke at some length, now sounding like a teacher or a parent, and Miguel's expression changed to one of respect.

"What are you telling him?" Barbara demanded.

"I told him about you," he said proudly. "He didn't understand why you were being so friendly, why you were talking instead of Mr. Holloway. Now he does."

She had Roberto explain that they would pay Miguel, and they would see to it that he had a place to sleep. And she wanted to tape-record the conversation. The exchanges became longer. He wanted to know why, Roberto said.

"Good," Barbara said to Frank. "He's sensible and intelligent." At her words, she caught a gleam of understanding in Miguel's eyes. "You can understand some English, can't you?"

He nodded and held up his thumb and forefinger about an inch apart. "Little," he said.

She suspected it was more than just a little, but she nodded and said to Roberto, "We think the man who hired him was engaged in an illegal activity. We don't think the men he hired are involved, but we need information. That's all, just information."

Presently they had the tape recorder working and Miguel, through Roberto, was answering questions.

He had been hired, he said, by a man in his village who explained that the gringo wanted four men to work for three or four days, that there would be a long drive first and they would be required to stay in the truck. The gringo wanted men who had no English; he was very firm about that. Miguel had no English, he said with a little shrug, and he needed the money. He had a wife and three children and no job. The gringo paid a hundred dollars a day, including the travel time.

When they got there, they had a big room with cots and showers, and plenty of food. They cooked for themselves. They weren't allowed to go outside.

"What did they do there?" Barbara asked. "What was the job?"

"He's coming to it," Roberto said patiently.

They made little boxes first, out of cardboard with print on it. And bigger boxes to hold the little boxes. They wore rubber gloves, doctors' gloves, and put medicine in little containers. They put cotton in the containers first, then medicine, more cotton, and they packaged them. That's all.

Frank got up and left, to return with a pad of graph paper. "How big were the boxes?" he asked Roberto.

Miguel held his fingers apart; five or six inches. Frank started to draw a box and Miguel said, "Señor, *por favor.* I show." He took the pad and sketched rapidly, a box about six and a half inches long and two inches wide. "Up," he said, and held up his fingers, then drew a line from the box upward about an inch and a half. He then drew a small cylindrical container, a pill bottle, one and a quarter inches high, and three-quarters of an inch wide. He looked at his work with a frown, then shrugged and handed the pad back to Frank.

"A little pill bottle," Frank said. "A *real* little pill bottle."

Miguel nodded and spoke rapidly to Roberto. Twelve

little bottles went in the box, he said, and twelve boxes in the big box. He shook his head and spoke rapidly again. First a paper was rolled up and fitted into the bottle. Rules? Miguel shook his head at the word and said something else. Instructions or something, Roberto said, printed paper, very small print, it went in first, then the cotton, the medicine, more cotton, and then the top was put on and sealed with a machine that melted plastic into a band.

"Good Lord," Barbara breathed. "Tamper-proof medicine bottles." Miguel nodded. "How many pills in each one?"

"Dos," he said promptly.

"Two pills? Only two?"

He nodded emphatically and then spoke for several seconds to Roberto.

"He says the pills were very dangerous; that's why they had to wear the gloves. They couldn't let them touch their skin, their fingers, anything. They were all very frightened by them and they were very careful."

"Could they have been radioactive?" Barbara asked, thinking out loud.

Roberto translated and Miguel shook his head and replied with another burst of rapid Spanish. No, the gringo wore the same kind of gloves when he handled them, but if they had been radioactive, he would have protected himself more than that.

"Can you read English?"

"Little," he admitted, and continued in Spanish for Roberto to translate. The instructions were not in English. He didn't know the language.

They kept at it for another hour. Barbara produced a bottle of aspirin and he nodded: Like that, one of the medicines, but smaller. Then he hit his forehead with the palm of his hand. In each little bottle they put one tablet like that, he said, and one different, a capsule, pink and soft. He sketched a slender capsule about an inch long. Pink, he said again. The medicines were kept in plastic jars, separated.

At twelve-thirty Frank said, "These fellows need some sleep, and so do I. Let's wrap it up for now."

Roberto suggested that Miguel go home with him. He could tell him about his school, and Miguel would like his mother's cooking. Miguel nodded. They all stood up. Miguel hefted his duffel bag, and Barbara said, "Just one more question, señor. Since you arrived in the dark and left again in the dark, how did you know that place was here, in Oregon, on that particular road?"

He flashed his big grin and explained to Roberto. They had heard shooting and had been frightened, but the gringo said not to worry and not to ask questions. But he began to think it was like practice, not like the army or bandits. The morning they left, he caught a glimpse of Gallead's sign, the long rifle silhouetted against the sky, and he put that together with practice, and suspected a rifle range. And on the last day, when the gringo's servant brought them some beer and chips, the cash register receipt stuck to the bag. He had been able to make out the words *Eugene, Oregon*, he finished, and spread his hands.

After they were gone, Frank prowled about the house checking door locks and windows, and then stopped at the kitchen table, where Barbara was working with a calculator.

"Bet he came back up with the idea of shaking down

Gallead, and his guardian angel said that was not a very good idea."

"I've been doing the numbers," Barbara said, frowning at her answers. "Each case holds one hundred forty-four individual bottles, and he said there were thirty or forty cases. That's between four and six thousand. Bailey said the truck makes a run about every six or eight weeks." She bit the end of the pencil. "That's not enough for street drugs."

"Could be a new psychedelic," Frank suggested.

"Or an aphrodisiac from Thailand."

"An invisibility pill. One to turn you off, one to turn you back on."

She grinned. "I like that."

"He wouldn't hire local help," Frank said after a moment. "Too risky. I'm surprised he hires anyone. Seems like he could handle it alone over a week or two."

She looked up at him. "I wonder if the Dodgsons know he brings in outside talent?"

Frank started to walk toward the hall and his bedroom. He stopped at the doorway and regarded her for a second, and then said, "Don't answer right now, sleep on it, but I'm thinking we may be in over our heads. This could really be time to talk to the FBI."

She had thought about it already, before Miguel Torres left, in fact. "If they believed us and went out there and broke down doors, what do you suppose they'd find?"

"I know," he said. "I know. Gallead's had time to clear out everything right down to virgin wood. But they'd start an investigation."

"Yes, and six months from now, or two years from now, or five, we might even hear echoes of it, and meanwhile, what about Paula Kennerman?"

Alone later, she continued to worry the question: What was in the little pill bottles valuable enough to pay two thousand dollars for illegal workers to package? Some kind of phony treatment for something incurable? Parkinson's, or Alzheimer's, or even AIDS? People would pay anything for hope. Where did the tablets and capsules come from? Miguel had said emphatically they did not make them at Gallead's place; they just packaged them.

She knew she was wasting time, but she couldn't leave it alone. So, she told herself, Craig picked up ten thousand doses of something somewhere. Where didn't matter, she decided; he said he went up and down the coast from Mexico to Canada, even to Hawaii. He could hide ten thousand doses easily enough, even if he was stopped repeatedly and searched for marijuana, coke, anything. All that was bulky, and he was dealing with very small items. His father had a supply of paper for the information sheet, or instructions; he could print and deliver five thousand to Gallead without involving anyone else. Same for the various boxes. That must be Dodgson's department, also. And Royce Gallead was the packager. Then, someone had to deliver them. Craig Dodgson, she decided. He had the perfect cover for numerous trips throughout the year—his involvement with the anti-abortion groups.

Her head was reeling when she gave it up at last to go to bed. Until they knew what the stuff was for, they were no better off than they had been yesterday, or last month, she thought tiredly as she went up the stairs.

TWENTY-ONE

SHE HAD BEEN up for over an hour before Frank appeared, looking grumpy and rumpled, wanting a cup of coffee, and no talk.

"I got hold of Carol Burnside," she said. "I told her we'd pay expenses, a room at the Hilton for two nights, the works. She said okay."

"Who the hell is Carol Burnside?" he growled, and then shook his head. "Don't tell me. Don't tell me anything yet."

"She's the photographer Dodgson bitched about. I need to spend a few hours at the office later on, reading to do."

"Don't talk," he mumbled, and carried his coffee back toward his room.

She followed him through the hall. "Where's there a pharmacy open on Sunday, with a working pharmacist?"

"Christ almighty!" He entered his room and slammed the door.

While her father shopped in a supermarket with a pharmacy, she browsed in the aisle of over-the-counter medications waiting for the pharmacist to finish up what he was doing. She held a container of baby aspirins, which she had opened, and another of Dramamine, and was studying a pink capsule that the label said was a time-release decongestant, when the pharmacist approached her smiling. The smile vanished when he saw the open medications. He was a bald, middle-aged man with thick glasses.

"Now, something I can help you with?"

"Maybe," she said. "I hope so. Can you think of any medication that would require two different forms, one like this baby aspirin and one like this capsule?" She held out her hand for him to see.

He looked at her suspiciously. "Baby medicine?"

"No. For an adult."

"Maybe if you tell me what it's for, I can tell you what it is," he suggested.

"I don't know what it's for," she said. "Only that one is a pink capsule and one is a white tablet, and they go together."

He shook his head. He glanced at the open containers with a pained expression; then he noticed the Dramamine. "For motion sickness?"

"I don't think so. But, tell me, does Dramamine come in different strengths?"

His suspicion increased. "No. Take one or two about half an hour before the problem is expected, and then again four to six hours later if it persists. Is that all, miss?"

"I suppose it has to be," she said, and started to walk away. "Oh, there is something. Can I buy the smallest pill container you have?"

"Just the pill dispenser? No medications?"

"Well, these," she said, holding up the over-the-counter medications she had opened.

He walked stiffly past her, back through a door into the pharmacy, and brought up a clear plastic container from under the counter. "Like this?"

"Is that the smallest?"

He slapped it down on the counter, looked again, and brought out a smaller one, about one and a half inches high. "They don't come smaller," he said.

That morning she had divided all her material into two stacks, one dealing with Paula and the Canby Ranch, and the other concerning the Dodgsons and Gallead. For several hours that afternoon in Frank's office she reread Dodgson's newspapers, consulting her notes frequently, making new notes more frequently. Her student researchers had done their work well. Under the various headings they had listed the papers by dates, the editorials and articles by page and paragraph. Frank had added his notes and cross-references. It was easy to find everything. And the office library, down the hall from her father's office, was up-to-date; in it she had found a medical reference volume on prescription drugs, which she consulted again and again.

She began to pace the long wide corridor. She liked the offices when no one else was around, the subdued lighting, the silence, the many closed doors that suggested secrets. She had a flash of déjà vu, a time when she had been eight or nine; her mother had brought her to the office one night, to deliver something to Frank, who was working late. Barbara had stayed in the corridor, walking back and forth, pretending she had an office here, that she was in charge, all this was hers, the library, the large stenographers' room, the little secretaries' rooms, all of it; everyone here worked for her. "You going to be a lawyer, honey?" her father had asked from his doorway, his arm around her mother's waist. They were both smiling, the way parents smile at children and make them stiffen and deny everything. "No way," she had said firmly. But she had known then that yes, she was going to be a lawyer. She couldn't be her mother, who had been very pretty but hadn't *done* anything. Now she knew how invaluable her mother's help had been to her father, but she hadn't seen it then. Frank had not tried a single murder case since the death of his wife. No more dealing with life and death, he had declared by his actions, never his words.

Barbara reached the end of the corridor near the reception room; the offices occupied twice as much space as they had at the time of her memory; now the corridor made a right turn and continued with another bank of closed doors on each side. The firm had taken over the entire third floor of the building. She turned to retrace her steps one more time, banishing the past, bringing her mind once again to the medicines. Finally she went back to Frank's desk, pulled the telephone closer, and punched in the numbers for Christina Lorenza in San Jose.

"Ms. Lorenza," she said when she reached the woman, "my name is Barbara Holloway; I'm representing a client in a murder trial in Eugene, Oregon. A few weeks ago, you very kindly talked to a detective about your experience with Craig Dodgson. May I ask you to clarify a point?"

"No! Leave me alone! I shouldn't have told her anything. She said no one would bother me again. Leave me alone!"

"Ms. Lorenza, just one question, please. Were the pills Craig gave you white and pink? Were they different?"

"Look, I'm calling Craig and telling him you people are after him. I'm not taking any more calls, no more questions, nothing. Go talk to him! Just leave me alone!" The phone banged down.

"Oh, dear God," Barbara breathed and redialed swiftly, to get a busy signal. Maybe she won't call him, she prayed, and pushed the redial button again. A minute later she did it again. She called the operator and asked for a verification of the number, and was told the phone was off the receiver. Don't call him, she said under her breath. *Don't call him!*

She was listening to the busy signal a few minutes later when she heard a tap on the door. It was after five. She should have called her father at five, she remembered, and said, "Come in." As the door opened and he stuck his head around it, she hung up the phone and said, "I can't believe I did anything so stu—"

Frank put his finger to his lips and opened the door all the way. Bill Spassero was behind him. "He dropped in," Frank said, pointing his thumb over his shoulder. "Thought you should hear what he has to say."

Was the man getting even blonder? Dyeing his hair lighter? She began to jam papers into her briefcase. "Well?" she said, not looking up. Suddenly she said, "What do you mean 'dropped in'?"

"I looked up Mr. Holloway in the records room and found the property transfer," Bill Spassero said. "Anyone can do it." He stood awkwardly at the door while

Frank entered all the way and dropped into one of the visitors' chairs. "Anyway," Spassero went on, "I kept thinking about something and today I decided you should know. I've been watching you in court," he said. "I know, you haven't really noticed. I wouldn't be looking over the audience much either the way the court is packed every day with *those* people, but I kept seeing this one man, Terry Bossert, and I saw that one of the police officers I know was keeping an eye on him too, so I asked about him."

Frank made a beckoning gesture. "Why don't you sit down and tell it?" he said.

Whatever it was, he already knew, Barbara realized. She nodded at Spassero, who was watching her for an invitation. "You might as well sit down," she said. "Who is Terry Bossert?"

Spassero took the chair next to Frank. He didn't look relaxed. "His real name is Terence Bossini. Up until he came here to work with Royce Gallead in the gun shop, he was a small-time crook down in Las Vegas— bouncer, messenger, gofer, hustler, you name it. He served time for extortion, got out on parole, and a couple of years later came up here. As far as the police know, he's been straight since then, but he lives in a pretty big house up on Spyglass Hill, not a cheap neighborhood. Everything's in the name of the woman he lives with."

Barbara studied him through narrowed eyes; he appeared perfectly guileless. Finally she asked, "Why are you telling us this? What do you want?"

"Remember when I asked you that?" he said with a hint of a grin. "Same answer you gave me. Nothing. I don't want anything. I just thought you should know if you didn't already."

"I already thanked him for the flowers," Frank drawled. "And for the tip that the Dodgson crew was heading for parts unknown last week."

"You did that, too?"

Spassero nodded. "I ran into Doneally and brought up the case, said I was really glad to be out of it since the way you were going after the Dodgsons made it appear they were involved. He said you wouldn't hound them for long, they were taking off. I thought you might want to know that, too. He might suspect I tipped you. Ran into him again and he cut me cold," he added with a shrug.

Frank stood up and said, "If you're done with those newspapers, I'll start putting them back. Bessie will have a fit if they're not where they belong." He picked up the stack that Barbara had put aside.

"I do want one thing," Spassero said then as he also stood up. "After all this is over, can I talk to you? I've been watching, making notes of your courtroom style."

Frank left the room while he was talking.

"I'd really appreciate it if you'd explain a few things later. Why you did this, not that. This question, this nuance, not that one. You've opened up this case in a way I wouldn't have thought possible. I'd like to learn how you saw it, how you knew where to go. You know: You mentor, me little brother. Would you do that?"

She stood up and came around the desk. "Mr. Spassero, I am grateful for your tip about the Dodgsons, and even the roses, and today especially. You've been very helpful." She held out her hand to him.

He ignored it. "You haven't answered my question."

"I'll have to think about it. I believe we're more than even now, don't you?"

He shook his head. "Not yet. You saved my life. All I've been able to do is maybe give a tiny nudge for your client. Not the same." He smiled. "I'll be in your debt forever, I'm afraid. Besides, as soon as you begin to think about being even, or if I might have the upper hand, your answer will be no. Won't it?"

She laughed. "Come on and shake hands and then get the hell out of here. I have work to do."

They shook hands very properly and he turned to leave. She followed. "Mr. Spassero—"

"Bill," he cut in.

"Bill then, no more flowers. No perfume, no candy. Okay? Really, they don't impress me."

He nodded. "As you say. I'll think of something that will, though."

As soon as she saw him out through the reception room and relocked the entrance door, she marched off to find her father.

"You can come back in now," she said tartly. "I have to tell you what happened."

His smile was benign when he emerged from Bessie's room and walked with her back to his office, but his expression became grim when she told him about the call to Christina Lorenza.

"If she gets Craig and he knows we're this far, she might be in danger," Barbara finished.

"She won't get him yet," he said, frowning. "He's out getting the yacht ready for a trip. He might come back in tonight, though. Maybe she'll cool off by then."

"And maybe she won't."

"Right." He was scowling at his desktop, drumming

his fingers, back in his own chair. She went out to the reception desk, turned on the computer, and called up airline schedules. When she returned to Frank's office a few minutes later, he was riffling through a card file.

"There must be someone I know down there," he grumbled.

"Forget it. I have a flight at six-thirty. I'm going down myself."

"You can't do that!"

"Save it for the car ride, Dad," she said, picking up her things. "Come on. I have to check in in twenty minutes or they won't hold the seat. We just have time."

"Barbara," he started, but she was already out the door.

In the car she said, "You'll have to put Lucille on in the morning and keep her talking. I'll be back by afternoon."

"We can send Winnie," he protested.

"She wouldn't have a chance. Christina knows her already."

"But look at you, how you're dressed."

She was wearing jeans and a T-shirt that had butterflies all over it. She shrugged; if it turned cool, she had a sweater. "And get on the phone to make sure they have a car waiting for me," she said. "I'll get there by nine, not too late for a drop-in visit. I'll call you or leave a message on the machine. Oh, sic Bailey onto Bossert, and tie in Gallead and Kay Dodgson before she left Las Vegas."

"I called Bailey already," he said. "Same idea. There's a link there, all right."

"Good. Anything else?"

He grunted and turned onto the airport road.

* * *

Christina lived in north San Jose in half a duplex house with a neat little dead lawn in front and a screaming child next door. Barbara rang the bell and smiled at the young woman who opened the door. She smiled back.

"Hi," Barbara said. "I'm looking for Christina Lorenza."

"That's me." She was short, five feet two, and plump without being too fat. She had long blond hair, much of it down in her face. Her smile was very nice.

"Ms. Lorenza," Barbara said, "I have to talk to you. You're in terrible danger."

She started to close the door; Barbara held it open. "I spoke with you on the phone a couple of hours ago," she said, "and I flew down here from Eugene, Oregon, to tell you that you're in danger."

"I'll call the police if you don't get out of here!"

"After I talk to you, you might really want to call the police, but first let me tell you why you're in danger."

"Who's there?" a man yelled.

"It's that lawyer from Oregon, the one who called before."

He appeared behind Christina, a slender, bearded man with horn-rimmed glasses. He looked out past Barbara. "You alone?"

"Yes." From next door came a more piercing shriek.

"Let her in," he said with a shrug, "and then we can toss her out again together." He grinned.

Grudgingly Christina opened the door and moved aside. She looked both angry and frightened. "You flew down here from Oregon? Tonight?"

"Yes," Barbara said. "You want to see the airplane ticket?"

Christina nodded and Barbara found it in her purse and handed it over. They both examined it.

"I really need to talk to you alone," Barbara said when she had the ticket back. "Five minutes is all it will take."

"You go ahead," the man said. "I'll finish up making the sauce." The fragrance of tortillas and chilies was mouthwatering.

"What do you want?" Christina demanded as soon as he vanished around a corner of the room. She had admitted Barbara to a living room without much furniture—one chair, a wooden sofa with a few pillows, and a lot of books everywhere.

"Have you called Craig Dodgson?" Barbara asked, keeping her voice low.

Christina shook her head. "He wasn't there. And then Dale came home. But I will tomorrow."

"Ms. Lorenza, Craig Dodgson is involved with some very dangerous people. You have information about Craig that puts you in a dangerous position. As long as they think no one knows about you, you're safe, I'm sure, but if they suspect you have told anyone—"

Christina was shaking her head. "You're just crazy," she said. "I don't know anything about him. I went out with him a couple of times, that's all."

Barbara reached into her purse, brought out the small prescription bottle, and emptied it into her hand, one baby aspirin, one pink capsule. "Did the medicine he gave you look like this?" she asked, holding her hand open before Christina.

"Yes," she said, startled. "I was seasick."

Barbara returned the tablets to the container and brought out the Dramamine. She shook one out and showed it to Christina. "This is for motion sickness. You take one or two every few hours, not a couple of days apart."

"But he said ... What did he give me, then?" She had gone very pale.

"I don't know for sure. But he mustn't suspect that you've told anyone about it, that you're at all suspicious. Will you please not call him?"

Christina shook her head. "What did he give me?" she whispered. "Why would he lie about it? Maybe another kind of motion-sickness pill? The pink one, it's a suppository. He said when you're so sick you can't take medicine by mouth. That sounded right. . . ." She shook her head harder. "It was for sea sickness!"

"Maybe it was," Barbara said. "And you're fine, so there's nothing to worry about, just as long as he doesn't know you've talked about it."

"I left a message on their machine," Christina whispered. "I just said it was Chris and I'd call back."

"Did you leave your number?"

"No."

"Does he know where you live now? Have you kept in touch?"

"Not since I got my job. I wrote him a postcard about the job. He knows where I work."

How many women named Chris did he know? Barbara bit her lip and then drew in a deep breath. "How long ago was that?"

"A couple of years."

Would he remember? Would he have kept the card? She said slowly, "I don't know how safe you are. In your place, I'd take a trip and stay away for a week or so. Could you do that?"

Christina looked ghastly in her pallor. "I don't know. I'll have to talk to Dale. But I can't tell him. . . . I don't know. I can't believe it wasn't exactly what he said. Why would he . . . ? How will I know when it's safe again?"

"You'll know," Barbara said. "Read the papers and you'll know." At the door she said, "I think you should tell Dale. From what I've seen of him, I think that he would be okay, that he'd be supportive." And if he wasn't, she thought, without voicing it, ditch him now before it's too late.

It was ten-thirty when she found a motel with a vacancy. She called her father and told him about Christina.

"Something Winnie could have done," he grumbled.

"Maybe so," she said, too tired to argue. "Get some sleep. See you in court."

She still had to go out and get something to eat and buy a toothbrush. She eyed the bed longingly, but went back out. So much for staying together, she thought, driving again, looking for a drugstore or grocery store or restaurant, whichever came first. There he was alone in that house that Bill Spassero had found without any trouble at all, and she was a thousand miles away in a strange town, starving. Togetherness, she thought bitterly.

That night she dreamed she was running away from the ocean where pink capsules and white pills formed waves that rose and rose and crashed down on her like a tsunami.

TWENTY-TWO

ON MONDAY, SHE was dismayed to see the haggard expression on her father's face when she spotted him on the second floor, outside the door to the little room they shared for meals. As soon as he saw her, he straightened and his expression changed to relief.

"God, you had me worried," he said, embracing her.

"Sorry, Dad. Stuck on a plane that wouldn't get off the ground. I think they had to glue the wings on or something. How'd it go?"

"Fine. Fine." He opened the door and they went in. "Lucille was grand," he said. "Not a dry eye in the house by the time she was done." He poured coffee from a thermos and handed it to her. "You look beat."

"Flying does that to me." She had stewed on the plane, which had been delayed two hours. Heath Byerson had met her at the airport, whisked her home to change her clothes, and then sped her to the courthouse. It was now a quarter till two. Fifteen minutes and she was on. She sipped the coffee. "What have you heard from Bailey? Winnie? What's been happening?"

"That will keep. Craig got back in last night. If he got that message from Christina, and if he remembers her, and they put that together with your vanishing act this morning, they know too much. We have to tread very softly, Barbara."

"I know," she said. "I have to call Roberto. There's something I want Miguel to do today."

"Tell me what it is; I'll call while you tackle the doctors."

She told him. She wanted Miguel to assemble facsimiles of the boxes he and his co-workers had put together at Gallead's place. Frank's expression darkened again, but he nodded.

Then, all too soon, it was time for her to be back in court, time to call the doctor who had examined Paula and have him explain the extent of her injuries before the fire.

She had two cracked ribs on the right side, he testified, and a bruise from her shoulder down the length of her left arm, as if she had been hit with enough force to drive her against a rigid, unyielding structure.

"Dr. Fellowes," Barbara asked, "would you say it was possible for someone with injuries like that to carry a can of gas that weighed eleven pounds for three hundred feet, and then to methodically throw that gas around using both hands, being careful enough to avoid getting any on herself?"

Fierst objected. The doctor couldn't say what was possible or not possible. Barbara rephrased the question, but it was the same question.

"In my opinion it would be most unlikely," Dr. Fellowes said. He described the muscles involved, how the nerve endings affected the muscle groups, the weakness that resulted.

In cross-examination Fierst said, "Dr. Fellowes, it has

been stated that it required two adult women to restrain
Mrs. Kennerman when they arrived at the fire. It would
seem that she had very good muscular coordination.
Isn't it possible—excuse me, likely—that—"

"Objection," Barbara snapped. "Mr. Fierst might as
well answer his question himself. He is leading the witness blatantly."

Fierst rephrased.

"Sometimes," Dr. Fellowes said, "the most grievous
injuries can be overridden by a psychological need to
act in a momentary situation of extreme anxiety."

"Do you mean that people can act even if they're injured badly?" Fierst asked bluntly.

"That's putting it in—"

"Dr. Fellowes, just yes or no. Can people take action
even if they are badly injured?"

"Well . . . yes. Sometimes."

During her redirect examination, Barbara asked, "Dr.
Fellowes, you said 'a psychological need to act in a momentary situation of extreme anxiety,' didn't you?"

"Yes. Those were my words."

"Let's break that down a little. Would an action that
requires five to ten minutes of cautious behavior be
what you mean?"

"No, absolutely not."

"Would you explain why not, please?"

"Yes. Cautious behavior indicates that the person is
conscious of every action and any possible consequences, and is taking them into account. In the psychological state I'm talking about the conscious mind is no
longer functioning in a normal way; it is bypassed by
the subconscious mind, which assumes control over the
body and does not allow awareness of pain to interfere

with its intentions. In that state a person behaves in a manner that often appears irrational, and is irrational in that the person is not taking into account the consequences of his or her actions. Pain is what prevents a person from adding further trauma when there is already an injury. A person in the state I am describing can and often does seriously aggravate an existing injury."

"And a person who is behaving rationally and deliberately could not ignore severe pain to such an extent that the original injury would be made worse?"

"A person might want to, but the body protects itself and prevents such actions most of the time. Tremors, weakness, even fainting may result if the person attempts such action."

The emergency-room doctor who had treated Paula after the fire and then the dentist who had treated her over a year ago followed in quick succession.

The marriage counselor was the next witness. She made it clear that although she had permission from Paula Kennerman to disclose information about their sessions, no such permission had been obtained from Mr. Kennerman and therefore she could not divulge anything he had said, or what she had said to him.

Barbara nodded when she explained this. "We'll stick to Mrs. Kennerman," she said. "Did she say why they were there?"

"Yes. She told me he had struck her and she would leave him if things couldn't be worked out."

"Did she have proposals to make, suggestions to offer?"

"She said if he ever hit her again, she would leave without any discussion. And he had to make a contribution toward the welfare of their child, her future education. Those were the two demands she made."

"How many times did they consult you, Mrs. Maggiore?"

"Four."

"And did they reach an agreement that they both accepted?"

She paused, then nodded, as if she had to consider if this was revealing what Jack Kennerman had said. "They had an agreement."

"Was it an agreement that satisfied Mrs. Kennerman's original demands?"

Again she paused, and then with some reluctance said it was.

"Did you advise Paula Kennerman to have psychological counseling?"

"No."

"Do you sometimes advise your clients to do so?"

"Yes."

"Did you so advise Jack Kennerman?"

She tightened her lips. "I'm sorry, I can't answer that."

When court recessed for the day, Barbara turned to Paula, whose eyes were puffy and red-rimmed. "How are you holding up?" she asked.

Paula shrugged. "Okay, I guess. None of this matters, does it? I mean, how things were before, what it was like before? They'll say that's past and done with. What matters is only that one morning, that one day."

"Hey," Barbara said. "We're making a case. You're tired or you'd see that we're making real progress. Don't fade out on me now."

Paula smiled wanly. "Oh, I'll be right here, won't I?" She stood up. "Lucille told them today that she offered you eight hundred dollars. She shouldn't have done that. It's for her kids. Eight hundred dollars! That's a laugh, isn't it?" Tears were standing in her eyes; she turned abruptly and nodded to the matron, ready to go.

"Okay," Barbara said as soon as she and Frank were inside his house. "Give."

"Bailey's coming over," he said. "Don't know yet what he's dug out. But Craig's getting the yacht ready for a long trip. Winnie dug up a good informant over there, and it seems that she knows each and every time that yacht moves an inch. For instance, Craig and Rich took off Monday after the death of that little girl. Went out for two hours, returned, drove back home." His forehead wrinkled. "Let's have a glass of wine. If there's anything else, it'll come to me."

"Did you get Roberto?"

"Oh, that. Yes." He led the way into the kitchen and got out the wine and three glasses and poured for her. "Here. We've earned it." He poured another glass and sipped it with approval. "Roberto and Miguel probably have the boxes done. I told him to keep away from here, to leave everything at Martin's for Bailey to pick up later. Roberto wants his committee to patrol this street," he added dryly. "Let's go out to the porch. This weather isn't going to last, but it's nice out there right now."

It was. The evening was cool, pleasant, the yard fragrant with blooms and grass. No trace of the drought was visible from the porch. Barbara wondered if her rhododendron had died; she felt she had been away from home for a very long time.

"Oh," Frank said, settling himself into a lounge chair, "Bill showed up in court this morning and left as soon as he saw I was at bat. Did he show up again?"

She shook her head. "I don't know. I didn't look." She couldn't remember any trial where she had so resolutely ignored the spectators.

She could feel the tension oozing out of her, feel herself relaxing, and she wanted only to go to sleep. Abruptly she put down her wineglass. "I think I'd better get something to nibble on," she said, standing up. "I just realized I haven't had a bite since breakfast. And that was seven-thirty." She went in for cheese, crackers, whatever she could find. In his house there were always good findings.

Back on the porch, eating cheese, she said with her mouth full, "When this is all over, I'm going to get drunk."

He nodded. "I did that a couple of times. Last time I did, the next day the judge summoned me to hear my penalty for contempt of court. I was in a sorry state, believe me, hung over like you wouldn't believe, red-eyed, bleary, unshaved, and the son of a bitch thought I'd been on a crying jag or some such foolishness. He said a hundred dollars and my remorse were punishment enough."

They both laughed. She never had seen him showing any effects of too much to drink. Another little secret he and her mother had shared, no doubt. And now, after a warning heart attack, he was off everything but an occasional glass of wine and, very rarely, a fine brandy after dinner. But she could drink, she told herself, and she would get smashed. She took another piece of cheese.

"This is a good time of day," Frank said after a moment. "You've put in the hours, every muscle in knots, and then you sit out in the cool of the evening and feel the knots coming undone. Remember that little table we used to have out in the backyard, with the shade umbrella? We'd sit there with a drink, a little cheese, and you'd play in your sandbox or on a swing, and I used to think if there's a god in heaven, this must be what he had in mind for us."

"We'd stay out until the sky turned dark enough to see the first star," she said, speaking as softly as he had done.

"So you could make your wish," he added. "We all wished on the first star. You never would say what you wished for, secretive little thing."

"I don't even remember what I wanted in those days," she said. She felt certain that what he had wished for was a little brother for her, a son. He should have had his son. Never by word or act had such a longing been expressed, but he should have had his son.

A long silence followed until he said, "What I wished for every damn night was just one thing. Never fudged, never cheated, went through the whole rigamarole—Star light, star bright . . . and always ended up with the same wish: Whatever it is she's asking for, let it be. Please, let it be."

She felt every muscle stiffen as if a synapse had fired, preparing her for flight. *No more,* she wanted to cry at him. It seemed that the still air had begun to vibrate with unspoken words. Just last year, at long last, all that wishing was coming true, they had both felt that, known that. *Don't you dare pity me!* she wanted to say. She set her glass down hard, but before she could say anything, Frank shifted and stood up.

"Then," he said brusquely, "wishing time over, bed for you, and back into the dragon mode for me—find a way to head them off at the pass, cut them off at the knees, mow them down one way or another." He had not looked at her during this brief interlude; he didn't look at her now.

"Were you ever sorry?" she asked, her voice hoarse with relief that he had stopped, that the unspoken words remained silent.

For a long time she thought he would not answer; he had never voiced any of the ambivalence that beset her. Calling that other persona his dragon mode was the closest he had ever come.

Then he said matter-of-factly, "Yes, I was. Times you see that your case is cooked, that you missed the boat and nothing you've tried is going to make it work out. You're sorry. Times you smell something so rotten it takes your breath away. You're sorry. Then you get mad again, and back you go. You can't unscrew the universe and fix yesterday, but you sure, by God, can work on today and tomorrow. If not us, who? The Doneallys of the world?"

He started for the door, but paused to put his hand on her head gently. "Honey, you're so good, you scare me sometimes. If not you, who?" He went inside.

He would be doing something about dinner, she knew, and felt not a twinge of conscience. He liked to cook. He could eat every meal out, or hire a cook, but he preferred to do it himself most of the time. The few times she had prepared dinner for them, he had been brave and excessively polite.

Then she thought about the things they had just said, the things they had not said, and she did feel guilt. For years after her mother's death she had refused to talk about her, had not let Frank talk about her. She had not understood it, could not have rationalized it in any way, and she was doing it again, she knew, and felt helpless to act differently. Frank wanted to talk about Mike, he needed to talk about him, and she couldn't.

The sky had darkened; if there had not been so much smoke in the atmosphere, stars would be visible. Would she have made a wish? She shook her head. Unscrew the universe, fix yesterday?

Abruptly she stood up. Bailey was late. She started to pace the length of the garden, and continued to pace until Bailey called hello from the back door.

"Where the devil have you been?" she yelled back.

He was laughing when she reached the house, and he had a glass of wine already. "Haven't they taught you not to throw rocks at the frog who might turn into Prince Charming at a moment's notice? Not even verbal rocks."

Frank stepped out of the kitchen down the hallway, and he yelled, too. "I don't mind cooking for you guys, but damned if I'll do it while you talk out of hearing. Get in here."

They sat at the kitchen table while he did mysterious things with pork chops. "Okay," Bailey said, "jackpot. It was Bossert/Bossini that did it. Should have spotted him myself, but, hell, I've never done anything except lose money in Las Vegas. Anyway, here it is."

Kay Dodgson, née Kay Darling—Barbara winced,

and he said he was sorry—was a dancer at a club down
in Las Vegas before she married Rich Dodgson. Exotic
dancer, he added with a leer. Later, when Rich was on
the road almost half the time, she took up her old profession after the boys started school, but only when
Rich was not home. And the assistant manager of the
club, he said, was Royce Gallead. Terence Bossini was
the bouncer.

"Boy oh boy," Barbara said. "Wow!"

"What I thought," Bailey said modestly. "Threw me off
because Gallead surrendered a California license when
he showed up here. He took a roundabout way when he
hightailed it out of Las Vegas, a couple of years down in
L.A., and then here. Once I knew to put him in Vegas
fourteen years ago, it was easy. He, at least, didn't change
his name."

"So fourteen years ago Rich quit selling, Kay quit
wriggling, Bossert quit bouncing, Royce quit managing,
and they all ended up here," Barbara said with satisfaction. "What do you know about that? They all hit the
jackpot at the same time, made a killing—enough to set
up two businesses, buy property. How about that!"

"Lady Luck smiles on her favorites," Bailey said, and
got up to refill his glass.

Frank had made pork chops with rosemary and garlic,
spinach with a yogurt dressing, and tiny red potatoes
crisped in butter.

"If I had a cook like you," Bailey said with pleasure,
"I'd never leave the house. And you'd never leave the
kitchen."

"It was wonderful," Barbara agreed. "I don't want to

move, but I have to get to the office before it gets much later."

"Tonight?" Frank asked in surprise.

"Yep, 'fraid so. About an hour and a half at the most."

He scowled over his glasses. "You might have mentioned it before. We could have eaten earlier."

"Have you rush dinner? Never!" She laughed.

"All right. All right. We'll run you over there and then go on to Martin's and pick up those boxes. Better take something to put them in, keep them out of sight. When will you be done?"

It was almost eight-thirty. "Ten," she said. "No later, I swear."

"Right. We'll come back at ten for you. Or thereabouts."

The office building had a small arcade on the street level with several retail shops, two elevators, and a stairwell. The upper floors were mostly attorneys' offices, and were never completely unoccupied; attorneys often worked strange hours. Lights shone through windows here and there on all six floors; dim lights were on in the shops on the ground floor. The building was a block away from the courthouse. This area was deserted after offices closed, with few pedestrians, no open shops; the attorneys' offices were the satellites around the center of government, and when lawyers worked at night, they worked alone.

When they emerged from the elevator on the third floor, there was a light on in one of the offices off to the left of the reception desk; Frank strode down the hall to see who was working late. "Les Smithers," he said, re-

turning. "He'll be in and out of the library. If his whistling gets to you, tell him to cork it." Les was one of the
junior attorneys who had a habit of whistling between
his teeth while he read.

Bailey and Frank left right away, promising to return
at ten, and she went to Bessie's office to collect the papers she wanted to reread. She took them back to
Frank's room and started, but realized that she could
hear Les whistling in the library, a dozen feet or so
from here. She closed the door, but in a second or two
she heard something fall, and he called out, "Sorry."
She gritted her teeth, gathered up everything, and
marched down to Bessie's office, around the corner
from the library, out of hearing no matter what he did.
Les, of course, was working with the library door open.
His whistling followed her until she closed Bessie's
door.

Her student researchers had been so thorough, she
marveled, reading her notes again. Three times in the
past year the *Weekly Valley Report* had been late, although the dates were right. She found the three papers,
and the papers for the following weeks, searching for an
explanation. In December, a snowstorm in the mountains had delayed delivery. In August of last year, a
power failure at the printing plant had occurred. And
one time there was no reason given. On Wednesday,
April twenty-third, the paper had been delivered that
had been due on Monday. She reread the editorial and
the news stories, and then folded the paper and put it in
her briefcase. *Cork it, Bessie,* she thought; *don't complain. I'll bring it back.*

She got up, turned off the lights, and went to the
door; fifteen minutes before ten; good timing, she

thought. She stopped after one step through the doorway, her hand still on the doorknob. Something was wrong. There was complete silence, and, she realized, the hall lights were off. She never had been here at night when the hall wasn't dimly lighted. Even as she thought this, the light from the library was turned off, and now the only light that showed anywhere was a tracery around Frank's door, which she had not closed all the way. She backed up and reentered Bessie's room, and pulled the door almost closed, listening. Had Les done something stupid to the lights? She shook her head; he would have yelled out about it. Then a flashlight beam shone on the corner door, Frank's door; it moved up and down, came to rest on the doorknob, and was turned off. She closed the door all the way, holding the knob, releasing it slowly to still a possible click. She backed away. She could not lock it; Bessie never had installed a lock. Some of the offices were locked each evening, others not. Her father kept his locked; Bessie didn't.

Faint light seeped in through the blinds, but she did not dare turn on a lamp. She didn't know if light would show around the edges of the door. She put her briefcase on the floor and groped in her purse for a tiny penlight, and, using it, she went to the desk and the telephone. She was starting to punch in the numbers of her father's phone, when she shook her head and hung up. Not him. Not anyone from this room. Whoever had gone to Frank's office knew she was not there; maybe he thought she had gone to the rest room; maybe he was on his way there. Or maybe he would start trying doors up and down the hall.

Rest room, she thought then, and played her light

around the side wall. There, a door to a bathroom Sam
Bixby and Bessie shared. She ran to it, and then had to
go back for her briefcase; he mustn't know she had
been in here, if he looked in. Sam's door would have a
lock, she felt certain. *It would have a lock,* she repeated,
and opened the door to the bathroom, as dark as a pit
inside. She reached across the tiny space, found the opposite door, opened it, and drew in a breath of relief.
The bathroom doors both had simple locks in the door-
knobs. She locked the one to Bessie's office and hurried
across the room to try the hall door. It was locked.

Now she ran to the desk and fumbled in her purse,
searching for her address book, still afraid to turn on a
light, using the penlight sparingly. She had to keep it on
when she opened the book and found Heath Byerson's
number. Everything was taking so long, she thought as
she did the numbers, listened to a distant phone ring.
No answering machine, she prayed. *Please no machine.*
She had left Sam's door open to the bathroom; her gaze
was fastened on Bessie's doorknob, which looked like a
pale ball floating in the dark. Enough. She would know
if it moved. Then a woman's voice was in her ear.

"This is an emergency," Barbara whispered. "I have
to talk to Heath. Is he there?"

"I can't hear you," the woman protested. "Can you
speak up?"

"No. Get Heath."

He was there almost before she finished. "Who's
that?" he demanded.

"Barbara Holloway. I'm at Dad's office, and there's
an intruder. Can you hear me?"

"I hear you. Stay cool. Two minutes." He hung up.

She replaced the phone, and then froze with her hand

still on it. The bathroom doorknob turned, and turned again, harder. He could force it, she knew; those locks wouldn't keep anyone out who really wanted in. Without a sound she pushed her briefcase under Sam's desk, crawled in after it, and crouched as low as she could. For what seemed a long time there was a profound silence, and then she heard the hall door being tried; the doorknob turned, turned. And silence again.

The offices were a labyrinth; he couldn't know which ones were locked without trying them all. There was the library, and a larger file room, and the stenographers' room, the secretaries' rooms. . . .

Two minutes, she told herself. Just two minutes. Maybe he would realize it was hopeless, leave. Stay cool, she ordered when she realized she was trembling.

It had to have been five minutes or longer, she thought in despair. Where were they? Maybe Heath hadn't called anyone. Maybe he was on his way. What if her father came first, surprised the prowler? She bit her lip and eased out from under the desk, crept to the door, put her ear to it, listening.

Then she heard someone shouting, "Ms. Holloway? Where are you? It's the police!"

She started to beat on the door, hesitated. A trick?

"Barbara! Barbara!" Her father's voice sounded panic-stricken.

"In here!" she yelled. "Sam's office."

The door was shoved open and Frank grabbed her and held her. He was shaking harder than she was.

Now she heard a siren, and many voices. "Did they catch him?" she asked, her words muffled against his shoulder.

"No. They're still searching." His voice was thick, almost unrecognizable.

She drew back and examined him. He was as pale as death. "I'm all right," she said. "It's over."

"He sneaked up behind Les. . . . It could have been you. God, it could have been you."

"How bad?"

"Don't know yet. Bad. Come on, let's go to my office and sit down." He kept his arm around her shoulders as they walked back to his room, where Bailey met them and put a glass into Frank's hand, another one into Barbara's.

"Take a drink," Bailey said, "and then look at this."

On the desk was a picture of Barbara, the glass smashed and Frank's paper cutter stuck in the middle of her forehead.

"Don't touch it," Bailey said. They all sat down and waited, listening to the police officers in the corridors, in the other offices.

Presently Heath Byerson appeared with a police lieutenant. "How are you?" Heath asked Barbara.

"Okay," she said. "What about Les? How bad is it?"

"They took him to the hospital. No report yet. He's alive, that's a plus."

"Look at that," Frank said, pointing to the picture. "How'd he get in here?" he demanded. "Where's the watchman?"

"We found him," Heath said slowly. "He took a bashing, too. He's alive, that's all I know. He was dragged under the stairwell, his keys gone. They're still gone," he added, and then said to Barbara, "You up to making a statement yet?"

She told them, and the lieutenant made notes. He asked

the questions after she finished. Although he was thorough and patient, she could add nothing. She had not seen him, had not heard him, didn't know who he had been.

"He wore gloves?" Bailey asked.

The lieutenant nodded. "They're lifting smudges, that's all." He glanced around Frank's office, the picture on the desk. "We'll do this room soon as you folks leave."

"And the weapon?"

"He kept it."

"Sounds like a pro," Bailey commented. "Not one of those crazies who've been hanging around."

"We're considering that," the lieutenant said. "Tonight we'll keep a man outside your house," he told Frank. "You can leave now. I'd change the locks here," he added grimly. One of the police officers came in with Barbara's purse and briefcase; she had forgotten them.

There was a brief discussion of how they would get back to the house. Heath wanted to drive them, but Bailey had his car in the parking lot, and finally it was decided that Heath would tag along, see that they got home safely, and wait there until someone came on duty.

"You're not going to like it when you get outside," he said. "Reporters. They'll follow us. I'm afraid your hideout is blown from now on."

Bailey went out to bring the car to the entrance, and Heath escorted them to it, with officers on each side of Barbara and Frank. The reporters were there, the television cameras, a crowd of onlookers. Flashbulbs exploded, questions were screamed at them, a microphone was shoved past one of the officers, who knocked it out of the way, and from the crowd a woman's piercing voice shrieked, "Next time you get it, bitch!"

TWENTY-THREE

WHAT IF SHE had not gone to Bessie's office? What if Les had not been there? What if her father had arrived to find an intruder? What if *he* had had a gun? What if she had called out to Les? What if she had not become alarmed by no lights in the halls? The thoughts chased themselves like a dust devil in her head. Bailey had started to talk about it, and Frank had said later, tomorrow. How carefully she and her father had examined each other, searching for what?

She had got to bed late, after twelve, and now her legs twitched, her head ached, her back hurt, and sleep was in the next county over. Twice she got up to look out a window to make certain the police were there. She summoned the sound of the wind in fir trees, whispering, whispering. . . . Finally, trying to make out the words, trying to understand, she fell asleep.

Bailey showed up even before Heath Byerson the next morning. "Thought I'd hang in close today, tomorrow, in case something comes up the last day or two the way it does sometimes," Bailey said in his offhanded way.

She wanted to order him to keep an eye on her father,

not get far from him, but she thought he already knew that. "Any word about Les?" she asked.

"In surgery. They flew him up to Portland last night. The watchman's in better shape, still in intensive care, still critical, but in better shape than Les Smithers."

Today there was a group of people outside the house—same people, same signs, same cameras, same shouted questions. "The neighbors will love this," she murmured to Frank.

"Fuck 'em," he growled, and, with a firm grasp of her arm, walked to the waiting car.

Outside the courthouse the crowd was larger, more unruly, and Frank was firmer, his hand on her arm harder. The bailiff met them and said she was wanted in the judge's chambers. He escorted her.

"Good morning, Barbara, sit down," Judge Paltz said when she entered his chambers. Fierst was already there; he looked harried, concerned. They exchanged nods. "How are you?" Judge Paltz asked Barbara when she was seated.

"Fine," she said. She suspected that she looked like hell warmed over.

He studied her for a moment, then nodded. "The jury is getting very perturbed over the length of this trial," he said. "I have reassured them twice already that it will end soon. And even though they are being sequestered, whenever there is so much outside tension connected to a trial, they seem to sense it, and even to echo it. Barbara, I have no idea what viper pit you're stirring up, but if it has nothing to do with the trial we are all enjoined to facilitate, I advise you to put down the stick until this trial is concluded." He held up his hand to forestall any response she might make. "I have never lost an attorney, for either side, during the course of a trial at which I acted in my judicial capacity," he said. "And I don't intend to now. Barbara, until this trial is concluded and a verdict is in, I am placing you and your father under full protection of this court. You will have police protection around the clock for the duration of these proceedings. And I want to know how long you estimate your defense will continue. When will you be done?" he asked bluntly.

"I'm hoping tomorrow," she said.

"Very well, that will leave Thursday for your summations, and for the jury to begin its deliberation." He stood up. "I hope you both will cooperate and expedite this trial to the fullest extent possible. No delaying tactics, no grandstanding. Is that understood?"

They both said meekly that they understood, and he said to Barbara, "You understand that the protection of this court will cease as soon as the verdict has been rendered?"

"Yes, sir," she said.

For a time he regarded her with no expression on his face, then he nodded. "Take care, Barbara. Take care." And he sent them out.

She reported briefly to her father before they were summoned to the courtroom. Frank had changed overnight, she realized. Last night he had looked haggard, like an old man, but today he looked mad as hell. And that was fine, she thought, because that was exactly how she felt—mad as hell.

Paula was very frightened; she clutched Barbara's hand and examined her. "Are you really all right?" she asked. "I heard the news, read the paper. . . ."

"I'm okay," Barbara said. "Relax. Look at it as a positive event, in fact. We're scaring the shit out of someone." She smiled at the young woman, and after a moment Paula smiled also, but it was not a good smile.

Barbara called her next witness.

Janey Lipscomb appeared to be too young to be a professional psychologist who dealt with the ugliest of human tragedies—domestic violence. As she recited her credentials, her work, it became clear that she was exceptionally well qualified, however.

"Dr. Lipscomb," Barbara said, "do you recall the day you and I talked? What I said to you?"

"Indeed," she said. She dimpled, and added, "I made notes as soon as I got to my desk."

"In your own words, will you recount our meeting?"

She did so succinctly.

After she finished, Barbara asked, "When you saw the child, Annie Everts, what was your appraisal?"

"She was extremely disturbed, traumatized by the events that she had assumed responsibility for." Annie had no memory of the day, she went on, but she was having nightmares, and had reverted to infantile behavior. They had talked that day, and the following week Mrs. Everts had brought Annie to the offices where Janey worked. Annie had played out the events there.

"Will you explain how the children 'play out' the traumatic events that bring them to you for help?"

Janey dimpled again, briefly. "We have cutouts—furniture, animals, trees, things of that sort, and dolls, a playhouse, other structures, boats, cars, a wide variety of stage props. The children select what is appropriate and position the objects in a way that satisfies them. Sometimes the scenes are fanciful, sometimes quite realistic. Often it is during this period of reconstructing where the events happened that there is a release of the repressed memories."

"So Annie set the stage and then played out the events using dolls?"

"Yes, that's right."

"Did you videotape her play?"

"Yes. We do that in order to watch it with the children and talk about the actions."

Barbara produced the videocassette and had her identify it, and then said, "Your Honor, I would like permission to play this cassette at this time."

"Objection!" Fierst cried. "May I approach the bench, Your Honor?"

Judge Paltz beckoned him and Barbara.

"Your Honor, the public defender represented Mrs. Kennerman at the questioning of that child. Defense and the prosecution both agreed not to call her as a witness because of her age, and to bring in further testimony that is not subject to cross-examination at this time is a direct violation of that agreement."

"Your Honor," Barbara said, "the day the child was questioned she was panic-stricken. Present were two police officers, one in uniform, neither of them trained in child psychology. Also present was William Spassero, who is not trained in child psychology. Annie said whatever seemed to satisfy them, and then she repressed the entire incident and became a very troubled little girl. I argue that this tape is the proper cross-examination of the prosecution's statement from her. They could have done it this way, if they had chosen. Dr. Lipscomb is a highly trained professional who is entirely neutral in this matter, as she has testified."

Judge Paltz looked off into space for a second or two, and then said, "In view of the fact that there were so many unqualified people present, none of whom appreciated the difficulty of obtaining a statement from a child, and none of whom objected to the method of the interrogation, we will view the cassette at this time. Meanwhile," he added, "I shall take under consideration if this is a proper procedure, and if I find that it is not, I will so advise the jury. You may proceed, Ms. Holloway."

There was absolute silence when the television came on to show a little blond girl at a table with a playhouse. She picked up some wooden dolls, only two inches high, and said, "They're going out to pick mushrooms. This is Mom." She put the Mom doll and a few other dolls behind a row of trees. The upstairs of the dollhouse had a bed, nothing else, and downstairs one room had a cutout TV and a couch, and another room had a refrigerator. Annie played both roles, one doll on the bed, the other one moving around it, then both dolls going to the TV, and the kid doll lying down on the couch. The Annie doll said in falsetto, "If you're just going to suck your thumb and go to sleep, I'm leaving." She walked her doll out the kitchen, through the door, and to the nearest tree. "The lady was tired," she said, and leaned another doll against a tree. "She's sleeping," the Annie doll said, falsetto, and then she reached across the table to an apple and began to bounce another doll up and down, and in a new voice, called, "Come here. See what I'm making." The Annie doll flew across the space. "That's an apple tree," Annie said in her normal voice, "not really a big apple. Fern can make crowns, not for real, but flower crowns."

"Where's the kid?" the Fern doll asked. "What were you doing?"

"Watching cartoons. She went to sleep."

The Mom doll was moved to the apple, and asked, "Where's the kid?"

Annie repeated what she had said, and the Mom doll was placed behind the trees again; the lady doll was moved to a point about halfway to the house, and in a moment the Annie doll and Fern dolls were put behind the trees.

Barbara stopped the cassette there. Annie had gone on to play out watching the fire, the ambulance, the police, all of it. "Dr. Lipscomb," Barbara asked then, "when you talked to Annie and watched the cassette with her, did she change any of the details we have just seen?"

"Nothing. This is what she remembers."

When Barbara said she was done with the witness a few minutes later, Fierst was taken off guard. It was evident that he had expected Janey to talk about Paula. He hesitated, and then tried to make Janey admit that she knew what information Barbara had wanted from the child. Janey was very pleasant, and very firm with him.

"Exactly how did this cassette come to be in the hands of the defense, then?" he snapped.

"After Annie began to respond to therapy, and then reverted to her normal behavior, her mother was deeply grateful. It was her suggestion that if the cassette would be helpful to Ms. Holloway, she should have it. Mr. and Mrs. Everts both agreed to release it to her. Ms. Holloway was quite surprised."

Poor Gerald Fierst, Barbara thought with almost malicious satisfaction. He had little left to do with this witness. She could imagine the long list of questions, accusations, innuendoes he had prepared, and would not be able to use. He tried, however.

"Dr. Lipscomb, did you visit Mrs. Kennerman in jail?"

"Objection," Barbara said. "Improper cross-examination; the matter has not been brought up in direct testimony."

"Sustained."

He had her talk about her practice. Did she treat women said to have battered-wife syndrome? Survivors? Rape victims? Janey talked fluently and well about her practice, but he could not connect her in any way to Paula. Finally he sat down.

"Just one more question," Barbara said. "How is Annie Everts now?"

Janey smiled. "She is a healthy, normal little girl."

"Everyone wants to take her home with them," Frank said during the recess.

"I want her to be a witness every time I'm in court," Barbara said.

"Have you looked around the audience this morning?"

"Nope. Why?"

"Do. You have groupies. And they're using a metal detector on everyone coming in. Good old Lewis." He handed her an envelope. "For both of us."

"Not again," she groaned, but this note was from Sam Bixby. The firm was behind her one hundred percent; anything she needed, just say the word.

"Seems someone let him in on the fact that the

barbarians aren't just at the gate but actually broke through," Frank said with a grin. "Now it's a family matter."

When they returned to court, she looked out over the people; the room held no more than forty spectators, and it appeared that half of them were from her neighborhood. Martin and his wife; Juanita Lopez, her next-door neighbor; most of the Delgado family; Mrs. Searles; even Roberto's mother. Paula's sister, Lucille, with her husband; the three students, who had been there every day. In the back row she spotted Bill Spassero. He grinned, and she nodded at him, at her friends. The others were still there, but they no longer made up a formidable wall of hostility.

She called Carol Burnside, a slender dark-haired woman in her thirties. She testified that she had gone onto the Dodgson property in order to get photographs of the elk one morning back in February. She indicated on the aerial map where she had stood, where she had photographed.

"But you didn't print them. Why not?"

"Too dark. And when there was just beginning to be enough light and I saw them, something scared them off. They turned back into the woods."

She identified the photographs as hers, and Barbara had them admitted, all without any objections from Fierst. He didn't care, she understood, how bad a picture she painted of the Dodgsons because he would agree that they were not nice people, but that it didn't matter.

Reggie Melrose was her last witness before lunch. She told again how she had gone to work at eleven; about Angela's phone call to the fire department; the smell of chlorine in the house. Barbara questioned her closely about the note to clean the refrigerator, about the usual procedure with the pool-room door. Mrs. Melrose talked freely, but her dislike for the Dodgsons was perhaps too apparent to make her a good witness.

"You say Mrs. Dodgson told you to go on home as soon as you finished in the kitchen. But you looked for laundry first? Why did you do that?"

"Well, it didn't mean much for her to say take the rest of the day off. And I knew he—Mr. Dodgson, I mean—would have a fit when he saw all those tracks in the living room, and a double fit if he saw dirty towels or dirty clothes around. So I looked, and then I went home."

"You didn't find any clothes or towels to wash?"

"No, ma'am. Not a thing, and then I thought, Well, I could always tell him she told me to leave, if he got on me about it."

"What kind of tracks were in the living room?"

"I guess Angela tracked in mud when she came in, and then Craig left wet tracks to his room. It was a mess, all right. That was the kind of thing they usually went on about, tracks on the rugs and such."

"Who hired you, Mrs. Melrose?"

"He did. Mr. Dodgson."

Barbara had her tell about the day she was fired. When she finished, Barbara asked, "Where was the floor stripper usually kept?"

"In the pantry, off the kitchen. I used up the last of it in March and he ordered a new gallon. That's where it was last time I saw it, in the pantry."

"Had you been using it for anything on Saturday?"

"No, ma'am. Back in March I did the floors."

"Was the container open?"

"I don't know. It must have been or it would have sunk, wouldn't it?"

Barbara nodded. "Mrs. Melrose, who usually gave you orders?"

"She did sometimes, like clean the refrigerator that day. He did mostly."

When Barbara sat down, she scribbled a note to her father. *Did they drain the pool? Who did the work?* She turned her attention to Fierst then. He had very few questions, and they emphasized the fact that this witness did not like any of the Dodgsons.

When he was done, Barbara asked, "Mrs. Melrose, did you see Mrs. Dodgson or Craig before Angela Everts arrived that morning?"

"No, ma'am."

Barbara thanked her and she was excused. Barbara could feel her toes tingle all the way up to her knees.

"Don't talk," she said when she and Frank were escorted to their room, this time out the jury door through the twisting halls with jury deliberation rooms on each side, up a back elevator. She hardly noticed. After a glance at her, Frank kept silent. He inspected their lunch while she stood at the window, and a minute later, when she opened the door and went out to the corridor to walk, he said nothing.

She started and looked at him without awareness later when he touched her arm in the hallway. "It's one-thirty," he said.

Her eyes focused again; she looked at her watch, and said, "Shit!"

"Yep. Come on."

Inside the room she picked up a sandwich, took a bite, and put it down again. Cardboard. "Dad, who do you know in the FBI?"

"A lot of them. Why?"

"You have to tell someone you trust that they have to keep an eye on the Dodgsons, Gallead, and Bossert tonight."

He snorted. "Tell Carter Heilbronner they're smuggling diamonds, is that enough?"

She eyed him curiously. "I don't know. Would it be enough?" Then she said with a touch of impatience, "I don't care what you tell him. They just have to keep all of them under surveillance tonight. Not the district attorney's office or the local police; the FBI." She put her coffee down and went to the door again. "I have to go to the bathroom."

"You think they're going to skip, all of them?"

Again she studied him with a curious intensity. "I think someone might try to kill Kay Dodgson."

TWENTY-FOUR

TODAY KAY DODGSON was wearing another of her designer outfits, coordinated down to her nail polish. A soft rose-colored cashmere suit, silk blouse, hose; she could have posed for a fashion magazine. Her jewelry was lustrous pearls—dangling earrings, a strand of pearls gleaming against the pink blouse, a pearl and diamond ring.

"Mrs. Dodgson," Barbara began, pointing to the aerial map, "was this gravel driveway there when you bought your property?"

"Yes, of course. It went from the private road out to Spring Bay Road."

"And you took out that end and put in your own driveway when you built, is that right?"

"Yes."

"Did you continue to use the remaining section of driveway?"

"Now and then, but mostly just for a way to get to the private road and take walks there."

"Later, after the Canby Ranch became a haven for women, you felt compelled to add the gate. Is that right?"

"Yes," she snapped.

"Did you put on a padlock?"

"Yes, we did."

"Do you keep the gate locked at all times?"

"Yes, of course. We don't want anyone taking a shortcut through our yard to Spring Bay Road."

"Where do you usually keep the key to the padlock?" Barbara asked.

"It's on a rubber bracelet that we hang on a hook near the back door. When I go out, I slip it on my wrist."

"Mrs. Dodgson, was the gate locked the morning of Saturday, April nineteenth?"

"Yes. I told you, we keep it locked."

"And you locked it when you returned from your walk?"

"Yes."

"How did Angela Everts get past it that morning? Did someone go out and unlock it for her?"

Kay Dodgson hesitated, and then said, "I don't know."

"Do you customarily give your housekeepers a key to the gate?"

"No," she said. Her clipped manner had changed, a new wariness had appeared.

"So if she simply opened the gate and drove through, you must not have locked it that morning. Is that right?"

"I don't remember," she said, almost defiantly.

Barbara nodded. That was the best possible response for a witness who didn't want to answer questions. "Is it possible that someone came after you, from the private road, along your gravel driveway, and that person forgot to lock the gate again?"

"No, it isn't," she said. "No one came until Angela."

"Did something happen that upset you, made you forget to lock it?"

"Objection," Fierst said. "The witness has already said she doesn't remember. How many times must she repeat that?"

His objection was sustained, and Barbara asked her about her walk that morning. Did she go to her gate and open it? Did she go back to her house as soon as Angela was in the Canby driveway? Did she return to the pond after that? Was she still there at eleven? Did she remember unlocking the gate? Did she remember tying her shoe? It took a long time; Kay Dodgson stuck to her original story.

She had been well coached, Barbara thought; it would have been surprising only if she had not been after all this time. "Mrs. Dodgson," she asked, "you have stated you are the bookkeeper–business manager of the Dodgson Publishing Company. Is that correct?"

"Yes, I am."

"Where did you go to school to learn bookkeeping?"

She moistened her lips. "I just picked it up."

"For a million-dollar business? You handle the insurance, the withholding taxes, pension plans, orders, all of it with no training?"

"Yes. We started small and as the business grew I kept learning more."

"Mrs. Voight testified that Mr. Dodgson paid her monthly by check. Did you ever see those check stubs or the check register with her name?"

"No. Yes." She had nearly worn her lipstick down to nothing. "I don't remember."

"Well, consider it this way. When you balanced the

checkbooks, where did you account for that sum? Was it a business expense?"

"Objection," Fierst said. "The witness has said she doesn't remember."

"The witness said she doesn't remember Mrs. Voight's name on check stubs or in the register. I am asking her about the sum, two hundred fifty dollars a month."

"Overruled," Judge Paltz said in his firm quiet way.

Kay Dodgson didn't remember.

"Who made out the payroll checks at the printing press?"

"I did."

"Did you sign them?"

"No."

"Who signed them?"

"My husband."

"Who made out the checks for household help?"

"I did. He signed them."

"Do you have a joint checking account?"

"Yes, of course."

"Do you use it often for your own purchases, your own personal items?"

"Yes."

"Do you sign those checks?"

Her cheeks flared, and the color washed out again rapidly. "Yes," she said in a near whisper.

"When was the last time you wrote a check for more than a hundred dollars that you signed?"

Fierst objected and was sustained.

"Who buys your clothes?" Barbara demanded.

Fierst objected and was sustained.

"Do you drive your own car?"

"Yes, of course."

"Is it registered in your name?"

She didn't remember.

"Who bought your car?"

Fierst objected and was sustained.

"Who hires the employees at the printing company?"

Her husband.

"Who hires household help?"

"He does. He likes to deal with people himself and I don't."

"Do you have any voice in the people he hires or fires?"

"Yes, of course. We talk it over first."

"Are you present when he interviews people he hires?"

"Usually."

"Were you there when he interviewed Mrs. Everts?"

"No. I mean, I don't remember."

"Were you present when he interviewed and hired Mrs. Melrose?"

"I . . . I don't remember."

"Did you discuss firing Mrs. Melrose?"

"Yes, of course. We had been thinking of it for some time."

"Where were you when he fired Mrs. Melrose?"

"In my room; I didn't feel well."

"Did you see the floor stripper container in the pool before your husband fired Mrs. Melrose?"

"Yes. We all saw it. He said leave it alone to show her why we were firing her."

"When did you see it, Mrs. Dodgson?"

She shook her head. "I don't know. I don't remember."

Barbara pressed her about it until Fierst objected.

"Mrs. Dodgson, did you ever question your husband about any items in his check register that you had to enter in the books?"

"No," she said faintly.

"So, if he is paying other informants two hundred dollars a month, three hundred, whatever the amount, you would not know about it. Is that right?"

"No!" she cried. "He wasn't."

"But how can you be certain if you never ask him to explain his checks?"

"He . . . he looks over it with me."

"Ah," Barbara said, nodding. "When he looks over the books with you, does he say this is for business, this is personal?"

She moistened her lips and hesitated. Barbara waited. Finally she nodded. "Yes, he does."

"So you simply enter items where your husband tells you, the way a secretary might do. Do you do the arithmetic?"

"I'm the bookkeeper!" she cried.

Barbara walked to her table and stood by it regarding Kay Dodgson, who looked her age and more now. Her lipstick was gone; her face was pasty. "You stated last week that before you and your husband came to Oregon to start a business he was a salesman and you were a housewife in Las Vegas. Is that correct?"

She nodded, then said yes.

"But were you not also a dancer, Mrs. Dodgson? Didn't you work for a casino called Aces Up?"

"No!"

"Weren't you what they call an exotic dancer?"

"No! No!" Her hand flew to her mouth, which was visibly trembling.

"Wasn't your stage name Kay Darling?"

"No!"

"And wasn't the assistant manager Royce Gallead?"

Kay Dodgson looked as if she would faint, or become hysterical. Both hands were pressed against her mouth hard, and her eyes were wild now, her gaze darting everywhere. She was shaking her head violently; the dangling earrings flew back and forth.

"I'm sick," she said. "I'm going to be sick!"

"For God's sake, leave her alone," someone behind Barbara yelled, and another voice rose, and another. "Stop attacking her! She's not on trial here! Get the baby killer!"

Judge Paltz was banging his gavel. "This court will be cleared. There will be a ten-minute recess for the witness to compose herself. The bailiffs will detain anyone making a scene, and those persons are held in contempt of court." He stalked off.

"The cat's in the fire," Frank muttered when they were alone. "Carter Heilbronner will see us both as soon as we're done here. At the house. Bailey will let him in. And Bill Spassero spotted Bossert in the corridor, carrying a cane. They grabbed him and seized it, just a cane. He was tossed out and told to stay out. He'll get a lawyer."

His words were staccato, his expression fierce. Altogether he looked exultant, and probably he was more excited than he should be, she thought. On the other hand, she could not account for her own feeling of great detachment, as if none of this had anything to do with her. What emotion she would feel if she dared let herself would be a terrible sadness, she thought.

"Bill Spassero again," she murmured.

"Someone else probably would have spotted Bossert, but it was Bill that did and got him out of here."

"Did Bailey find out about the pool-cleaning company?"

"You bet. They pumped it out on Tuesday, the day Dodgson fired Mrs. Melrose. Bailey's talking to the guys who did the work now."

"They're gluing Kay Dodgson back together," she said, and went to the door. "I'll be back in a minute." She went to the rest room that had been put off limits to everyone except those who had proper identification. The women who worked up here must be hating this, she thought. She washed her face with cold water and reapplied her own lipstick and then regarded the stranger in the mirror. "Shark," she murmured to the face.

The glue job on Kay Dodgson had been hasty, Barbara thought when she resumed. Kay Dodgson was pale, and she was very frightened; her gaze flickered here, there, everywhere but on Barbara. She kept looking out over the audience as if searching for someone.

"Mrs. Dodgson," Barbara said in a conversational tone, "you know that the state of Nevada keeps a register of those who work in the various casinos, don't you?"

"I don't know."

"They do. Did you work as a dancer in a casino called Aces Up?"

"Maybe, when I was very young."

"Before you married Mr. Dodgson?"

"Yes."

"And later, when he was working as a salesman and

was away from home for many months of the year, didn't you return to work?"

"We needed the money," she said. "I worked a little, just to help out, when one of the girls couldn't make it. Not full-time."

"I see. Did this continue, your part-time job as a dancer, until you left Las Vegas and moved to Oregon?"

She was moistening her lips already. She nodded. "Just part-time, not often."

"Was Royce Gallead the assistant manager of the club where you danced?"

"I don't know."

Barbara shook her head. "Mr. Gallead was assistant manager of the club where you danced until the summer of nineteen seventy-eight, the same year you and your husband moved to Oregon. You knew him very well, didn't you, Mrs. Dodgson?"

"I don't remember," she whispered.

"Did your husband approve of your dancing while he was out of town?"

"He . . . he . . ." She shook her head helplessly.

"Did he know you were dancing all those years?"

"I don't know. We didn't talk about it."

"You never told him, did you, Mrs. Dodgson?"

She hesitated and then said, "We didn't talk about it."

"Mrs. Dodgson, didn't you have a separate checking account, all your own, your own money that no one made you account for?"

"I was saving," she whispered, "so we could move, start the business."

"Did you make a contribution to the business?"

"No," she said in such a low voice Judge Paltz asked her to repeat it.

"You couldn't, could you?" Barbara asked then. "He would have demanded to know where the money came from. Isn't that right?"

"I don't know," she whispered. She was so pale, her makeup looked garish in contrast to her pallor.

"Did Mr. Gallead ever threaten to tell your husband about your work?"

She looked down at the dais before her. "No," she whispered.

Barbara went to the exhibit table and picked up the photographs taken by Carol Burnside. "Mrs. Dodgson, do you recognize the background in this picture?"

After no more than a glance, she said, "No."

Barbara pointed out the details, showed the spot where Carol Burnside had stood to take the picture, reminded the jury of the resultant call Rich Dodgson had made to Mrs. Canby, and again held the photograph out to Kay Dodgson. "This is the fence around the Gallead property, and this is his truck. Someone is opening the gate, and five men are standing near the truck, one of them stretching. Mrs. Dodgson, were you aware that Mr. Gallead was importing laborers in the dead of the night to do some work for him?"

"Objection!" Fierst called. "We don't know anything about that shadowy photograph, or the figures in it. Counsel is making unwarranted assumptions without proper groundwork."

He was sustained.

"Wasn't Mr. Gallead the one who became angry over the incident?" Barbara demanded. "Didn't he insist you get rid of those women before something else happened?"

She was still studying the photograph. "I don't know," she said.

"Mrs. Dodgson, on the morning you spoke with Angela Everts and she told you the Canby house would be empty, didn't you see it as the answer to Mr. Gallead's insistence that you do something? Didn't you go home and call him and tell him the house would be empty? Didn't you go back out to watch for him, to see if he would actually dare do anything? Didn't you see him that morning?"

Fierst was yelling objections and Judge Paltz was banging his gavel, but Barbara got it all out in a furious, demanding voice, and she knew Kay Dodgson had heard every question.

While Fierst was stating his just cause for objecting, Kay Dodgson said in a low voice, "Yes." Fierst shut up to stare at her.

"Yes what, Mrs. Dodgson?" Barbara asked.

"I called him. I thought I saw someone. I wasn't sure who it was, or that I even saw someone. And I ran back home."

And then the cat was really in the fire, Barbara thought as the courtroom erupted into a cacophony of voices and the rustle of people scurrying out—reporters, she thought, without looking around. She kept her gaze on Kay Dodgson and waited for Judge Paltz to deal with the pandemonium in the room. She removed the photograph from before Kay Dodgson and returned it to the exhibit table, and then stood with her arms crossed, waiting.

When order was restored, she said, "Mrs. Dodgson, will you please tell us exactly what you did that morning?"

Kay Dodgson did not look up. In a low voice she repeated, "I called him."

Barbara sighed. "You called from where? Which room?"

"The kitchen."

"Did you go into the family room?"

"No. I just went back outside."

"Was Craig swimming when you called?"

"Yes."

"Then what did you do?"

"I went back out to the private road, down to the pond, and watched for him."

"And you saw what?"

"Just a shadowy figure. I wasn't sure. I'm still not sure what I saw. I was afraid and hurried back home."

"Where did you see the figure?"

"If I did," she said, not looking up. Her voice was faint; the courtroom was absolutely silent now. "Up past the Canby driveway, crossing the private road."

"Mrs. Dodgson, did you see the women and children leave the Canby house that morning?"

She shook her head. "I wasn't paying attention."

"Come now, Mrs. Dodgson. You had made the call, you knew they had to be out of the house before anyone entered. Human nature would have made you watch. Didn't you see them leave?"

"I couldn't have seen them," she cried. "The grass and weeds were too high."

"Not in April. From the end of the road you had a perfect spot to observe the space between the house and the woods. Didn't you watch until you saw them all leave, and didn't you then kneel down to tie your shoe?"

"No!"

"Weren't you signaling to someone that the house was now empty?"

"No!" she screamed. "Leave me alone! For God's sake, leave me alone! What more do you want?"

"The truth, Mrs. Dodgson." Barbara walked back and forth. "When Mr. Dodgson came in that morning, did you tell him what you had done?"

Kay looked up and cast a swift glance over the spectators, and then looked down at her hands. "No," she said.

"You haven't told him in the intervening months?"

"No."

"Why didn't you tell the investigating officers you might have seen someone crossing the private road?"

"I . . . Rich said Paula Kennerman did it, and I believed him. I thought I must have been mistaken," she said in a low voice.

"Were you afraid that Mr. Gallead would tell your husband about your dancing during his absences?"

She cast another desperate look about and ducked her head again. "I wasn't afraid," she said, nearly inaudibly. "I just wanted the past to stay buried. There was no reason to bring it up now."

"Monday, April twenty-first, your husband and your son went out on the yacht, but you didn't go with them. Why not?"

She gave Barbara a startled look. "I was sick."

"Did you go to the office that entire week?"

"No, I was sick."

"Mrs. Dodgson, your husband controls the business; he controls the household affairs; he buys your clothes and gives you an allowance, doesn't he?"

She shook her head. She looked agonized now.

"That Saturday when he came in, didn't you in fact tell him exactly what you had done, and didn't he beat you? Weren't you afraid that if he learned of your dancing, your private funds, he would beat you severely? Wasn't that why you were in the power of Royce Gallead, because you are deathly afraid of your husband?"

Fierst was screaming objections; Barbara ignored him. "Mrs. Dodgson, do you understand the meaning of battered-wife syndrome?"

Judge Paltz's voice rose and Barbara looked at him now. "Ms. Holloway, you will stop piling questions on questions. You will stop leading this witness. You will conduct yourself properly. Do you understand?"

"Yes, sir," she said.

Kay Dodgson was sobbing into her hands; her entire body convulsed. Judge Paltz glared at Barbara; he looked at Kay Dodgson, then back at Barbara, and beckoned her and Fierst to the bench. "How much longer do you intend to take with this woman?" he demanded.

"Only a few more minutes, Your Honor."

"I don't want this to continue into the morning," he warned. It was twenty minutes past four.

"Your Honor," Barbara said before he could raise his gavel for another recess. "I would like to suggest that Mrs. Dodgson be made aware that she can have protection if she so desires."

His gaze held hers for a long time, it seemed, before he nodded. "She will be so told out of the hearing of the jury." He raised his gavel then and called for a recess.

* * *

"Ah, Bobby," Frank said. "How on God's little green earth did you know that?"

"She told me. Everything she said, every gesture, her fear. She told me."

"Honey, it's over. You can rest the defense today; you've done it."

She shook her head. "Not yet. There's one more witness, remember? I want him, Dad. I really want him in that chair."

She went to the window and looked out. *They* were still there, patrolling. And then in her mind's eye she saw the look on Paula's face only minutes ago when she had returned to the defense table. A look that was a mixture of fear and revulsion.

"Mrs. Dodgson, just a few more questions," she said when they began again. Kay Dodgson had washed her face and reapplied lipstick, but there hadn't been enough time for the mascara, the blush, all the rest. She looked haggard. More, she looked defeated. "Did you not tell the authorities the truth about that Saturday because you were ordered not to speak of it?"

"No," she said dully.

"You know Mr. Gallead has a gun shop and he runs a firing range, but do you know of other activities he is engaged in?"

"No." Her voice was toneless.

"Do you know if your husband and Mr. Gallead are business associates?"

She repeated her denial without a change of expression or voice.

"Do you know if your son Craig and Mr. Gallead are business associates?"

A flicker of life came into her eyes. "No, they aren't!"

"What about your other son, Alex? Is he associated with Mr. Gallead?"

This time the life flared to a flame. "No!" she screamed. "Alex doesn't know anything! He has nothing to do—"

"Yes, Mrs. Dodgson? He has nothing to do with what?"

"Nothing. I don't know what you're talking about!"

Barbara regarded her coolly for a moment, then returned to the defense table. "No more questions," she said.

Fierst stood up as if undecided, then said he had no questions. He would try to undo some of it at summation, Barbara knew, but he understood it was over as well as she did.

TWENTY-FIVE

GETTING OUT OF the courthouse to the car was hellish; there were more reporters today than onlookers and demonstrators, more flashbulbs, more TV cameras, more shouted questions, more pushing, yelling. . . . At the house it was marginally better. As Frank propelled her to the door, it swung open and Bailey stepped aside for them to enter, slammed the door and locked it.

"They had to put a cop in the backyard," Bailey said cheerfully. "They were coming over the fence taking pictures of the tomatoes."

"Christ on a mountain," Frank muttered, and headed for the back door. A man emerged from the living room. "Oh, Carter. Right back." Frank went out through the kitchen.

"Ms. Holloway, I'm Carter Heilbronner." He extended his hand. He was a slender, dark-haired man, fifty or fifty-five, very well dressed in a dark suit, maroon tie.

She shook hands with him; he looked exactly the way an FBI agent should look—discreet, well-mannered, pleasant. "Please," she said, "make yourself comfortable. I'll just be a minute. Bailey, why don't you give Mr. Heilbronner a drink?" She went upstairs to change her clothes, wash her face, rid herself of the briefcase and purse, and just to sit and not do anything for a few seconds. Finally, in jeans and T-shirt, she went back down.

Heilbronner and Bailey were in the kitchen, where Frank was sorting tomatoes and peppers, cursing. "Damn fools, look what they did!" He held up a smashed pepper. "Goddamn idiots!"

Bailey asked her if she wanted wine and she said no, she wanted what he had. Heilbronner was not drinking. Then, with bourbon and water in her hand, she sat at the kitchen table. "As good a place as any," she said, motioning Heilbronner to a chair. Frank's curses became almost inaudible.

"Your father asked us to put certain people under surveillance," Heilbronner said. "And of course we can't do that without cause. Ms. Holloway, will you tell me why you made such a request?"

She sipped her drink. "I think right now the Dodgson group is considering the murder of Royce Gallead, and possibly his stooge, Terry Bossert. And I think those two are trying to figure out how they can get to the Dodgsons without being caught. And meanwhile, I think Kay Dodgson expects to get the hell beaten out of her, if not tonight, then tomorrow." She took another drink, bigger this time. "If that scenario isn't quite right, then some, or maybe all of them, are likely wondering if they can get to me overnight, or else they might be checking airlines for parts unknown. And they really should not be allowed to skip, not just yet."

Heilbronner's expression did not change even a fraction.

She sighed. "I asked Judge Paltz to advise Kay

Dodgson that she could have protection if she felt the need."

"Ms. Holloway, you know very well that isn't enough. We need real data or our hands are tied, as you also know."

"If I told you enough to make you call out the dogs, what would you do? Arrest people? Search and seize? Bring them in for questioning? All of the above? I can't do that because I haven't concluded my defense of Paula Kennerman yet, and my primary commitment must be to my client. As soon as the jury starts its deliberation, I'll tell you everything I know, everything I suspect, give you everything I have, but I really would like to know that all those people will be alive and healthy then." She picked up her glass and added moodily, "And it would be really fine if they didn't get together and discuss things overnight."

Heilbronner regarded her for another minute, then shook his head. His face revealed nothing. Did the FBI have lessons in that? she wondered irritably. Neutral Expression 101?

"You know, don't you," Bailey drawled, "that the news hounds out there are national as well as local. We got their attention."

"For Christ's sake, get off your high horse," Frank snapped from across the kitchen. "What's it going to cost you? If you lose, you lose big. Cover your ass!"

Heilbronner continued to watch Barbara. She finished her drink and waved Bailey away when he reached for her glass. She was so tired another drink might make her fold.

"You understand," Heilbronner said, "that the FBI doesn't involve itself in local crimes, not even murder."

"Of course, I understand that," she said. "Look, I'm really beat. Tomorrow, as soon as the jury is charged, I'm asking Judge Paltz to convene a meeting in his chambers. The D.A. will be there. Come if you want." She stood up. "If some of the people we discuss turn up dead or missing, well, I tried."

When he remained deadpan, she shrugged and turned deliberately to Bailey. "Anything new on Les Smithers or the watchman?"

"Les was in surgery for eight hours; he's critical but stable. They say that's a good sign. The watchman will make it."

Heilbronner got up then. "I'll be on my way," he said. Bailey went with him to lock the door again.

"What do you think?" Barbara asked Frank.

"You kidding? They'll be watched. Didn't do your case any harm at all, bringing up Les and the watchman." He was still scowling at his ruined vegetables.

Barbara went to the stairs and stepped up, down, up, down.

"What are you doing?" Bailey asked.

"Exercising." Up, down, up.

"That can't be good for her," Bailey said to Frank in the kitchen.

"You staying for supper? If so, go on out there and pick some beans."

Barbara stepped up, down, up. . . .

Rich Dodgson was what people meant when they said a fine-looking man, Barbara thought the next morning, studying him. He was fifty-nine, a few pounds overweight, not enough to be unattractive. His eyes were light blue, his hair dark, almost black, with gray at the temples.

He was dressed in charcoal-colored slacks, with a lighter gray sports coat, shirt open at the neck, no visible jewelry, not even a wedding ring.

She asked him to fill in his background for the jury, and he did so concisely. When he was done, she shook her head. "You are too modest, Mr. Dodgson. You say you were a salesman, but weren't you, in fact, at the time of your retirement, the sales supervisor of the entire western district for the Doud Pharmaceutical Company?"

"Yes."

"How long were you with the pharmaceutical company?"

"Twenty years." His voice was level, almost bored. He looked at her infrequently, as if he found her tiresome. He was very much at ease. He smiled and nodded to someone in the room behind her.

Today she had her own little cheering section again: her neighbors, Bill Spassero, Lucille and her husband. She had seen Kay Dodgson and Craig in the audience, and a lot of *his* people. *They* were being very quiet.

"If you had remained five more years, you could have retired with a full pension and medical insurance, couldn't you?" she asked.

He shrugged. "Probably."

"But you chose to leave in order to start your own business, is that right?"

"Yes."

"Were you and your family dependent on your salary, Mr. Dodgson?"

Fierst objected. She didn't dispute him.

"Mr. Dodgson, when you came to Oregon you bought land from Mrs. Canby, and a year later built your house, didn't you?"

"Yes, we did."

"And you bought the printing plant, the building housing it, added new equipment, computers. Is that correct?"

"Yes."

"Seven years ago you bought your yacht. Is that correct?"

"Yes."

"How much does your newspaper cost, Mr. Dodgson?"

For the first time he hesitated, but only for a second. "Fifty cents an issue. A subscription is fifteen dollars a year."

"And how many copies do you print?"

He shrugged again. "About a thousand."

"How long have you published on a weekly basis?"

He glanced at her and away. "About two years. Before that we were a monthly."

"So the newspaper has never been your primary source of income from the company. Is that right?"

"Yes, that's right," he said, a sharpness entering his voice, as if he had lost patience with her and her questions. "We always printed whatever jobs came along. We are a printing company. And we have advertisers."

"Your Honor, I object to this line of questioning," Fierst said, rising to his feet. "Mr. Dodgson's company, his occupation, have nothing to do with the matter before this court. Counsel is simply fishing."

Judge Paltz sustained the objection, and then said, "Ms. Holloway, I suggest you get to another topic."

Barbara nodded. When she looked at Dodgson again, she caught a hint of a gleam in his pale eyes, before he registered indifference once more.

"Your masthead lists you as the publisher and editor of the paper, Mr. Dodgson. Do you have reporters?"

"No."

"You write all the material yourself?"

"Yes."

"What are your news sources, Mr. Dodgson, if you have no reporters?"

"People tell me things. I write them," he said. He raised his arm and looked at his watch.

"You are solely and completely responsible for the content of your newspaper?"

"That's what I said. That's what I meant. Should I say it again?"

"You wrote this?" She picked up the top newspaper from a stack on the defense table and read: "The so-called feminists are screeching at the gates, folks. Pay attention. What they want now are classes for our boys to teach them what they call nurturing. What that means, folks, is they want to teach our boys how to cook and sew and baby-sit while they go out and steal away men's jobs. What can you do? Scream back at them, for openers. . . ." She looked at him. "You wrote that?"

"Objection!" Fierst yelled. "Mr. Dodgson's private philosophy is not on trial. We have and honor freedom of speech in this country. He can write what he wants."

"Your Honor," Barbara said, "I agree absolutely with Mr. Fierst. However, it is possible that the witness misspoke when he said he writes all his own material. This editorial, for instance, appeared in three different local papers in the state. I think Mr. Dodgson deserves the opportunity to clarify his statement, if he spoke hastily."

Judge Paltz overruled Fierst.

"The question, Mr. Dodgson, was, did you write that?"

"Yes. They might have copied it, if anyone actually published that same article."

"Oh, someone did," she said, lifting another paper. "This is the *Belham County Bugle*, a monthly, I believe. The editorial in it is from February, nineteen ninety-one. Your article is dated May, nineteen ninety-one. How do you suppose they copied it before you published it, Mr. Dodgson?"

"Objection!" Fierst cried. "Counsel knows that's an improper question."

"Sustained."

"I suppose it was," Barbara murmured. "Mr. Dodgson, here is another copy of your editorial, dated January of the same year, and a fourth one, dated June. Mr. Dodgson, I ask you, did you write the editorial?"

"Yes. I said I wrote it."

"And you can't account for the exact editorial appearing in these other papers?"

"No, I can't."

"Very well," she said, handing the papers to the clerk to be admitted. "Let's take this one." She lifted another newspaper, and watched his gaze leave her, fasten on the stack of papers on her table. Well, she thought, she had his attention. He no longer looked bored.

She read another editorial, this one attacking birth-control pills, with three duplicates. He said he wrote it. Another one, about IUDs, with two duplicates. He said he wrote it. A third one about the morning-after pill, one duplicate. He said he wrote it. He had become steely-eyed, his jaw set; he was grating the words now.

Barbara could well understand why Kay was terrified of him.

"Mr. Dodgson, the last three editorials all deal with birth control of various sorts. Is it a fair assumption to understand that you are opposed to all birth control?"

"Those aren't birth-control methods. They're murder methods," he said with cold precision. "I am morally opposed to any and every kind of murder of innocent children."

"I see," she said, and picked up another paper. This one bewailed the use of spermicidal gels. "Mr. Dodgson," she asked after she read it, "do you claim that the use of a spermicidal gel is also murder?"

"If the girls don't want to get pregnant, they should stay out of the bedroom."

"Do you claim that the use of spermicidal gel is murder?" she repeated.

"It can be considered murder."

"Mr. Dodgson, will you explain to the jury what a spermicide is?"

"It is an agent that kills male sperm." He was staring at her with an almost hypnotic intensity. His eyes looked inhuman with a metallic sheen.

"You mean it kills the sperm before it reaches the ovum?"

"Yes. I mean that."

"So the ovum cannot be fertilized? Pregnancy cannot take place?"

"You know that's what I mean."

"Yes, I know that. And you state in this editorial that it's another form of murder." She put the paper down, grateful that no one had challenged it; there was no duplicate of that editorial. She picked up the next paper.

"Mr. Dodgson, what is the substance you wrote about in this editorial, RU-486?"

"It's an abortion agent."

"It isn't used in this country, you say here, and yet you have a long editorial about the dangers it presents. Why is that?"

"There is intense pressure to have it approved here. It's a very dangerous drug used to murder babies, and one that has killed countless women in Europe."

"I see. It is used in France, England, and Sweden, approved by their governments. Are they aware of its dangers?"

"Objection!" Fierst called out. She withdrew the question.

"In the past two years you have published one hundred thirteen issues of your newspaper, one a week. Of that number, eighty percent have dealt with birth control, pregnancy, illegitimate births, single mothers, teenaged mothers, feminism, or abortion. Ninety editorials. You have railed against every form of birth control available to women except abstinence. Many of your articles and editorials are duplicated throughout the state. Mr. Dodgson, are you part of a national network to propagandize against the use of birth control for women?"

"I write the truth as I see it."

Barbara read: "The sperm is the sacred bearer of life. With its penetration of the ovum, the ovum itself becomes sacred, and the body that carries it to birth is sacred." She put down the paper. "Until the ovum is penetrated it is not sacred. Is that what you mean?"

"You read it. You know what it means," he said. "Alone the ovum is nothing."

"Is the body that produces the sacred sperm also sacred?"

He stared hard at her and nodded. "It is."

"And the body that produces the ovum, is it nothing until there is fertilization?"

"Woman was created to carry the seed of life to birth. If she shirks that God-given blessing, she is nothing." He enunciated the words carefully.

"And you believed the women at the Canby Ranch were shirking their duty?"

"They ran away from their husbands," he said.

"Were they shirking their duty?"

"Yes. They were."

"So in your eyes they were nothing. Is that right?"

"If they were counseling abortions, performing abortions, they were less than nothing. They were murderers and accessories to murder."

"You didn't know that," she said. "All you knew was that they were seeking refuge from situations that had become intolerable. Were they nothing?"

"In my opinion, women who run away from their husbands are nothing," he said flatly.

"Is there never a sufficient cause for a woman to leave a husband, then?"

"Objection," Fierst said. "This line of questioning is nothing but an undergraduate debate. Mr. Dodgson's philosophy is irrelevant." The objection was sustained.

"Mr. Dodgson, your wife came to court beautifully dressed every day. You buy her clothes, you run the household, you oversee the domestic help. She lives in a doll's house, doesn't she, Mr. Dodgson? Is that your duty to her? To maintain her like a beautiful possession to show off to the world? And if she gets out of line, is

it your sacred duty to chastise her? To beat her? Do you
beat your wife, Mr. Dodgson?"

"Objection!"

It was sustained and the jury was told to disregard
her remarks, and then it was time for a recess.

"Disregard them, hah!" she muttered to Frank as
Judge Paltz left the courtroom.

"Mr. Dodgson, is this your editorial? Did you write it?"
She read: "All over the country so-called Safe Houses
are springing up.... What can you do? Be alert!...
Visit the house, demonstrate against this assault on every family value you hold dear. Write a letter to the editor, talk to your neighbors. Don't let them get away
with it!" She read the entire editorial, and he said yes,
he had written it.

"This exact editorial appeared in six different newspapers within the state within a month's period, Mr.
Dodgson. I ask you again, are those your words, is that
your original editorial?"

"Many people have access to the same national
news—"

"Mr. Dodgson, please. A simple yes or no. Did you
write those words as if they were your original thoughts?"

"Yes!"

"Do you make a distinction between your editorials
and the articles that pass as news?"

"Of course."

"Do you check the sources of news information for
accuracy?"

"If possible. I trust my sources and don't—"

"Do you check them for accuracy?"

"Sometimes, if there—"

"Mr. Dodgson, just a simple yes or no, that's all that is required. Do you check for accuracy? Yes, you do, or no, you don't."

"No," he snapped. "There's no need with the people I deal with."

"Where did these figures come from, Mr. Dodgson? I quote, 'Sixty percent of women who have abortions have severe psychological problems that must be treated by qualified medical specialists'?"

He shrugged. "I read it in a medical article."

"Where? What was the article?"

"I don't remember. I read a lot of articles."

"Was it in the print media? A magazine?"

"I don't remember."

"Was it, perhaps, an item you downloaded on your computer?"

Fierst objected. The witness had said he didn't remember; he couldn't be forced to remember.

"Are you aware of national networks that issue regular lists of books to be banned by religious or political organizations?"

"Yes, I know about them."

"Do you subscribe to them?"

"Yes. As a publisher I need to know what—"

"You subscribe, yes; isn't that your answer?"

"Yes," he snapped.

Through the same process she forced him to admit that he subscribed to other networks that issued facts and figures about abortion, birth-control methods, morning-after pills, IUDs. . . .

Finally she demanded: "So, when you write these editorials in which you make claims about the dangers of the birth-control pill, you are simply relying on your network. Those words are not yours; you did not write them; you did not check the sources; you accepted the networks you subscribe to for your information. Isn't that correct?"

"There's no need to cross-check—"

"You accepted without question whatever information came through the network, isn't that correct?"

"I'm trying to explain—"

"I don't want any explanation," she snapped. "Did you simply accept whatever they told you? It's a simple question."

"Objection," Fierst said. "This is not proper examination of a witness. Counsel is trying to browbeat the witness into making unwarranted statements."

Judge Paltz looked at him thoughtfully and then said, "Overruled. I think the witness can answer the question directly." He turned to Dodgson. "Sir, do you recall the question?"

Dodgson's expression was murderous. "I recall it," he said. "I accepted what my sources told me."

"Did you ever inform your readers that many of your editorials and articles were not your original thoughts, that you were simply repeating what distant and unknown masters were dictating?"

Fierst objected violently this time and was sustained.

"Mr. Dodgson, do you agree with your son that there is never any acceptable reason to resort to abortion?"

"Yes. Absolutely."

"Did you believe the Canby Ranch was being used for abortion counseling, possibly for abortions?"

He hesitated. "Yes."

"Why didn't you write an editorial, a series of articles denouncing it?"

"A reasonable man doesn't act without proof of some kind," he said. "I was waiting for proof."

"Did you ever demand proof for any of the information you accepted from your computer network affiliations?"

He hesitated, as if expecting Fierst to intercede; when Fierst didn't, he said, "No. I knew those people."

"Did Mrs. Canby warn you that if you published any unwarranted accusation about her property and its use as a refuge for battered women, she would have you and your family investigated from the day of your birth?"

"No! She did not!"

"Did you know the Canby Ranch property was being used as a refuge for battered women? Didn't Mrs. Canby inform you of that?"

"Yes, we talked about it."

"You printed a number of articles and editorials denouncing the use of safe houses, denouncing the principle of providing a haven for women fleeing their husbands, did you not?"

"Yes. I believe such action—"

"The answer is yes," Barbara said. "You printed articles advising neighbors to spy on neighbors, to inform, to demonstrate, and yet you tolerated such a house on the property next to yours without a murmur. Why?"

"I suspected there was more to it than merely providing a haven," he said. "I was gathering information."

"For over two years?"

"Yes."

"You were being cautious, is that what you mean?"

"That's what I said."

"Did you personally write this article and this editorial, calling Paula Kennerman a baby killer, the fire an arson fire, an attempt to hide the murder?" She read the opening of the article.

"Yes, I did."

"This newspaper is dated April twenty-first, the Monday following the death of Lori Kennerman and the arson fire at the Canby Ranch. That was ten days before the police released a statement that there had been a murder and arson. Who gave you that information, Mr. Dodgson?"

He shrugged. "I don't remember. Maybe I figured it out myself."

"I see. Days before there was an autopsy, before the fire marshal made his report, you just figured it out yourself, that a murder had been done. And you printed your opinion as if it were factual. Is that what you are saying?"

"I was right, wasn't I?"

She turned to Judge Paltz. "I ask that the witness's comment be stricken and that he be ordered to answer the question directly." When this was done, she repeated: "Did you print your opinion as if it were factual?"

"Yes, I did. It was."

"The words following 'Yes, I did,' will be stricken," Judge Paltz said. "Mr. Dodgson, you are required to answer the questions without further comment. Do you understand?"

"Yes."

"Did you send, or arrange to have sent, copies of your paper to Jack Kennerman?"

"No."

"Did you arrange a cash payment to him of three thousand dollars?"

"Of course not. I don't even know him."

She asked that his comment be stricken. He was staring at her through narrowed, glinting eyes as cold as death.

"Were you aware that four other newspapers through the state ran your original article and editorial verbatim in the weeks of early May?"

He shook his head. "Sorry, the answer is still no."

"On Saturday, April nineteenth, where were you all morning?"

"Cutting the grass with the tractor mower."

She led him through the morning. He had seen Angela driving in and had started to go in when Craig came waving him down. He returned to his house at about twenty minutes past eleven, just about when the fire engines arrived.

"Then what did you do?"

"Nothing. There was nothing any of us could do. We stayed home, out of the way."

"Did Mrs. Dodgson tell you she had called Mr. Gallead?"

"No."

"Did she mention seeing, or possibly seeing, a figure crossing the private road?"

"No."

"It has been stated that you usually went to the office on Saturday afternoon to prepare the paper for Monday morning distribution. Why didn't you do that on that Saturday?"

"My wife was not feeling well. She was upset by the death of the child."

"So you stayed home the rest of the day?"

"Yes," he snapped. He looked at his watch and then checked it against the clock on the rear wall.

"And you remained home all day Sunday?"

"What difference does that make?" he demanded. "Yes. So what? I was rethinking my front page and my editorial."

Again she asked that his comments be stricken from the record.

"Had Mrs. Melrose left yet when you returned to the house?"

"I don't know."

"So if she was still there she might have overheard something you or your wife or son said. Is that true?"

"Objection," Fierst said. "That's a hypothetical question."

It was sustained.

"Why did you fire her, Mr. Dodgson?"

"She was incompetent."

"She was with you for fourteen months. Was she incompetent all that time?"

"She was."

"But you waited until you had proof of her incompetence? Was that it?"

"I fired her when I got tired of her messing things up," he said. "Fouling the swimming pool was the last straw."

"When did you first discover the empty floor stripper container in the pool?"

"Sometime on Monday. I left it there to show her why I was firing her."

"And it floated around from Saturday until Tuesday," Barbara murmured. "Did you find that strange?"

"Objection," Fierst said. "Isn't all this rather irrelevant?"

"It is not irrelevant," Barbara said. "Mr. Dodgson possibly has manufactured an excuse to fire his housekeeper who might have overheard something he did not want repeated."

"You're crazy," Dodgson said in a soft voice that sounded menacing. "There are many ways to get rid of someone; you don't have to go to the expense of cleaning out a damn swimming pool."

Judge Paltz rapped his gavel and admonished Rich Dodgson once more. He sustained the objection.

"Or maybe," Barbara said, going to her table to pick up a piece of paper, "Mr. Dodgson fired his housekeeper as an excuse to clean out his pool."

Fierst objected and was upheld.

During this brief period, she watched Rich Dodgson, who had become very still, the way a predatory cat is still just before it leaps, she thought. "Mr. Dodgson, is this the invoice from the Sweet Waters Pool Maintenance Company?" She placed the paper in front of him. His eyes were like pale ice.

"I will not answer any more of this woman's questions. I object to allowing this woman to meddle in my private affairs. I object to having been called to testify in a matter that I know nothing about. I object to this public persecution. This woman is on some sort of personal feminist crusade to obliterate truth and decency. What is happening here is a travesty of justice, a mockery—" He had started in a low, intense voice that gradually rose until he was shouting. He was drowned out by the furious banging of Judge Paltz's gavel.

"Sir," Judge Paltz said, "the court will adjourn at this

time until one-thirty. At that hour, you will present yourself in the witness chair and conduct yourself properly. You may consult with your attorney if you choose, but, sir, you have been called as a witness, and you will testify."

The noise in the courtroom was like an explosion when the judge left.

He had cut the luncheon recess short, but it was too long, Barbara thought, pacing, too restless to sit still, too restless to consider food. She wanted to walk in the woods, by the river, in her old neighborhood, anywhere. On the beach. That was what she wanted, to walk on the beach, for hours and hours.

"That's how he must be before he hits her," she said with a shudder. "Remote, icy, monstrous." She went to the window. "He put on that last performance on purpose," she added. "Controlled all the way. Buying time to think, to plan."

"You rattled his cage, all right," Frank said. "He must be going nuts trying to figure out where you're leading him."

She turned away from the window—she had not seen a thing out there—and faced him again. "I'll nod when I want the stuff," she said. She had told him this already. She bit her lip and went to the rest room to wash her face.

"Mr. Dodgson," she said, "I showed you the invoice from the pool-cleaning company and asked if you recognized it. Do you?"

"Yes."

"It's correct to your knowledge?"

"I don't know."

"But you paid the bill; you must have accepted it at the time. Didn't you?"

"Yes."

She held up the invoice. "The man who did the work reported here that he started the pump on Tuesday and returned when the pool was empty on Wednesday and scrubbed down the sides with detergent to remove an oily residue. Mr. Dodgson, a floor stripper chemical is not oil based, is it?"

"I don't know what it is."

She handed the invoice to the clerk. "When you lived in Las Vegas, were you acquainted with Royce Gallead?"

"No."

"Did you know that your wife danced in the club where he was assistant manager?"

"No."

"Did you know she continued her professional dancing while you were away from home?"

"Yes," he snapped. "We have no secrets."

"Is Mr. Gallead a business associate of yours?"

"No."

"Do you speak French, Mr. Dodgson?"

Fierst objected and she withdrew the question. Dodgson's eyes were narrowed, his jaw hard and tight again.

"Is your printing company capable of printing in foreign languages?" she asked.

While Fierst was objecting, she glanced at her father and nodded. He was at the defense table, not behind it as he had been throughout the trial until now. She faced Dodgson again, aware of the rustle of paper behind her.

"Is it possible that Mr. Gallead is not a real associate of yours, that he is instead merely a customer? Someone you do printing jobs for?"

He was watching Frank with an intense stare. His lips had all but vanished.

"Mr. Dodgson," she said. "Did you not hear the question?"

He moistened his lips and then said in a low voice, "I've done printing work for him."

"And you wouldn't necessarily know what the work was, especially if it was in a foreign language. Is that right?"

He turned his gaze to her, and then looked past her. There was a slight commotion. She turned to see Craig Dodgson pulling away from Kay Dodgson's hand. Craig hurried from the courtroom.

"Mr. Dodgson," she said. "Did you hear my question?"

"I heard it," he said with a flash of fury. "I don't know what the work was. It was in a foreign language, on a computer disk. I just did the printing."

"Ah," she said. She walked to the table and regarded the pyramid Frank had constructed, the cardboard carton on the bottom, the case-size box on top of it, the small box on top of that. She turned and approached him again with her hands in her pockets. "Mr. Dodgson, do you recognize these?" She withdrew her hand and opened it. Dodgson turned the color of wet putty.

"Objection!" Fierst yelled. "Your Honor, this is a fishing expedition pure and simple. What is counsel doing playing games with boxes, hiding something in her hand?"

Paltz glanced at him almost absently. "Overruled. Mr. Dodgson, did you hear Ms. Holloway's question?"

"I don't know what they are," he said in such a low voice, Judge Paltz asked him to repeat it.

Barbara approached the bench and said, "It's baby aspirin and a time-release decongestant, Your Honor. But it looks very much like the combination drug RU-486."

There was a cry behind her; she turned to see Kay Dodgson running from the courtroom, closely followed by half a dozen other people. Reporters, she thought, and looked at Dodgson again. He was stone-faced and very pale. She read murder in his expression, cold, merciless murder.

"Mr. Dodgson, did you print labels for boxes similar to those on the defense table for Mr. Gallead?"

"Yes."

"How many did you print?"

"I don't remember."

"Well, was it in the hundreds? Thousands?"

He hesitated, then shrugged. "In the thousands."

"Did you print information sheets for him?"

"I don't know what it was."

"Was it in French?"

"Yes. I don't read French."

She walked to her table, thinking, Here goes. She had warned him, had coached him, had led him all the way to the next question. Enough? She hoped so. She faced him again.

"When you were cutting the grass at your house on Saturday morning, April nineteenth, did you see anyone on your property who didn't belong there?"

He hesitated briefly, then nodded. "I thought I did."

"What did you see?"

"Just a shadowy figure dart across the road, go behind the trees, out of sight."

"Did you recognize that figure?"

He was hesitating after every question now. This time the pause was longer. "No," he said.

"Where did he come from?"

"I don't know. I just caught a glimpse of someone on the road."

"Across the road from your property is the Gallead property, isn't it? Did he come from that direction?"

He drew in a long breath and said yes.

"Did you simply continue to cut the grass?"

"Yes."

"Mr. Dodgson, you hired spies to keep an eye on your property, you were so alarmed at the thought of intruders, yet when you saw a strange shadowy figure, you simply kept mowing the grass? Is that what you did?"

"Yes!" he yelled. "Yes, that's what I did! I thought I'd been mistaken, and I cut the grass."

"Before the fire, did Mr. Gallead pressure you to try to get the Canby Ranch closed as a refuge for women?"

"No." He ran his hand over his face, and then said, "Yes, he did. He asked me repeatedly to call Mrs. Canby. I don't know why."

"But you obeyed him. Why was that, Mr. Dodgson?"

"I wanted them out, too."

She felt almost sorry for Fierst when it was his turn. He stood up and then sat down again. "No questions," he said tiredly.

TWENTY-SIX

THE SUMMATIONS HAD been brief. Fierst had reconstructed the prosecution's case and stated that all the other material that had been introduced was irrelevant, but his performance was lackluster, spiritless. Barbara had also reconstructed the state's case, and item by item destroyed it, and the jury was out.

Now Frank and Barbara were being ushered into Judge Paltz's chambers, where others had already gathered. The district attorney, Larry Coltrane, was there, along with Fierst and another assistant. Carter Heilbronner and an assistant were there. Judge Paltz was behind his desk, his senior clerk at his side and a stenographer in a chair pulled back a few feet.

"Come in, come in," Judge Paltz said. He made the introductions, and then said, "Barbara, please sit over there." He indicated a chair, and then waved Frank to another one. He peered at Barbara. "You asked for this meeting, so I turn it over to you at this time. Since this is irregular, notes will be taken." He leaned back in his big handsome chair.

"Before we start," Larry Coltrane said, "I want it on record that my office is very aware of the leading nature of counsel's questions, and we are considering action.

We believe she deliberately led witnesses to make statements that she knew were lies." He folded his arms over his chest and glared at her.

She shrugged. "People on the stand lied from day one. Are you objecting because a few of the lies helped my client instead of hurt her? Where do we start examining the lies given as evidence?"

"Not here, and not now," Judge Paltz said. "This is not a good beginning. Barbara, what is RU-486?"

She glanced at Heilbronner. "Will any of them have a chance to wipe computer disks, flush stuff down the drain?"

He shook his head.

"Good. RU-486 is a drug combination that induces abortion with virtually no side effects. It mimics an early spontaneous abortion, commonly called a miscarriage, with as few aftereffects as a miscarriage. It's widely used in Europe, and is illegal here. There's been terrible pressure to keep it from being licensed in this country; no company here will touch it for fear of massive reprisals in the form of boycotts, demonstrations, whatever. There is evidence that Dodgson and Gallead have a source for it, and they are smuggling it in, packaging it, and distributing it to selected doctors. If it were legal, it would cost about seven hundred fifty dollars; on the black market, who knows what they charge for it? All Dodgson's diatribes against birth control, abortions, and all the while he was making millions with RU-486. And Craig's demonstrations against clinics while he was actually delivering the stuff. This has to be the most cynical, the most hypocritical black-market enterprise on record!" She was too furious to continue.

"You can prove any of this?" Judge Paltz murmured. His eyes were gleaming.

"Not enough," she admitted after drawing in a long breath. She told them about Miguel Torres, how he and three other men had spent four days packaging a medication. "We have the picture showing the truck with five workers at a different time. We have people who will testify that the Gallead truck brings in workers every six to eight weeks. This is a multimillion-dollar operation. They are packaging from four to six thousand doses at a time, six or more times a year! We have the names of four doctors Craig Dodgson visited in Denver, all gynecologists; I have no idea how many doctors may be involved. I talked to a woman who was given medication that looked like the baby aspirin and decongestant I showed Dodgson in court. She had what she thought was a spontaneous abortion following it."

No one had moved or made a sound as she talked. Now Larry Coltrane made a disgusted sort of noise, not quite a snort. "If they're making that kind of money, where is it, why doesn't it show?"

"This isn't an open-ended racket," she said. "The day RU-486 is legalized, they have to close shop, and I imagine the day after that, they all planned to vanish."

"By this time," she went on, "Gallead believes the Dodgsons are throwing him overboard, framing him for the murder of Lori Kennerman. And, no doubt, he believes that Dodgson is going to plead ignorance of what Gallead was doing. Dodgson said he can't read French, remember. All he did was print orders from time to time. I think Gallead will talk, he'll want to deal." She added, "It seems likely that Gallead got hold of someone with the drug years ago and looked around for a partner, and who better than a pharmaceutical rep?"

"All that nonsense about a shadowy figure," Fierst protested. "It's not worth a damn. You can't pin the murder on Gallead with nothing more than that, and you know it."

"I never said I could," she said. "Right now they all know we're onto the RU-486 operation, and the Dodgsons know that I'm asking dangerous questions about the arson fire and murder of Lori Kennerman. Let me tell you one more scenario, the only one that makes any sense. The one that the Dodgsons will do anything to keep under wraps, even if it means framing Gallead."

Fierst set his mouth in a tight line and didn't speak.

"They must have been desperate to close down the refuge after Carol Burnside took those photographs. But if they stirred up too much trouble Mrs. Canby would have had the Dodgsons investigated; she told me that. And real investigators were more dangerous than someone stumbling over their operation. Then, less than two months after that incident, Kay met Angela and learned that the house would be empty. She hurried back home." Barbara scowled at Fierst and added, "Carrie Voight saw her, remember? Kay and Craig saw their chance to get rid of the Canby place, to burn it down. She wrote the note to Mrs. Melrose to clean the refrigerator in order to keep her in the kitchen. She opened the pool-room door, the door to the family room, turned the music on loud, all to establish that Craig was in there swimming naked. And then she went back toward the end of the road to watch for the departure of the women and children at the Canby house. From the pond area she had a clear line of sight. But she didn't know Angela's little girl was there, so when the second little girl ran out, she thought that was the last one, and she stooped down to tie her shoe. She couldn't see Craig through the trees, but he could see her very well in her pink running outfit. Then she went back to the house to wait for him, to open the front door for him. He must have been covered with blood and gas. Maybe in shock. No one expected a child to show up to witness the arson." Her voice hardened. She took a deep breath and continued. "Anyway, there he was, reeking, filthy, and at any moment someone could have walked in. So he jumped into the pool, clothes and all, maybe even with the gas can; he stripped under water, anchored everything out of sight. They couldn't risk anyone's seeing the clothes, the can, or smelling gas. Kay ran to get his robe, and then Angela appeared while she was still carrying the robe. Having Angela appear at the front door must have been almost as great a shock as seeing Craig covered with blood and gas."

There was complete silence while they all considered it. Finally Larry Coltrane said, "That's why they had to pump out the pool and scrub it down. There could have been some gas left in the can."

"And why Craig and Rich went out for a short cruise on Monday," Barbara said. "To dump the clothes and the can at sea." She gave Coltrane a bitter look. "I suspect he left footprints on the flagstones, on the carpet, somewhere. Something that made it necessary to send Mrs. Melrose home early before she noticed. I'd press Mrs. Melrose about the footprints she saw. And I'd see if they redecorated the house after that—new carpets, for instance."

"Barbara, if I may ask," Judge Paltz said, looking

thoughtful, "what made you even think of this particular scenario, true or not, as time will tell?"

"The missing clothes," she said. "Craig testified that he changed in the dressing room, but Mrs. Melrose didn't find any dirty clothes there, and no one had gone to get them. She had no reason to lie about that. Or anything else. He put on the robe that his mother provided. And there was no reason for her to take him a robe if his own clothes were available. That and the fabrication of an excuse to clean the pool and get rid of Mrs. Melrose at the same time."

"Even if there's a shred of truth," Larry Coltrane said after a moment, "there's no way on earth to prove anything. Just another story."

"And what was it when you set your eyes on Paula Kennerman?" Barbara demanded. "Every shred of evidence pointed away from her, but you never wavered. Battered-wife syndrome, blame the mother, no more questions."

"Statistically we were right," he said. "It usually is the mother, or the father."

"Paula Kennerman isn't a statistic! If you want a battered woman, look at Kay Dodgson. Without Rich to tell her what to say and how to say it, she'll tell you whatever you need. She's put in a lifetime of serving men. You saw her in the courtroom! She cracked wide open! Without her men, she'll talk. If she thinks for a second that she can keep her younger son Alex from being involved, she'll beg for a chance to talk. Or if she thinks for a second there's a chance for Craig to get off with manslaughter instead of murder, she'll sing and dance for you." She was shaking, and stood up, jammed her hands in her pockets. "I need a cup of coffee. Are we finished here?"

"What the hell was all that shit about Gallead, then?" Coltrane yelled. "Just muddying the waters?"

"Don't be an idiot!" she snapped. "What if I had brought up this picture? Gallead would be out of it. The whole damn smuggling operation would be out of it. And Craig would have got off, and you know it. Without the smuggling, Craig has no motive worth a damn. The Dodgsons have done everything in their power to get a quick conviction of Paula Kennerman. My God, Craig's a murderer, Kay's an accessory before and after the fact, and Rich is an accessory after the fact! They'll give you Gallead in a basket to save their skins, and you need Gallead to start talking to save himself. He knows the difference between taking the rap for peddling an illicit drug and the rap for murder. No one knows what all I suspected, how much I actually know. Keep them separated and they'll all talk! I rather imagine they all think they have enough money stashed away to buy their way out of anything." Her fury was increased by her awareness that she couldn't seem to stop shaking.

"Sit down, Barbara," Judge Paltz said kindly. He nodded at his stenographer and clerk. "I think you can go now, and see that someone brings in coffee, will you please?"

Heilbronner and his assistant moved toward the door. "I'll be going, too," he said. "Ms. Holloway, after court adjourns we'll have to talk. I'll want those doctors' names, Miguel Torres, and the name and address of the woman who took the medication."

"The doctors and Miguel," she said. "Not her, unless she comes forward."

He regarded her for a moment, and then left without speaking again. But he would be back, she knew, and thought, Fuck him.

The jury took under an hour to bring in their verdict of not guilty, and the courtroom erupted; some of Dodgson's people were loyal and loud, but most of them left as if dazed. Paula broke down in sobs, and her sister sobbed with her. Jurors pressed around, some patting Paula's shoulder; one woman, also weeping, embraced her; one man shook her hand awkwardly and said, "I'm sorry. I'm so sorry."

When the crowd thinned out, Barbara said to her, "Go on with Lucille and get some rest, some fresh air, some good food. Give us a call when you're rested. Dad has come up with a list of real options for you to consider. Okay?"

Paula nodded. "Janey came to see me last night. She said she has a group, that I should think about joining it. I will, if I can afford it. She said I should start thinking about my future, what I want to do."

"I think after you talk to Dad you'll see that you can afford Janey's group," Barbara said. "That's a fine idea."

"I want to go to school, do what Janey does, help other women and children," Paula said, and then, without warning, she flung herself at Barbara, who held her and stroked her hair and did not mind at all that her nice silk jacket was getting tear-stained.

TWENTY-SEVEN

SHE HAD BEEN at the coast for three days. It was pointless even to wonder how many miles she had walked
on the hard sand, how many dunes she had scrambled
over, how many cliffs she had climbed up and down.
Now she stood at the cliff overlooking Little Whale
Cove. Below, the water was so dark it looked bot-
tomless. Every day the weather had been calm and
warm, the waves had been gentle, but on the hori-
zon she could see a dark wall of clouds moving in,
bringing a Pacific storm. She would wait for it, she
decided, although earlier she had planned to go home
this evening, after this last stop. First the storm, then
home to her little miserable house, which was being re-
painted.

An erratic gust of wind swept her hair into her face,
and she thought she should get some decent clothes,
at least get her hair cut, look more like a respectable
lawyer.

The water below was beginning to churn, as if in an-
ticipation of the coming storm, as if the distant low-
pressure area was already having an effect here. It was,
she thought then; nothing was not connected. Last February she had stood here, rain and wind lashing her,

and in February Carol Burnside had taken her photographs: such isolated incidents, both necessary. Connected.

Below, a whitecap formed, vanished. Another rose. "This is what I do," she whispered into the gusting wind. "This is what I am." The words belonged out there with the note she had thrown into the sea.

She watched the churning water, the wind tangling her hair, until she finally turned to walk back to her car, to drive back to the rented cottage with a view of the ocean.

By the cottage door she saw Bill Spassero. She nodded as she got out of the car, and went to unlock the door. "Dad told you," she said.

"I kept pestering him, I'm afraid," he said. "He said I might as well carry a message. They're all singing like trained birds. His words." He spread his hands, palms up. "No present," he said. "I don't think there's anything I could buy or steal or make that would impress you. I figured out what will, but it will take a long time. First I have to learn how to be a good lawyer, and then I have to be the second-best lawyer in the state. A long time. You said you'd think about talking to me about the case."

She laughed. "Where are you staying?"

He pointed to another cottage.

"What I'm going to do," she said, "is get a scarf and then go down to the beach and walk until sunset, or until the storm moves in, whichever comes first. If you want to take a walk, fine. But, Bill," she added, "I'm not ready for anything else. Understood?"

He grinned a huge grin that made him look like a

sophomore. As if he knew she was thinking this, he said, "When I'm ninety, you'll be ninety-six."

Then, with her scarf tied on, with a wind increasing from the sea, they walked on the beach, talking.